Beverly Thyson's astonishing rise in the ruthless world of women's fashion amazes everyone – including herself. But her personal life (including a failed marriage and an exciting but unfulfilling affair) makes Bev feel she is lacking as a woman. Using all her strength and intuition to reach the pinnacle of success, she is still constantly searching for love.

Helen Van Slyke draws upon her own experience in the glittering world of the powerful to tell a fascinating story of the people she knows so well: their successes and failures, their triumphs and tragedies – their public smiles and their private tears . . .

Also by Helen Van Slyke
A NECESSARY WOMAN
SISTERS AND STRANGERS
NO LOVE LOST
and published by Corgi Books

Helen Van Slyke

with James Elward

Public Smiles,
Private Tears

CORGI BOOKS

PUBLIC SMILES, PRIVATE TEARS

A CORGI BOOK   0 552 12240 8

Originally published in Great Britain
by William Heinemann Limited

PRINTING HISTORY
Heinemann edition published 1982
Corgi edition published 1983
Corgi edition reissued 1983

This book is set in 9½ pt. Caledonia

Corgi Books are published by
Transworld Publishers Ltd.,
Century House, 61–63 Uxbridge Road,
Ealing, London W5 5SA

Printed and bound in Great Britain by
Cox & Wyman Ltd., Reading

Editor's Note

When Helen Van Slyke died, in 1979, she left behind the complete manuscript of her ninth novel, *No Love Lost*, and a half-finished manuscript and an outline of *Public Smiles, Private Tears*, a book she had every intention of finishing had she lived. After many unsuccessful tries by many writers to complete the book, I was about to give up and leave it in the trunk. And then I remembered James Elward, a writer I'd worked with a few years ago, a writer who has always impressed me with his sensibility and adaptability. I asked Jim to try his hand and he wrote a magnificent second half. Here's the finished book and I think it is practically seamless in quality and spirit of feeling. I'm terribly pleased with *Public Smiles, Private Tears*, and I think Helen would feel we'd done her proud.

Lawrence P. Ashmead

New York, N.Y., 1981

1

Beverly Thyson was the second happiest woman at her wedding to Ed Richmond in June of 1946.

The happiest was Angela Thyson, the twenty-two-year-old bride's mother.

It was what Angela had been waiting for, this hushed, solemn ritual in which Beverly would be safely married to a handsome, gentle young man who adored her. 'Safe' was the operative word. Every night for two troubled years, ever since Bev left home, Angela had prayed for this moment. Given her choice, she would have liked to have seen Bev married with all the trimmings—the big church, the long white gown and veil, six bridesmaids. Knowing her modern daughter, she had not even suggested it. Don't press your luck, Angela, she told herself. Just thank God she's getting married. There had been many times when Angela had feared she never would.

They were not close as some mothers and daughters were —or at least as some pretended to be. Bev had always been a good child, a loving and respectful daughter, obedient to her parents' wishes, reluctant to worry them in any way. But Angela never felt that she really knew her only child. And since Beverly had had her own apartment, her absorbing job, and her personal, private life, she was even more like a courteous stranger in her family's presence. Angela was told little, but she guessed much, some of it so terrifying that she deliberately thrust aside her suspicions, firmly classifying them as the product of an overactive imagination. Beverly was not a girl given to easy confidences. Even when she was growing up she was different—a fact which did not go unnoticed, either by her friends or her mother.

Angela gazed steadily at the bride's slim, straight back as her daughter stood calmly at the altar of the little chapel on Madison Avenue. Bev seemed so tiny next to Ed, who had chosen to wear his Air Force uniform for the brief, almost impersonal service. But only in stature was the bride more delicate than her husband-to-be. Inside the tiny frame, beneath the pale blue crepe dress, Bev was more ambitious, more determined, perhaps less idealistic than the man she had chosen. Not that she did not have her gentle, vulnerable qualities. She was a compassionate, a loyal, even highly moral girl, despite the fact that she had probably broken most of the important rules by which well-brought-up middle-class young women lived in the 1940s.

Angela did not know for certain that Bev had broken the rules. It was one of the things she had made up her mind not to think about.

Beverly had thought about those rules a thousand times in the past two years. Even now, speaking her vows, knowing she would keep them, her recent life kept coming into her mind. Ed is right for me, she repeated silently. We'll make each other happy. Everything that came before was a mistake, a stupid rebellion. She looked up at his handsome, loving face. He's so good, Bev thought. I'm not sure I deserve him. She still had not shucked the guilt feelings incurred by defying the mores of her formative years—the code of the 'nice girls,' the behavior patterns she had broken for two men, once innocently and once in a kind of reckless desire for self-destruction. She blamed herself for the things she had done. In this she was wrong. She should have blamed the peculiar period of time in which her values were molded, and the culture in which she lived.

For Beverly and young women like her, the 1940s were a special time to be young and female. These post-flapper, pre-liberation years produced a strange, ambivalent kind of girl-woman whose like had never been seen before and never will exist again. Neither thoroughly emancipated nor totally enslaved, conditioned by convention and conscience, her ingrained timidity was strangely at odds with her determination to be independent and free.

The 'nice girl' of this period was a hybrid with values

somewhere between the passive conventional behavior of her middle-class mother and the total sexual freedom and demand for recognition that would mark the daughters she was yet to bear. Clinging to idealistic standards and romantic fantasies, she was uneasy, confused, and somewhat ashamed of her mixed emotions. On the one hand she instinctively sensed her potential as a complete person. On the other, she was a product of her time, conditioned by rules of 'respectable' behavior and spoon-fed generous helpings of society's recipe for happiness: an innocuous blend of modesty, femininity, and above all, virtue.

Beverly, hungry for life, was afraid to taste it. In high school she and her friends were not 'easy' girls who put no value on virginity. They necked heavily but always stopped short of 'going all the way.' Promiscuity, they agreed, was for cheap girls—or madcap heiresses whose money and position presumably put them above normal moral behavior. Nice girls were brought up being told that their parents 'trusted' them. Broadly speaking, this meant they would do nothing to shame the family. Specifically it meant that they would not go to bed with a man to whom they were not married. Many of them did, indeed, cling to their virginity right to the edge of their marriage beds, fortified by their early training, their unshakable ideas of self-respect, and their not inconsiderable fears of pregnancy out of wedlock.

Those who did not wait for the formal vows justified their fall from grace with the honest, innocent conviction that premarital sex was a pledge of true mutual love which would be publicly acknowledged at the altar . . . always presuming their young man survived the war. Trembling, they climbed into their first illicit beds believing themselves in love, certain that the men who desired them were emotionally as well as physically involved, and rationalizing their betrayal of morality with the self-protective belief that this was no careless animal urge. They equated sex with love and love with permanent commitment and permanent commitment with marriage, home, and children. This was the way they felt; this was the way they naively believed their partners felt as well. And besides, with their young men in service, there was so little time.

And yet, with this almost Victorian attitude about sex, they were the most unfettered young women modern history had ever known. They smoked and drank, drove their own cars, sometimes took—over their parents' reluctant objections —their own apartments, and were often seriously, though fleetingly, 'career minded.'

Their career ambitions came right out of the pages of *women's* novels or straight off the surface of movie screens and ran to the kind of jobs portrayed as glamorous and exciting. They dreamed of being gorgeous but intelligent war correspondents, sophisticated magazine editors, highly paid retail executives, or beautifully dressed and frightfully clever heads of cosmetics companies, couture houses, or advertising agencies. They admired Dorothy Shaver, the president of Lord & Taylor, and stood in awe of tiny, dominant Carmel Snow, editor of *Harper's Bazaar*. But their real idols were Rosalind Russell and Katharine Hepburn, those strong, sure-of-themselves women who lit up movie screens with a sophisticated assurance that cloaked a normal weaker-sex need to be dominated by Cary Grant or Spencer Tracy. For though they fantasized about achievement and public recognition, most of these well-brought-up middle-class girls did not honestly believe that any career, no matter how dazzling, was woman's ultimate achievement. Marriage to a strong, handsome provider who would find their ambitions laudable but transient was, in their minds, the only enduring vehicle for true female fulfillment. When the films ended 'happily,' with Roz or Katie giving up her high salary and lofty position for the rewarding love of a tolerant but demanding man, they were satisfied with the outcome; they tacitly wanted to be 'kept in their place' by dominant men—having, of course, first sampled the sweet fruits of accomplishment. They approved of a story in which a rebellious Katie was lovingly and firmly squelched by a smarter, tougher Spencer. They nodded in understanding when a rapier-tongued Roz was outwitted but still respected by a suave, almost amused Cary. It was easy to identify with these high-spirited, identity-seeking female stars who ultimately 'came to their senses' through the persistence of assured and irresistible leading men. Their screen heroines accepted these normal roles of male and female, even up to and including a premarital double standard. Why should they, lesser mortals, question the way things were meant to be?

There were, of course, exceptions. And one of them was

Beverly. Not that she was so much different from the girls she grew up with. She shared their life-style, their attitudes and actions, including, for the first twenty years of her life, the precious price they placed on chastity. Beverly, too, had parents who constantly reiterated their trust in her, emphasizing that if they did not have such complete confidence in her they would never have allowed her, barely twenty, to take her own little apartment.

'We know what kind of a person you are, darling,' Angela Thyson had said. 'Neither your father nor I will lose a minute's sleep worrying about you.' She brushed back a tear. 'Not that we're really happy about this move, Beverly. It just doesn't look right for an unmarried girl to have her own place in the same city where her parents live—you're very young to be living alone. It's going to be lonely without you. And hard for you, too, dear, working in the store all day and trying to take care of an apartment and cook for yourself.' Angela sighed. 'But we know it's what you want. I suppose it's time for you to leave the nest. And, as I say, it's not as though we didn't have complete trust in you.'

'You and Dad don't have to worry about me, Mom,' Beverly had said patiently. 'I'm going to be fine. Good Lord, it isn't as though I'm moving to China! I'll only be across Central Park. I'll probably be here for dinner five nights a week!' She smiled at her mother. 'Besides, you know the *real* reason. It's much more convenient to the store, and now that I have my promotion I'll be working all hours, probably six days a week.'

'Stop being an overprotective parent,' Harry Thyson had said. 'My God, Angela, your baby is grown up. Who else do you know who has a kid who's an assistant buyer at her age? I'm proud as hell of her. She's going to be a big executive one of these days. You can't keep her on your apron strings forever.'

Bev glanced gratefully at her father. He'd wanted her to go to college, but she'd pleaded not to. Instead, she'd gotten a job as a salesgirl in the better dress department of Welby's Fifth Avenue, the most expensive specialty store in New York. She was only eighteen, but even at that most romantic of all ages she had begun to question the validity of woman's secondary role.

She and her best friend Ruth Wells had argued about it a

11

lot in the past year, particularly after seeing one of those boy-meets-girl, boy-loses-girl, boy-gets-girl films. Beverly did not find the predictable ending as satisfying as Ruth did.

'I think it's crazy,' Bev would say. 'Why couldn't Roz have kept on running her cosmetic business even after she married Cary?'

'Because, dope, you can't do that to a man's ego. He wants to be the breadwinner.'

'Who made up that rule? For God's sake, Ruthie, who decided there could be only one ego per family—Spencer Tracy?'

Ruth sighed. 'Nobody made up the rule. It's just the way things are. Honestly, Bev, I'm your best friend, and *I* don't understand you! Don't you want to get married and have kids?'

'Sure I do. But I don't see why I can't do both. Have a job and a family, I mean. Other women have.'

'Like who, Eleanor Roosevelt?'

Even Bev had to laugh. Then she turned serious again. 'No, really, I don't see why it can't work if you marry an intelligent man. I do want a career, Ruth. This selling job is only a first step for me. I'm going to be a buyer at Welby's, maybe even a merchandise manager one day, like Sylvia Schlesinger. There's an example for you, by the way. She has a nifty husband *and* a terrific job.'

'Sure. And you told me it took her three tries. Two divorces before she found that "nifty husband." Not for me, thanks. I'll settle for the vine-covered cottage instead of your business jungle. Bev, you're trying to go against the laws of nature. Men work and support their families. Women get a lot more out of life when they're good wives and mothers.'

'Aren't we supposed to be equal?' Bev asked. 'If I have a brain and ambition, am I supposed to forget it?'

'You're hopeless,' Ruth said. 'Like refusing to go to college with the rest of us.'

'It's a waste of time. I'm learning and getting paid for it. While you're getting fat on sorority-house food and looking for a husband, my friend, I'm going to be making a name for myself. As soon as I can afford it, I'm going to get my own apartment. But don't mention that to the folks. They have no idea.' She smiled at her friend's troubled expression. 'Don't look so worried, for Lord's sake. Maybe I'm just "going through a phase," as Mother would say. I'll probably end up like the rest of you—a happy suburban housewife. But Ruthie, there's something inside of me that has to be satisfied first. I'll never rest until it is. Maybe that's dumb, but that's how I am.'

'You're special, Bev, you've always been much more independent than the rest of us. But I hope this *is* a phase. Personally, I don't understand why you want to kill yourself working in a store, but that's your business. Anyway, it'll probably all change when you meet the right guy.'

Bev laughed. 'You and my mother! I think she'd rather see me unhappily married than not married at all. As long as I'm "Miss Thyson" I'll be a failure in Mother's eyes even if I get to be *president* of Welby's. Dad's different, which I must say surprises me. He fought me like a tiger about not going on with my education, but now I think he's kind of pleased that I'm talking career instead of marriage. I guess fathers don't really like the idea of "giving their little girls to some young upstart." He'd probably like me to be a virgin all my life.'

Three years later, acting as her friend's matron of honor while her husband served as best man, Ruth Wells Eliason, wife and mother, recalled that serious conversation. Bev had predicted both their futures with uncanny accuracy. Ruth had quit college at nineteen to get married, and Bev had become assistant buyer of Better Dresses and now was co-buyer of the Import Shop at Welby's. She had had her own apartment for two years, and today she was getting the understanding, indulgent husband she'd visualized. Like Angela Thyson, Ruth suspected that in between there had been bad times for Beverly. But like Angela, Ruth's suspicions were only that. Bev kept her own counsel, led her own life, did not even cry out for help when she needed it. Ruth correctly surmised that there had been times in these past years when Bev had desperately needed reassurance and support. She wished that they could have stayed closer. Even now, though she knew that her friend loved Ed Richmond, Ruth felt a strange uneasiness. It was as though Bev were settling for marriage because it was expected of her. Something was missing. There was almost an air of resignation about the bride, indefinable, perhaps imaginary. Ruth could only compare the atmosphere to her own wedding day when she had been suffused with happiness, an unreluctant virgin eager to give her life to Geoffrey Eliason. She'd not regretted it for a moment during the last three years. She found herself silently praying that Bev's fulfillment really was complete. She had her job, which she had no intention of leaving, and her tall, handsome husband, who was inordinately proud of her success. She also had, Ruth felt, more than her share of haunting memories. She's barely twenty-two, Ruth told herself, but she acts like a woman who has lived a lifetime and who's reaching, like a fifty-year-old, at a chance for security and companionship and peace.

There were others in the small chapel who loved Beverly Thyson dearly and who shared, to some degree, the vaguely disturbed feelings of her best friend. Beverly's boss, Sylvia Schlesinger, seated with her quiet, devoted Herman, had come to know the girl well. She liked her as a person, respected her ability, and had been instrumental in Bev's rapid rise in the retail world. But she saw in Beverly something of herself at that age—an almost schizophrenic desire to be a docile wife *and* a dominant executive. It had taken Sylvia almost the span of Bev's lifetime to realize that these qualities were incompatible in most women. She had had to live through two unsuccessful marriages and know the agonies of self-reproach before facing the fact that she was one of those strong women who could only exist happily with a noncompetitive man. It was a hard realization to accept. In the eyes of the world, Herman was a failure. That was not easy for any wife to live with. It had taken her twenty years to stop fighting the engendered idea that a husband must always be brighter, stronger and richer; that there was something disgraceful about a marriage in which the woman was the breadwinner. Sylvia was thirty-five years old before she stopped caring what 'they' thought. She was happy with Herman and he with her. But it was also a situation that one could understand only through experience. Ed Richmond, Sylvia believed, was very like Herman—a man without envy, arrogance, or the insecure need for masculine domination. He would make Bev a good husband. Sylvia's worry was whether Bev was mature enough, realistic enough, to recognize Ed's gentleness and not share the world's view of him as a weak man.

Sitting in the front pew 'on the groom's side,' Marion Richmond also found herself speculating on the durability of this union. She loved her brother and she loved Beverly, but she had not wanted to see them marry each other. And yet, the very evening she brought them together she knew uncannily that this would happen. Marion had introduced Bev last fall. She remembered how it had come about. Ed had come to the showroom of Marion's small, exclusive dress shop to pick her up for dinner. He was just out of the Air Force, disoriented and lonely. It was hard to imagine him as a navigator on a bomber in the Pacific during World War II; Ed was such an easygoing, nonviolent man. But he had loved active duty, had been actually sorry when he had to become a civilian again, faced with the prospect of finding a job, picking up a new life, even, Marion thought ruefully, being forced to make decisions on his own. She adored this only brother, but she had always known he was disinterested in status and success. She had also known that he would gravitate toward a woman with the capabilities and strength of Beverly Thyson. And that Bev would instinctively reach out for a man she could consciously mother and unconsciously dominate.

Bev had been in the showroom, writing the last order of the day for Welby's, the afternoon Ed arrived. She and Marion had become good friends through business. It seemed natural to ask Bev to join them for dinner. The romance started that night and ended on this sunny afternoon in the quiet little church. Marion wished she felt more content for both of them. Ed was in heaven, marrying this lovely, bright girl. And Bev was obviously devoted to him. But Marion felt they were wrong for each other. They would stick, Ed because he was loving and Bev because she was loyal, but it was a mismating of personalities. Marion knew it. So, she suspected, did the groom's mother, who sat quietly beside her.

In this she was not accurate. Jane Richmond had reservations about her son's marriage, but they were thrust somewhere back in a mind that was filled only with relief and happiness for Eddie. Widowed at forty-five, Jane had gone to work in a dress shop to support herself and her son; Marion, already twenty-five years old, was recently divorced and the owner of a small but flourishing dress business. Eddie was only sixteen, still in high school. He had always been—was to this day—the most loving and undemanding child. Jane had put him through college over his protestations that she couldn't afford it. She had worried about him all through the war. And now he was home, safe and sound and marrying this lovely girl. In her heart, Jane knew that Ed was intelligent but not brilliant, probably not likely to become a great success. But she believed that he would 'find himself' and she chose to believe that the strength she saw in Beverly was exactly what her son needed to start him on the normal, inevitable road to a successful, well-rounded business and personal life. The idea that he was weak—in the world's definition of the word—never crossed her mind. A little unmaterialistic, perhaps. Not as eager for fame and fortune as some. But this, Jane told herself, would change now that he had responsibilities. Bev would understand how hard to push him . . . and exactly how far.

The two men who were indirectly responsible for Bev's marriage to a man like Edward Richmond were not in the church. One of them read about the wedding in the *New York Times* the next day. The other had no idea it was happening. He read only the bulldog edition of the *Daily News*, which came out late at night. It was long on gossip columns and sports news, short on social notes.

2

The spring of 1944 was the happiest time Beverly had ever known. In March, the long-hoped-for promotion to permanent assistant buyer came about, thanks to the hard work of the appointee and the not entirely unselfish assistance of Sylvia Schlesinger, who not only liked Bev but recognized good executive material in the making.

The new job with its small but satisfactory increase in pay made it possible for Bev to have a roof of her own. It was a modest one, a small living room, bedroom, kitchenette, and bath in a big East Side apartment building. (Angela and Harry had made only one stipulation: Bev must live in a good part of town and in a building with a protective doorman and elevator operator.) Without great difficulty, she found a charming flat for which she paid—in those now-hard-to-believe days—ninety dollars a month including utilities. Bev adored it, and even though her budget was tight, she insisted on buying everything new, from furniture to kitchen equipment. She gently refused financial help from her father and offers of household goods from her mother. She wanted everything to be the product of her own efforts. She wanted to cut her ties with the past. Not that she planned to divorce herself entirely from her family. She was truly fond of them. She realized now that she had grown up in the Depression not really knowing that it existed. The Thysons were people of only moderate means, but they had deprived her of nothing within their power to give. She was grateful, and she would never willingly hurt them, but she knew somehow that she could not really relate to her parents. She was never able, as girls like Ruth Wells were, to be open and uncomplicated with her mother and father. She was incapable of sharing her thoughts with them. They did not understand her because she did not really understand herself. On the surface they were a quite ordinary, well-adjusted family. In reality, they were three totally different kinds of people.

In June, a week after her twentieth birthday, she moved into her own place. In July she fell madly in love with a man who she thought must have been made to order for her.

Frank Burroughs was twenty-eight when they met, a good-looking young Army lieutenant from Virginia currently stationed on Governors Island, the base just outside New York. Impeccable in his custom-tailored uniforms, Frank was a romantic dream. A well-born family had equipped him with a lightly accented prep-school voice, beautiful manners, and the head-turning deference to pretty young girls that somehow men learn early. They met at a cocktail party, and Frank was drawn immediately to this healthy, happy, independent creature who radiated excitement and anticipation.

Each of them had come alone to the party. They left together. Over dinner at Billy's restaurant, 'the oldest gas-lit bar in New York,' they talked for hours about their lives. Bev told him about her family, her job, her wonderful new apartment. He told her about his mother and father, brothers and sisters, all in Roanoke, about his cushy job in the Army which permitted him to keep an apartment in the city, and about his first marriage which had ended in divorce four years before.

'It was one of those kid things that never should have happened,' he said. 'We met in college. It lasted two years. She's a nice girl. We just weren't right for each other. Or for marriage.'

'You didn't have a child.' It was more a statement than a question.

Frank gave a strange smile. 'No.'

'Do you ever see her?'

'Never. I think she lives in Texas. I heard she got married again. But I really don't want to talk about my past, Beverly. What about your love life? Have you been married or anything?'

She shook her head. 'Not married or engaged . . . or anything.'

He understood what she meant. In those days, twenty-year-old virgins were not that rare.

18

After their fifth date they began to go steady, and Bev's conviction that she had found her husband-to-be grew stronger with every meeting. Thoughts of Frank took precedence over everything, even over her job. Suddenly her future as a career woman seemed less important than it had before he came into her life. Without discussing it, Bev knew that Frank Burroughs was not the kind of man who would want a working wife. He planned to return to Virginia after the war and go into his father's law firm. He spoke with genuine affection of his mother, his two sisters, of the kind of gentlemanly life that he looked forward to resuming once he 'got out of this damned monkey suit.'

As the romance progressed, so, of course, did their physical desires. They spent long hours in her apartment, kissing and embracing on the living-room couch. Bev let him roam searchingly over her clothed body, touch her breasts, put his hand between her thighs. But always she drew back. She would not touch him where he begged to be touched, or let him take her into the bedroom. Sometimes, in those next three months, he became angry. She felt she deserved his anger. She hated girls who were known as 'teasers.' She wanted him desperately. His kisses and embraces were insistent, his explorations agonizingly exciting. And still she held back, frightened of the irrevocable step, waiting for the promise that would make it all right. She could not tell him that she was only waiting for him to ask her to marry him, but she thought that if he did not they would explode with frustration. Some nights when he finally left she wondered whether he had gone off to find relief with some girl whose demands were less permanent. She shook with fear that she would lose him. And yet, without a declaration, she could not bring herself to give up the chastity she had been taught to guard. She knew she was a fool. She adored him, trusted him, ached for him. And yet her ingrained sense of right and wrong persisted. She fought it and could not win.

And then, in that magic year, it seemed that God rewarded her for her self-discipline. One night in her apartment when his caresses had brought them both to a frenzy of desire, Frank said the words she had prayed to hear. His mouth was on her breast, his hand almost rough as he pulled up her dress, reaching for the warmth that beckoned.

'Darling,' he said, 'please, please—'

Bev held him tightly, light-headed with desire.

'Marry me, Bev. I love you so much. I'll love you forever.'

Miracle. Reassured, overjoyed, free of guilt, she raised his head and kissed him fully and deeply.

'Oh, yes, my darling, of course I'll marry you. I love you —more than anything in life.'

In her bed she ventured a shy question. 'Sweetheart, can you . . . take care of things? You know I've never . . .'

In the dim light his face looked troubled. 'I know, love. It's all right. We can't have children, Bev. I'm sterile. Are you going to mind terribly?'

For a moment, the unexpectedness of it broke the mood, left her surprised, even dismayed. Her thought processes since knowing Frank had so completely turned around that she felt a twinge of loss at the thought of a childless future.

'Are you sure? How do you know?'

'I found out during my marriage. We wanted to have a baby. We went to doctors. I was the one who couldn't.'

He had moved a little away from her, waiting.

In an instant she gathered him into her arms, touching him now as he'd so often begged to be touched. 'It's you I want, my dearest. Frank darling—beloved—it's only you I want. Now and always.'

His relief was almost pathetic, his passion overwhelming. Sex was the beautiful, wonderful thing she'd known it would be, not frightening or possibly painful as some of her school friends had darkly predicted. It was a velvet cloud, a roaring, soaring flight of mindless bliss, purer and more exquisite than she'd dreamed, as natural as it was shameless. Over and over she loved and was loved. And much later, when she was alone, she convinced herself that she was actually happy about Frank's sterility. It had no relationship to his potency, and in a way it would almost make their marriage better. She had always been slightly repelled by the preplanning that contraception involved. She had imagined that it would somehow destroy the joyous spontaneity of sex, whether it was her responsibility or his. Now there was no need. They could have a wonderful, carefree physical union any time, anywhere, undisturbed by cautious interruption or the fear of an inconvenient pregnancy. She anticipated no feeling of deprivation. The maternal instinct was not strong with her. Had Frank wanted them, she would have had children happily. But with the feel of him still in and around her, she knew that the prospect of childlessness was nothing compared to the dread she'd had that her own priggishness would drive him away. If they wanted children one day, they could always adopt. It didn't matter. Nothing mattered now except that the man she loved wanted her beside him always.

Foreseeing a different kind of married life now, Beverly allowed herself to entertain a small hope that Frank might change his mind about going back to Virginia after the war. If there was to be just the two of them, why couldn't they live in New York? Who needed roomy old Southern mansions unless they were to be filled with kids? He could never have the kind of family he grew up in. Perhaps she could make him see that New York was right for them. Perhaps he would join a Manhattan law firm and she could go on with her career. She had been willing to give it up in exchange for marriage and motherhood. But if this was not the way it could be, why did she have to go and live in some dreary Southern town where there'd be nothing to do but garden, play bridge, and wait for Frank to come home at night? She didn't really want to stop working. She would have, she still would if Frank insisted. But maybe now there was a way to have the best of both worlds.

Wisely, she said none of this to her fiancé. But she could not resist pushing him to set a date for their marriage. He seemed to avoid it, invariably ending the discussions by picking her up in his arms and carrying her to bed, where he teased her about her impatience.

'What's the matter, old lady? Afraid you're going to be too old to marry? You have a point there. You're pushing twenty-one.'

'But darling, why should we wait? We're sure how we feel. You can give up that silly little apartment and move in here. It will be such a wonderful day when the girls at the store call me "Mrs. Burroughs" instead of "Miss Thyson." I don't want to miss a minute of being married to you. I want to sleep with you all night.'

He smiled at the last statement. Bev's sense of propriety excluded him from sleeping over. Even if it was five in the morning she insisted he go home after their lovemaking. Waking up with a man who wasn't her husband was still

21

wrong, according to her code of ethics, still something that 'nice girls' didn't do.

He propped himself up on his elbow and looked at the tousled head on the pillow beside him.

'Bev,' he said gently, 'I don't think we should get married until the war is over.'

She sat bolt upright. 'What are you saying? That's the most ridiculous thing I've ever heard! The war could last for years! Besides, except for your days at the base and the nights when you have the duty, it's as though the war doesn't even exist.'

'That's exactly the point. I may not be at Governors Island forever, sweetie. I hope I will, but nothing's certain in this man's army. What if I were shipped overseas? Even though we seem to be winning in Europe, the Pacific war could go on forever. There might be years of separation. It wouldn't be fair to you.'

Beverly could not follow this line of reasoning. 'Even if the worst happened,' she said, 'even if, God forbid, you were sent overseas, it wouldn't change anything. We're already married, Frank, at least as far as I'm concerned. I wouldn't behave any differently. I'd die of loneliness for you, sweetheart, but it's not quite the same as if you were to leave a woman with children who had to be cared for by one parent. I don't see what all this has to do with our being married.'

He kissed her. 'Baby, I understand you better than you understand yourself. You'd be in limbo. An unmarried wife, dying, as you say, of loneliness and too conventional even to have an innocent date. I'd go out of my mind worrying about you. Because in spite of what you say, you *would* feel different with a wedding ring on your finger. Without it, you might at least consider some harmless diversion if I were away for a long time.'

'But I wouldn't,' she protested. 'Not the way I feel about you.'

'I still think we should wait, darling. What's the big rush? I haven't even met your parents.'

'I know. And they're anxious to meet you. I haven't told them how serious it is, but I've hinted a lot about my beau.'

It was true. For the first time in her life she had come close to telling her parents everything about her deep feelings, her future hopes. Well, not everything. She would never let them know that she'd already slept with Frank. But she

22

talked about him almost incessantly when she had dinner with Angela and Harry. Her absorption with this new young man was unmistakable. Her mother and father exchanged knowing looks, asked casual questions, and waited to meet this Frank Burroughs who was so important to her. She had made no mention of an engagement or marriage, but there was no mistaking the tone of her voice when she spoke of him, even if the actual words remained unspoken.

He kissed her now. 'We'll make the family call soon. I guess I just haven't been able to face them. I feel like a dirty old man who's deflowered their precious child. But we'll go see them, I promise. Right after I come back from leave.'

At the mention of his leave, Beverly's face fell. He was going home for ten days. She'd hoped he'd ask her to go with him to meet his parents, but he had not. It was strange, she thought. In a way, Frank seemed to feel more guilty about their relationship than she did. She had expected to feel ashamed, but she didn't. They were in love; they would marry. It was only a matter of when.

The ten days he was gone seemed endless. She invented excuses to work late at the store, came home and listened to records, went to bed and dreamed of her lover. She supposed this was what he'd meant about the pattern she'd follow if he went away for a long time. But he was wrong. She could have endured the loneliness better if they had really belonged to each other in the eyes of the world.

She was radiant when he returned, eager to make love to him, joining in his laughter when he accused her of turning into a sexpot. The only thing that disturbed her was his continuing reluctance to meet her parents.

'They don't have two heads, darling,' she said. 'Daddy won't bite. And Mother will welcome you like a savior. I'm sure she's convinced I'm doomed to a life of spinsterhood!'

'We'll do it soon,' he promised again.

He was never to meet them at all. The end came explosively and unexpectedly two months later on the evening that Frank walked into her apartment obviously nervous and visibly upset. He didn't want a drink. He wasn't hungry. His kiss was strangely quick and cool. As though he had to get it over with quickly, he said, 'Bev, I have some bad news.'

Stomach churning, she tried not to show her fear. He was

going overseas; that's what it was. She tried not to sound as terrified as she felt.

'What's happened?' she asked lightly. 'You look like you're about to announce the end of the world.'

He didn't look at her. 'I guess I am. I'm getting married in two weeks.'

At first she didn't understand. For a hopeful moment she even thought that he was teasing her, that this was his whimsical way of saying that he had finally decided to set the date for their wedding. But he wasn't kidding. One look at his face told her that.

'What is this, Frank, some kind of childish game?'

'I wish it were, Bev. My God, how I wish it were! It's all a ghastly, stupid mistake.' He seemed unable to go on. 'Maybe I'll take that drink after all, if you don't mind.'

Wordlessly she handed him a whisky, her hand as cold as the ice she automatically dropped into the glass. Frank took a long swallow.

'It happened when I went home on leave. There's this girl. We were kids together but it was never a romance, I swear to you. I hardly ever thought about her. Never even bothered to mention her name to you, it was that unimportant. Especially after I met you. I'd almost forgotten she existed. But she hadn't forgotten about me. She was waiting when I got home, and we had a few dates. Christ, Bev, I don't know what happened. Maybe it was being back there, like I'd never been away, like the war and New York and everything else didn't really exist.'

And like I didn't exist either, Beverly thought. But she said nothing. Frank put down his drink and came over to her. He got down on his knees in front of her chair and looked into her face.

'She's pregnant, Beverly. The child is mine. I've spent all day on the phone with her and her family and my mother and father. They insist we get married right away.'

It was a nightmare—except that she was awake and looking into the beloved eyes so full of pain and remorse. For long seconds Beverly couldn't speak. Then she became hysterical.

'But it must be a mistake! It's impossible! Frank, you're sterile. It can't possibly be your child. You're being used, don't you see that? How can you allow yourself to be railroaded into this, knowing what you know?'

24

He shook his head. 'The baby's mine. Obviously the doctors were wrong.'

'The doctors were wrong! What about us? What about all these months? Why haven't I gotten pregnant if the doctors were wrong?'

'I can't answer that. God knows if I had to get somebody pregnant, Bev, I'd want it to be you. It's you I want to marry, not Sally. But I'm the father. I'm sure of that. Sally was a virgin.'

Bev didn't answer. The obvious spoke for itself.

'I don't know why I did it. It meant nothing to me: magnolias and mint juleps. And now this. I'm trapped. No way out. But you must believe that it's you I love.'

'Love!' She spat out the word. 'What kind of love? The kind that pushes me out of your mind and turns you into a tomcat the minute you're away from me? Is that what you call love?' The enormity was just beginning to hit her. 'I don't think you ever loved me, Frank. I don't think you ever intended to marry me. I don't even believe you thought you were sterile! Maybe you were crazy enough to take chances with me the way you did with your virginal Sally. You got away with it with me, but it didn't work with her, did it?'

He tried to quiet her. 'You know none of those things are true. I do love you. I do want to marry you, but now I can't. As for believing I was sterile, of course I believed it. I'm not crazy or stupid. I had every reason to think the doctors were right. Even if I didn't believe it, isn't that proof that I was willing to take a chance that you'd get pregnant because I knew I wanted to marry you? But that isn't the way it was, Beverly. I did think I could never father a child. My God, if I'd had any inkling, do you think I'd have been so foolish as to have that idiotic fling with Sally?'

She was crying now, confused, wounded but still fighting for her life.

'All right, Frank, you did something despicable, but we can forget it. You don't have to marry her.'

'Yes I do, darling. A man has to do what's right. He has to face the consequences of his acts. That's what I've been brought up to believe.'

She faced him angrily. 'And what have I been brought up to believe? That's not important, is it? I was a virgin too. Just like your precious Sally. I gave you months of love. She gave

25

you a few evenings. Does that entitle her to the rest of your life? Let her get an abortion. Or let her have the damned baby without you and your lousy code of honor!'

'You know I couldn't do that, Bev.'

'I don't know anything! For all I know you may have been engaged to her the whole time you've been pretending with me. Maybe she's not even pregnant. Maybe this is just your rotten, devious way of doing something you've had in mind all along.'

He walked slowly to the door. 'Think anything you want of me, Bev. Hate me if it will help. But as God is my judge, I love you.'

With all the dignity she could summon, she turned her back on him.

'Go away, Frank,' she said. 'Just go away.'

3

Frank's totally unexpected betrayal produced a feeling of numbness that Beverly could not shake. After the tears she shed in his presence, she did not cry again. Some mornings she awakened with relief, believing for a few happy seconds that the whole episode had been a bad dream, only to revert, once again, to a bleak, wooden, walking-dead state of existence.

She held silent conversations about what had happened. They went on inside her head, endlessly and unproductively. In the beginning, womanlike, she wondered what she should have done differently, where she went wrong, how she could have prevented what happened, or what she could have said to convince Frank that it was wrong to sacrifice his life and hers for an unrealistic ideal of chivalry. Later, her thinking changed. Now the dialogues of her mind were filled with bitter condemnation of Frank and unanswered questions about his honesty, right from the beginning. She would never know the truth about Sally, past or present. She would never know whether the whole sterility story had been invention. One brief sexual experience did not qualify her as an expert on such matters. Perhaps it was she who was incapable of childbearing. There was no logic to her thinking. She was unable to put the events into focus, and for a long while she was too stunned to know where to place the blame.

When, at last, she pointed a finger at the culprit, the accused was, once again, herself. She became scornful of her own naiveté, filled with self-hatred and unknowingly obsessed with the desire for punishment. There was no one to fulfill this subconscious need for chastisement except Beverly herself. She had made a fool of herself, had been a trusting, blindly romantic child who saw love as the all-encompassing answer to the questions of life, and in her muddled mind she believed she had to pay.

She remembered how she had spat the word 'love' at Frank on that last evening. In that, at least, she'd been right. Frank did not know its definition. No one did. Love, Beverly thought, is a master of disguises, the Houdini of happiness. Skilled in the art of subterfuge, tricky, clever, and hypnotic, love is an evil magician, adept at a sleight of hand that is quicker than the eye of the innocent.

For the young and hot-blooded, like herself, love masqueraded as sex, an enduring power that could conquer all. For the aging and lonely, she supposed, it was a final embrace. The inherently compassionate confused love with pity while the arrogant equated it with power. It was emotional displacement, a tug-of-war between decency and desire. Only the realists could define love in one cynical word: liar.

In this period of bitter scorn for herself, Beverly withdrew from all but the necessary contacts with other people. She pulled her shame around her like a heavy cloak, hiding her 'stupidity' from the curious, the sympathetic, or the wise. She might have gone to any one of several women for solace or encouragement or advice. She had no wish to. Her mother, had Beverly been able to explain to her, would have opened her maternal arms to a hurt child, but Angela would have had no frame of reference for understanding. Ruth would have listened, as she always had, to her friend's self-questioning and responded with pat reassurances that Frank was a heel and it really was for the best. But Ruth would have had only a surface awareness of Bev's unutterable despair. Like Angela, she had never lived through anything as degrading and gut-wrenching as this. Lucky Ruth was too involved in her own happiness, her recent marriage to the dependable Geoff Eliason, her enviable position as having made a 'good catch.'

Had she dared, the woman Beverly would have liked to confide in was Sylvia Schlesinger, a woman she sometimes guiltily wished were her own mother. But she was not close enough to Sylvia to pour out this unhappy story. Nor could she intrude on the employer-employee relationship in such a suddenly personal manner. Sylvia, Bev thought, might understand the way she despised herself. It would not have surprised Bev if this worldly, tolerant woman had not, at some point in her life, suffered the same self-loathing. But it would be impertinent to make that assumption. It would be an unthinkable imposition.

So she kept her suffering and her self-punishment to herself, fed on it, nurtured it, determined never again to permit such vulnerability, equally and unreasonably convinced that somehow she should atone for her misplaced trust.

It would not be fair to say that in this period Beverly was deranged, but certainly her confusion, particularly her unconscious desire for self-abasement, could reasonably be considered a temporary kind of madness. On the surface, she showed no particular change. She was as efficient as always at her job. She looked and acted the bright, well-dressed, well-organized young assistant buyer. But beneath the crisp unchanged exterior, Beverly Thyson was a robot, going automatically through the duties expected of her at Welby's, solving departmental problems, assisting the buyer, Miss Jamieson, whose job she hoped soon to have, conferring frequently with Sylvia Schlesinger, who had given Bev subtle hints that she would be promoted when Miss Jamieson retired.

She did not, during this period, see either Ruth or Angela and Harry Thyson. It was not unusual for her not to see Ruth. Although she was the only one of Bev's childhood friends with whom she kept in touch, sometimes months went by without the two girls meeting. Avoiding her parents was more difficult. She invented excuses for not coming to dinner, fielded questions from Angela about her 'young man,' promised she'd go to Central Park West soon for a long-delayed visit. Her mother suspected that something was wrong, but she did not press Beverly. She knew, as well as her daughter, that they did not share the kind of easy rapport they both might have wished for. The Thysons had never met Frank Burroughs, had only heard Bev mention his name in what she thought was a casual, offhand manner. Angela, even more than her husband, had sensed Bev's serious interest and waited hopefully for something solid to develop.

Now, in this long period of withdrawal, Angela was certain that Beverly's absence had something to do with the romance. Bev, for some reason, did not want to visit her parents as she had done weekly since the day she took her own apartment. One Sunday Angela Thyson discovered why.

Reading the society section of the *New York Times*, her eye was caught by a picture of a pretty young girl in traditional wedding dress. The caption read 'Sally Crawford weds Lt. Frank Burroughs.' A description of the wedding in Roanoke, Virginia, followed, including the information that the bridegroom was stationed in New York, where the couple would make their home. Angela knew that Bev's Frank came from Roanoke and that he was posted to Governors Island and—clincher because they had laughed about it—that his father's name was Robert Lee Burroughs.

Angela's impulse was to call her daughter. Instinctively she resisted. If this was the reason for Bev's absence, and Angela was sure it was, the child must be terribly hurt. True to form, she would be hiding away to lick her wounds. Even as a little girl she had kept her disappointments to herself, refusing concern, which she thought of as curiosity, or help, which she proudly but foolishly equated with pity. Angela knew better than to speak first. Bev was jealous of her privacy. When and if Frank Burroughs was ever mentioned again, the subject would be brought up by Beverly. Her mother could do nothing but wait. She's only a baby, Angela consoled herself. She'll get over a broken romance. I only hope she hasn't done anything foolish.

In Angela's definition of 'foolish,' Bev had. She had offered her precious chastity to a man whom she would not marry. By Bev's definition she had been foolish only in being open and honest and expecting a man to be the same. She vowed never to make that mistake again, a resolve that was strengthened when she too read the *Times*. The picture of a smiling, secure Sally Crawford hardened her heart. It also, surprisingly, shocked her out of her immobility. The final, printed confirmation forced her into the hateful realization that she had to go on living, even pick up some kind of life outside of the store. She had to get back into the world, but this time she would return selfishly, looking for fun and games, giving nothing, expecting nothing, because she deserved nothing. It was a dangerous and uncharacteristic attitude, destined to

30

lead her into a chapter of her life which only a few weeks before she would have found unthinkable.

It began harmlessly enough through the friendly intervention of Midge DeLuca, a chirpy, cricketlike girl of Bev's age. Midge and Bev had come to Welby's at about the same time as salesgirls. They had never been close because they had nothing in common, not background, standards, or ambition. But they liked each other. Midge admired Beverly's poise and brains; Bev found the easy cheerfulness of the little Italian girl pleasant and warming. Midge was incapable of malice or envy. She was delighted when Bev was promoted, knowing that this was what she wanted. Midge wanted something quite different: her job was no more than a holding action until her beau, Tony Marino, doing war work as a welder, was financially able to marry her.

It would have surprised Bev to know that lately Midge was worried about her. Underneath Bev's semblance of composure, Midge recognized a troubled and unhappy young woman. It has to be man problems, she rationalized. Nothing else makes a girl look so drawn and unhappy. All this was pure conjecture, of course. Bev did not socialize with the staff. Even Midge called her 'Miss Thyson' in front of the others, though she used her first name when they were alone in Bev's office. In the locker room one morning Midge made a startling statement to the other girls.

'I think Miss Thyson's awfully unhappy about something,' she said. 'Any of you kids notice a difference in her?'

Karen Landers shrugged. 'Not especially. She's always been a block of ice as far as I'm concerned.'

Jean Brandt disagreed. 'I think Midge is right. She acts sort of—well, *automatic*. Like she's got a lot on her mind. You think maybe she's not going to get old Jamieson's job after all? Maybe they're going outside for a new buyer. That would really throw Thyson.'

Midge shook her head. 'I don't think that's it. I think it's something personal. Like maybe a broken love affair.'

'Oh, for Christ's sake, Midge,' Karen said impatiently, 'you don't even know whether she's ever *had* a love affair! I'll bet she's never even been in the hay with a guy.'

'Karen's right,' Jean said. 'I agree with you that Thyson's

upset about something, but you're jumping to conclusions. Anyway, what the hell can you do about it?'

Midge stood her ground. 'Maybe nothing, but I'm going to try. I'll bet you five bucks she's dying of loneliness. I'm going to ask her to go out one night with Tony and me. If she has a fella, she'll bring him. If she doesn't, I'll offer to introduce her to somebody. Look, she can't kill me for making a friendly gesture, can she?'

'Depends on what you call death,' Karen said. 'You could end up with the brush-off of your life, closely followed by a new assignment to bras and girdles.'

Once again, Jean agreed. 'I think you ought to stay out of it, Midge. You don't know for sure what's eating Thyson. I know you started here at the same time, but you've never been buddies. You're only guessing about her love life. Remember, a person never gets in trouble keeping her mouth shut.'

'Maybe so,' Midge said, 'but she never helps anybody either. When the time's right, I'm going to try.'

The time came a few days later when Midge went into Bev's cubbyhole office to ask her to okay the return of an evening dress.

'It's that same lady who always brings back the glamour job she bought the day before. Will you sign the credit?'

'Reluctantly,' Bev said, reaching for the paper and scrawling her initials on it. 'It's against policy. If she weren't such a good customer in other departments I'd put a stop to this business of bringing back evening clothes.'

'Maybe she buys them for big dates that don't come off,' Midge said.

Beverly managed a half smile. 'Maybe. More likely she wears the dress one night and brings it back. She's a chronic returner, Midge. You know that. One of these days we're just going to have to clamp down, good customer or not.'

'Sure. But she always looks so apologetic when she comes in. Like she has a lot of disappointments. Plans that fall through. You can almost read that kind of thing in a woman's face.'

Bev looked at her curiously, not answering.

Nervously, Midge rushed on. 'Look, Bev, I hope you won't be offended, but I've been worried about you. These ast few months you've seemed . . . different. Is there anything I can do? I mean, I know we aren't really friends, but I hate to see you looking so sad all the time. Some of the other girls have noticed it too.'

For a moment Beverly was angry. How dare they gossip about her, speculate about her problems? But Midge's earnest, troubled little face stopped her from making a cutting reply. They cared, these girls. They liked her, respected her, even though she had kept aloof from them. Perhaps with most of them it was just curiosity, but with Midge she knew it was genuine concern. She was touched by it.

'It's dear of you to offer, Midge, but there really isn't anything you can do.'

Midge looked like a spanked puppy. 'I'm sorry. I guess it's none of my business. It's just that I've always liked you and I know something's bothering you. Maybe I had the dumb idea you needed somebody to work it out with.' She laughed self-consciously. 'Well, excuse me for butting in. I'm sure you have plenty of friends to talk to.' She started for the door, but Bev stopped her.

'Midge. Wait.' To her surprise, Bev found herself wanting to tell this girl about her troubles. It was idiotic to pick someone she barely knew as the only person she felt able to confide in, but then it was easier sometimes to talk to strangers than to those really close to you.

'I'd appreciate it if you'd keep this to yourself,' Bev said, 'but you're right. The details are unimportant, but I have been having a bad time. A broken engagement. It hit me pretty hard, but I didn't know it showed so conspicuously. I'm glad you told me. I'll try not to act so much like a road-company Camille from now on.'

Midge hadn't the faintest idea what a 'road-company Camille' was, but the way Bev said it was pathetic.

'I'm sorry. It must be tough to lose somebody you love. But you're so terrific, Bev. Somebody better will come along.' Midge stopped. 'Now, that's gotta be the dumbest thing I *ever* said! If I were in your shoes and somebody handed me that kind of canned sympathy the first thing I'd do would be clobber 'em.'

Bev smiled. 'If you were in my shoes, Midge, what's the next thing you'd do?'

'Well, I wouldn't just sit back and wait for something to happen. I'd go find another guy as fast as I could. Nothing heals a broken heart faster than a new romance.'

'And where would you go to find it, wise one?'

Midge considered that. 'I guess I'd put out the word that I was on the market again,' she said. 'You oughta let your friends know that you're free. There must be lots of people who could introduce you to new men. I'll bet you've been running home from the store and moping every night. That's no good. You'll never get over it that way, not by yourself.

'Good advice,' Beverly said, 'if I knew how to implement it. Meantime, you'd better get back on the floor with that okayed return before your wounded dove is too old to be interested in another evening dress she can buy and return.'

'Holy cow! You're right!' Again Midge started for the door. Encouraged now by Bev's unexpected openness, she paused. 'Listen, I've got a crazy idea. Can I come back at lunchtime and try it on you?'

'Of course. And Midge . . .'

'Yes?'

'Thank you. Thank you very much.'

The crazy idea which Midge returned to explain was an invitation for Bev to join Midge and Tony on the following Thursday evening. It was, Midge explained, her birthday, and they were going to celebrate with dinner and dancing at their favorite place, Valentino's, a restaurant-bar on West 52nd Street. She chattered enthusiastically about the idea. She'd told Tony so much about Beverly, he was dying to meet her. And he had this nice friend, a lawyer named Paul Young recently discharged to civilian life. Another couple was going along, the Fitzgeralds. It would be fun. Lots of laughs. The food wasn't bad and there was a great combo. Please say yes, she begged.

Bev's immediate impulse was to decline politely. There was no reason to go, and every reason not to. She was not a snob, but she had always made it a point not to hobnob with the girls who worked for her. Much as she liked Midge, she knew that her crowd was from a different stratum. She probably would have nothing in common with them. As for the blind date, Paul Young, the whole idea was unattractive. Midge, out of pity, was trying to fix her up with a new man.

34

She didn't want her pity; she recoiled from the idea that Midge saw her as some poor, forlorn creature who couldn't get a date on her own. And yet, Bev thought realistically, that was not too far from the truth. She had dropped all her old friends for Frank Burroughs. The men she used to date occasionally no longer called, and she was too proud to call them.

She admitted to herself that she was lonely. The last thing she wanted was a new emotional attachment. But perhaps that was all the more reason to accept Midge's candidate —someone with whom she could not possibly get involved. To her amazement, she heard herself accepting the invitation. She had to do something, even if it was only to run away from herself and her own self-hatred.

Midge was delighted. 'That's great! Shall we pick you up at your apartment about eight?'

'No!' The answer was so quick and sharp that it startled both of them. Embarrassed, Bev tried to cover up. She could not say that she wasn't yet ready to face meeting another man in the place where she had spent so many ecstatic hours with Frank. Poor Midge. She probably thought that Bev didn't consider her and her friends good enough to come calling at the smart East Side address. Bev quickly tried to explain. 'I have a date for drinks that night,' she lied, 'so I'll meet you at Valentino's, if that's okay.'

Midge looked relieved. 'Sure. Fine. We'll be there a little after eight. Just ask for Mr. Marino's table.'

Half a dozen times in the next few days, Bev came close to telling Midge that she couldn't make it on Thursday. It was ridiculous for her to get mixed up, even for one evening, with these people. But she couldn't hurt Midge's feelings, not after the way the girl had dared to extend a friendly hand. She'd go and escape as soon as she decently could. She had never been in Valentino's, but she knew about it—a typical jazz joint, not unrespectable but a far cry from any place Frank would have taken her. The thought made her angry at herself. If Frank had had half the compassion of Midge and her friends, she wouldn't be in this absurd situation. She had to forget Frank. At least someone was trying to help her do that. Filled with gratitude, she took herself to the cosmetics department and bought Midge the most expensive compact in stock—a flashy fake-jeweled copy of a design by Van Cleef & Arpels—as a birthday present. Midge would love it.

On Thursday night, almost timidly, she presented herself at Valentino's. In the cab she had been tempted to turn back. It seemed too much effort for nothing. But it was not for nothing, she told herself. It was only ordinary politeness in return for consideration.

Midge's group was assembled when she arrived, five nice-looking young people seated at a disconcertingly conspicuous table right next to the bandstand. Midge beckoned enthusiastically and performed the introductions when Bev reached the table.

'I'm so glad to see you!' she said. There was a trace of relief in her voice. Had she suspected that Bev might not show up? 'These are my friends, Julie and Tom Fitzgerald, Paul Young, and the fella who's stuck with me, Tony Marino. This is my boss, everybody, Miss Thyson.'

Bev pretended horror while she acknowledged the greetings and took the chair that Paul Young held out for her. 'Please, Midge! You make me feel like a stranger. The name is Beverly. And I hope you like this little birthday remembrance. Many happy returns.'

Midge tore open the Welby's gift wrap.

'It's gorgeous, Bev, you *shouldn't* have!'

'It's not nearly enough to thank you for inviting me. I've looked forward to meeting you all, and I'm so flattered that you included me in the party.'

It was not true. She still had misgivings about being there. Yet they all seemed pleasant enough. Tony Marino was a good-looking young man who obviously adored Midge. The Fitzgeralds, slightly older, appeared to be their best friends. And even her blind date, Paul Young, was a perfectly respectable-seeming, decent-looking lawyer in his early thirties. A mixed bag, Bev thought. My Italian host and hostess, their dear Irish friends, and a Brooks Brothers-suited WASP for me. All in all, better than she had expected. In spite of feeling that, at least for business reasons, she shouldn't be there, Beverly found herself enjoying it. They were a gay group, full of laughter and good-natured teasing as Midge opened the other gifts in front of her plate. She was childishly excited and pleased by the attention, and yet Beverly was aware that she was just a little nervous about the presence of her boss. She kept glancing at Bev often, obviously anxious to be sure she was having a good time, probably hoping, Bev thought with affection, that Paul Young would like her and vice versa.

Paul did seem to like her, and she found him intelligent and articulate. But no bells rang for her, and she was quite sure they did not ring for him either. Instead, something else quite extraordinary was happening.

Right from the start of the evening, Bev felt another pair of eyes on her: the insolent, interested, almost challenging eyes of the good-looking black-haired drummer in the band. Whenever she looked up, he was staring at her, a half smile on his face. At first she returned the smile noncommittally, then uncomfortably, and finally not at all. She tried not to look at him, but her chair faced him directly and his concentration on her was so intense that it was impossible to ignore. Midge picked it up quickly.

'Do you know Neil?' she asked.

'Neil? Who's Neil?'

'The drummer. Neil Farrentino. He acts like he's seen you before.'

Bev shrugged. 'Never set eyes on him in my life. He a friend of yours?'

'Not really. Tony and I have talked to him a few times. He seems like a nice fellow.'

'He sure has eyes for you, Bev.' Tony laughed. 'He's been looking at you all night.'

'I may have to punch him in the mouth,' Paul said lightly.

Bev joined in the laughter, but inside she was trembling. It was absurd to be so upset by the rude stare of a musician, yet she could feel the vibrations between them. There was a raw, sexual pull building up. With no contact, without so much as a word, Beverly was excited by the man. I must be going insane, she thought. My imagination is running away with me. To hide her distress she excused herself to go to the ladies' room. When she came out, Neil Farrentino was waiting in the corridor.

4

The affair with Neil was a spiritual suicide in which Beverly sought to obliterate all traces of the rules she had been taught to follow. It was also, in her mind, a secret revenge on Frank Burroughs. During the unlikely weeks that followed, she sometimes thought with bitter amusement of how her actions would have horrified her first lover. Her reckless behavior was because of him, and he would have had an even greater sense of guilt had he known about it—or so, in her contorted mental state, Beverly believed. As for her, this was, at last, the punishment she sought. Neil represented retribution. In return for her blind devotion to Frank she had received rejection. She was in mourning for her own stupidity. The loss of her precious virtue did not trouble her nearly as much as what she saw as her idiotic, ill-founded trust in men. It was a lesson learned the hard way, and she thought that in return for this hateful new knowledge she deserved to be humiliated. Neil was the perfect vehicle for her anger, which was turned inward in a bizarre and totally unrealistic way.

She remembered, later, how he had looked, lounging in the dingy hallway outside the ladies' room, smoking a cigarette, waiting for her to appear. Neil was handsome as one imagines the devil is handsome—dark, seductive, compelling. She had never seen eyes like his, black, bottomless, unreadable. There was a promise of excitement and danger about him, but his smile gave no hint of that. It was open, friendly, almost boyish.

'You took a long time,' he said without preamble. 'I was afraid I'd have to go back on the stand before you came out.'

'Would that have been so terrible?'

'Noooo. Not terrible. Disappointing, maybe.' He seemed to be appraising her. 'The fact is, I'm curious.'

Bev didn't answer.

'Don't you want to know what I'm curious about?' He moved closer. She smelled expensive cologne, was intensely aware of the lithe, muscular body under the conventional dinner suit. He did not touch her, but she knew what it would be like if he did. She made a pretense of casualness.

'All right. What are you curious about?'

'You. You don't fit. I can't peg you.'

'That's strange,' Bev said. 'All evening you've made me feel like a bug under a microscope. By now I'd have thought you had me all figured out.' She smiled. 'Let's leave it as one of life's little mysteries, shall we? You have to go back to work, and I have to go back to my friends.'

He didn't move. 'They're not your friends. They're not your type.'

'Really? And how do you come by that instant diagnosis?'

'Lady, when you've played clubs as long as I have, you figure out people pretty fast. We get all kinds here—the tramps, the uptown snobs slumming, the middle-class jerks like the ones you're with. You don't fit any of those. You're not a rich doll, but you've got class and you're bored out of your mind. So what are you doing here?'

'At the moment I seem to be trapped in a hallway.'

Bev thought he was going to grab her, but he just stood there, smiling. Then he stepped aside, making room for her to pass. 'Okay. Sorry. Guess I had a wrong hunch.'

It was, as he well knew, exactly the right thing to say. Now the curiosity was on her side.

'And what was your hunch?'

'That you're a nice girl wishing something exciting would happen to her.'

The accuracy of the statement startled her into an involuntary response.

'And if I were?'

'Well,' Neil said slowly, 'if you were, you'd let your date take you home and then you'd come back here. I quit work at two.'

Beverly brushed past him. 'Sorry. It's not my style.'

Neil made a mock bow. 'I know,' he said. 'That's exactly the point.'

40

For the rest of the evening Bev was aware of his eyes on her, mocking, challenging, half amused by her discomfort. She did not know that he was surprised by his own interest in her. Normally, he had nothing to do with the drop-in trade who came to Valentino's. He didn't covet the well-dressed, silly young girls who came with their uniformed boyfriends. A lot of them looked at him appraisingly, even invitingly. But Neil gave them no more than an insolent recognition which he knew they would not follow up. He didn't want them to. His kind of girl was like himself—sexy, not overly bright, and, above all, transient. There was a plentiful supply of easy, uninhibited bodies at his disposal, demanding nothing but physical satisfaction and a few mutually recognized lies about how much he loved them. They were the regulars who drifted in and out of his night circle. They were his bed mates on the evenings when they weren't being paid for their services. Neil never paid. He didn't have to.

It was unlike him to go chasing what his Italian immigrant mother called 'a good girl.' Neil was sure that Bev fell into that category. If so, she could be nothing but trouble. She wouldn't understand the rules, this little bird dying to try her wings in the big scary world, this protected kid who was looking for danger. Neil sensed when women like this one were itching for new kicks. The problem was that they didn't know when to get lost. He didn't know what had prompted him to make a pass. She excited him, but he hoped she wouldn't come back. And yet he knew she would.

When she rejoined Midge and the group, Bev truly had no idea of taking Neil Farrentino up on his offer of the late date. It was more than a cheap idea; it was foolhardy. The man was a stranger who might be anything—a drug addict, a sadist, who knew what? She had never in her life been picked up. It was weird to consider the experience under *any* conditions, and insane to even toy with the thought under *these*.

And yet, when she bid Paul Young a polite good night at her front door, deftly fending off a kiss with a polite handshake and a thank-you, she knew she was going back to Valentino's. She felt frightened and excited getting into a cab at one o'clock in the morning, trying to sound very cool as she gave the driver the address. As she had on the earlier trip, she was tempted midway to turn back, but, as before, she did not.

The band was taking a break when she came into the club. Neil, sitting at the bar, motioned to her and she joined him there. She was strangely offended that he did not seem surprised to see her.

'Hi,' he said. 'What are you drinking? They've got a few bottles of Scotch tucked away.'

'Fine. With plain water, please.' When the bartender was out of earshot she spoke again. 'You don't seem very surprised that I came back. Are you always so sure of yourself?'

'Usually.'

'Which means you do this often, I suppose.'

Neil looked at her expressionlessly. 'As a matter of fact, I don't. Girls like you are bad news. I was hoping you wouldn't come.'

Bev clutched her purse. 'I can always leave,' she said. 'I don't know what I'm doing here anyway.'

'Sure you do. You're looking for a good lay."

She turned scarlet, shocked by his crudeness. She got down off the barstool. Neil took her arm.

'Get back up here,' he said. 'If you want an apology I'll give you one, but it won't change my mind. I still think that's what you're here for, even if you don't know it. So what? What's so bad about a good screw with a few laughs thrown in? Drink your drink and relax. What can you lose? By the way, you might tell me your name.'

'Beverly,' she said. 'Beverly Thyson.'

'Pretty name. Pretty girl.' He took her hand and held it almost tenderly. 'You're trying to work out some kind of problem, aren't you, Beverly Thyson? Maybe you've got a crazy idea that you can work it out with me. Well, maybe you can. But maybe you won't like it.' He glanced at the bandstand. 'Gotta go do the last set. Be back in twenty minutes. Then, if you want to, we'll go out and see how the other half lives.'

While he was gone, she tried to make her mind behave. You've started something, she told herself. For God's sake, be woman enough to finish it. Don't be surprised by this vulgar musician's gutter language and insulting accusations. Something has brought you here, and he knows it. Let it lead

42

you, mindlessly, wherever it will. Almost irrelevantly, she wished she hadn't given Neil her right name. Not because she minded his knowing it, but because she wanted to be another person. Beverly Thyson would never behave this way.

When he came back she was determined to join him in whatever lay ahead. That first night he took her to a seedy joint on Eighth Avenue where they ate hamburgers and drank until four in the morning. She told him where she worked and lived and that her parents were in New York. She did not tell him about Frank Burroughs, but she did say that she'd recently had a bad experience with a man.

'Husband?'

'No. Fiancé.'

'What was the matter, couldn't he cut it?'

For the first time, Beverly smiled. 'He cut it,' she said, 'but with somebody else.'

'So he cheated on you and you walked out in a huff. Typical. Jesus, girls like you never learn, do you?'

'It wasn't that way, Neil. He walked out on me.'

'Why? Are you lousy in bed?'

'I don't know. I haven't had much experience in that direction. I believed that I was loved, very gently, very tenderly, and very honestly. Somehow I messed it up.'

'So you messed it up. Big deal. Probably the first time. Feeling sorry for yourself, aren't you? Baby got hurt, didn't she? Think maybe the big, crude, sexy drummer can make it all well?'

She cringed from his directness and his uncanny accuracy.

'Listen, Beverly, we better get a few things straight. I can show you a world you don't know anything about. It isn't nice and polite and pretty, but it's honest. I can introduce you to a lot of people you might wish you'd never met. And I can screw you until your head comes off. But I won't fall in love with you, I won't marry you, and when it's over, it's over. If you want to play with me by those rules, you can play.' He paused. Then, abruptly, 'You got a diaphragm?'

Stunned, Beverly shook her head.

'Get one tomorrow. Jesus, no wonder you messed it up! Come on. I'll put you in a cab. When you're ready, you know where to find me.'

Next day, as though in a trance, she went to a doctor and

43

was fitted with the contraceptive device. That night, wearing it, she went back to Valentino's.

Every night thereafter she met Neil when he finished work. Usually they would join a group of musicians, gamblers, and hangers-on, uneducated, rough young men and their flashily dressed women. They sat in on jam sessions in closed nightclubs, ate indifferent food in Chinatown, frequented dirty little Italian restaurants. At four or five in the morning they would go to Neil's hideous little room in the West 20s, where he would make violent, selfish love to her, apparently disinterested in her satisfaction, concerned only with his own.

His sexual demands were incessant, his language foul and laced with obscenities which he used to describe her timid body and her still strangely innocent reactions to his uninhibited behavior in bed. He never struck her, but he was often rude to her in the presence of others, sometimes ignoring her for hours while he flirted with another girl. She accepted it all, welcoming the crudeness, the ugliness, the debasement. It was as though she were going through some kind of cleansing with dirty water.

It might have gone on for a long while if sheer physical exhaustion had not mercifully put an end to it. She hated everything Neil represented: the carelessness of his way of life, the cheapness of his friends, the limitations of his mind. But to her own shame, she responded to his lovemaking. For all its brutality, it was expert and exhilarating, even to the point of sometimes making her forget the sleazy rooming house and the untidy bed from which she crept at six o'clock every morning to dress and go home to her own apartment.

But there was a limit to how much punishment she needed or how long she could go with only four or five hours' sleep in every twenty-four. Five, sometimes six days a week she rushed home from the store, had a cup of soup, and went to bed, setting the alarm for midnight. Then she got up, dressed, and spent the rest of the night with Neil, returning in early daylight to bathe and dress for work. On her day off and on Sunday she slept all day, sometimes fourteen hours at a time. She did not see Neil on Sunday. That was his day with his mother and the seemingly endless numbers of brothers

44

and sisters, in-laws, nieces, and nephews which comprised the Farrentino clan she never met.

Not that Neil had ever met the much smaller and far different Thyson family. They did not know of his existence. No one in Beverly's normal life did. She could never have explained this 'romance' to anyone. She could not even explain it to herself. All she knew was that as suddenly as she started it, she ended it. Sitting, bruised and exhausted, in a taxi at six o'clock one morning, ignoring the leering, curious eyes of the driver watching her through the rearview mirrow, Beverly knew it was over. She was physically exhausted, but she was also blessedly drained of the madness that had led her into this obsessive behavior. She wanted to be Beverly Thyson again, to lead a life that made sense to her, to attack her job with the energy she'd been unable to summon since Frank had left. She wanted to see the family she had avoided. She wanted to sleep alone, in the clean sheets of her own bed, have dinner at Schraffts, go to an eight-o'clock movie. Dumb things, normal things. She thought about them with anticipation and relief.

That night she did not go to Valentino's. She went to bed at ten o'clock and awakened at seven the next morning, dimly aware that the phone had not rung. She was not surprised. Though no words had been spoken, Neil would know what her absence meant. He might even be glad that the affair was over. In any case, he had no need for explanations and he would do no soul-searching, engage in no reminiscences. If he thought about her at all it would be without emotion. Neil had no capacity for introspection. He was a healthy, selfish animal whose life had been briefly touched by this 'kid,' as he often called Beverly. He'd used and enjoyed her body, perhaps even liked her company, but he would accept her disappearance from his life as casually as he had fitted her into it. To him it was just another, perhaps slightly more unusual affair. Neither of them had ever thought it would last. Neil did not consider such a thing, and Bev knew, even in her bewilderment, that a Neil Farrentino was no permanent answer. She had taken a sixty-day retreat from reality. It was what she had wanted—a world as far removed from Frank Burroughs as it was possible to find. It had served its strange purpose, and now she was sane enough to go back to the things she had believed in for most of her life: to marry a husband she could be proud of, to establish a social life with her peers, and to find some self-satisfying degree of success in the business world. For the rest of her life she would wonder what she had hoped to accomplish through this short, sordid episode. The answer forever eluded her. She could only believe that she was temporarily deranged with grief, self-hatred, and remorse. At least, she thought, this time there were no scars. Neil had not hurt her except in the way she wanted to be hurt. In a way, she had used him for some deep, complex purpose of her own. He had filled a need. She found she could think of Frank now without the awful pain. She thought of Neil barely at all.

While Beverly had been able to avoid the searching eyes of her parents and friends during this period, she had not been able to escape the scrutiny of Sylvia Schlesinger. As merchandise manager and self-appointed patron, Sylvia had noticed the change in Bev and been disturbed by it. It was not just the physical change. God knew the girl looked as though she hadn't slept in weeks! There was also a listlessness that was very unlike Beverly. She did her job scrupulously, never missed a day at the store, didn't, apparently, foul up. But it was as though a spark had been snuffed out. The excitement and flair that had shone through were suddenly missing. Sylvia worried about her, personally and professionally. So much so, in fact, that she broke one of her almost inviolable rules and discussed the problem with Herman.

'I think,' Sylvia said one evening at dinner, 'that my pet protégée has a problem.'

Her husband looked surprised. Sylvia rarely discussed the store. He wouldn't have minded if she had, but he knew that she firmly believed that men do not like to listen to an account of their wives' career problems and/or achievements. She would never get it completely through her head that he was not like either of her previous husbands. They had resented Sylvia's success; it threatened their own superiority. Herman had no such insecurities. He had never been a success in anything he'd tackled, from real estate to clothing manufacturing, and it had never made him unhappy. Oh, he'd have liked to be a rich, important person, he supposed, but he knew he was not cut out to be one. He was a sweet man, a good man. He would have made a fine college professor, perhaps, or even a psychiatrist if he'd been trained for either of those fields. Instead, he had finally settled on a low-paid but intensely rewarding job as a social worker. It suited him fine, probably better than the unlikely role of tycoon.

He sometimes thought, almost tenderly, that his lack of accomplishment subconsciously worried Sylvia more than it did him. They loved each other deeply, and he sensed that Sylvia, without realizing the generosity of her spirit, did not wish to rub her success in his face. He appreciated that, even though it would not have mattered. He was proud of his wife and found happiness in her presence, comfort in her strength. They had searched a long time for each other, and they'd had five years of perfect contentment. Herman, early on, had analyzed and accepted his role, a not uncommon one among the husbands of dynamic businesswomen. He was friend, lover, companion, willing escort, and sensibly untroubled 'kept man.' He knew, realistically, that he gave Sylvia more than her affluent previous husbands had ever been able to offer. In the Schlesinger marriage Sylvia would always be the provider. It was for her sake, more than his, that they maintained the private and public charade that Herman was 'head of the house.'

Years ago this reversal of roles would have troubled them, probably even destroyed their precious marriage as it had destroyed so many others. But they had both learned by experience to accept, serenely, the roles for which they were destined. They were older and wiser now. They couldn't have cared less about what 'society' thought were the differing obligations of male and female in monetary or prestigious contributions to a marriage. It was only because Sylvia did not want Herman to be hurt that they even pretended to have a more orthodox arrangement. They were sensibly, considerately happy, which was more than they could say for most of the other married couples they knew.

And so when Sylvia deviated, that evening, from her normal avoidance of any shoptalk, Herman knew that it was really important to her, not only on a professional level but on an unusually personal and emotional one.

'By protégée, I assume you mean Beverly Thyson,' he said. Syl had had Beverly to the apartment once or twice for a

47

drink, an event rare enough to signal Herman that she liked the girl. 'Nice child,' he added. 'What's wrong, honey? She falling down on the job?'

'Not in any way you could put your finger on. Still as efficient and polite and pulled-together as ever. But there's a personality change. It's like she's gone into a shell. I don't know what it's all about, but something sad has happened to her. I get the goddamnedest feeling that no matter what she's wearing on top, there's really a hair shirt underneath.'

'No clues?'

'None. But naturally I suspect it's a man.'

Herman smiled. 'Naturally. We're all beasts.'

Sylvia returned his smile. 'Right. And you're the worst.' She looked pensive again. 'Seriously, that child is eating herself up over something. I wish she'd talk to me. Maybe I could help.'

'But you wouldn't presume.'

'I couldn't, Herm. You know that. It's her private life. I have no right to interfere, especially when her work isn't suffering. At least not in any way that I can pinpoint.'

'Then, darling, I guess you'll just have to keep your pretty trap shut until *she* comes to *you*.'

'Not likely to do that, I'm afraid,' Sylvia said. 'Hell, what am I worrying about? These kids work out their problems, or if they can't they can always go to their mothers. Bev has a mother. Why am I making noises like one?'

This time Herman laughed. 'Latent maternal instinct, no doubt. Sooner or later it was bound to crop out, my love. You're just a little retarded.'

She joined his laughter, feeling a little foolish. 'But you don't think I'm turning into the sentimental clucking type, do you? My God, how unattractive at this late stage of my life!'

'Sylvia, dear, if I were to search the world for a non-clucker, I would look no farther than you. Sentimental, yes. And generously, compassionately troubled, thank God. I'm grateful that I'm one of the privileged people who know that beneath your expensively dressed, very-much-in-charge exterior beats the heart of a Jewish mother. Sweetheart, I'm not a bit surprised that you're concerned about a nice kid you happen to like. And I know it's a real concern, not just the fear of losing a potentially good executive.'

'But I'm being stupid about it.'

48

'Are you? I don't think so. What were you like at twenty-one? A little like Beverly Thyson, maybe? Different from the other girls? More ambitious than your friends and yet more frightened and confused and vulnerable? What are you really doing, Syl, worrying about Beverly or identifying with her?'

She relaxed, grateful for the thousandth time that her third try at marriage had been the right one. Herman understood her as no one else ever had. He was tuned into her insecurities the way she supposed she was tuned into Bev's. She saw a long-gone reflection of herself, going from loneliness to frantic pursuit, being hurt and hiding it, playing a role that probably hadn't fooled anybody, even then. And all the while yearning for the unquestioning love and acceptance it had taken her nearly forty years to find. Herman was right. She was painfully identifying with a girl she barely knew, yet one whom she believed she understood. She didn't want the things that had happened to her to happen to Beverly.

And when, after what seemed an eternity, Bev began to slowly come back to be the person Sylvia had known, she couldn't wait to report to Herman.

'Whatever it was,' Sylvia said, almost proudly, 'I think she's pretty well got it licked. Oh, Herman, I'm so relieved she's snapping out of it. I don't know what happened. I probably never will. But whatever her sickness was, she's recovering. I can see it. Just little signs, but she's going to be okay.'

'Thank God she got better without chicken soup,' Herman teased. 'You're a wonderful woman, Sylvia, but you make lousy chicken soup.'

5

For three months after she stopped seeing Neil, Beverly led a peacefully routine life in which her job consumed most of her waking thoughts. She was still a burned child as far as men were concerned. She went out on a few dates, most of them engineered by her friend Ruth Wells Eliason, married to her Geoffrey and determined, like all brides, to match-make at every opportunity. But none of the young men moved her even remotely. For one thing, this being 1945, most of Ruth's candidates were in the service, and Bev admitted to herself that she probably was still uniform-shy. All the khaki and navy and white reminded her of Frank. There were few suitable civilians around in that period, and those who were in mufti were 4F, deferred because of some physical disability or indispensable defense job. She wondered how Neil had escaped the draft. Maybe he had some underworld connections with enough pull to keep him out of the service.

The lack of a steady date did not bother her. It was a relief to feel none of the emotional torment of a love affair. She turned her attentions to her career and to the task of mending her fences—not only with Ruth but with her family. She went faithfully to see Angela and Harry at least once a week, and though she suspected that she did not entirely fool her mother, she was pleased to discover that Harry Thyson did not question her months-long disappearance or find anything unusual in her dutiful reappearance.

'Guess they've been working you pretty hard at the store, baby,' he said. 'We've missed you around here.'

'It's been a hectic time,' Bev agreed, avoiding Angela's

gaze. 'But it looks as though it's going to pay off sooner than I expected.'

Harry was all ears. 'That so? What's up?'

'Mrs. Schlesinger says that Miss Jamieson probably is going to retire earlier than planned. Maybe in a couple of months. I guess they're going to be crazy enough to make me the buyer.'

Her father looked as though he might explode with pride. 'You hear that, Ange? Your daughter's going to be a big executive. I'll be damned. That's really something! Not even twenty-two and smart enough for a job like that! There's something you can brag about at the bridge club!'

Bev looked pityingly at her mother. Poor Mom, she thought. While all her friends have been arranging weddings for their daughters, she's probably been making lame excuses about my spinsterhood. The buyer's job will be small consolation. She'll only be happy when she can brag about being mother of the bride.

Angela's forced smile confirmed Bev's assessment, but she managed to make her congratulations sound sincere. 'It's wonderful, darling,' she said. 'We're so proud of you.'

'Well, let's not make a public announcement until it really happens,' Beverly said. 'Don't worry. You'll be the first to know. Provided I live through the rat race long enough to accept the job, when and if it's offered!'

'You will,' Harry said confidently. 'By the way, Bev, what does it pay?'

'I'm not sure. Not as much as Miss Jamieson's getting, of course. She's been there for thirty years. I don't know. Probably around ten or twelve thousand.'

Her father whistled. 'That's some money for a girl your age! Look at her, Angela: cool as a cucumber. Next thing you know she'll be up in the twenty-thousand-dollar bracket. Our Beverly's going to be famous. You just wait and see. Better start her scrapbook now. You're going to have a full-fledged career woman on your hands one of these days pretty soon.'

The prospect obviously did not thrill Angela. She would rather have had a photo album full of pictures of grandchildren.

'By the way, Bev,' she said, 'are you seeing any nice young men?'

'A few. Nothing serious, Mom.'

Angela decided to take the risk of being rebuffed.

'Whatever happened to that chap you used to go out with? What was his name, Frank something?'

You know damned well what happened to him, Bev thought. You read the Sunday *Times* just like I do.

'Frank Burroughs?' Bev's tone was innocent. 'Oh, he got married quite a while ago. Some girl he'd grown up with.'

'I see. I do hope you're having some fun, dear. You know that old saying about all work and no play.'

Harry snorted. 'For God's sake, Angela, leave the child alone. She'll settle down when she's ready. Anyway, all the good men are still overseas.'

'Mom's afraid I'll get so important and make so much money that I'll scare off all the eligible men,' Beverly said. She knew that was exactly what was in Angela's mind.

'It *has* happened,' Angela said quietly.

'Women!' Harry said impatiently. 'Always looking on the dark side. Pretty and bright as Bev is, she can have her pick when she decides to get married. Personally, I hope she won't rush. She's already accomplished twenty times as much as any of those silly girls she grew up with. When the time comes, she'll show 'em up in the husband department, too.'

A few months later Bev was able to tell her parents that the buyer's job was official. She was a bit short of twenty-two, very young for the responsibility, but very much up to it, as Sylvia Schlesinger assured her. They had become quite close lately. Every ten days or so Bev had dinner with Sylvia and Herman, whom she had come to know and adore. Bev envied their happiness, though she wondered sometimes how Sylvia could respect a man who everybody knew had failed at all the things he'd tried. Respect was an important word to Beverly. She believed that love was built on it. Darling as Herman was, she thought, she could never be married to a man like him. Strong women needed stronger men. Even Sylvia must sometimes wish she had a man she could lean on. But if this were the case, Sylvia certainly showed no sign of it. Her devotion to Herman and her happiness with him were wonderful to see. Perhaps the situation was right for them, Bev told herself. It would be terribly wrong for me.

Her new friend Marion Richmond agreed with this analysis. Marion, older than Beverly, was a divorcée who ran her own successful dress business, one of Welby's best resources. She and Bev had progressed from a pleasant business relationship to a solid friendship which both of them welcomed. Marion was the first contemporary woman friend Bev had made in her adult life. She admired this sleek, bright, rather exotic woman with whom she shared so many interests. Not only did they have business in common, they also liked the same things: concerts, the ballet, the same books and restaurants. They also shared the same attitude toward men. They did not believe that marriage was the answer to everything. Marion's had disintegrated after two years, mainly because her young husband had felt emasculated by her success. 'We fell out of love,' Marion said simply. 'He resented my business and I recognized his jealousy. It was an amiable parting, but it taught me a lesson. I doubt that I'll ever marry again. I just hope José lives forever.'

José was Marion's lover, a married man whom she saw three times a week. It was a good arrangement, she told Bev. They went out to dinner, sometimes to the theater, always back to Marion's apartment for a few hours. He was adorable: sexy and exactly right for her. She was crazy about him, but she wouldn't have married him even if he'd been free.

'He's the perfect lover,' she said, 'but he'd be a lousy husband for me and I'd be a worse wife for him. Spaniards don't go for wives with careers any more than they go for divorces. A working paramour is okay, but a crazy, ambition-ridden wife wouldn't be tolerated even if such a thing were possible, which it isn't. This suits us both perfectly.'

For all her pretended sophistication, in areas like these Beverly was remarkably naive. It was not the infidelity that amazed her, it was the openness of it. She was surprised that Marion and José were seen so flagrantly in public. She had always assumed that an affair with a married man would have to be discreet, a love life carried on in typical 'Back Street' fashion, hidden as far as possible from friends and, above all, from the man's wife.

'Aren't you likely to get into some kind of trouble, being seen with José?'

'Darling, you just don't understand the Latin mind,' Marion said. 'A man like José is expected to have a mistress, especially when he's been married for twenty years. Good Lord, you don't think we could spend all our time squirreled away in my apartment like a couple of lovesick teenagers, do you? We'd be bored to death in three months! We go out all the time. I know a lot of his friends, and he's met most of mine. We are, as Dorothy Kilgallen would say, "a thing,"'

'But his wife must know,' Bev said. 'Doesn't she care?'

'I doubt it—that she cares, I mean. And it wouldn't do her much good if she did. She's Spanish too, remember, and that upper-class European background gives her quite a different view of things than puritanical American wives. It's all a matter of early indoctrination. She knows she's the señora for keeps, no matter how many ladies the señor may have. She has her children and her bridge games and her big apartment with all the servants, just like the good old prewar days in Madrid. Besides, José's really very considerate. He gives her everything she wants, and they keep up appearances. I'm sure he really loves her—in quite a different way than he loves me.' Marion smiled. 'Does all this shock you?'

'No. Of course not. It's very civilized.'

'Liar. If you were José's wife, you couldn't buy it. Well, I'll tell you something funny. If *I* were José's wife, I couldn't either. But that's because of the way we've been brought up. American girls don't play second fiddle. They walk out in righteous indignation, get a divorce to save their stupid pride, and spend the rest of their lives regretting it. We can't help it, but it's dumb. Impractical, lonely, and dumb. The señora, love, is *not* dumb.'

It was like being introduced to a strange drawing-room-comedy world. Bev had never known a 'kept woman,' and Marion certainly did not fit her preconceived idea of one. Of course, in the strict sense of the word, Marion was not really 'kept.' José gave her beautiful presents—lovely furs and jewelry—bought her expensive dinners, and took her dancing at El Morocco. But Marion paid her own rent and had her own successful business and her precious independence. José would have been happy if she'd given up all three, but Marion flatly refused. She would have been miserable as an idle woman with nothing to do but wait for her lover's visits. She adored her business and had fought hard for the self-reliance which both it and her charming apartment represented. Besides, though she was in love with José and faithful to him, Bev suspected that Marion could never have the feeling of permanence about an affair that she would have had about marriage. Her condemnation of marriage was just a little too vehement, her admiration for the liberal European viewpoint about sex just a little too pat. Marion knew that José had no other girl friend, but she had to know that he also performed as a husband. Bev could not quite accept that. She didn't think she could sleep with a man who was also sleeping with someone else, even if that someone was his wife. Any more than she could sleep with more than one man at a time, especially if one of the men happened to be her husband.

She agreed with Marion that all this was a middle-class hangover at odds with the tolerance and freedom of thought which she professed to espouse. God knows she'd been no angel. And she did not condemn Marion and José for their affair; in fact, she admired them for their cool acceptance of the terms, especially Marion, who seemed never to be jealous, demanding, or possessive. Bev found this most admirable in a human being. She had been all three, and it had gotten her nowhere. She hoped she was learning by her friend's example. Maybe next time—if there ever was a next time—she wouldn't make the same childish mistakes she'd made with Frank. If she ever fell in love again, she'd hold him on a loose rein, the tightest bond of all. She wouldn't be overanxious to please, or totally committed, or boringly eager to be taken for granted. Next time, she told herself, she'd be cool and wise, as Marion was.

They usually had brunch together at the Plaza on Sunday, José's unalterable day at home with his wife and children. Funny, Bev thought; Sunday had been Neil's 'family day' too. It was also a day, Bev had come to notice, on which Marion was unusually quiet, almost moody. There was no showroom or designing board to distract her, no phone to bring José's voice from his office. When you were in love with a married man, Sundays were like Christmas and holidays. You were off limits on the best days of the year. But on this particular Sunday, Marion seemed unusually cheerful.

'Guess what?' she said. 'My baby brother's coming home tomorrow.'

Beverly looked up from her eggs Benedict. 'Your baby brother? I didn't even know you had one.'

'Well, he's not exactly a baby, even though he's a disgusting nine years younger than I. I guess he just seems like a kid to me. I had already left home when Dad died. Eddie and Mother shared the apartment until he went into the army —except, of course, for the time he was in college. He's been in the Pacific in the Air Force for the last two and a half years. He's been discharged. I can't wait to see him. I'm crazy about him. Everybody is.' Marion grinned. 'You ought to see Mother. She's out of her mind with excitement. I think she's cooked every dish Eddie ever mentioned he liked since he was a baby. And, honey, you can whip up a lot of recipes going back twenty years!'

Beverly smiled, happy for Marion and for Mrs. Richmond, whom she didn't even know. 'That's wonderful news. Is he married?'

'Nope. After college he kicked around. Had a few odd jobs. One summer vacation he hitchhiked across the country and almost married a girl in San Francisco, but thank God it didn't come off. He enlisted in the RAF even before we got into the war, then transferred to our side when he could. He's a nut about aviation. Like a kid. I've been tripping over his model airplanes since he was ten.'

'What do you think he'll do now that he's out of the service, get a job in aviation?'

Marion looked suddenly troubled. 'I haven't a clue. He's one of the world's greatest guys, but there's a little Walter Mitty in him. God, he used to have the craziest, most impractical schemes when he was growing up. He was always going to start an air-freight service or be part of a flying circus or some goofy thing. I can't imagine Ed coming home after all these years in the wild blue yonder and facing the facts of life like getting a job and planning a future. He has gallons of charm and I suspect not an ounce of ambition, as you and I know it. My father was like that too: adorable and unrealistic. Everybody worshiped him, but when he died there wasn't a bean. Mom went to work to support herself and Ed. She was determined that he get an education, and he did: liberal arts. I don't know what he's really equipped to do, Bev. Almost twenty-eight years old, and if he has a career plan I'll eat my John Frederics hat.'

'I think you're worrying unnecessarily,' Bev reassured her. 'You haven't seen him in a long time. The war may have made him grow up more than you think.'

'Possibly. I hope so, for his sake. Not that Eddie won't always get along. But niceness doesn't pay the rent. If being sweet and fun were the ingredients for success, my brother would own the Chase National Bank. Instead of which,' Marion said wryly, 'it will probably own him. Among other things, Ed has always had the well-known champagne tastes on a beer pocketbook. I blame Mother for that; she spoiled hell out of him: her only male child. And so much like my father, at that.'

They fell silent. Then Bev said, 'I can't wait to meet him.'

'Oh, you will. But you have to make me a promise. Don't fall in love with him, okay?'

'What a crazy thing to say! I've never laid eyes on your brother, nor he on me. Aren't you getting a little ahead of yourself?'

'Bev, dear, I just told you. Everybody falls for Eddie. He's just plain goddamn lovable! And I have a funny hunch you're going to be just his type.'

'Meaning?'

'Meaning pretty and gay and bright and . . .'

'And what?'

'Well, I hate the word, but I can't think of a better one: strong. My hunch is that Eddie will eventually marry somebody who'll mother him, expect the minimum from him, and be the dependable member of the family, instead of its being the other way around. That's not your thing, Bev. You're not Sylvia Schlesinger on the third try. Don't be snowed by Eddie's charm. He's an angel. But I think he's a passive fellow. The kind *you* don't need. I love you both, but I don't want you to marry each other.'

Beverly was startled. 'Marion, you idiot,' she repeated lamely, 'we haven't even *met*. Anyway, I've told you I'm not sure I ever want to marry anybody. And even if I change my mind about that, it will have to be somebody strong, successful, and disgustingly rich. Which seems to reduce my chances of becoming your sister-in-law to a very safe minimum.'

Marion began to laugh at herself. 'I guess I do sound a little goofy, don't I? One minute building up Ed as the greatest thing since nylon and the next minute putting him down as a futureless failure. Anyway, you'll meet Edward Patrick Richmond as soon as I can get my paws on him. Maybe you two will have a roaring love affair. That would probably be good for both of you. But no marriage, okay?'

'Don't buy the maid-of-honor dress yet. Or is it matron of honor? Where does a divorcée stand in things like that?'

'To the left of the bride, smarty. But if it ever comes to a wedding, I'll be a worried spectator in the first pew on the groom's side. I wouldn't be an accessory after that fact.'

'You're really nuts.' Bev laughed.

Marion nodded. 'You catch on slow, don't you?'

6

As danger-filled as his life was, as uncomfortable as were his quarters in the hot, steamy air bases of the South Pacific, Sergeant Ed Richmond had really enjoyed his tour of duty in the Air Force and was almost sorry when the war ended. He was nearly twenty-eight years old, handsome, moderately intelligent, and totally lacking in direction. Amiable and outgoing, he was incapable of envy and unimpressed with civilian achievements. Basically unaggressive, definitely non-competivive, he was, as his sister had said, an easygoing, thoroughly likable man.

Before he enlisted, Ed had lived at home with his mother, a pleasant, long-widowed, handsome woman who had, since the time of her husband's death, worked as a vendeuse in a small dress shop on Madison Avenue. He returned to his mother's apartment on Central Park West when he got back to New York, stowed his gear in his old room, and somewhat reluctantly faced the fact that he'd now have to go out and get a job.

Not that Ed was lazy. Between college and the Air Force he'd always had jobs, mediocre ones that didn't interest him but enabled him to offer to pay room and board to his mother, who refused it. Marion had long since been gone from the family apartment. Ed was only twelve when she married and almost fifteen when she was divorced. He admired his sister, but he knew that they were very different. She had drive, ambition. Look at the way she'd scrambled to set up her own business and how hard she worked to become successful. He wondered sometimes how happy Marion really was. Maybe, indeed surely, public recognition meant a great deal to her. In this, they were very different.

Ed was never initially motivated toward success. And later he'd seen so much dangerous living and unnecessary dying in World War II that conventional accomplishments and stereo-typed life-styles became even less important to him. The thing was to live, love, and be happy. He liked money, of course, but he was not obsessed by it. He didn't need to be rich, any more than he needed fame or power or the other yardsticks of success adopted by those of his friends who were already bucking for heart attacks. Ed did not think that ulcers were a concrete example of heroism under fire, like the Purple Heart. He could not picture himself locked in an office with his name on the door, ass-kissing the boss and shuffling a lot of ridiculous papers that they would have used for toilet tissue in New Guinea. The sense of life's priorities that he'd had even as a teenager was reinforced by his war years. He knew his values were unorthodox, but a lack of anxiety about living by the rules also made him a contented man.

He had a couple of good discussions with Marion after his return. She was a very understanding woman who seemed much older to him than the years which separated them.

'Everybody has to do it his own way, Eddie,' she'd said. 'I can make a place for you in my business if that's what you want, but I think you'd hate it. I just don't see you a dress salesman somehow.'

His look of absolute horror at the idea made her burst into laughter.

'Don't panic,' she said. 'I wouldn't ask you to do it. But what do you want to do? Any ideas?'

'Not really. Except I think I'd like to stick with something in aviation. It's too bad I'm not a pilot, but I couldn't pass the physical to become one. Flying is the only thing that interests me. I thought maybe I could get a job as a steward on one of the commercial lines. What do you think of that idea? Too menial? Not classy enough?'

'Don't be a jerk,' Marion said. 'If that's what you want to do, go do it. There's nothing disgraceful about it, God knows. I don't know what kind of future it offers, but I'm not sure that's the biggest consideration in your life.'

'You're quite a girl,' he said. 'You really understand, don't you?'

'I think I understand *you* right now. The kind of job you're talking about will be interesting, respectably if not stupendously well paid, and it will keep you where you love to be —in the air. I don't know if it's what you'll want forever, Ed. But as a holding action, I don't see anything wrong with it.'

That had been three weeks ago. Getting a steward's job with one of the big lines had been easy. The war was still on. There was still a shortage of employable young men. And Ed's flying experience plus his charm made the personnel director eager to sign him on. He liked it. He didn't mind catering to the passengers, and he was quite used to taking orders from a captain. It was true, as Marion had said, that it was a job without much of a future. But that kind of thing didn't concern him. He had no one to look out for but himself. His mother was self-supporting, his sister successful. He was not a man to fret about the future. It was stupid to worry about tomorrow; the flak over Japan had taught him that. Today you could be having a beer and laughing at a joke. Tomorrow you could be dead—killed by a Jap fighter or a taxi on Fifth Avenue. There wasn't much point in worrying about anything in between.

Meeting Beverly changed his mind. That first afternoon in his sister's showroom, he'd found her unusually attractive. They had a lot of laughs over dinner. Ed was full of stories about the Air Force, all of them amusing, designed to make the war sound no more serious than a bunch of kids playing soldier. Marion's devotion to this irresistible brother with his nonsense and his relaxed attitude about life was unmistakable. Bev could understand why Marion loved him. She also began to see why any woman could become entranced with Eddie.

Halfway through the meal he turned to his sister and pretended to scold her. 'Fine friend you are,' he said. 'You've been holding out on me. I've been back in civilization for three weeks, and this is the first time you've introduced me to Beverly. What's the matter with you, Marion? Ashamed of me?'

Beverly answered for her. 'On the contrary. I think she was afraid to expose me to your charm.' It was said teasingly, laughingly, but Marion recognized the veiled declaration of interest on Beverly's part as well as on Ed's. I'm a witch, Marion thought. I knew this was going to happen.

Ed picked up the half-serious statement. 'Well? Was she right?'

Bev smiled. 'She's always right. Haven't you found that out by now?'

'Don't let it go to your head, little brother,' Marion said tartly. 'Bev's charmproof. Besides, she's got her future all mapped out. Don't get your hopes up. The lady's on her way to being a big executive. Flyboys, even charming ones, don't fit into the picture.'

They looked at her in surprise. It was not like Marion to be so snappish. Bev understood, though she hadn't expected her friend to be so vehement. Eddie wondered what was behind this nearly nasty remark. It sounded suspiciously like a serious warning.

Again, it was Bev who picked up the conversational ball. 'Marion flatters me,' she said. 'I've done all right for a high-school graduate from the West Side, but I'd hardly call myself a big executive or anything close to it. Anyway, that's not important. What about you, Ed? Marion tells me you've gotten a job with Trans-State Airlines. Do you like it? What exactly do you do?'

Deliberately, he told a lie. 'I'm what they call a passenger supervisor. Do a lot of flying, overseeing the performance of the crew, kind of a management spy.'

Marion looked at him wide-eyed. He was taking a chance that she wouldn't tell Bev that he was a steward. It was unlike him to be phony. Obviously he wanted to impress Beverly, and he was counting on her not to give him away. She said nothing, but she took some satisfaction in noticing that her startled gaze produced a slight blush around his collar. It was not a serious lie but a significant one. He was trying to build himself up, to create an impression of importance, something he'd never before felt the need or desire to do. At first Marion was angry with him, her anger mixed with disappointment that he would stoop to such a petty deception. Then she felt sorry for him. There was no way he could get away with this story. Bev was bound to find out what his job really was, and then she'd put him down as a liar and a fake. Poor Eddie, his sister thought, how quickly you've learned that status is an aphrodisiac in this materialistic world you've come back to.

Emboldened by her silence, Ed went on, describing his

imaginary responsibilities, his plans for the future, his ideas of how the aviation business could expand in the postwar years. What happened, Marion wondered, to the young man who only a couple of weeks ago had been content to take a quite ordinary job? Maybe he'd changed his mind. More likely, he'd realized that his work wasn't classy enough to make him interesting to a girl like Beverly Thyson. There, she was right. As Bev listened to this seemingly ambitious young executive, she felt vindicated. She'd told Marion that perhaps the war had changed her brother, had made him grow up, and obviously it had. She was interested in him. But, as he had correctly guessed, she probably would not have been quite as attracted if he'd told her the truth about what he was doing and how little he really cared about becoming somebody important.

Being important mattered to Beverly. Frank had been a man of substance; part of his attraction for her had lain in the confidence he exuded, the secure future that was ahead of him. It was one of the reasons that even if Neil had been a gentleman she could never have visualized a future with him. A musician? No chance. She realized her attraction to success and power and was a little ashamed of its shallowness, but at least she faced this failing head on. Status did not mean a great deal to Beverly—her own and certainly that of any man she could be deeply attached to. She was glad to know that Ed Richmond was not the drifter that Marion had remembered.

She called Marion the next day to thank her for the evening. 'You were so right about Ed,' Beverly said enthusiastically. 'He's a dreamboat! And Marion, I was right, wasn't I? He's really ambitious. Look how fast he got a good job. You must be so happy and relieved.'

I should tell her the truth right now, Marion thought. Blow the whistle on this pack of still-innocent lies before she gets involved. If she's any kind of person, she'll like him no matter what he does for a living. Hell, what's so terrible about being a steward, anyway? Eddie could be happy with a job like that for the rest of his life. But Beverly wouldn't be happy for him. That's what's wrong with the whole setup. I felt it in my bones even before they met. I just didn't know that Ed would realize so quickly that his job would matter to Bev.

'Marion?' the voice on the phone said. 'Hey, are you still there?'

'I'm here. Sorry. I was looking over some sketches when you called. Guess my mind is still on them. What were you saying, Bev?'

'I said I'm sure you're relieved and happy.'

'Oh, yes. Very.'

'Ed's taking me out tonight. Just a dinner and a movie. Will you join us?'

'No, thanks.'

'You're seeing José, I suppose. Give him my love.'

'Sure. Have fun.'

Bev stared at the phone when she hung up. Marion hadn't sounded like herself at all. Distracted. No, disapproving somehow, even though she hadn't put it into words. Remembering the breakfast conversation at the Plaza, Beverly knew that Marion had been in earnest when she'd told Bev not to fall in love with Ed. It was as though she'd had a premonition. But that was ridiculous! They were only having their first date. People didn't fall in love at first sight. Anyway, this wasn't the Ed that Marion had described. Even his sister must realize that. He had all the endearing qualities she'd remembered, but he was no longer a baby brother. He was a very grown-up, strong, and attractive man. One a woman could be proud of. She didn't understand Marion's attitude. Had she not known better, Bev would have thought she was jealous. She did not realize that Marion, in her own way, was trying to be protective of them both, and already aware of the futility of it.

The romance took off like a skyrocket, even though at first Beverly was wary. The wounds were still there, but the desire for love persisted and the devotion of Ed Richmond was unique. She had never met a man like him. Always before it had been she who was the giver, the servant. Now she was the served. Whatever made her happy made him happy. It was a heady new experience, a much-needed, ego-building one. Cautiously, liking the feeling of power, enjoying the return of desire, she began to let herself fall in love with him. On their fifth date they made love and found it good. On the one-month anniversary of their meeting, Ed gave up his old room at his mother's and moved into Bev's apartment.

They kept this fact a secret from everyone except Marion. Ed told his mother that he was moving in with one of the other stewards. It was a crumby place, he said, but more convenient to the airport. He went to see her once a week, on the same night that Bev had dinner with her parents. They were fortunate that neither family expressed any desire to visit their children's lodgings. The answer was food. Jane Richmond's greatest pleasure in life was fixing Eddie all the things he liked to eat. As for the Thysons, they had long since come to expect Beverly to have dinner with them in their home. She lacked any talent as a cook, hated the sight of a kitchen.

They became expert at fooling their families. Ed lied that he and his friend were on the waiting list for a phone; meanwhile he would call his mother regularly. Bev hired an answering service. They let the phone ring at night, checking later for messages, Bev returning the Thysons' calls and Ed getting his messages from the airline the same way. For Marion they invented a code: ring once, hang up, and call again. It was all complicated and tricky, but the inconvenient deceptions were well worth it. Thank God, they said, their families were born New Yorkers. The eleventh commandment was 'Thou shalt not drop in without phoning first.'

After the first cool reception, Marion seemed to accept the inevitable fact of Bev's involvement with her brother. She hoped that it would just continue to be an affair; she approved of that for these two. And for a while it seemed this would be the case. When she and Beverly talked about it, the girl still insisted that she didn't want to get married.

'It's perfect the way it is,' Beverly said. 'I think marriage would spoil it.'

'Right,' Marion agreed. 'You're both blossoming.'

Ed did not see it that way. He was deeply, desperately in love. He hated all the secrecy, the rigmarole of the phones, the fact that he could not brag to the world about his beautiful, successful girl.

'This is silly,' he said after six weeks. 'We're free, we love each other for keeps. Why the hell shouldn't we make it legal?'

Bev tried to laugh him out of it. 'Seems to me the tables

are turned here. You want me to make an honest man of you. Darling, give it time. Of course we love each other, but it's too soon for such a permanent move. Too soon for both of us, Eddie dearest. I only plan to marry once, and I'm betting on you. But let's really know each other.'

'Don't we?'

'Yes, but not like we should. For one thing, that damn job of yours makes this a part-time relationship. You're away as much as you're home. I'm not sure that would make for a good marriage. It's tough enough to put up with the separations even at this point.'

He was quiet. He had never told Bev the truth about his job, still uncertain that he would not lose face. His frequent trips were as easily explained by the 'management supervisor' duties as by those of a steward. Both required taking flights three or four days a week, often staying overnight. And it was not only the danger of her disappointment that worried him. She might not only be disturbed that he was not a rising executive, she might actually be disgusted with him if she discovered that he had lied to her. Marion had been a good Joe not to tell Bev the truth. Apart from her, he had few worries about being unmasked. They saw only Bev's friends, never his, who might let the truth slip. He disliked deceit, but he couldn't bring himself to tell Bev that he was not the junior executive she thought him to be.

He had reason. Bev even thought that being a part of middle management was not good enough for him and that being a passenger supervisor was far beneath his talents. Ambitious herself, she was sure he shared her drive. He had been right in his first instinctive appraisal: She enjoyed her own success, but the culturally conditioned, dependent part of her nature sought a mate who would surpass it. Besides, now that she was truly in love, the one she loved had to be larger than life. Ed recognized this ambivalence in her and, knowing his own nature, had qualms about what was expected of him. Soon she was hinting that perhaps he should leave his job and look for something with a greater future.

'Darling, you know you're wasting yourself in that organization,' she said. 'With your brains and looks and personality, you'd be a vice-president somewhere else!'

He hesitated, savoring the confidence and wishing that he really wanted to fit the mold she saw him in.

'I don't know, Bev,' he answered. 'It's not a bad job, and nothing's to say I can't move up. Maybe not as fast as in some other business, but it's a field I like. Besides, I don't know what else I'd be good at. The only thing I know is flying.'

'Sweetheart, stop underselling yourself. My God, look at the idiots who are holding down big jobs! You have more brains in your little finger than they do in their whole fat heads!'

He loved what she said, but he resisted feebly.

'Baby, I wish I had your opinion of me. That's a big cutthroat world out there. They're tougher than the Japs. I knew how to handle those little S.O.B.s Working warriors may be something else.'

She had put her arms around him, snuggling her slim little body close to his big one in the double bed.

'All right, I'll tell you another reason I'd like you to quit. I *do* believe there's a bigger future for you somewhere else, sweetheart, but I'm afraid my major motivation is selfish. I hate your being away so much. I want you to have a job right here in town where we can be together every night.'

She was irresistible. He held her close, feeling the desire in both of them. For all her drive and ambition, she was so completely feminine and soft. He adored her beyond anything. Beyond his own happiness. Even beyond his own doubts that he could be the kind of hard-hitting executive that she believed he could become. He put aside his reservations. Maybe Bev was right. The big break could be just around the corner. He'd never really looked for it. Besides, he too hated the idea of his being away from her. She might meet someone else while he was traveling half the week. He didn't really believe that; he knew she was a one-man woman. But maybe if he changed jobs she'd change her mind about becoming Mrs. Richmond.

'When *are* you going to marry me?' he said.

The one-word answer came with her mouth against his. 'Soon.'

Next day he handed in his resignation. His boss was sorry about it.

'We hate to lose you, Ed, but I understand. Smart young guy like you has to be thinking about more of a future, I guess. Wish we could promise you something better immediately. You've got another job, huh?'

'No. I've just decided to ground myself. My girl misses me when I'm away.'

His superior looked dubious. 'None of my business,' he said, 'but sometimes separation can be a good thing. You know—absence makes the heart grow fonder. Don't mean to be a wet blanket, but I've seen some traveling men live to regret your kind of decision. It's not just that they're unhappy changing their way of life. The women sometimes find out that they're better off when the guys aren't around all the time. That way they're gladder to see them when they do get home.'

Ed laughed. 'No sweat in this case. Not with my Bev. To match clichés with you, I'm not afraid that familiarity will breed contempt. We want to be together. We don't want to waste half our lives being alone.'

'Good luck to you,' the older man said. 'When you're president of U.S. Steel, see if you can find a job for me.'

Bev was overjoyed when he told her what he'd done, and undismayed when he worried about how long it might take him to find a new job. 'Who cares?' she asked blithely. 'We have a roof over our heads and enough to eat. And drink. Oh, darling, it's so wonderful to know you're going to be around and I don't have to feel like a part-time widow!'

'How about being a full-time wife?'

'Soon,' she said again.

'Bev, what are we waiting for? If you're going to support a lover you might just as well support a husband.'

She kissed him. 'Dummy! That has nothing to do with it!'

'Then why don't we get married?'

'Darling, I told you, I want both of us to be sure. I know I love you. I know I always want to be with you. But it's such a big step.'

He looked hurt. 'You're afraid that I'm not good husband material just because I backed away from it once before. Marion told you about the San Francisco thing, didn't she?'

She smiled at him, her eyes full of love. 'You really are such a wonderful silly ass,' she said. 'How stupid do you think I am? A kid's idea that didn't jell? You were nineteen years old, darling. That was no engagement, that was teenage lust! No, I'm not worried about your being good husband material. Maybe I'm more worried about my being good wife material. You deserve the best. And I've got a closetful of

70

faults, beginning with selfishness and ending with ambition.'
Seeing the pain in his face, she changed her tone abruptly.
'But I will make you a damned good wife,' she said. 'I know a
good buy when I see one! Let's just not rush, dearest. Things
are so good, and I love being wickedly "engaged." We'll get
around to City Hall soon. I promise.'

It took her four months to fulfill the promise. Four months
in which they were joyously, childishly happy. Even Ed's
inability to find work for the first three months did not spoil
their delight in being together. He had dinner waiting when
she got home from the store. They exchanged news of their
day—hers harried and exciting, his frustrating but always
optimistic. They went to bed and made love rapturously.
Sometimes he was still asleep when she left for the office.
She would stand over the bed looking at him with an almost
maternally protective smile on her face. Poor baby, she
thought. He's been so uncomplaining about quitting his job
and so good about keeping up his spirits. Maybe today will be
the day.

When he got the first job, selling advertising space for a
fashion magazine, they celebrated by going out to dinner. It
was Bev's suggestion.

'Let's go to the Stork Club,' she said. 'This is a big night!'

'Honey, I can't afford that.'

She pretended to frown. 'What's that "I" stuff, all of a
sudden? We share, don't we?'

'Not much sharing,' Ed said. 'For months now you've been
paying for everything: rent, food, booze, even my new suit.'

'Darling, it doesn't matter to you, does it? It doesn't matter
to me.'

He grinned. 'No, it doesn't matter as long as you don't
begin to love me less for it.' Suddenly he turned serious.
'Sometimes I think that I ought to worry more than I do
about your footing all the bills, even temporarily. It doesn't
seem important to me where the money comes from, but
that's probably wrong. One of these days you might get fed
up with a guy who can't support you.'

'Past tense,' Bev said. '*Couldn't*. You're a big magazine
tycoon now, remember?'

'Some tycoon. I've been given the worst accounts in the
place. Mail-order stuff. And the pay is lousy.'

'But you're on your way, darling! This is just the beginning. You'll make fabulous contacts. I'm betting you won't be in that job a year. Wait and see. You'll get a terrific offer.'

She was half right. He was in the job only two months when he quit. He had made no contacts and he had had no offer, terrific or otherwise.

'It's a waste of time,' he told Bev. 'All the other guys have been there ten, twenty years. They're not about to let go of any of the big accounts. I could spend the rest of my life selling ads for toilet-bowl cleaners and hand-crocheted pot-holders.' He watched her face. 'I'm sorry, love, but I couldn't take it. Was I wrong to quit?'

'Of course not! Who needs it? You'll find something better.'

'You're wonderful,' he said. 'I came home early and fixed us a great dinner. While you're changing I'll whip up a nice cold bowl of martinis.'

Under the shower, Bev tried not to feel anxious. They'd been married a month. The fact that Ed had been hired by the magazine was, she admitted to herself, part of the reason that she'd finally agreed to the irrevocable commitment. She felt guilty. He had given up the job he loved to please her. He had taken this one in good faith and stood it as long as he could, an unmistakable display of his attempt to 'make something of himself' for her sake.

She faced the fact that his success was terribly important to her. More important, she feared, than it was to him. She wished with all her heart that Ed really shared her concern for the future or even for the achievements of the present. Her values were more shallow, she supposed, and her insecurities more threatening. All she knew with unhappy certainty was that in his place she would never have quit unless she had another job waiting. Still, she loved him wildly. She was a mercenary bitch to want him to stay in a job he hated. He'd get another, better one.

She was to make that speech to herself more than once in the years ahead. As her own career prospered, Ed's stood still or even went backward. He got and lost a job as a professional fund-raiser. That time, in fairness, he was let go when the staff was reduced. A few months later he went to work for a printing firm, selling its services to businesses who used outside printers for brochures, pamphlets, and other material. He found it dull and the people stupid. He began to complain about the filthy office in the West 30s and the dreary buyers of printing who haggled with him over prices and expected kickbacks for placing their orders with him. When he quit that job, it was a long time before he found another, selling insurance for a major nationwide company. As usual, the pay was small, but, as he did with every new job, Ed went into it with optimism.

He had not changed since their marriage. No, that was not quite true. He was as warm and loving as ever. He seemed to take more delight in Bev's increasing prominence than she did herself. He showed no sign of resentment over her success, contrasted with his failures. He predicted, constantly, that she would be president of the store one day, even as he insisted that his own great opportunity was still waiting for him. The only change in him was that he seemed more and more lethargic about getting or holding a job. Sometimes weeks passed before he even went looking for one. He accepted without comment the fact that Bev would pay the rent and buy the necessities of life. When he was working he bought her foolish, extravagant presents. Ashamed of her own thoughts, she began to wish that he'd share the household expenses instead. She found herself resenting his seemingly easy acceptance of almost constant unemployment, his apparently untroubled attitude about being supported by his wife. She hated herself for her growing impatience with this man who, she knew, would give his life for her. Moreover, she had brought it on herself. She had instigated the first move and he had complied to please her. Now he was growing more and more dependent on her, while she grew cold inside when he bought a suit and charged it to her, or invited friends in for cocktails made with liquor she paid for.

Her reaction to her disappointment in him was expressed in little ways. There were no arguments. No healthy fights in which she might have screamed out her growing scorn. It was all very civilized and understanding. Guilt for the way she felt only increased her politeness and tenderness for him. She refused for a long time to admit to herself that her feelings were becoming less those of a wife than a mother. But as respect diminished, so did desire. They made love less frequently. Ed could not help but notice her withdrawal, but he did not inquire, much less insist.

When he got the job selling insurance, it did not fill her with elation as it once would have. She tried hard to appear delighted about it, but it was a poor act, so poor that even he could not ignore it.

'You think this one will be like the others, don't you?'

'Of course not, darling. It sounds wonderful.'

'It's the right one. I know it. You'll see.'

That had been two years ago. To her surprise and relief, Ed still had the job, though she detected the by-now-familiar beginning signs of restlessness. He didn't understand why he hadn't been promoted. He'd lost out on two good accounts because of office politics, he said, but he was damned if he'd be an ass-kisser like the rest of them. Maybe they ought to chuck the whole scene and start fresh, he said one night. They could go to Australia. He'd been there during the war. It was the last great land of opportunity. They were dying for bright guys, especially Americans. Maybe he could even start some kind of local air service, he said enthusiastically. If not that, then there was sure to be something better than selling insurance with a bunch of thieves.

He was saying—without putting it into words—that he didn't want to compete. Bev knew that his wild ideas about Australia signified other things too. Ed still lived in a dream world where he was free of the hard realities of survival. It was why he loved flying, she supposed. There were no dreary streets to be walked, briefcase in hand. No rigid office reception rooms where one waited for an appointment and pleaded for a sale. Ed was like a big beautiful bird who could not adjust to the confinement of the cage he'd entered to please her.

And Bev was just the opposite. The thought of Australia horrified her. The idea of leaving her job was unthinkable. She loved the challenge of business, the 'come and get me if you can' attitude of New York. She loved her husband. She was a fool to have tried to change him. What frightened her was that he didn't understand her respect for achievement, and she couldn't endure his disregard for reality. She wondered how much of her fears he secretly shared.

'You're not going to leave the job, are you?' Bev asked. 'You seem to be doing so well.'

'No, honey, I'm not going to leave it,' he said quietly. 'All that talk about Australia was just a lot of adolescent nonsense because I had a bad day.' He came close and kissed her. She simulated response when he tried to arouse her. Pretending passion, she let him carry her into the bedroom. As so often happened lately, the lovemaking did not go well.

7

In another apartment, a Park Avenue duplex penthouse not more than ten blocks from the Richmonds', another couple's marriage was also proceeding, more obviously and much more vocally, on a collision course. At the very moment that Beverly was unsuccessfully trying to simulate passion in response to Ed's desire, Marilyn Powers was telling her angry husband that she wanted a divorce.

'I'm sorry, Arthur,' she said, 'but it just hasn't worked out. We've tried for a year. You're a nice man. I like you, but I don't love you. I've made arrangements to leave for Reno next week.'

Arthur Powers couldn't believe what he was hearing. He was a well-preserved forty-two, looking five or six years younger. He was rich, sophisticated, and famous both in the fashion and financial worlds. As sole owner of Powers Textiles, the company he'd inherited from his father, he was a working executive who ran the company even better than his grandfather, who founded it, or his father, who expanded it. He had also done so without the single-minded, all-consuming dedication to business that his forebears had found necessary. There had been plenty of time for living on a grand scale, and Arthur had done a lot of it. There had always been women flocking around him, attracted by his looks, his money, his fame. He'd had dozens of affairs and three marriages, which had produced a daughter by his first wife and two sons by his second. He supported both ex-wives and the children and never saw any of them. He didn't really like them.

His first marriage at the ridiculous age of eighteen was strictly playboy stuff. He'd carelessly impregnated a sexy, simple-minded showgirl who'd blackmailed him into marriage. He stayed with her long enough to see Joanna born and talk his disapproving father into making a generous settlement for child and mother, and then he got the hell out of the whole stupid blunder.

At twenty-three, pressured by his parents with threats of disinheritance, he'd married 'suitably'—the dull daughter of his father's best friend. The union lasted for ten boring, blatantly unfaithful years and produced the twins James and Christopher Powers. He might have been trapped forever if his mother and father had not died within a year of each other, relieving him of parental threats and marital bondage. Within six months of their passing he was free again, enormously independently wealthy, thirty-three years old, and determined to have no more of marriage.

For eight years he'd held steadfastly to his freedom. He'd loved his bachelor life, his penthouse, his chauffeur-valet, and his women. Inundated with invitations, chased by the richest and best-looking girls in town, Arthur stayed uninvolved until the evening, a little more than a year before, when he spied Marilyn at a cocktail party. She was in her late twenties, the most strikingly beautiful creature he'd ever seen and, intriguingly, not the least interested in him. She barely acknowledged the introduction and immediately turned away to talk to some nondescript couple. Arthur was sure she hadn't even listened to his name.

'Who's the beauty in the black sequin dress?' he asked his hostess.

'You don't recognize her? Arthur, I'm surprised! I thought you kept up with the fashion business. That's Marilyn Flynn. She's been a top fashion model for the past five or six years. She's been on at least twenty covers of *Vogue*. Sensational-looking, isn't she?'

'Married?'

'Not at the moment. She outgrew one husband when she got famous.' Arthur's hostess, a famous gossip columnist, gave a bitchy little laugh. 'Maybe she's sorry now. Poor Marilyn. She's just about had it in the modeling business. The magazines are getting tired of her face. Anyway, she must be at least twenty-six or -seven. The camera is a heartless seeker of youth. I hope she's had sense enough to save her money, but I doubt it. Models are narcissistic by necessity. They never think they're going to be over the hill one day. And they're rarely equipped to make a living any other way.'

Arthur could not suppress a smile. What a crazy business this fashion world was. Models were like baseball players, through in their late twenties, most of them. And like the rare athletes who became managers or radio sportscasters, only a few of them were bright enough to open model agencies or become fashion editors. The rest took lower and lower modeling jobs as long as they could. First with the low-paying publications, then with catalog photographers, until finally they were reduced to the lowest form of camera work: posing for bra and girdle ads. The lucky ones got married before this happened. Some of them ended up selling cosmetics in Macy's. They seldom went back to wherever they came from—usually hick towns in Nebraska or Illinois—too ashamed to let the folks know that they were no longer goddesses. He wondered whether Marilyn knew she was at the end of her career. If so, he wondered what she was going to do about it.

The idea, as well as the woman, intrigued him: not only her physical perfection but her aloofness, her projection of supreme confidence, and most of all her blatant disregard of him. Arthur was not used to being ignored. He never had been. Just as he'd never been rejected.

Strategically, he made no attempt to speak to her again that evening, but three days later he sent flowers and a note asking her to dine. When he called to confirm the invitation, she said politely that she was busy every night for the next two weeks. Perhaps some other time.

Annoyed, Arthur was tempted to forget it. Instead, he heard himself asking, almost meekly, for her first free evening and being ridiculously pleased when she set a date three weeks away. He had no suspicion that she had plenty of open spaces in her engagement book in between.

Marilyn was no fool. All the things the columnist had said about her were things she already knew. She saw her high-fashion modeling career drawing to an end, and she was damned if she'd grub for fifteen-dollar-an-hour catalog jobs. She also knew that she wasn't capable of, or even interested in, starting some new kind of work. Her best bet was a rich man, and the best rich man in town was Arthur Powers.

She had put on a good act that first evening at the cocktail party, pretending complete disinterest in him. She knew all about Arthur, had talked to girls who had slept with him, editors who had been to his parties. She had once heard somebody say that 'New York was only made up of six hundred people,' meaning that sooner or later everybody in a certain stratum met everybody else. She had always meant to meet the great Arthur Powers. In fact, she had only gone to that dreary cocktail party because she knew he would be there.

Marilyn congratulated herself on her performance. To have gushed over him, to have been obvious, would have been the worst thing she could have done. She knew enough about this spoiled man to know that he would be fascinated by her apparent disinterest. It had worked out just as she'd planned. The next step was to drive him crazy. She would not go to bed with him; she would break dates, invent a serious rival; and most of all, she would act as though she didn't give a damn whether he ever called her again.

Because she did not love him, these things were easy to do. She remembered something her mother had once said to her. 'If women could treat the men they love the way they treat the ones they don't care about, most romances would work out better. Men like to think of themselves as pursuers, the conquerors. They seldom marry pushovers, Marilyn, and don't you forget it.' It had been strangely cynical maternal advice, but solid. It worked with Arthur.

For three months after their first date, Arthur was a frustrated and thoroughly bewildered man. He was totally spoiled, complacently sure that his money, his manners, and his good looks were irresistible. They always had been. He couldn't remember not being able to get any woman he'd wanted—married or single. And it was always he who decided when the affair ended, when he'd had enough of the same woman. Marilyn's cool handling of him made her a challenge, one which became so obsessive that he finally decided he was madly in love with her and that no matter what it took he would make her marry him.

It took four months, two rejected proposals, and incredible self-discipline on Marilyn's part before she finally said yes. It was not that she had any great physical desire for Arthur. She liked him well enough. She enjoyed the expensive evenings and the extravagant gifts and particularly the feeling of being in control. The discipline lay only in not jumping at the first marriage offer he made. She had to play him like a marlin on a line, making sure that he wanted her so much that he didn't back away when she finally accepted. It was well known that Arthur never planned to marry again. He'd announced his intention to stay free openly and with conviction many times over the past years. Friends who knew that they were going out together were making bets that the whole thing would never end in marriage. They even said so to Marilyn, who agreed with them, knowing they would repeat her words to Arthur, adding a nice touch of fuel to the fire.

When he proposed for the third time, she knew it was time to let him take the bait. Even so, she pretended hesitation.

'Are you sure, Arthur?' she said. 'After all, you've told the world you'd never marry again. Why me?'

'Because you are the most beautiful, the most exciting, the most sensuous woman in the world.'

Not 'I love you.' Not 'I want the world to know you belong to me.' Arthur was not conscious of what he didn't say. He was not even conscious that he was winning a battle rather than fulfilling a dream. He was mad about Marilyn, mostly because he was not sure that she was mad about him. He would change all that. Her acceptance of him was, he firmly believed, the triumph of his life.

It was, indeed, a disaster that he refused to admit. Far from being sensuous, she was, if not frigid, certainly cold in bed. Perversely, her lack of response only increased his desire. He was an expert lover, but he could not seem to awaken her. He was insistent; she was coolly acquiescent; and this irreverence for his 'manhood' drove him wild, increasing, rather than diminishing, his passion for her. He could not understand it, would not accept it. He was virile, vigorous, and experienced, and yet he could have been making love to a robot.

After six months he insisted she see a psychiatrist. She thought the idea was ridiculous.

'You have your satisfaction, Arthur,' she said. 'What difference does it make whether I go wild with you?'

'It makes every difference! My God, you make me feel ineffectual, something less than a man! You have some

81

hang-up, Marilyn. I adore your body. I want you every minute, and I want you to enjoy my lovemaking.'

'You want me to feed your ego,' she said calmly. 'If I don't go out of my mind with ecstasy I've somehow destroyed your precious confidence, isn't that it? Maybe you're the one who needs the head doctor, Arthur, not I.'

She had never seen him so angry. It was frightening. Frightening enough, in fact, to make her agree. Ironically, it was also the beginning of the end of the marriage, because for the first time in her life Marilyn fell in love—with her doctor, and he with her.

She had heard of such things happening and put them down as another of the myths about shrinks. But this was real on both sides. Her doctor was nowhere near as rich as her husband, but she couldn't have cared less. She knew now what her mother's warning meant. She literally threw herself at her psychiatrist, openly worshiping him. But this time it worked. Within a few weeks the patient-doctor relationship disappeared and they became lovers. He asked his wife for a divorce at the same time that Marilyn told Arthur she was going to Reno. They both denied to their respective spouses that there was anyone else. The doctor's wife, weary of her unfaithful husband, knew better, but she put up no resistance. This was not the first time, by far, that he'd taken up with another woman, but it was the first time he'd decided to marry one of them. Theirs was a marriage she'd be well out of, and he'd pay dearly for his freedom.

Arthur's reaction, predictably, was exactly the opposite. He accepted the fact that there was no other man. His first shock of disbelief was followed by raging accusations of other kinds. He cruelly suggested that she was frigid, probably a lesbian. She simply smiled and did not answer. He accused her of being a shell of a woman, too involved with herself to give anything to another human. He threatened her. She'd not get a penny out of him. She was a washed-up has-been who'd probably end up making stag films. She became angry then, at last, and told him she didn't want a damned dime. And as a parting shot she suggested that he might examine his own sexual prowess. 'Maybe you need a new press agent,' she said. 'You don't live up to your reputation.' It was not any more true than the things he said about her. They simply knew, too well, how to wound each other.

In November, Marilyn Powers left for Reno. Right up to the last minute, Arthur couldn't believe it. He wasn't shaken by her remarks about his lovemaking. He knew he was good. It was simply that he couldn't believe a woman—any woman —could walk out on him. Arthur did the walking. Arthur had never been discarded until now. His unhappiness was not caused by the loss of Marilyn. He knew now that he'd never really been in love with her, and the last year had been no more satisfying than sharing a bed with a Saks Fifth Avenue window mannequin. He simply could not tolerate rejection. It ate at him, undermined his security, and left him bewildered and bitter. Some day he'd teach her a lesson. He didn't know how, but she'd pay for what she'd done to him. In late December he received a copy of the divorce decree. He threw it angrily into a desk drawer.

'Bitch!' he said aloud. She hadn't even wanted alimony. It was incredible that her freedom was something she craved more than money, more than him. He mixed himself a bicarbonate of soda and water. He was drinking a lot these days, and his stomach was giving him trouble. It was that goddamn Marilyn's fault. Until the past few months he'd had the digestion of a sixteen-year-old. He still was at the emotional level of one.

No two men could have been less alike than Arthur Powers and Ed Richmond, yet they had qualities and problems that were strangely similar. Neither until this point in his life had ever experienced the feeling of being abandoned. Both had desperately wanted the women who were slipping away from them, one overtly and the other reluctantly but surely. And both faced these facts with an unreasonable reluctance to believe that they were really at fault. Arthur, even with concrete proof of Marilyn's rejection, did not believe that the trouble lay within himself. Ed, with a growing suspicion of Beverly's unhappiness, felt helpless and unsure of what had happened to this once-idyllic union.

He was well aware of Bev's increasing malaise, but he did not doubt her love. He did suspect that he had been forced to try for a role that was more for Bev's satisfaction than for his own, but he refused to believe that lack of business success was the cancer that was killing his marriage. Nothing that unimportant could destroy what he and Bev felt for each other. It was too superficial, too silly, all this stress on big titles and big salaries. That wasn't what life was all about, and if Bev thought so he was disappointed in her. Besides, he told himself, for four years he'd done the best he could. It wasn't his fault if he simply wasn't geared to take the whole structure of power and dominance very seriously. If such things satisfied some need in Bev, that was okay with him. He didn't think that ambition had a gender. Sure, he'd have liked to have been a big shot for her sake. He'd have liked anything that made her happy, and it did worry him that nothing seemed to work out right for him. He was getting discouraged, and what Beverly mistook for increasing weakness was really only bravado. When he quit a job and did not hurry to look for the next one, he was being subconsciously defiant, really testing Bev and the strength of her love. If she cared for him, she would stand by, the way his mother had stood by a father who refused to let man-made rules get in the way of the enjoyment of an all-too-brief life.

He did not envy Bev her success; he was proud of it, undismayed that she made more money than he, even when he worked. He saw nothing wrong in the fact that he was the cook. He was good at it, and Bev was almost helpless in the kitchen. Ed could not know that he was really twenty-five years ahead of his time in his attitudes about the man-woman relationship, about the equality of the sexes, about the roles of husbands and wives which the next generation would explore under the unheard-of name of 'liberation.'

He did know that he had unresistingly allowed her to dominate him, to lovingly try to direct his future, to make the decisions, set the directions, assume the leadership in their marriage. Such things still did not disturb him, but he was coming to the realization that they troubled Bev. It seemed, bewilderingly, that the more he gave her her way, the more she resented his doing so. At moments he almost felt that she hated him for being so untroubled by her success and so disinterested in his own. He did not understand that what she really wanted of him was some strange standard of good marriage. For Ed, just being with her was a good marriage. But they weren't together as they were in the beginning. They seemed to be losing communication, mental as well as physical. With helpless anxiety, he felt that it was Bev who had changed because she had expected him to change.

84

Perhaps she had always subconsciously sensed that he couldn't. Perhaps that was why she had been reluctant to marry him for so long. We should talk about it, he thought. We should have it out, once and for all. Maybe we both can give a little more than we have in the past. But he didn't dare bring his anxieties into the open or ask Bev to confess hers. It could mean the end for them. And that he couldn't bear.

Much the same thoughts were in Beverly's mind as she lay awake night after night beside her husband, knowing she was failing him in and out of bed, angry at herself for the lack of respect which colored her attitude toward him. And yet a kind of scorn gnawed at her. Why was he so easygoing, so content to play a secondary role in the matrimonial drama? His calm acceptance of her progress and his lack of it seemed unnatural to her. She was a strong woman. She yearned to look up to her man. It was a stupid, outmoded attitude, and yet it bore heavily upon her every action. It had almost gotten to the point where she couldn't bear to have him touch her. And it was all ridiculous. He was still the same gentle, adoring, unselfish Eddie she'd fallen in love with. She should have nothing but admiration for him. He probably was the finest person she'd ever known. And yet her disappointment lay deep. Without a man's outward manifestations of superiority, she felt less of a woman. She should have been thanking God for bringing her someone who loved her so selflessly. She had what few others had: a loyal mate, generous in spirit, tender in every thought. And yet this same docility made her scornful of him.

She knew that the marriage was in trouble unless she came to terms with it. Marion had been right. Eddie was not going to change. She would have to accept him as he was, forgetting her dreams of glory for him, or leave him. Neither possibility seemed tenable. Staying would increase her frustration to the point of ugly, open hostility. Walking out would be like abandoning a child whose only crime was an endless effort to please her. It was a problem that could have no happy solution. Perhaps, Bev thought, it could have no solution of any kind. Perhaps they would go on year after year with their public smiles and private tears, growing more and more like the polite strangers they were rapidly becoming.

They were playacting now, behaving more like people

who'd been married forty years instead of less than four. On the rare occasions when they went out, they gave the appearance of a handsome, happy young couple. At home they talked little and never argued, occasionally tried to make love and found that it satisfied neither of them. Ed plodded on at the insurance company, coming home early to prepare their dinner and spend most evenings lost in his endless supply of aviation magazines. They no longer spoke of his great future. Bev was grateful that he was at least sticking to one job, even though it seemed to be going nowhere.

At night they both lay with their own troubled thoughts, not daring to talk about their disintegrating relationship, still loving each other, still faithful, frightened, and confused.

By the fall of 1949 Bev had almost convinced herself that divorce would be the best thing for both of them. She was numb with disappointment and self-reproach, but she was incapable of rekindling the passion she'd once felt for Ed. Without respect for him, she could only feel pity. She could not summon desire. She felt dead. If it had not been for the excitement and stimulation of the store, she thought she would have become a weary old woman at twenty-five, drained of hope for personal happiness and fulfillment.

More important, she rationalized that, without her, Ed would be forced to find his own way. Without a prop he would have to stand on his own feet, perhaps making something of himself if he wanted to. At least he would be free to do whatever he enjoyed—start a new life in Australia, go back to the mediocre job at the airline, do whatever would make him happy. She wanted his happiness. Even if he would not believe it, she felt that she was standing in his way. He deserved a woman who could accept him as he was. She was not that woman, filled as she was with this awful guilt and stagnation.

It seemed to her that all through her life, whenever she'd had a problem, there'd been no one to talk to. It was that way now. Her parents would not understand. They adored Ed, rightly so, because he adored their child. Even if she tried to make them understand how he had 'failed' her they would be uncomprehending. They probably would even reproach her. Her husband was loving, faithful, and, though there'd been some hard times, he had a respectable job and could support her if she'd only let him. Her mother would recommend that she have a baby. Bev could hear it now. 'There's nothing like a child to make a man realize his responsibilities,' Angela would say. 'It's about time you gave up that job and started a family, Beverly.' How could she explain to her mother that she didn't have enough confidence in Ed to take such a risk? How could she say that though she loved him she had no faith in his ability to support her, much less a child?

She could not bring herself to admit her failure to Marion, either. Not, she supposed, that Ed's sister didn't guess that things were less than perfect. They saw her fairly often, and Marion was not easily fooled even by the most skilled acting. But Marion had opposed the marriage from the beginning. She would not say 'I told you so,' but Beverly was too proud to admit that Marion had been right. Besides, how could one expect her to give dispassionate advice when it involved the future of her dearly loved brother?

But perhaps there was someone, even more emotionally tied to the problem, who could listen with compassion and speak with the wisdom of experience. Jane Richmond had had a husband very like Bev's. Though Eddie was her son, he was also part of that man and probably reacted to things much as his father did. If anyone could help Beverly sort out her loyalties and her sorrows, Jane could. It was a feeble straw, but Bev grasped at it in the hope that somehow her mother-in-law could miraculously, mercifully, put things right.

On a gray November Sunday afternoon when Ed had gone to a football game, Bev called his mother.

'Doing anything special, Jane?'

'Only waging my weekly duel-to-the-death with the *Times* crossword puzzle. What's a seven-letter word for "emotionally disturbed"?'

'Try "Beverly." Listen, would you mind if I ran up to see you?'

'I'd be delighted. Come ahead.'

As she waited for Bev, Jane Richmond knew what it was about. She saw her son and daughter-in-law rarely, but often enough to have formed some vaguely disquieting opinions about their marriage. She had recognized the symptoms of trouble and hoped these two would overcome them. Apparently they had not. Bev's call was one she had somehow anticipated. It would not be Ed who would confide in her. He never had.

8

At first, Beverly didn't know how to begin. Facing Jane Richmond in that composed woman's cosy living room, Bev wondered whether she had not made a mistake in choosing her husband's mother as the audience for a recital of her marital troubles. How could she possibly expect Jane to be impartial? It seemed indecent to ask her.

'It's wrong of me to burden you with my problems,' Bev said in a low voice, 'but I'm going out of my mind talking to myself.'

'I'm flattered that you feel we *can* talk. It's Eddie, isn't it?'

'Yes. No. I mean, I'm not sure whether it's Eddie or me or both of us. I think maybe it's more me than Eddie.'

Jane waited, saying nothing.

Suddenly Bev was pouring out the whole story of her life, all the years that preceded her marriage. For an hour she talked, uninterrupted, about her childhood, about the things she'd been told to believe and the 'respectability' that Angela and Harry had done their best to teach her. She went over the questions in her own mind about 'right and wrong.' She told Jane about Frank Burroughs and even, with shame and bewilderment, something of her experience with Neil. She spoke of meeting Ed and of her instinctive reluctance to marry him. It all came flooding out in waves of relief, as though she were in a confessional and Jane Richmond had the power to grant absolution. All the anguish she had bottled up, her self-loathing, her repugnance for the things she had done and felt, became remorseful realities when she was able, for the first time, to put them into bald sentences.

Jane listened, expressionless, not interrupting these unexpected, sometimes shocking, and always touching revelations. Only when Bev came to the end did she speak. The girl was crying now, shedding all the hurt she'd held back over the years.

'I'm sorry,' Bev sobbed. 'Sorry that Ed and I fell in love. You hate me for the miserable creature I am. I'm not good enough for him. What's wrong with me? Why can't I stop trying to make him different? He's better than any man I've ever known, and yet he's like a little boy, and I don't want a little boy. If I did, I'd have one. It's wrong of me to blame Eddie. I'm the one who's driven, not only for myself but for him. And he's tried so hard to please me. I think he's given up. The more I've tried to push him, the more he rebelled. I've watched him slip into a passive state, and he's not a passive man. I find myself condemning him for it. I can't respect him. And yet, in my demented way, I love him. What am I going to do, Jane? What's best for both of us?'

Jane chose her words carefully. 'Bev, dear, you know I can't answer that. God knows I don't judge you for the things you've done in the past. I can only sympathize for the way you feel. I'm disappointed, of course. I wanted to see you two make it. When I sat at your wedding I felt that you were the very thing Eddie needed—the woman who was strong enough to help him in a way he's never cared to help himself. I guess I've sensed for quite a while that you're the best and the worst thing that ever happened to Ed. And, I suppose, vice versa.'

Bev nodded miserably.

'My dear, it would be presumptuous of me to give you advice. Presumptuous, dangerous, and impossible. I like to think that I have some degree of objectivity even about my son, but I'm human and I am his mother. To further complicate it, I love you both. I know it would break Ed's heart if you left him. But it will harden yours if you stay.' She looked compassionately at her daughter-in-law. 'This may sound strange, but after three and a half years of marriage and almost half a year of living together before that, how much do you really know about your husband?' She smiled at Bev's startled expression. 'You left out the living-together part of the story, but you didn't really think I was deceived by that idiotic story about a roommate with no telephone, did you? I was glad you were doing it. I thought you'd iron out the rough spots before marriage or discover that the wrinkles were too firmly embedded on both sides. Anyway, that's not the question. The question is, What do you really know about Ed?'

Bev looked puzzled. 'Just about what I've told you, I think. That he's a kind, loving, loyal man who doesn't want to face the realities of life. At least not my kind of realities.'

'I mean, what do you know about Ed's life before you met him?'

'Bits and pieces,' Bev said. Suddenly she realized that she knew surprisingly little, and most of that gleaned from Marion. 'I know that his father died when he was sixteen and that you put him through college. I know he hitchhiked across the country and almost married a girl in San Francisco. I know he volunteered for the RAF and then switched to the Army Air Force. He spent a hellish time in the Pacific.' She stopped. 'Funny. I never thought of it, but neither of us has ever gone deeply into our early lives. Ed doesn't know any of the things I've told you, Jane. About how I was before I met him. And apparently I am just as ignorant of what he was like.'

'Isn't it strange,' Jane said, 'how people can live together in the deepest kind of intimacy and know so little about each other?' The question was rhetorical. 'It never ceases to amaze me. Like you. All you know about Eddie is the bare bones of a life. The vital statistics, like something you'd read in a *Who's Who of Anonymous People*. You know how your early years affected you, Bev, but you've never thought of how Ed's may have affected him, how they may be shaping his life and yours today.'

Bev listened attentively. Jane took a deep breath and went on.

'Do you know, Beverly, that you're probably the first person in Ed's life who ever asked him to measure up? The only one who's ever really demanded anything of him? Of course, you don't. How could you? But it's true. And most of it is my fault. Ed's so like his father that it's scary. My husband had the same sweet, adoring attitude about me that Ed has about you. He also had the same kind of dreamy unreality about life. Of course, he didn't have an independent wage-earning wife, so he couldn't just abdicate responsibility the way Eddie's been able to. But he'd probably have reacted to the protection of a strong woman the same way his son is reacting now.'

'But you're a strong woman too,' Bev said.

'Not in the way you are. I didn't dream of going to work when my husband was alive. For one thing, I had two children. He knew that if he didn't pay the rent and put food on the table, nobody would. It was only after he died, leaving us nothing, that I had to get a job and support the family. I was strong in other ways, Bev. I bolstered Ed's dad when he'd get fed up with the world, when he failed at job after job. I reassured him that he was right in his attitudes and everybody else was wrong. I only wanted him to be happy, and I gave him whatever strength I had in the form of faith and approval. I don't know now whether I was right, but that's the way I played it. Eddie grew up watching an idealistic, unrealistic father and a blindly acquiescent mother. He never saw competition in this house. He never heard complaints from me that we should have more money, or more security, or more status. I didn't feel martyred. I accepted my Stephen as he was, but more out of ignorance than out of nobility. I wasn't equipped by talent or desire to be a successful person in my own right. I convinced myself that the materialistic things in life were secondary to peace of mind. Serenity was all-important. And when Stephen died, I took the same tack with Eddie.

'I took over the same self-appointed job of protecting him from the world, the way I'd protected his father. I never thought of either of them as weak. They seemed special to me. Even when Ed got out of school and picked up odd jobs, I wouldn't let him pay room and board. I was delighted that he could earn a little money for his own pleasure. I didn't say, as maybe I should have, "Well, now, son, you and I are *mutually* responsible for picking up where your father left off." I just wanted him to be happy, the way I wanted his father to be happy. Maybe this was my ego thing, Bev, the way your desire for a success is yours.'

'Do you think that if you'd demanded more of Ed it would have made a different person of him?'

'I don't know. I don't find that kind of hindsight very helpful. I know that I never asked him to assume any responsibility or feel any pressure. I let him drift, just be loved and looked after. First by me, then by the Army. And now, of course, by you. Except that you're unwilling, or maybe unable, to settle for that. You have a healthy, selfish desire to be looked after yourself. Oh, you want to be independent and to have a career, I know that. But I suspect that even more you want to feel you have someone you can rely on and be proud of. Someone whose accomplishments you can point to and brag about. There's nothing wrong with that. Most women feel that way. The trouble is, Bev, that Eddie hasn't been conditioned to think in those terms. It has dawned on you that Ed doesn't even give lip-service to the world's idea of success. He saw his father happy without it. He saw me happy without it. And now I'm sure he's seeing you unhappy without it, but I doubt that there's much he can do about it even if he wanted to. His values, like yours, are too firmly entrenched. At thirty-two he's hardly likely to take a whole new attitude about what's necessary for a full and happy life.'

Jane paused. 'This sounds self-accusatory. I don't really feel that way. You see, I'm not sure that Ed is wrong, or that I made a mistake in fostering his belief that life is made for living and loving and that side benefits like fame and money are pleasant but rather inconsequential. If they happen to fall into one's lap, fine. If they don't, okay. I can accept that, Bev. But I share your grave doubts that you can or ever will. Eddie isn't going to change even if he tries to pretend that he wants to. And from what you tell me, he's pretending less and less. If there's any changing to be done, Beverly, it will have to be on your part. I know that sounds unfair. It *is* unfair. But it's realistic.'

'And if I can't change?' Bev asked.

'Then you should leave him, dear. But don't make that judgment hastily. You have to decide what counts most in life. Specifically, in your life. Think about it selfishly. You should. You're still young and desirable. There's still time for you to find the kind of man you may need. But at the same time, Bev, don't overlook the years to come. Ed will wear well if you let him. And perhaps his rare kind of loyalty and devotion may count for more in the long run than the part-time attention you'll get from a man who makes the pursuit of money the most important part of his life.'

Bev stood up. 'You must be terribly disappointed in me, Jane.'

'Disappointed in you? Not at all. I understand, Bev, and I don't blame you for wondering whether you should leave Ed. If you did, I'd be sorry, but I could never hate you for it. Your whole life is ahead. Ed won't die of a broken heart if you become truly convinced that you'll be happier without him. People just don't do that; they pick up and go on. But I beg you not to act rashly, for your own sake as well as his. It would be good if you had a little vacation from each other, perhaps. Give you time to think it over quietly and put things in perspective. Do you think that's possible?'

'I don't see how. This is our busy time at the store.'

'Yes, of course. I, of all people, should know that.' She kissed Bev warmly. 'Thank you for talking to me, Bev. I hope I've been some help. Anyway, I'll say a little prayer for both of you.'

While she waited at home for Ed's return from the football game, Bev mulled over all the things that her mother-in-law had said. They explained a lot. But they did not solve the basic dilemma. She hadn't really expected a solution when she went to see Jane, any more than she had expected to bare her soul in that impulsive but somehow healing outpouring of the past. And yet she had gained a great deal, both from her own confessions, as if what she had told Jane had been a poison trapped inside her now finally released, and from the older woman's sensible and acute view of her son. It would be so easy to blame Jane for what was wrong with Eddie. It was beginning to be the fashion for every magazine to have articles about what mothers had done to their children. But it would be as wrong to blame Jane for Eddie's lack of drive as it would be to blame Angela for making Bev into what she was. Only, if she and Eddie were to change, how was it to happen? As always, Bev had gone instantly toward what was practical, what could be done. But at the moment she could find no answers, except to set the table and start preparing supper for the man she had married and, apparently, did not know at all.

The next morning Bev was at the store early, going straight to the small cubicle she shared with her two assistants. Dinner had been peaceful. Eddie had filled in the meal with enthusiastic accounts of the game, not noticing that she had little to say. When he finally asked if something was wrong, she pleaded a headache and went to bed as soon as the meal was finished. Am I going to become like that? she thought as she got into bed. One of those women with chronic headaches because they don't want to face an ardent husband they're no longer sure they love? That thought was too painful to be examined, and Bev had forced herself to sleep. In the morning she made a special effort to be cheerful. But she left the small apartment earlier than usual. Acting a charade, she thought as she took the bus to the store, was not the best way to start a day.

She had hoped to have a few minutes to herself before the working day began, but she had hardly hung up her coat when the phone range. It was Sylvia, already in her office, ready to start tackling the day and the week ahead of her.

'Can you come up, Bev?' she asked.

Bev agreed almost eagerly. Anything would be better than being alone with her thoughts, she decided. As always when she walked through the store before the doors had opened to the public, she found her spirits reviving. Each aisle held so many things that were beautiful and fresh and, above all, *new*. Each rack of dresses, each display case of glittering cosmetics, promised changes in life, something exciting to happen in the future if you bought this shade of lipstick or tied a new Italian scarf in a certain way. The quiet counters seemed to say, Forget the past . . . try something different.

But much as she loved the store itself, it was when Bev stepped into the elevator and asked for the executive floor that she always felt her spirits rise with her body. A symbol of power, of course, moving upward; she was aware of that even on this morning. But there was something else she felt and, to be honest with herself, envied on this corporate floor, so beautifully decorated, so quiet and calm even when the rest of the store was a madhouse. It was the sense of security. The people who had reached this level had done so because they knew what they wanted; the thousands of decisions they had made over the years had built Welby's into one of the most important stores in New York and, in consequence, in America. They had known what was right. Bev could only envy that kind of assurance.

Not that she envied Sylvia exactly, her one real contact with the people who shared this executive level. Oh, without jealousy she could envy the manager's vice-presidential title, her position and her success, evidenced in the silk-and-satin office that Syvia occupied. But most of all, Bev envied the older woman her happy marriage. Unconsciously she sighed as she took the little armchair beside the delicate French desk.

Sylvia pushed her glasses up on top of her head, lit one of the endless cigarettes in the gold holder that was her trademark, tilted her head, and looked with narrow-eyed appraisal at Beverly. The sigh had not escaped her.

'Good morning to you too,' she said. 'No good can come of a week that begins with Monday. What's the matter? Was your weekend too bad or too good?'

Bev managed a smile. 'It was okay. I spent a lot of time with my mother-in-law yesterday.'

Sylvia groaned. 'Oh, my God! You poor baby!'

This time Beverly laughed. 'It's not like that at all. I really love her. She's a fabulous lady. You know that, Sylvia. You've met her.'

'Only at your wedding for a second. I don't really know her. I apologize. I guess I'm brainwashed by my own two unfortunate experiences with the breed. What did you and Eddie do?'

'Not much. He went to the football game.' It was obvious that Bev was not in the mood for small talk. That's okay, Sylvia thought. She will be in a minute.

'Listen, kiddo, how would you like to run away from home?'

Beverly amost literally jumped.

"Don't look so startled,' Slyvia said. 'I'm not suggesting you jump the marital ship permanently. What I want to know is how you feel about making the Paris buying trip with me in January. I got the okay this morning for you to go to the couture openings. It'll be a five-week trip, over on the *Queen Mary*, back on the *Elizabeth*, two weeks or so in Paris, and a few days in London. Think you could stand being cooped up with me that long? Unfortunately, our skinflint store sees no reason why we can't share boat and hotel accommodations to save a little money. Well? What do you say?'

'I say I can't believe it!'

'You can believe it. You can also believe that you'll work your behind off. But we'll have some fun too. Do you think Ed will come down here and kill me?'

Bev had somewhat recovered. Her tone now nearly matched Sylvia's.

'He'll be despondent,' Bev said airily, 'but he's the nonviolent type. Actually, I think he'll be happy for me. He knows I've never been out of the country.'

'Good. Then plan to leave on January twentieth. You'll need a passport, smallpox vaccination, all that, so you'd better get right on it. We'll be back around the first of March, give or take a day or two. By the way, are you a good sailor?'

'I don't know. I've never left my native shores in anything bigger than a sailboat—but I've never been seasick, even on Long Island Sound.'

'The Atlantic is rougher in winter, but the *Queen*'s steadier and a helluva lot more comfortable. I only ask because we're sharing a stateroom. Can't abide green-faced shipmates. Or difficult roommates. You don't snore, do you? Or do constant laundry? I loathe being smacked in the face by wet nylons when I go into the bathroom.'

Bev left the office smiling, not only at the excitement of the news but at the absurdity of Sylvia's questions. Here was Beverly Thyson Richmond about to take a trip she'd hardly dared to dream of, and Sylvia was concerned with seasickness and wet stockings! Of course, the semiannual Paris buying trip, reinstated after the war, wasn't such a big deal to Sylvia. She'd made it many times before the elegant doors of the haute couture were closed to the free world's retailers and press, and she'd gone three or four times since the French designers had resumed showing their collections. Sylvia took the European trip for granted. To Beverly it was the ultimate recognition of her success in the fashion business. Only very important people went to Paris in January and July.

From the personal side, the 'holiday' had come at just the right moment too. The short separation from Ed that Jane had thought might help her sort out her thinking was now possible with no need for explanation. In five weeks, she would know how much she missed Ed, how it felt to be without him for the first prolonged period in nearly four years. She truly hoped that the trip would work wonders. Please, God, she said silently, make me so anxious to get back to him that I'll want to swim the last mile to the pier.

When she told him the news that evening he was genuinely happy for her.

'It's a great compliment to you, dear,' he said. 'Not that there's any doubt about how the store feels about you. You're going to be a very big wheel in the fashion business. I've always told you so, but this confirms it, doesn't it? Too bad All-American Insurance doesn't have a Paris office. Maybe they'd send me over to write a whopping policy on Mr. Christian Dior.' There was no rancor or envy in the remark, just pride and an implied wish that he was going along. But Beverly felt guilty, knowing how much she wanted to get away from him.

'Maybe next time you can go with me,' she lied. 'We could make it a July holiday.'

She felt that he saw right through her, that he knew how much she wanted to escape, but all he said was, 'That's worth thinking about.'

That night she made love to him almost the way she used to. He did not comment on the difference, but in his quiet way he understood.

For the next month she was caught up in preparations for the trip, absorbed in planning her wardrobe, thrilled at the sight of her first passport, undismayed, as most people are, by the terrible identification picture on it. Sylvia rolled her eyes heavenward when Bev showed her the commercial photograph. 'My God,' Sylvia said, 'you look like a Lithuanian refugee. More like somebody getting *off* a boat than getting *on* it! I hope they don't pick you up at Immigration for carrying a phony passport.'

Bev laughed. Who cared what the picture looked like? In another six weeks or so she'd be on her way to Paris, the Mecca of every aspiring merchant. Her enthusiasm was contagious. Even the girls in the department were happy for her. Midge DeLuca, now Mrs. Tony Marino, working only until she became pregnant, extended congratulations when she heard about it. They had not seen each other again socially since that one evening at Valentino's. Bev felt slightly self-conscious about it, wondering whether Midge knew the outcome of her birthday party. If she did, the bright-eyed young woman gave no hint. She continued to be friendly and apparently fond of Bev, but she did not suggest another outing. Only now, when she told Bev how pleased they all were for her, did she make even an oblique reference to the past.

'I told Paul Young about your trip,' Midge said. 'Remember him? He was your date the night we all went out together. He's married now too. Anyway, he said to wish you bon voyage for him.'

'Thanks, Midge. That's nice of him. Did he marry a nice girl? Is he happy?'

'I guess so. We don't see them very often.'

Bev hesitated. 'Do you still go to Valentino's?'

'Once in a while. It hasn't changed much.'

They let it go at that. She knows, Bev thought. Well, what difference? All that was a hundred years ago. By now it seemed like a hazy dream, a nightmare lived by someone she'd only heard about. The last vestiges of remorse had somehow been swept away by telling the story to Jane Richmond. Neil Farrentino had happened to a creature who wasn't Beverly Thyson. Just as Frank Burroughs had been part of another, more naive girl's life.

Her present life was built around the eagerly awaited trip and what it would reveal about her feelings for Ed. He had never been more selfless than in those next few weeks. One night he asked her to pick out some luggage; it would be his Christmas gift to her. She protested.

'That's too big a present. Luggage is awfully expensive.'

'I want you to have it. You don't have any decent suitcases. Besides, I can afford it. Just made a pretty good commission on a policy.' For the first time he sounded slightly sardonic. 'I'd better be careful,' he said. 'Next thing you know I'll be offering to pay half the rent.'

She didn't answer. They still lived in the apartment Bev had taken on her twentieth birthday, almost six years before. By now she could have afforded a better one, but some perverse streak made her refuse to move. She'd have liked a more spacious place, but only if her husband were paying for it.

Instead, she said calmly, 'I'd love the luggage, Ed. I'll look for some at the store tomorrow. With my discount I can keep it within reason. What do *you* want for Christmas?'

'Nothing. I have everything I want when I see how happy you are.'

There was no hint of sarcasm, no accusatory note in his

voice. He really means it, Bev thought. He really doesn't know that I've come within inches of asking for a divorce.

When Bev told her mother-in-law about the trip, Jane responded happily. 'I'm glad. You and I both know why. You'll have plenty of chances to think things through, Beverly. Think right.'

The Thysons were overwhelmed. 'Paris, France!' Harry said. 'How about that? I never even got to see it in World War One.'

Angela was equally delighted. 'I'm glad Mrs. Schlesinger will be along to look after you,' she said. 'Goodness, imagine going where they don't even speak English!'

Bev and Ed laughed. 'Mother, it isn't darkest Africa,' Bev said. 'Besides, a lot of Parisians speak our native tongue.'

'Sure, Mother T.,' Ed added. 'And if your baby gets lost she can always ask a nice gendarme to take her by the hand to the American Embassy.'

Angela looked defensive. 'You can laugh if you like, but I hear there are still a lot of Nazis in Paris.'

'Oh, sure,' Harry said. 'And they're all hiding in those big fashion houses where Beverly'll be spending her time. Angela, stop being so silly. Your baby is a married woman, a full-fledged buyer. I don't think you'll believe she's grown up until she hands you your first grandchild.'

An awkward silence fell over the room. In his blundering way, Harry had barged into a delicate area. It was true. It was what Angela was waiting for. She did not know that Bev and Ed had talked about children early in their marriage and decided to wait until he was firmly established in business. In those days they had agreed that they wanted children, even if Bev kept on working. In the last couple of years they'd not discussed the subject at all.

'Speaking of children,' Bev finally said, 'I'm having lunch with Ruth Wells tomorrow. I mean Ruth Eliason. I'll never get used to calling her by her married name. You know she has three little boys, don't you, Mother? Absolute darlings.'

Angela sniffed. 'That's because Ruth never had any silly ideas about being a career woman.'

'No,' Ed said easily, 'that's because she had the good sense to marry a very rich young man . . . which is more than your daughter was bright enough to do.'

From habit, Bev sprang to his defense in front of other

people. 'I wouldn't trade my life for Ruth's, no matter how content she is with her brood. Motherhood's great, but it isn't the be-all and end-all of the world. Not for every woman. Some of us find satisfaction in other things.'

They were on dangerous ground again. This time, Ed got them off it. 'Anyway,' he said, 'the Eliasons are a terrific couple. They're our closest friends. After all, they stood up for us at our wedding. We feel like we have three kids without the fuss, to say nothing of the expense.'

On the way home from the Thysons, Ed was unusually quiet. Bev knew exactly what was on his mind. He adored children, and the Eliasons' were no real substitute for their own. He knew, too, that Bev would not consider getting pregnant at this point. Maybe he suspected that she'd never consider it. In any case, he didn't bring up the conversation with Bev's parents. And neither, of course, did she.

On Christmas Eve, the family they loved and felt closest to was suddenly struck by tragedy. Geoffrey Eliason, flying home from a business conference in Chicago, determined to get back in time to help trim the tree, was one of the passengers in a plane that crashed trying to make an approach to LaGuardia Airport in a blinding snowstorm. There were no survivors.

Ruth's mother, trying to control herself, called Bev a few hours after Ruth was notified. Ed and Beverly rushed over. They found a stunned, haunted-looking young widow who sat motionless and dry-eyed in a chair in her living room, staring at an untrimmed Christmas tree. As she rushed to her friend, Bev's tears were the ones that wet the cheeks of the two young women. Ruth seemed frozen, unable to move or to speak.

Ed drew Mrs. Wells aside. His firm voice was very gentle. 'I suppose someone is making arrangements?'

She nodded. 'Geoff's father has gone to claim the body.'

'What about the kids?'

'We haven't told them. In a way, Ed, I thank God they're so young. Even Philip won't really comprehend this horror.' Mrs. Wells began to cry. 'Why do things like this happen, Eddie? They were so happy, so young, so in love. They had everything to live for.'

He held her close. Always the same questions, he thought.

He'd asked them of himself hundreds of times during the war. Why did Joe or Pete or Antonio or Les have to die? They, too, were young, with everything to live for. Some of them left widows and children, just like these; some of them never even had a chance to know what love was all about. At least, Ed thought sadly, soldiers died for a cause. The taking of Geoff's life seemed so senseless, so without purpose. He was needed, looked up to, adored. Ed's heart ached for Ruth and for the three soundly sleeping babies who might never even remember their father. He closed his eyes. Geoff, he said silently, at least you made your woman happy. You left a lot of yourself behind.

He joined Bev, who was crouched beside Ruth's chair, holding her hand. Kneeling beside the bereaved young widow, he took her face tenderly in his hands. 'He was everybody's best man, Ruthie,' he said. 'Not only yours and mine.'

The simple words opened the floodgates of tears. Bev cradled her close. 'We know,' Bev said over and over. 'We're here, Ruthie. We're here.'

The last thing she said to Ed as she kissed him goodbye at the gangplank of the *Queen Mary* was, 'Look in on Ruth whenever you can, will you?'

'Of course I will,' he promised. 'Don't worry about her too much, Bev. She's been remarkable these past few weeks. She's very strong. Just like you, love.'

Bev shook her head. 'No, she isn't. She's not strong. And she's nothing like me. She has a lot of pride and a lot of dignity, Ed, but she's more like you. Underneath she's all soft and gentle and easily hurt. You both pretend, but neither of you fool me for a minute with your take-it-in-stride attitudes.'

He looked at her curiously. It was a strange little going-away speech.

'I'll stay close,' he said again. 'Don't let it spoil this trip for you, dear. Nothing can undo what's happened. Ruth will have to make a new life for herself. She knows that, and she can do it. She isn't the first person who's had to.'

He'd never seen Bev look so sad. 'No,' she said again, 'she's neither the first nor the last.' Then, in an abrupt change, she smiled at him. 'Take care of yourself, Eddie. Let me hear from you often, okay?'

'Okay. And you take care of you. I'll miss you, darling.'

She kissed him again, harder this time. Suddenly he was afraid to have her leave. Maybe he'd lose her. It was the same feeling he'd had in the beginning when he'd lied about his first job. He couldn't bear living without Bev any more now than he could have then. Maybe even less.

9

Paris in late January of 1950 was what visitors always hope the city will be and what it so rarely is—softly romantic, sweetly seductive. Even the winter weather seemed determined to cooperate. The sun shone warmly enough to permit surprised café owners to serve coffee at the little round outdoor tables on the sidewalks of the Champs Elysées. The air was gentle, almost an April air. The city seemed to have a benevolent attitude as though, like the French themselves, it finally dared to relax from the rigors of occupation, reveling in its release from intruders who did not know the meaning of finesse.

Things, the Parisians told each other, were finally getting back to normal. After five years of liberation, they had now literally and figuratively erased the Nazi heelmarks from the footboards of their Louis XIV beds. They congratulated themselves over their endless cups of bitter coffee and said yes, of course, it had taken time. But look what was happening at last. The great hotels were once more full of tourists, the fine restaurants offered prewar cuisine, there were automobiles instead of bicycles in the streets. It was comforting to learn that the unique symbols of elegance—the houses of haute couture—were about to present collections as elaborate and glamorous as ever.

It was good to see the rich American buyers and even some wealthy private clients pouring back into Paris to spend their much-missed dollars on the creations of Monsieurs Dior and Balenciaga. George was smiling behind the bar at the Ritz. The Americans were his old friends. The store people, fashion editors, manufacturers of textiles and clothing appreciated George. The Ritz, Paris, and the couture, possibly in that order. A few brave ones had come right after the war. But 1950, surely, was the beginning of a decade of solid prosperity. The personnel of great American fashion stores such as Bergdorf Goodman, I. Magnin, Neiman-Marcus, and J. L. Hudson had returned en masse to buy originals and copy them, seam for seam, for their customers in New York, Los Angeles, Dallas, and Detroit.

The fashion-magazine people were here in droves—sleek young women editors speaking a language of their own in finishing-school voices; wild-eyed, frequently effeminate young male photographers with a bevy of camera-carrying assistants; tall, beanpole-thin American models imported for magazine sittings which went on through the night. The magazine people probably worked harder than any other group in Paris. During the day they saw every collection, and at night—when the couture was not showing—they feverishly photographed what they had seen. Messengers raced frantically from studio to studio, carrying armloads of expensive dresses to *Harper's Bazaar* and *Vogue* and *Glamour* and all the other slick publications which would show the newest French creations to a presumably fashion-starved American buying public.

Twice a year, in January and July, Paris became a frantic, breathless game of chance which revolved around the genius of designers and the skill of buyers and editors in selecting the most beautiful, extravagant products of France. It was a game for high stakes. The couturiers staked their reputations on their collections; the editors gambled theirs on selecting the few dozen best garments to show from a parade of hundreds; the buyers, entrusted with thousands of dollars of their stores' money, held their breath and hoped they bought best-sellers.

Stepping off the boat train from Le Havre after five days on the *Queen Mary*, Beverly sensed an excitement in the air that was above and beyond the frenzy of the Paris railroad station. She seemed to be walking into a supercharged atmosphere that had nothing to do with the Gare du Nord. It was as though she had come alive again to be reborn in this lusty, reckless new world.

Crowds of people made the platform almost impassable, porters virtually inpossible to find, but Sylvia had managed to buttonhole a disinterested baggage handler and in her bad

French was now trying to convince him to take their luggage to a taxi. Her flat New York accent rose sharply amid the rapid inflection-filled voices around them.

'*Monsieur! Nous désirons un taxi, s'il vous plait!*' Sylvia was screaming. '*Un taxi,*' she repeated. '*Pour le San Regis.*' Shrugging, he loaded their suitcases onto a hand truck and set off at a half run, plowing his way through the masses, shrieking imprecations at anyone who got in his way. The two women trotted breathlessly behind him, weaving and dodging like football players, trying to keep him in sight.

'Bloody independent bastards,' Sylvia gasped. 'They're all the same. Damned glad to have the American buck and hellbent on making you pay for the privilege of spending it! Not just porters who make it tough on you. Waiters, shopgirls, taxi-drivers—every one of them plays the same little game. Never know what you're talking about. Not much, they don't! You can be saying all the right French words, but if they come out with a Yankee accent you might just as well be speaking Chinese. I don't know what in God's name makes them all so ornery.'

'Maybe it's their way of showing pride,' Bev said as she puffed along beside Sylvia. 'After all, they were a defeated people for a long time. If we were in their shoes we'd probably want to show some independence, too.'

'Why take it out on us? Who the hell liberated 'em? No, they were the same before the war. I admire the French, but I can't say that I love them. They make it impossible. Here we've come a million miles to help, and all we get is contemptuous tolerance.'

They were nearing the entrance where people were queued up for taxis. Their porter miraculously had one waiting for them. The driver was probably his cousin. Trying to ignore the angry glares of the people in line, Bev climbed into the cab while Sylvia paid off the porter, who mumbled something that might have passed for '*Merci, madame.*'

Sylvia slumped into the seat of the rickety taxi, vintage God-knows-what. Their bags were strapped precariously onto the roof. The interior smelled of wine and stale cigarettes. It took another three full minutes to make the ancient driver understand that they wanted to go to the Hotel San Regis. Sylvia's fury was mounting.

'Relax,' Bev said. 'We'll soon be at the hotel. A drink and a nice hot bath will make you feel better. Oh, Syl, I can't believe I'm here. Isn't it wonderful?'

'What's wonderful? A maniacal train station and a hostile porter who practically spat at me when I overtipped him. *That's* wonderful?'

'You been in Pennsylvania Station lately?'

Sylvia managed a half smile. 'Okay. You're determined to love Paris. Far be it from me to disillusion you. Just tell me how you feel a week from now when you're doing eight hours of collections every day, figuring out the buy every evening, *and* being treated like a leftover crepe suzette.'

'I am going to love every minute of it. I know it'll be hard work. But isn't everything?'

Sylvia subsided momentarily. She was clenching her fists and looking at her shoes, trying to ignore the wild ride through Paris that they were now embarked upon. The driver was navigating traffic at death-wish speed, hanging out the window to curse pedestrians and other drivers, plunging into circles and intersections with the obviously unshakable conviction that no other car would dare violate the sacred privilege of the vehicle with the right-of-way. Amazingly, no other car did, though there seemed to be a terrifying number of near misses as they tore through a city which had no speed limit and no traffic lights.

'Someone once wrote a column about Paris taxis,' Sylvia finally said. 'They said the only way to survive in them is to put your *parcels* on the seat and *yourself* on the floor. Damn it.' She leaned toward the driver. '*Doucement!*' she yelled. He ignored her. So did the placid French mongrel who lay on the front seat beside him. 'A dirty cab, a crazy driver, and a dog.' Sylvia closed her eyes. 'What a way to go.'

Bev was too interested to be frightened. If anybody drove like this at home she'd be paralyzed, but here it seemed to be part of the joie de vivre. She was sure the driver was enjoying himself, probably giving vent to all his pent-up frustrations in this headlong dash up the Champs-Elysées. She could see the Arc de Triomphe in the distance; she could imagine what this broad avenue looked like when the French and Americans had come marching down it once again. There were shivers down her spine as the cab turned left down the beautiful Avenue Montaigne and left again on Avenue François Premier and round a little circle to pull up, triumphantly, in front of the hotel on a tiny side street with the melodic name rue Jean Goujon.

In a few minutes they were in the tiny foyer of the San Regis, being welcomed by a suave concierge and a sleepy-eyed French girl at an inefficient-looking switchboard behind the desk. Messages and invitations to showings were thrust into Bev's hand as she squeezed into the ridiculous, snail-paced lift. With a flourish the concierge ushered them into a minuscule bedroom and sitting-room suite furnished with the most beautiful antiques Bev had ever seen. The room was filled with flowers from couturiers, from the head of Welby's Paris buying office, and from the publishers of fashion magazines. It was a moment of wild confusion, but lovely. Like a movie sequence of the thirties. And if she was not the star, she was, at least, the supporting actress.

Even before she took off her coat she rushed to the French windows, opened them, and stepped out onto a little balcony. They were there, the rooftops of Paris. She could see the Seine and beyond it the ugly majesty of the Eiffel Tower.

'Sylvia, come and look!' she called.

'I've seen it. Come in and shut that goddamned door. You're freezing the roses. Besides, we have to make a hundred calls before we go to the *Harper's Bazaar* party. My God, I dread that phone! That beauty downstairs has a well-deserved reputation as the most inefficient switchboard operator in a town of incompetent telephone operators. I think she's constantly tiddly on French wine. But then, I think the whole country is.'

Reluctantly, Bev came back inside. If all of France is a little drunk, she thought, I can understand it. So am I.

Arthur Powers had arrived in Paris a week before Bev and Sylvia. He had business to do before the collections started. In fact, the showings, though they were important to him, were less significant than his visits to the French textile manufacturers, where he arranged for the purchase of new patterns and designs to be reproduced in America. He also was a big buyer of French silks and brocades, among other fabrics, and he was heartily welcomed by these offshoots of the couture industry.

The whole business of Paris bored him. He had done it so often it was like making a trip to Pittsburgh, but it was part of the job, part of his image. In New York, Arthur didn't mix much with the fashion people. He might take the editor-in-chief of a magazine to lunch at the Colony, or dine with a top store president at Le Pavillon. But by and large he reserved his appearances for collection time. In those two weeks he reinforced useful contacts, kissed all the right flustered hands, gave the lower echelon a chance to glimpse the glamorous Arthur Powers. He was invited to the collections, to dinners at Maxim's and lunches at the Crillon. He went to as many places and saw as many people as he could, doing penance, as he thought of it, for aloofness during the other eleven months of the year.

This January the task was unusually distasteful. The fashion people reminded him of his ex-wife. Marilyn would have loved it. Or maybe not, he thought nastily. She'd hate seeing all those young models who were just beginning their careers. There'd be plenty of them tonight at the cocktail party that *Harper's Bazaar* was giving. He dreaded it. He knew exactly how it would be—'madly authentic.' Meaning that it was to be held in the apartment of the magazine's resident Paris editor, an ancient, formidably lady who lived in a chic, rickety Left Bank building so old it had been designated a historic site. As he made his way up the dimly lit stairs (why were Paris elevators constantly out of order?), Arthur could hear the clamor of voices on the third floor—a blend of good French, unmistakable England-English and overtones of Americanese from effette Eastern to flat Midwest.

He put on his professional smile and braced himself for another exercise in inbreeding. One lived on a constant diet of cocktail parties in Paris, but the ingredients never varied. The food and drink were always the same. So were the guests. Only the location and the hostess changed from night to night.

Arthur did a quick, practiced survey of the room and headed for the hostess, who appeared to be suffocating in a crush of overdressed bodies. Near her stood a doughty, eighty-year-old grande dame of the retail world, a wispy French designer, and a magazine photographer who was recording the whole scene for posterity and the April issue. Arthur kissed the American editor on both cheeks, and she rewarded him with a conspiratorial smile.

'Doing your duty, I see,' she said.

He looked hurt. 'Francesca, what a thing to say! Some parties are a bore, but never this one. I'd hate to fall off your guest list.'

The venerable matriarch sniffed. 'Only falling you're likely to do, Arthur, is through this floor. If one more person comes in this room the whole thing is going to give way.'

Arthur smiled. 'Let's hope the people below are friendly.'

'Seems doubtful,' his hostess said. 'I'm sure that the natives don't approve of business cocktail parties any more than you do. Can't say that I blame them. An uncivilized institution.'

The arrival of a new batch of guests saved him from more of this inane conversation. Ignoring the waiters who were trying to circulate with glasses of champagne, he headed for the bar and ordered a double vodka. It was then that he saw her, standing quietly, alone near the window. She didn't look forlorn or uncomfortable. On the contrary, she was like a fascinated child, curious and interested by the spectacle, as though it were a puppet show and she an absorbed onlooker. Arthur watched her for a minute. She was a pretty woman, not beautiful by any means, but there was a quality about her that was arresting. It might have been the contrast of her composure against the overanimated, shrill-voiced women in the room. She wasn't his style. Too understated and almost certainly too unimportant to interest him. And yet he found himself joining her in the little island of sanity she seemed to have created.

'Hello. I don't think we've met. I'm Arthur Powers.'

She extended a delicate hand. 'Beverly Richmond.'

He shook the hand instead of kissing it. 'Nice to know you. You with the magazine?'

'No. I buy for Welby's in New York. What do you do?'

The question amused him. 'I make fabrics,' he said.

Beverly reddened. 'Oh, *that* Arthur Powers! I've heard of you.'

'I won't ask what you've heard. Lies, I promise you. Nothing but lies. At heart I'm a sweet, simple, unaffected, hard-working rag man.'

'That's exactly what I've heard,' Beverly said.

He found himself laughing. It was the first time he'd laughed in weeks.

111

'This must be your first trip to Paris,' Arthur said. 'Otherwise I'd have seen you.'

'The very first. It's overwhelming. I can't believe I'm here. I've dreamed about it.'

'And is it everything you dreamed?'

Bev smiled. 'So far, yes. We only arrived this afternoon.'

'We?'

'I'm traveling with my boss, Sylvia Schlesinger. You know her, I'm sure. She's a vice-president of Welby's. She's been to Paris often.'

'Sylvia? But of course! Marvelous lady.' He was lying. It was a name he'd heard. Probably he had met her on some trip to Paris, but for the life of him he couldn't have picked her out in the room. She wasn't high enough on the fashion ladder for him to have noticed her in New York. 'Sylvia will show you the couture,' he said. 'She knows her way around. But that's only one part of Paris. I hope you're going to see more of the real city.'

'Naturally. I'm going to steal every minute I can and walk for miles. I want to see everything I can . . . every little shop and bistro and flower cart. I'm going to the Louvre and Notre Dame and the top of the Eiffel Tower. I hope to get to Versailles, if there's time.' She paused, embarrassed. 'I must sound like the typical tourist to you. Like some kid from Iowa instead of a grown-up woman on a business trip.'

His voice was kind. 'You do sound a little ingenuous. But it's nice. It's refreshing.'

Bev made a face. 'That's an awful word, Mr. Powers: "refreshing." You make me feel more gauche than I already do. At home I have quite a reputation as a career woman. Some people even think I'm quite sophisticated.'

He was mock-serious. 'I'm sure you're very sophisticated, Miss Richmond.'

'It's Mrs. Richmond. But I'm more comfortable with Beverly. Or Bev.'

For the first time in a long while, Arthur's stomach didn't hurt. It was easy to talk to this girl. Uncomplicated. Five minutes before, he'd had no intention of saying anything to her beyond a polite hello. Somewhat to his own surprise, he found himself anxious to prolong the encounter.

'Sylvia can steer you through the fashion side of Paris, and any good sightseeing guide can give you a conducted tour of the monuments,' he said, 'but how about letting me show you the after-dark part of the town? I know it pretty well for an American who speaks lousy French.'

Bev hesitated. 'I don't know, Mr. Powers. . . .'

'Arthur. Never Artie. Or Art.'

'Arthur,' she repeated. 'It's nice of you, but I think Sylvia expects me to stay with her. She said something about dinner after this.'

'Let's go make it right with Sylvia,' he said.

Minutes later, Arthur was helping her into the big black Cadillac that waited downstairs. It was a ridiculous car to have in Paris. It had trouble getting through the side streets, backing and turning to navigate in the narrow old sections of town. But it was typical of Arthur, just as the expensive restaurant he took her to seemed to suit his strange mixture of elegance and flamboyance. It was an elaborately overdone place with red velvet walls and banquettes, electrified table candles with shirred-silk shades, and, as a final theatrical touch, a band of strolling violinists who seemed to know Arthur Powers and hovered near his table, playing over and over the current hit, the zither-music theme song from the film *The Third Man*. It was Arthur's favorite song. The melody stayed in Bev's head. She would never hear that music again without thinking of this night. Arthur was a knowledgeable host, an attentive companion. She was having a wonderful time. This was every woman's dream of Paris: an elegant restaurant, superb food and wine, a handsome, interested man whom everyone treated with respect. There was just the slightest hint of flirtation between them in the way he held her on the dance floor, in the way she brushed his hand as he held his lighter to her cigarette. It was harmless, Bev told herself, and it was exciting. It was like some fantasy world and she was Cinderella, except that at midnight the Cadillac didn't turn into a pumpkin. It took them to tiny bars on dark streets where Arthur assured her they were the only foreigners. It waited for them at Les Halles, the famous wholesale food and flower market, where they ate onion soup at four in the morning in a café filled with workingmen, and where Arthur bought great bunches of mimosa at a flower stall and filled her arms with them. It took them, finally, back to the door of the San Regis, where he

113

kissed her hand and said, 'Thank you for a wonderful evening, Bev.'

'Oh, no. Thank *you*. It was the most glamorous night of my life.'

He rang the bell and they stood silent, waiting for a sleepy concierge to open the locked door.

'There's much more I'd like to show you,' Arthur said. 'Are you busy tomorrow night?'

Her face shining above the fragrant flowers, Bev shook her head. 'No. At least, I'll arrange not to be.'

He looked pleased. 'I'll call you about seven. When you get back from the collections. We'll make plans. Good night, Bev.'

'Good night,' she said.

Sylvia awakened when she tiptoed into the bedroom.

'Have a good time?' she asked sleepily.

'Indescribable.'

'Good. Sleep fast. Our first appointment is at nine at Dior.'

Bev undressed quietly while Sylvia went instantly back to sleep. She found a vase in the living room and put the mimosa into it. The fragrance was overpowering, as sensuous as the blossoms were delicate. There was no sleep in Bev, but she forced herself to go to bed. It was after five o'clock. 'You'll feel like death when you have to get up in two hours,' she told herself. It didn't matter. She felt happy and totally new. Not at all like the entrapped Mrs. Edward Richmond but elegant, desirable, and precious. Nothing would come of it, her good sense told her, but one thing could not be argued: Arthur Powers was a man who knew how to make a woman feel thoroughly female.

At the Ritz, Arthur examined his feelings with almost detached interest. He'd had a good time. Beverly Richmond was an unusual girl, curiously unbrittle in spite of her fashion-world appearance and her not-insignificant place in a tough competitive business. She had attracted him in a totally new way. There was a sexual pull, but he had not made the overt moves that were his normal pattern with a woman to whom he was casually drawn. He realized that he knew very little about her, beyond the fact that she was married to somebody in the insurance business. Happily or unhappily married? He had no idea. It occurred to him that he had spent most of the evening talking about himself, carefully editing the details of his previous marriages to make them no more than disappointing experiences, untinged by bitterness. If he had been good for Bev's ego, she had been even better for his. Her obvious admiration took away the memory of Marilyn's indifference. For a few hours he'd been able to forget. It was the reassurance he needed. Satisfied from the beginning, he looked forward to the next few weeks. Maybe Paris wasn't going to be such a crashing bore after all.

10

Even after a month without him, Ruth Eliason automatically reached out her hand to touch Geoff when she woke each morning in the big double bed they'd shared all their married life. The empty place beside her was a reproach to God. She would turn over on her side and stare dry-eyed at the undented pillow, seeing, in her mind, the strong, peacefully sleeping man around whom she had once complacently planned her life.

Everyone had been so kind. Almost too kind. They had not let her alone for a moment, as though the sheer weight of company could keep her from remembering, could somehow wipe away the past. She did not want to forget. It was sweet to remember. It was all that was left—memories of Geoff. She was not morbid about it, but it was more difficult not to 'dwell on it,' as her friends and family urged, than to gradually and realistically accept. She had to learn to live without her children's father, her first and only lover. She did not want pity. She needed quiet recuperation. Instead she was surrounded by anxious eyes that pretended not to watch her, conversation that touched every subject except death in any form. She wanted to talk about Geoff, to evoke his memory in gentle laughter. Instead, she was required to act as though somehow nothing had happened, as though dying were some kind of disgrace that shouldn't be mentioned lest it weaken the survivors' belief in their own immortality.

Only one person seemed to sense Ruth's need for cold, therapeutic confrontation with fact: Ed Richmond. A day or two after Bev sailed for Europe, he'd called Ruth and asked her if she had any feeling about going out to dinner.

117

'Maybe you think it's too soon after Geoff's death,' he'd said, 'but maybe two lonely people can help each other.'

She was grateful to him. It was the first time anyone had spoken to her as though she were a mature woman, capable of accepting the fact of death.

'I'd like to have dinner with you, Ed. Very much. In fact, I've been thinking of calling you. I have a favor to ask.'

'Shoot.'

'It's Philip. He's the only one of the boys who has any awareness of what's happened. He knows his daddy died in a plane crash and he's developed a terrible fear of airplanes. Even when one flies over the house he runs and hides in a closet. He misses Geoff terribly and nobody will talk to him about his father. I try to, but I think he needs man-talk. Would you mind terribly trying to make him understand about Geoff's death? I know I'm asking a great deal, Ed, but I'm worried about Philip. I don't want his life scarred by this.'

'Of course I'll try to talk to him,' Ed said. 'But, Ruth, he's so young. Only six. Are you sure he isn't just reacting to a strange new situation without being as troubled as you think?'

'I'm sure. He's an exceptionally bright and sensitive little boy who's living in a conspiracy of silence. Next to his father, you're the man he's always admired most. He knows you've done a lot of flying too. I think that may help. I'm not dramatizing it, Ed. He's a changed child. Almost every night he has terrible dreams about planes crashing. And yesterday I found a kind of bomb shelter under his bed. Pillows, flashlight, that kind of thing. He said it was where he was going to hide when an airplane fell through our roof.'

'Sweetie, I'll try,' Ed repeated. 'Poor kid. But my approach is bound to be highly unscientific. If it keeps on, he may need professional help.'

'I've thought of that. But I'd like it to be a last resort, and I don't think it will be necessary if somebody will just level with him about his father's death. I haven't been able to get through. Too emotionally involved, I guess. And nobody else will even mention Geoff to him. They think that's the kindest way. They mean well, but I believe it's only contributing to his vivid imagination and the facts he can't quite grasp.'

They settled on dinner for two nights later.

'I'll pick up Philip after school tomorrow,' Ed said. 'You tell him we're going to spend a few hours together in the afternoon, doing things fellas do together. Then I'll report to you when I see you.'

'I can't tell you how grateful I am, Eddie.'

'Let's wait and see how successful I am. Frankly, at the moment I don't know where the hell to begin.'

The next afternoon when he collected Philip in front of the child's private school, Ed saw instantly why Ruth was concerned. The other kids bounced out the door in high spirits, yelling, shoving, full of first-grade horseplay. Philip walked out alone, silently, not even hurrying. He looked, Ed thought, like a sad little old man.

'Hi, Phil! Your mother tell you I'd be here?'

The high-cheekboned little face that was so like Geoff's lit up just a little.

'Hi, Uncle Ed.'

'I'm glad to see you, buddy. It's been too long since we've spent time together.'

Philip didn't answer. The baby knuckles had a tight, tense grip on the notebook he held.

'Listen,' Ed said, 'I borrowed a car. How about we go have a hot dog and then take a ride?'

'Where to?'

'That's a surprise. Okay? Don't you like surprises?'

'No.'

'Sure you do! Everybody likes surprises.'

Looking at the quiet child, Ed cursed himself for his stupidity. Geoff's death was Philip's worst surprise, he thought. Damn it, I should be more careful about what I say! Then, remembering his conversation with Ruth, Ed reversed his thinking. On the contrary, I should say whatever comes naturally. There's been too much tiptoeing around this boy, too much unnatural editing of everything that's been said to him. If people aren't themselves around him, how can he ever learn to be himself again?

'Well, like it or not, pal, this is your afternoon for surprises.' Ed helped him into the front seat of the car. 'First of all I'm going to introduce you to the wildest hot dog you've ever eaten in your life. It's called a kamikaze. Comes with everything—chili, cheese, hot relish, peanut butter, and two

119

kinds of pickles. Only place they make it is in a little diner out on Northern Boulevard. You game?'

Philip nodded. 'Okay. If you want to.'

'Tell you the truth, Phil, I helped invent it.'

He was regarded with the first flicker of interest. 'You did? How come?'

'Well, a long time ago, even before your Aunt Bev and I were married, I worked not too far from this diner. At LaGuardia Airport, to be exact. I had a job with Trans-State Airlines, and a bunch of us used to have lunch at this place pretty often. That's when we invented the kamikaze. You know what the word means, Phil?'

They were speeding out of the city now. The child sat quietly beside his big friend. At the mention of the airport and the airline, Ed saw his face go white, but he said nothing. As though he hadn't noticed, Ed went on, not waiting for an answer to his question.

'Kamikaze is a Japanese word,' Ed explained. 'It was the name given to Japanese pilots in World War Two—the war your daddy and I both fought in. Anyway, these pilots were the most honored and respected in the Japanese air force and the ones most feared by our side. You see, Phil, their mission was to crash their planes into our ships and sink them, even though they knew they were going to die doing it. It was called a suicide mission. It was hard for us to understand, but they were willing to give their lives for what meant most to them.'

He glanced casually at Philip. The child was swallowing hard, and his breath was coming in short, nervous gasps. Oh, God, Ed thought, don't let me blow this. Let it be right. He wished Philip would say something, anything, even ask him to stop talking about men killing themselves in planes.

They were nearing the diner now. Ed tried to act as though he were not making a point. 'So, that's why we named these sandwiches kamikaze. A bad joke, maybe. Supposed to mean that they were as dangerous to the digestion as an enemy plane filled with explosives was to American fighting men.'

Philip looked as though he were going to be physically ill.

I've done a horrible, insensitive, cruel thing, Ed silently accused himself. Richmond the dummy. As usual. He pulled into a parking space in front of the diner, turned off the car engine, and sat looking at Philip.

'Any questions?'

The child bit his lip. 'Uncle Ed, why did my daddy have to die? He didn't try to, did he? He wasn't like those Japanese men.'

'No, Phil, he didn't try to die. It was the last thing he wanted. He didn't want to leave you and your mother and Sam and little Geoff. But if he'd had to, he would gladly have given his life for you, the way those pilots happily gave their lives for their country and their emperor. You see, Phil, your daddy's death was a terrible accident, but he lost his life doing what meant most to him—trying to get home to the people he loved. Your father was a brave man. He took a plane in bad weather. He took a risk. Maybe he even knew it was a risk, but he figured that the chances were very good of his getting through safely. Most planes do, you know. Crashes are very sad, but thank God they are very unusual. Your dad knew that. He wasn't afraid of airplanes. And I don't think he'd want you to be.'

The little boy began to sob. Ed held him very gently for a long while. 'I *am* afraid of airplanes, Uncle Ed. They fall down and kill people.'

'Sure they do, Phil. Once in a great while. And a lot of people are afraid to fly in them. Most people, I guess. But there's a difference between being nervous in a plane, like maybe your father was, like I've been lots of times, and thinking that there's something evil about airplanes themselves. They're beautiful, efficient machines. That's all. They're not dragons. An airplane didn't kill your daddy. Some men in charge of it made a mistake. A very rare but human error. Wherever your daddy is, he knows that. He has forgiven them, Phil, and you must too. Your mother has. I have. When your brothers are older, they will. That is, if you set the example for them. You're the head man in the Eliason family, buddy. You're awful little for that responsibility, but your father left it to you. Can you be as brave as he was?'

The sobs were subsiding. Ed wasn't sure how much of all this Philip had understood, but he sensed, with relief, that he had gotten some of it through to the child. There'd be other conversations between them. Ruth had been right.

Philip needed a man to reassure him about strange things like airplanes, even about most men's inherent heroism. He hugged the boy and repeated his question.

'Can you, Phil? Can you be as brave and strong as your dad was?'

'I'll try, Uncle Ed.'

'I know you will. So does your mother. The best thing is to remember your father as he was. He was quite a guy. And so are you.'

Philip dried his eyes on Ed's handkerchief. He wasn't sure about all that had been said, but somehow he felt comforted as no one else had been able to comfort him. If his daddy died trying to get home to them, that meant he really loved them. He hadn't just gone off and left them, the way Phil thought. But he was still scared of airplanes. Even Uncle Ed couldn't change that.

'How about the kamikaze?' Ed asked.

'No thanks, Uncle Ed,' he said politely. 'I think I'd like to go home now.'

Ed reported the conversation to Ruth next night at dinner. 'I hope I did right,' he said. 'I sure didn't get him over his fear of airplanes, but I think I made a little headway in his thinking about Geoff.'

'You did.' It was the first time he'd seen her smile since that terrible Christmas Eve. 'He told me last night that his daddy was very brave because he'd tried to get home to us the night of the accident. He seemed to grasp the fact that his father loved him very much and that he hadn't deserted him. I've read enough books on child psychology to know that kids often think that the death of a parent is a deliberate abandonment of them. They resent it. You've helped Philip get over that part of his problem. It's a big step, and I don't know how to thank you. You're really very good with little boys.'

'Used to be one myself. I was a lot older than Phil when my father died, but I remember how I almost hated him for leaving us. Mother was great. She still is. But it was a lopsided life. I don't want to see that happen to your kids, Ruth. God knows it's too early to talk about it, but I hope you'll marry again and reasonably soon. Those boys need a father.'

'I know. I can't even make myself think about it now, but I will one day. Being happily married is the only life I've ever wanted.' Her face took on the look of memory. 'Bev and I used to talk about it when we were growing up. We never saw our lives quite the same way, but we both knew that a good marriage was necessary for girls like us. I'm so glad that Bev has you, Eddie. She needs your stability and your kindness, as well as your love. You're very lucky, both of you.'

He didn't answer. They were very unalike, these girlhood friends, brought up in almost identical ways yet so differently motivated. He suspected that Ruth would have adored Geoff even if he hadn't been rich and successful, the qualities that were so important to Bev. He didn't blame his wife for the standing she craved. It was as much a part of her as Ruth's natural gravitation to the less complicated role of wife and mother. The thing both women shared, Ed thought with a sudden flash of insight, was a wish to be proud of their husbands. Geoff had been able to make that wish come true. Ed was not certain that he'd ever be able to.

What gave him the first ray of hope was a conversation he had two weeks later with his boss. At three o'clock, Joe Taylor sent word that he'd like to see Ed in his office. Ed had been nervous when he'd gone in. Jesus, don't let him fire me, he'd prayed. I've been working hard. Even closed a pretty good deal last week. It wasn't my fault that I muffed the O'Dwyer policy. Taylor wouldn't can him for that. Hell, nobody batted a thousand.

But the reason for Joe's summons was quite different. It was to tell him that he was being considered for the assistant manager's job in the New York office. Taylor smiled at the stunned look on Richmond's face. Joe was an up-by-the-bootstraps type, a poor boy who'd made good. A hearty, cornball, rough-edged go-getter, he was addicted to big cigars, heavy-handed locker-room humor, and an understandable desire to control the destinies of smart-ass college graduates. It made him feel important, knowing that a classy guy like Ed Richmond was scared just walking into Joe's big office.

Yet, with the instinct of a winner, Joe Taylor did not allow his resentments to get in the way of his business judgment.

Ed Richmond might sometimes act like he was too good to sell insurance, too irreverent in his attitude toward the company, but Joe recognized quality when he saw it. And college boy or not, he must need the job, need the money. Taylor had heard that Richmond's wife was some kind of hot-shot lady buyer. Shrewdly he guessed that Ed also needed the prestige of a title and that he'd work his tail off if he saw the opportunity to get on the executive level.

Ed's reaction verified his instinct. The guy looked like he'd won the Irish sweepstakes when Joe told him about the possibility.

'That's just great, Joe!' he said. 'I really had no idea that I was being considered. I mean, most of the other men have seniority. I figured one of them would get Chuck Wampole's job when I heard he was leaving.'

'Yeah, they probably figured the same. But the recommendation is up to me. Of course, the final say-so will be in the main office. Not that I expect any flak. I think I can say modestly that the brass respect my judgment. Hell, I've given 'em the best damned thirty years of my life! If I say you're the man for the job, I'd be surprised if they didn't agree.'

Ed tried to look properly respectful.

'You see, kid, you got something very important—style. Of course, I'd like to see you act like more of a go-getter. You need more chutzpah, Eddie boy, but I think that'll come with the title. I've told the front office that you'll show plenty of muscle once you're in the job.'

Once more, Ed thanked him. 'My wife's going to be the happiest girl in town. Or rather, in Paris. That's where she is now. On a business trip. She's the Better Dress buyer for Welby's.'

'I know. By the way, it wouldn't be a bad idea if you could get some of the store's business. Maybe write a few executive policies. Not that that has anything to do with your promotion. Still, if you brought in a few big ones right now it couldn't hurt.'

'I'm not sure about that. Bev and I never interfere in each other's work.'

'Sure. It was just a thought. Like I said, probably wouldn't make any difference one way or another. You're still my candidate and I'm ninety-five percent sure that's all it'll take.'

'Ninety-five percent?'

'The other five doesn't mean a thing. Just grapevine stuff. I hear one of the V.P.s has a nephew he's pushing pretty hard, but the kid isn't in your league. Take it from me, Ed, you can count on it. Just make sure that you're as busy as a one-armed paperhanger with the hives for the next couple of weeks, in case the powers-that-be send somebody around to look you over. Don't worry. In another ten years or so you'll be right here in this chair giving some other guy his big break.' Taylor smiled confidently. 'Of course there's no use mentioning it until it's official. All those Nice Nellies out there will be teed off soon enough. Okay, that's it. I'll let you know when things are final.'

Ed wanted to ask a few questions about salary and benefits, but Joe Taylor was already shuffling papers. That's what I'll be doing, Ed thought. I'll be boxed in between INCOMING and OUTGOING for the rest of my life. Deliberately, he focused on Bev. She'd be so pleased, so proud of him. In ten years he'd be New York manager. Big job. Sixty, seventy thousand dollars a year plus benefits. Even now he was sure of a substantial increase in salary. They could move to a bigger, better apartment; he could buy Bev some nice things. Maybe in a year or so, when he felt really secure, they could have a baby. Maybe eventually she'd even have enough of working. They'd move to the suburbs, buy a house, have two or three kids. The thought of kids reminded him of Philip. He'd been seeing him every couple of days, warmed by the child's admiration, bolstered by his own ability to communicate with the little boy. He was getting through much better now. In a few days he was going to suggest that they take a sightseeing plane ride over New York. He'd discussed it with Ruth, and she'd agreed that it would be a great stride forward if Phil would do it.

While all these thoughts were careening through his mind he was still sitting in the chair in front of Joe Taylor's desk. The manager finally looked up, surprised to see him still there.

'Something else on your mind, Ed?'

'No, no. Sorry. Thanks again, Joe. I really appreciate the break.'

A distracted nod was all the acknowledgment he got. Elated now by the future he visualized, Ed swung jauntily out of the office, stopping for a moment at the receptionist's desk.

'Got a couple of appointments,' he told her. 'Probably won't be back in the office today, but I'll check later for messages.'

He had no appointments. Instead, he went to the apartment and placed a call to Paris. It was 2 P.M. New York time. Bev had been gone for two weeks and two days.

For a girl who had insisted all her life that she needed eight hours sleep a night to 'feel human,' Beverly had been walking proof for ten days that excitement is an infallible antidote for lack of rest. She and Sylvia were out of the hotel by nine every morning. They returned at seven, reviewed their work, and discussed the next day's showings. Then Bev would bathe, dress, and be picked up at nine by Arthur. She seldom got back to the hotel before three or four o'clock the next morning. She flourished on it. She never looked or felt better.

The collections were, as Sylvia had warned her, hard work. There were two, sometimes three a day. Each lasted close to two hours—slow-paced, elegant spectacles unlike the hurried presentations of Seventh Avenue. The great salons were packed with rows of hard little gold chairs, the men and women on them squeezed in like stylish sardines with barely enough room to raise their pencils to their notebooks and write the numbers of the styles that interested them. They sat mute and nearly motionless through mind-boggling parades of a hundred and fifty or two hundred coats, suits, and dresses disdainfully presented by sullen-looking young women who glided through the silent smoke-filled rooms.

The mannequins, as Bev learned to call them (in France, she discovered, 'models' meant the garments themselves), were very like the French working people Sylvia had described. They seemed to be antagonistic, almost daring the onlookers to dislike the creations they wore. Some certainly were downright sadistic. Like the gaunt, ugly creature at Balenciaga who carried her card with the identifying number half hidden or sometimes even upside down so that the eager buyers almost literally stood on their heads to see it. Bev learned to ignore the hostility. It was all part of the act. Like the heavy smell of perfume and of flowers, the totally absorbed viewers, the incredible, cathedral-like hush, rapt and reverent. This was the Vatican of the fashion world, and Bev felt privileged to be granted an audience.

After each collection, she and Sylvia made an appointment with the salon directrice to return later to place their orders. They would not spend any money until they had seen all the collections once, and they would return to the best of them two or three times. At the prices charged, they had to be quite sure they were making the right selections, getting 'exclusives' for Welby's couture department, in some cases buying what *Vogue* or *Harper's Bazaar* planned to show in their Paris Report issues. The pages in these magazines would give important credits to Welby's. Being the store mentioned as carrying the photographed clothes helped maintain Welby's high-fashion image and attract the relatively few customers who could afford custom-made copies of the originals. Bev and Sylvia were not only buyers, they were publicists and sales-promotion people as well as molders of fashion direction in America. It was a heavy responsibility.

Between showings they lunched with manufacturers, couturiers, and editors, visited milliners and shoe designers, shopped for new jewelry, handbags, and accessories. By the time they got back to the hotel their eyes were bleary and their minds straining under the pressure of trying to recall the hundreds of things they'd seen that day. It was the same every evening. While Bev ordered a drink, Sylvia kicked off her shoes, fell into a chair in the tiny sitting room, and stared bleakly at the two bulging black notebooks that were the badge of their trade.

'I warned you,' Sylvia said on the fifth evening. 'The ASPCA wouldn't put up with treatment like this for a carriage horse in Central Park.'

Beverly laughed. 'Most people at home think we're having a paid vacation. They're green with envy.'

Her companion grunted. 'I'll buy that green part. Around the gills.'

Bev was only half listening. She was waiting for the regular call from Arthur.

'That's quite a little number you have going with the great Arthur Powers,' Sylvia said suddenly. 'The whole American contingent is talking. A fling is one thing, but trying to get along on three hours' sleep a night can kill you. Just being *in bed* isn't the same thing, luv.'

Bev looked at her with genuine surprise. 'I haven't been to bed with Arthur,' she said. 'He's just been showing me the most wonderful time anyone could imagine.'

'Oh, come on, Beverly.' Sylvia looked around the room. The suite bulged with the flowers that Arthur sent every day —masses of tulips, a huge tree of apple blossoms, and vase after vase of mimosa. 'This place looks like a classy bordello. Or a mobster's funeral. Or a thank-you for some pretty special favors.'

Sylvia sounded almost nasty. She's jealous, Bev thought for a moment. She wishes she were the one Arthur had picked out at the party. She's angry at the idea that a man prefers me to her. Especially a man like Arthur Powers. Probably Sylvia would have been in bed with him long ago. Instantly she was ashamed of this disloyal reaction. It was ridiculous to think that Sylvia was envious. She did not lack invitations. She went out every night for dinner, but there obviously was no one special person to whom she was drawn —or who was drawn to her. The exotic, assured, much-married Sylvia Schlesinger was actually feeling overshadowed by her innocent assistant. Bev couldn't let this hostility persist. Nor could she behave like a middle-class moralist.

'There are no special favors, Syl,' she said calmly. 'But if there were, is that such a crime?'

'Only with a guy like Arthur Powers. He's bad news. A professional charmer with a penchant for marriage, even though I can't say much for his staying power.'

Bev laughed with relief. Sylvia wasn't jealous after all. She was just genuinely disturbed that Bev was taking the whole thing too seriously. A few dates wouldn't have troubled her, but this public pursuit was something else.

'Don't worry, Syl. I know it's just the first-trip-to-Paris syndrome. I recognize an unreal world. It's not going to mix me up. I know damned well that my life certainly won't include Arthur once we get back to the States.'

'Spare me,' Sylvia said contemptuously. 'Right now you're playing with the idea that Arthur has something more permanent in mind than a two-week romance in Paris.'

'He does,' Bev said mischievously. 'He's going to London

with us. And he has return reservations to go back on the *Queen Elizabeth.*'

'Where do you plan to bunk, his stateroom or ours?'

'Sylvia, stop it! I am just having fun.'

'Not you. You're not the type to file and forget. I'm not agin a little harmless extramarital activity for those who can live with it, but I don't think you can handle a full-fledged affair. And if I ever saw anybody ripe for one, you're it.'

Bev actually blushed. 'Does it show that much?'

'It's shown for a long time. At least I've sensed that you were restless in your marriage. Probably a mirror image. I knew when I offered you this trip that it meant more to you than career recognition. You needed to get away from Ed, didn't you? Maybe you even needed a chance to decide whether you want to stay married to him. I've been through it, Bev. I understand. I'm sorry, though. I thought you had just the right kind of marriage for a girl like you.'

'What do you mean . . . a girl like me?'

'Mirror image again. You're very like me. Or like what I used to be. Ambition-driven and hating my ambition. Aggressive without really wanting to be. Domineering and loathing the role. We're not bad people, Bev. Silly, maybe, and certainly selfish. Only a basically solid, noncompetitive man can put up with our kind of ego. I hate to toss clichés around, but we really are insecure people under all the outward confidence. We're afraid all the time. Afraid *not* to feel needed and in charge. And yet afraid of what will happen to us if we never find a man we're forced to admire. I've been around that course. You're just at the starting gate. My first two husbands wouldn't put up with my nonsense. I finally found one who understands that it's all a front. Herman is so secure that he can defy society's approval and still understand my dumb need for it. I'd hoped that Ed was the same kind of man. I think he is. But I don't think you're smart enough to separate realism and romance. You're a babe in the woods, my young friend. You haven't learned the soothing effect of compromise, so you're going to blow a good marriage just because you can't have it all your own way.'

'It's not that I want it all my way,' Beverly said defiantly. 'I just don't think I can live such a one-sided existence. I appreciate Ed. I think I still love him. I try to respect him for not caring more about making money or being important, because in my heart I know these things are superficial. But they matter to me, Sylvia. I can't help it. And so I can't respect him. And that changes everything. God knows I try to weigh his goodness against his lack of ambition, but I really want him to be successful.'

'Do you? Or do you just want to manipulate him into the kind of success that makes *you* look better? The kind *you* can take credit for? What would you do if he struck it rich and started giving orders? Suppose he suddenly became successful and demanded that you give up your job, stay home, and have babies? Would that make you happy? I doubt it. You want it all: home, career, husband, but on your terms. You know what I think, Bev? I think Ed's easygoing attitude really makes you feel that *you've* failed. And you can't stand that. You want to be proud of him for *your* sake, not *his*. And it's all a mirage. Maybe you'll get wise one day, but the day has not yet arrived. I hope it will for you, as it has for me.' Sylvia laughed. 'God, I haven't given that long speech since I won the Fashion Leader of the Year Award!'

Beverly was devastated. 'Am I all that terrible?'

'You're not terrible at all. You just don't match the charts. You know, the ones that say you're supposed to get married, be happy, and thank the Good Lord every night that you're not a dried-up spinster like your Aunt Mathilda. You grew up knowing about those charts. They're written in invisible ink on the bedroom wall of every nice middle-class girl. Trouble is, you can't make yourself fit them and it's eating you. It's just too bad that you can't handle an occasional escape from the reservation without making it a turning point in your life. I'm sure now that you haven't gone to bed with Arthur Powers. I wish you could without feeling guilty and committed. You'd get a lot of things out of your system, and you'd end up being happier than ever with Ed.'

'But I loved Ed when I married him,' Bev repeated. 'I think I still do. He's a wonderful human being. I believed he only needed to find himself. I thought I could help him and that we'd have a wonderful, evenly matched life. I wasn't any angel, Syl. I'd been through a bad time. Two bad times. But I didn't marry Ed on the rebound. I really felt sure it was right.'

'I don't argue that your motivations were lofty and your heart, at least, pure. But you seem to have mixed up love and

130

ego-building. You found a warm, sweet, gentle slave, and now you think you want to turn him into a whip-cracking sultan. Well, I've got news for you. It won't work. You'd better learn to live with your "basic disappointment" and be damned grateful that somebody that kind and tolerant and attractive is so nuts about you.'

'Is that the way you feel about Herman?'

'It sure as hell is. I cheat on him every now and then. That shocks you, doesn't it? It shouldn't, because it's meaningless. I do it only when I'm in one of those states like you're in now. I know exactly why I do it. It satisfies my need to be pushed around and made to feel all dumb and helpless and inferior. I'm female too, believe it or not. I like feeling all weak and womanly sometimes. But I don't confuse it with my real life, which is going to be spent with somebody who really honest-to-God would kill for me.'

'But don't you ever feel guilty?'

'Not really. I know I have romantic lapses that are real but temporary. I've learned to live with that conditioned reflex to the quote true role of a woman unquote.'

'And has Herman learned to live with it too?'

Sylvia smiled. 'I don't flaunt my affairs in his face. I suppose he guesses, but he really understands me, Bev. Just as I understand him. I'm sure Herman must stray now and then, as I do. But when the chips are down it has nothing to do with the way we feel about each other and our marriage. And it never will.'

Bev shook her head. 'It's all too Noel Coward for me. Maybe I'm too provincial. If I cheated on Ed I could never look at him again.'

'We're all different,' Sylvia said. 'I'm not suggesting that my hard-nosed attitude would work for you. Maybe an affair would destroy you. I do think, though, that you're unwilling to see yourself as you really are, Bev—a good person, a loyal wife, a sensitive woman with physical and emotional needs that can be satisfied without destroying your own life or that very nice guy's.'

'Even if I accepted what you're saying, I don't know whether I could ever do that. I think I'd feel . . . rotten.'

Sylvia was very serious. 'Why don't you say it? The word is "dirty." But that's because you think that all I'm talking about is sex. That's only part of it. The main thing is to get this martyr monkey off your back whenever you feel its claws digging in. Look, friend, there are worse things than infidelity, especially if you know *why* you need to be unfaithful. No marriage is perfect, Bev. Human needs aren't measured out like precise quantities in a cake recipe. Some of us need frowned-on things like the excitement of a rotten bastard named Arthur Powers to counteract the unquestioning but occasionally boring devotion of an Ed Richmond. Sometimes what one gets from the former only strengthens the love for the latter. At least it takes the pressure off, if you can live with it. And that, friend, is a big "if." '

'I wish I were as honest as you,' Bev said. 'You're the least hypocritical person I know.'

'Maybe I'm just the most experienced," Sylvia said wryly. 'If I've made my view of infidelity sound like therapy, it's only because to me an occasional escape has nothing to do with my faithfulness to Herman. I've simply quit fighting a part of my nature that makes realistic demands. Believe me, Bev, I'm not recommending the same course for you. I'm just telling you what I've learned. In the end, you'll do it your way. And you should. You don't *have* to live with Ed, but you'll always have to live with Beverly.'

Bev didn't answer. Why can't I be that unemotional and intellectual about my psyche? I wish I could have an affair with Arthur and go back to Ed feeling purged and content. It would be simple and uncomplicated. It would make sense for us all. But I'm not Sylvia. She's like a man who wouldn't give up his wife for anything in the world but who needs an occasional break in the routine.

At that moment the phone rang. It was not, as she expected, Arthur. It was the overseas operator with a person-to-person call for 'Madame Reechmond. From New York.'

11

She lay listlessly in the big French bathtub, letting the warm
water soothe her weary body and her troubled mind. She'd
be late meeting Arthur if she didn't get out of the bath. And
still Bev didn't stir. She wished she could stay forever in that
big porcelain womb, safe from the threat of her desire for
Arthur, removed from the prospect, now inevitable, of
returning to Ed.

His phone call, minutes before, had told her what she
must do. At first, when it came through, she was sure that
something terrible had happened. It had to be bad news.
Maybe, in a way, it was, though the content of the conversation was just the opposite. Her first words reflected her
concern when she heard her husband's voice.

'Ed? Is something wrong?'

The connection was dreadful. The words kept fading in and
out, with long pauses. They had to shout at each other.

'No! Nothing wrong,' Ed yelled. 'Great news, honey! I'm
going to be made assistant manager!'

'I can't hear you! What?'

'Assis-tant man-a-ger. Joe Taylor just told me. I'm getting
the job!'

Mercifully, the line cleared. 'That's wonderful!' Bev said.
'When do you start?'

'Soon as Chuck Wampole leaves, I guess.' He didn't
mention the need for top-level approval or the existence of
another possible candidate. It wasn't deception. Taylor had
dismissed the possibility of a snag, and so had Ed. 'Listen,
Bev, this could change a lot of things for us. I'll be getting a
big increase along with the title. Straight salary. No more
lousy commissions.'

'That's wonderful.' Didn't she know any other words? 'How much will it be?'

He laughed. 'Tell you the truth, I was too stunned to even ask. But it's bound to be enough to keep my wife in style. How is my wife, by the way?'

'I'm fine. How are you?'

'Great, but lonesome. Did you get my letter about Philip?'

'Yes. It's dear of you. How's Ruth?'

'Doing okay. Sweetheart, are you having any fun, or are they working you to death?'

'A little of both.'

There was a pause. 'Bev, you *are* pleased about my promotion, aren't you?'

It was the little boy seeking approval. Look, Mom, I got A in algebra. Aren't you proud of me? She was ashamed of her instinctive comparison.

'Bev? Hello? Are you still there?'

'Yes, dear, I'm still here. Of course I'm pleased, Ed. Darling, we'd really better hang up. This call is costing a fortune. Write me all about it. Better send it to the Dorchester in London. I'll only be here another week.'

'I know. God! It seems like you've been gone forever! I don't know how I'll last another three weeks. I'll be at the pier when you get home.'

'Fine. Take care of yourself, Eddie. And give my love to everyone.'

'You too, sweetheart. And my best to Sylvia.'

Dabbling her hand aimlessly in the warm bathwater, Bev knew what she had to do. No more tug-of-war in her head about whether or not to break up her marriage. Ed had done what she wanted—gotten and held a job and was moving up the ladder. It was all for her. This was what she protested she wanted, wasn't it? A successful husband. One she could respect. The assistant manager's job wasn't anything to set the world on fire, but it was the first real sign of advancement. In her heart she knew that Ed probably didn't give a damn about it. Probably he hated it. But if it made her happy, he would push aside his own boredom and disdain for 'the nine-to-five nonsense,' as he'd once called it. You'd have to be a heartless bitch to walk out on a man like that.

Reluctantly she stepped out of the tub, drying herself in the terrycloth peignoir that French hotels supplied instead of towels. There's something else I have to do, she thought. I have to stop seeing Arthur. She'd tell him so tonight. He must not go to London with them or sail back on the *Elizabeth*. There was a limit to temptation. She'd nearly succumbed to it, and restlessly she faced the fact that she still wanted to. But she was not Sylvia. Now that she knew she was going back to Eddie, she'd do so with her marital vows intact. That much, at least, she owed him.

She thought again of the significance of his new job. Probably he could support her now—though how typical of him not to have even asked what the salary would be. But, assuming he could take over, was she willing to let him? She knew what she should do. She should quit her job, make it clear to him that there was no money coming in, that if he didn't make good, they'd starve. It was what Ed needed. He'd made a beginning. She probably could ensure great progress by forcing necessity on him. It would be the best thing she could do for him. But she couldn't do it. She was selfishly afraid to take away the props. She didn't have enough faith in him to entrust her future to him. It was a bleak but honest admission. Even if she could give up her personal ambitions, there had been too many years of past disappointments to overcome. She prayed that the new job would be real and lasting. Maybe after a while she would have confidence in his ability to take full responsibility for their lives. Or maybe she'd never reach that enviable state. Maybe she didn't really love him enough to live through him, not merely with him.

Midway through dinner, Arthur picked up her hand and tenderly kissed the palm.

'You're very quiet tonight, little one. Anything wrong?'

It was the perfect opening and she didn't take it. 'I guess I'm just a little tired.'

'I shouldn't wonder! Working the way you do all day and then staying out with me most of the night. I'm a selfish bastard. I don't have your schedule. I can pick and choose the collections I want to see. Sleep late if I like. I even have time for a nap at the end of the day.'

'Lucky you,' Bev said.

'Yeah, lucky me.' He paused. 'Anyway, my love, you're going to get a couple of days off. I have to go to Lyon

135

tomorrow to see about a big fabric order. Be gone till Wednesday. Promise me you'll have dinner in bed for the next two nights.' He smiled at her. 'Alone, naturally.'

She felt a pang at the thought of even this brief separation. How would she feel when she told him she was never going to see him again? She should do it now. To cover her distress she took out her compact and pretended to powder her nose. Her hand shook. Arthur was watching her carefully. Alert. Undeceived.

'You haven't given me your promise,' he said at last.

She hoped she sounded casual. 'What promise?'

'About having dinner in bed for the next two nights.'

'Oh, I will. Believe me, I can use the rest.'

He took her hand again. 'Will you miss me?'

She looked straight at him. 'Yes. Very much. Terribly.'

They were talking to each other with their eyes, his full of questions, hers pleading with him not to ask them.

'Bev?'

'Um-hm?'

'When are we going to stop playing games? You know I love you. I want you. Am I crazy to think you feel the same?'

She toyed with her champagne, not answering. The bubbles went round and round. She made them go faster with the little gold swizzle stick from Cartier, the present he'd given her two nights ago as a joke because she had become such a champagne fiend. He didn't know that it was not only the wine she loved. It was the whole ambiance it represented: the dark restaurants with their exotic food, their solicitous waiters, their strolling corny but wonderful violinists. Life with Arthur was leaving a bottle of champagne half full on the table behind them as they dashed off to the next adventure. It was Maxim's and tiny bistros on the Ile Saint-Louis. It was the Folies-Bergère and a lesbian nightclub called Carrol's. It was Piaf and Paris and Arthur Powers.

He cupped her chin in his hand, tilting her face toward him. 'What a beautiful, frightened little creature you are,' he said softly. 'Sometimes I think you're a ten-year-old playing grown-up. But then I know, like now, that you're a woman I want to make love to.'

She could put it off no longer. 'Arthur, I can't. Not now. Not ever.'

He was expressionless. She didn't know what she expected. Rage? Scorn? Disappointment? No emotion showed in his face. He didn't even ask why not.

'I talked to Ed this morning,' she said. 'He's getting a big new job. He's so happy about it because he knows it's what I've wanted. I can't cheat on him. I can't do that to him, Arthur. I've told you enough to make you understand why.'

It was true that she had told him something of her state of mind. She'd hinted that her marriage was shaky, that she had a sweet but unsuccessful husband whom Arthur correctly surmised she'd been supporting. He'd made it his business discreetly to find out more about Ed Richmond from the Americans, who knew just enough bits and pieces to confirm his suspicions that Bev's husband was 'a nice guy who didn't amount to much.' They'd not dwelt on her current marital problems, any more than they'd gone deeply into his own recently solved ones. But in their long hours together, a word here, a half jest there had given Arthur a reasonably complete and quite accurate picture of where the Richmond marriage stood.

He knew, too, that when they met, Beverly had been at her most vulnerable and had remained so until this evening. He had not made a serious attempt to take her to bed. She'd let him kiss her deeply in the privacy of the car, his hand moving searchingly on her breast. But that was as far is it had gone. Once or twice he'd made light references to her 'seeing his digs at the Ritz,' but she'd laughed them off, and he'd let her. He could have kicked himself now for all the missed opportunities. Until tonight he could have, with a little persuasion, made love to her. She would have felt guilty, of course. She was really a very puritanical young woman. But she probably would have been able to justify her infidelity in her own mind on the grounds that Ed Richmond had failed her, that she owed him nothing. Now she felt indebted to him. Now an affair was out of the question. If she were ever to—as she so quaintly put it—'cheat' on Ed, it would have been a week ago while she was still feeling put-upon and injured.

'Well,' he said after a long while, 'where does that leave us, Bev?'

'I guess it leaves us nowhere.' All the wretchedness she felt was in that small sentence. 'I don't think we should see each other any more, Arthur. I can't take it. You know I love you.

You know I want to go to bed with you. I don't think I'm strong enough to be around you and remember what's the decent thing for me to do. Not only decent for Ed and me. Decent for you.'

Suddenly he was angry. 'Now, that's all very neat and tidy, isn't it? You're so goddamned noble and self-sacrificing! One call from your husband and I'm supposed to disappear like a rabbit back into a magician's hat. Suppose I don't choose to disappear, Beverly? Suppose I'd rather go through with the plans as scheduled—another week here, a week in London, and a trip home by sea? You can't make me just go away like a naughty dream. I love you. And now I know you love me. You flatter yourself, my girl. It's perfectly possible for me to be around a woman without insisting on sex. I'm not an animal.' He thought of his frustrating courtship of Marilyn. 'But I'm not walking out of your life for another three weeks. I won't ask you again. But frankly, I won't refuse if you offer.'

His words surprised him almost as much as they did her. He recognized that she'd gotten to him more than he'd known. In a furious way he was demanding her presence, even on her terms. It was unlike him. Maybe I really am in love with her, Arthur thought suddenly. Maybe I even want to marry her. Until now the idea had not seriously occurred to me. He wanted to get Bev into bed. Had almost since the first moment he saw her. But he hadn't thought of anything permanent. Only when she ordered him away did his thinking change. It was a little like the business with Marilyn. Rejection sat badly on Arthur Powers's broad shoulders; its presence increased his determination to beat it. He wasn't sure of his feelings for Beverly any more than he was sure of what remained of his emotions about his ex-wife. Sometimes he was convinced that he was still in love with Marilyn. He still felt something for her, but whether it was love or a scream for revenge he couldn't be certain. In a way, Bev was doing to him what Marilyn had done—dismissing him. He would not tolerate it.

Bev was looking at him uncomprehendingly. He softened his voice to an almost seductive whisper.

'Forgive me, sweetheart,' he said. 'I didn't mean all those terrible things. I respect you for your decision. God knows there are few enough compassionate people in this world. Ed Richmond's lucky to have you. I envy him and I swear I won't do anything to make things harder for you. Just give me the three weeks of joy in being able to see and touch you. Give *us* those weeks, Bev. We're entitled to them.'

'It won't work,' she said feebly. 'We'll end up lovers.'

'We're lovers now, my darling. Sex is only a technicality.'

She wanted to be with him more than she had ever wanted anything in the world. If he meant what he said, if he truly would help her keep the fidelity that was all she had left to give Ed, she'd be a fool to give up the little time of happiness that remained. But it was idiotic to think that they could be together for three more weeks and not succumb to the physical yearning. She didn't believe that Arthur could be around her without wanting to make love. It would all be up to her. He'd not force himself on her, she knew that. But it was too much to expect that she could maintain such self-discipline. Even a saint wouldn't be capable of such control! And you're not a saint, Beverly, she told herself. You know what it is to be a sinner. But maybe you can do it. Maybe you can store up enough memories to last through all the monotonous years ahead. Nothing has changed, really, she thought. You always knew, in spite of everything, that you wouldn't leave Ed. Just as you always knew you couldn't go to bed with another man while you were married to him. Haven't you been cheated enough? Aren't you entitled to this one last harmless experience?

Arthur was waiting for her answer. 'We're lovers now. Sex is only a technicality,' he'd said. Not so for her. Yet in a way he was right. She'd already been as unfaithful to her husband as she was likely to be. She tried to convince herself that there'd be no pleasure in Arthur's lovemaking while a feeling of wrongdoing hung over her. She could carry off three weeks of a platonic relationship if he could.

'Can we really do it, Arthur? Can we see each other and stay out of bed?'

'I told you, love. If that's the way you want it, that is how it shall be. I'm selfish. I would rather see you, even if I can't have you, than not see you at all.'

She was so pathetically willing to be convinced, so reluctant to give up this magic. Once again, she wished she saw things as Sylvia did, and once again she knew that it was not possible for her. She touched Arthur's hand gently.

'It's crazy,' she said, 'but let's try.'

139

'Half a loaf,' Arthur said.

'Even crumbs.'

He smiled at her. 'All right, but there is a condition.'

'What?'

'If we're to be together, even with this new understanding, I won't allow anything to change. We'll go to the same romantic places, we'll kiss and touch. I'll send you flowers and buy you presents. You must allow me to pretend that nothing is different except for my efforts to seduce you. Doing things for you is my pleasure, dearest. I won't be deprived of the joy I see on your face when you know you are loved.'

She nodded, so touched she couldn't speak.

'And when I say nothing is to change, I mean it. Like tonight. I had something planned. I don't want you to read a meaning into it that you might not have read earlier.'

'I don't understand.'

'Remember the first night we met? I told you I could show you things that Sylvia or a tour guide couldn't?'

She nodded.

'Before I picked you up tonight and you changed the whole course of our lives, I'd already arranged to take you to an exhibition.'

She had no idea what he was talking about.

'It's quite the thing to do in Paris,' he explained. 'You watch people having sex. It can be erotic or sometimes very funny.'

She was stunned. Pornography, the little she'd been exposed to, did nothing for her. She preferred to create her own ecstasy rather than read about it or look at pictures. As for an actual live 'exhibition,' it sounded disgusting. Her face registered the shock she felt at this unexpected suggestion. Arthur did not look surprised.

'Forget it,' he said. 'I just thought it would be a novel experience for you. Part of your Paris education. A once-in-a-lifetime kind of thing.' He paused. 'No, I'm lying, Bev. When I set it up I did it deliberately. I hoped it would excite you into wanting to make love to me. Now it's become an idea fraught with suspicion. You'll think I'm being even more devious, trying to change your mind about us. Stay here. I'll go make a call and cancel the appointment.'

'No. Wait. You said nothing must be different in the next

140

three weeks. If this is what you'd planned, it's what we should do. We agreed to that, didn't we? We'd have gone if I hadn't told you my decision, wouldn't we?'

'Yes, probably. Unless you'd hated the idea. But I won't hold you to this part of the bargain, Bev.'

'Then already we're acting differently. It will spoil everything if we start making exceptions. If we have to be careful about everything we say and do from now until the time we get back to New York we might just as well call it off now.'

'You amaze me,' Arthur said.

Bev laughed. 'I amaze *me*. Okay, where does one go to witness an exhibition?'

'Where else? In what you would politely call a "house of ill repute." But I still think we should skip it. I have a feeling it's not your kind of thing. Especially not now.'

'No, let's not skip it. Let's do it.'

'You're sure you want to? I don't mind spending the money, but it is expensive and there's no point if you're going to run out screaming with embarrassment.'

'No. Honestly. I'd like to see what it's all about. I admit the idea makes me nervous, but I can't be an ostrich all my life!'

In minutes they were entering an elegant house on a sedate street in a good neighborhood. Beverly was surprised. She'd expected some sleazy whorehouse. Instead, this was a richly appointed mansion where they were greeted by a well-dressed, soft-spoken woman who might have been the matriarch of some aristocratic family. She spoke cordially to Arthur, whom she obviously knew, and graciously acknowledged the introduction to Beverly.

'I am so sorry, Mr. Powers,' she said in her gently accented English, 'but we are very busy tonight. I can offer you and the young lady only Denise and Michelle. You would perhaps not find them amusing.'

Arthur glanced inquiringly at Bev.

'I have no idea,' she said. 'It's up to you.'

A faint smile crossed Arthur's face. 'Maybe it's even better,' he said. 'At least, it's bound to be funnier.'

The madam looked more closely at Bev. Then she nodded. 'Possibly,' she agreed. 'At least your charming companion will, I suspect, find it more extraordinary.'

She led the way to a bedroom on the second floor. It was empty. Close to the big double bed there were two chairs flanking a low coffee table on which reposed a chilled bottle of champagne and two glasses. The proprietress motioned them toward the seats. 'Enjoy yourselves,' she said and departed, leaving them alone in the ornate room.

Arthur poured the wine, looking with amusement at a nervous Bev. 'It's not too late to back out,' he said. 'We can still run for our lives.'

She returned his smile. 'I'm okay. I just hadn't expected to be quite so close to the scene of action.'

'I love you. You're fantastic.'

Bev took a sip of wine and choked. Through the door had come two naked women. She had thought the 'Michelle' mentioned was, of course, 'Michel,' a man. The girls smiled at their audience and skipped onto the bed. Bev turned white.

'The tall one,' she whispered to Arthur. 'She's strapping a . . . a thing onto herself! Like a man!'

'I know, darling. That's why I thought it would be funny. And you don't have to whisper. They don't speak English.'

For two minutes Bev was silent, riveted in disbelief. The women on the bed began making love ardently, apparently totally unaware, after that first sign of recognition, that there was anyone else in the room. Beverly was revolted, horrified. And then the ridiculousness of it struck her. She began to laugh. It was too silly, she and Arthur sitting in this gaudy bedroom watching two women pretending to enjoy sex with a fake penis! They probably weren't even lesbians, she thought. Just a couple of trained seals going through their ridiculous motions for the benefit of some rich American tourists. Her giggles were contagious. Arthur began to laugh with her. The two on the bed seemed not to notice. Finally simulating a mutual climax, they stopped and lay back panting but watchful. Then slowly they both smiled. They were delighted to have pleased the audience.

The smaller one sat up. She was a pretty little thing, not more than nineteen or twenty. Provocatively, she looked at Arthur and said something in French.

'Don't tell me they want you to *join* them!' Bev said.

He could hardly contain himself. 'No, my angel. They want *you* to join them.'

For a moment she thought she hadn't heard correctly. Then, like a child, she clapped her hand over her mouth and collapsed in laughter. 'Let's get out of here,' she said. 'I've had enough. I don't believe any of this. It's all absolutely too absurd.'

They raced back to the Ritz bar. At the table, Bev turned solemnly to Arthur. 'If that was supposed to make me passionate,' she said, 'it wasn't entirely a failure. It just makes me regret missing the real thing all the more.'

He kissed her lightly. 'Then it was a hundred bucks well spent,' he said. 'Not that I expect a return on my investment.'

On the night that Bev and Arthur were watching the exhibition, Ed Richmond was having dinner with his mother. It was the first time he'd seen her since Bev's departure. He was fond of Jane. He supposed he loved her, but she produced in him such a disquieting variety of emotions that he didn't often seek her company. Sometimes he unfairly blamed her for his father's premature death. He wrongly suspected that she had pushed his father. Pushed him so hard that he killed himself trying to live up to her expectations. He didn't know why he thought that. He could remember nothing in his early life that would indicate that this woman was anything but loving and devoted and happy with her husband and her children. Still, he recognized the strength in her, the independence and durability that made him feel somehow inadequate. In his distorted view she was, in many ways, very like Bev: strong, ambitious, self-sufficient. Her business success was thwarted early by the limitations of her talent and the responsibility of two children, he supposed. Had she started working fifteen years earlier, she probably would be exactly like Marion and Bev, two almost frighteningly competent career women. Instead, she had stayed home to be a wife and mother until his father's death. To give her credit, she had uncomplainingly become the support of herself and her child. She had never asked Ed for anything. He often wished that she had. It would have made him feel more a man.

He did not realize how closely his feelings about his mother resembled his intuitive worries about his wife. But he sensed that Jane might help him sort out his troubled thoughts, if only he could relax enough to discuss his nagging fears.

143

She had been glad when he called her at the shop and suggested dinner.

'Want to come to the apartment?' she asked. 'I'll be home about six. I can pick up a steak and some salad mixings on the way.'

'No, I'd like to take you out, Mom. We'll go somewhere quiet, okay?'

It was fine, she told him. She'd look forward to it. And here they were, in this dim little restaurant where the food was overpriced and overcooked, the service slow, and the captain condescending. The place had only two virtues: the tables were far enough apart to make a private conversation possible, and it was expensive enough to make Ed feel important.

They had two drinks, chatting casually about Bev's reports from Paris, Jane's rich and difficult clients at the dress shop, Ruth and Philip, and Ed's job at the insurance company. He told her about the forthcoming promotion. By now it was, to him, a reality. He made it sound as though it were a fait accompli, and Jane was delighted. In fact, she was almost too exuberant.

'Darling, I'm thrilled for you!' she said. 'I know Bev must be too. This is going to make all the difference in the world!'

Her pleasure struck him as more like relief.

'You seem excessively excited about it,' he said.

She pretended innocence. 'Not at all. Is it so unusual for a mother to be happy when her son gets a big promotion?'

'Only when she obviously didn't expect that he ever would.' He knew he sounded cruel and surly. Damn it, he thought, why does she do this to me? He couldn't stop himself. 'You never thought I'd amount to anything, did you, Mother? Well, you've had reason, up to now. You're a smart lady. You know I've let my wife support me for the past four years. That's practically a federal offense, isn't it?'

The minute the words were out, he'd have given anything to take them back. He must be crazy. Why was he attacking her this way? All she'd done was react happily to a piece of good news, and suddenly all the pent-up resentment he felt against the world came rushing out to engulf them both.

'I'm sorry,' he mumbled. 'I don't know what got into me. You just sounded so damned *relieved* when I told you about the new job.' He paused. 'I guess the truth is that I know Bev

144

is going to react the same way when I see her. Like it's a major modern miracle that I've finally gotten myself a decent spot. Neither of you can believe I have any real capabilities. That's what really gets to me. I feel like a backward third-grader who suddenly got promoted.' Ed smiled apologetically. 'I don't know what's come over me lately. I used to love every day of life, doing it my own way, not worrying about tomorrow. Now all of a sudden I feel like I constantly have to prove something.'

'To whom, Eddie? Me? Bev? Or yourself?'

He was no longer angry. He was just a troubled man facing a difficult decision, weighing the merits of trading all his lifelong beliefs and attitudes to regain the respect and love of the woman he had married. It had not been necessary, for a long time, for Beverly to put her disappointment into words. But it was not a one-sided disappointment, he thought defensively. She had changed from the unconcerned, unconventional girl he'd thought her to be. He'd believed she understood and shared his convictions about the priorities of life. Not true. She didn't comprehend how unimportant success was. She saw it in terms of material advancement at the expense, if necessary, of inner peace. Ed still viewed success only as the ability to live fully, richly, lovingly—to be a whole man, scornful of the standards which pronounced some people failures. Failures at what? Making money? Running corporations? Garnering titles that were only momentary monuments to ego? He didn't fault Bev for her ambitions. He simply knew, regretfully, that they were not his. He could have lived in a small town; on a farm; even, as he had quite seriously suggested, in the remoteness of a country like Australia. Complete contentment in the total scheme of things was freedom to relish the pleasures of an all-too-brief lifetime, with the woman of his choice at his side. The world—and Bev—called this lack of ambition. He thought of it as extracting the best out of whatever years God would allow him to live on this earth. What's real? What's important and indestructible? What's life all about? Four years ago he thought he knew. Today, to his own dismay, he had begun to question his views. Perhaps he was lazy or overidealistic or stubbornly defiant. If he wasn't ever going to be the man Bev really wanted, he knew he was going to lose her. And for reasons that were so trivial, so shallow. *She* was his life, a life that he feared was coming to an emotional, if not literal, end.

It seemed hours, rather than minutes ago, that Jane had asked him to whom he had to prove himself. It was a question without an answer. He didn't have to prove anything to anyone. Not even to himself.

This he finally said to his mother. 'I can't pretend,' he said. 'You've never asked me to prove anything. I've never felt a personal need to. As for Bev, I thought that the giving of myself was enough for her. If there are other conditions attached, I probably can't meet them. And if the marriage hinges on that, then the marriage won't last. I can't change my outlook. Not even for her.'

'Are you sure she wants you to?'

'Yes, I'm sure. It's in every little move she makes. More importantly,' he said ruefully, 'in every one she doesn't.'

'Have you talked it out?'

'No. Not in so many words. But we don't have to. I know she thinks I've failed her because I haven't made it big. She's been steadily withdrawing. I can feel how bottled up she's been. I sense what she's going through. She was so glad to go on this trip that she was guilty about it. She's tried not to care that I'm not the hotshot she thought she'd married. I know that. But she can't help caring. Any more than I can help *not* caring about all the things she puts so much stock in.'

Jane tried to be reassuring. 'But all that could change now, Eddie. The promotion. You're finally on your way.'

'To what? A dumb little rut that gives me nothing but the appearance of respectability? I tried to feel excited about it. I really did. So help me, I tried to tell myself that this *was* the answer—the first rung on that ladder Bev respects so much. But I don't want it. I can't con myself into believing I do.'

'Not even for Bev's sake?' She looked at him searchingly. 'Compromise, Eddie. That's what it's all about. Make it work, because that's what will make Beverly happy. And in the end your happiness depends on hers. She loves you very much and she's worried about the future. She blames herself much more than she blames you.'

'What makes you so sure?'

'We had a long talk last fall.'

His amazement was genuine. Then he laughed. 'Well, now, that's beautiful. What more do I need to say to you,

146

Mother? My wife can talk to her mother-in-law but not to her husband. My God, why doesn't she come out with it to me? If she can unburden herself, why not to the one who's causing it all? That's how far apart we've drifted. We can't even talk to each other.'

'You're being either blind or stupid, Ed. Don't you see that Beverly had to talk out all the things that are eating her without risking hurting the person she loves? She couldn't tell you the shame and self-disgust she feels. You'd have stopped her. You'd have taken all the blame on yourself. She needed a psychiatrist or a priest or a close friend. Someone to listen as dispassionately as possible. Not,' Jane said, 'that I can be considered an objective audience. But I was the closest thing she had.'

'Why wouldn't she go to her own mother? Why mine?'

Jane Richmond smiled. 'You, of all people, should understand that, dear. It's not easy to face up to one's failings; real or imagined. And the hardest thing of all is to confess them to someone who has pride of ownership in you. You know, Eddie, I think this is one of the few times you and I have ever talked quite so openly. Can't you imagine that Bev would find it equally difficult to tell her mother that she considers herself a failure as a wife?'

He looked at her incredulously. 'Bev considers herself a failure? What are you talking about? I'm the one she considers a failure. She's succeeded at everything she's ever wanted to do.'

'We're back to definitions of success, aren't we. Ed, in college did you ever read anything by Karen Horney?'

'No. Who's she?'

'A psychoanalyst who wrote, among other things, a book called *The Neurotic Personality of Our Time*. She has some interesting things to say about success or the lack of it, and particularly the way people react to one or the other. She believes that Americans put too much emphasis on success and that the striving for it takes a great emotional toll. We center our lives on winning or losing, she says, and so we are all in a kind of constant competition in which nobody comes out happy. The losers are tormented by envy and self-hatred. The winners know that they're admired grudgingly and often with hostility, so that makes them unhappy too. That's my loose layman's understanding of what Dr. Horney says. From what I know of Bev, the world thinks of her as a winner, and she recognizes herself as the recipient of the hostility along with the admiration. But in her own mind she's a loser in the things at which she really wants most to succeed. Like putting her future in somebody else's hands, learning to trust, giving respect even when, in the eyes of the world, it isn't deserved. She's full of self-hatred, Ed. She's probably full of envy for people like Ruth Eliason who are untormented by self-doubts about what they're really meant to be. She's a winner on the surface and a loser in her heart. Just as you are basically the opposite. It's a rough situation for people who really love each other. They can't come to terms with their mates *or* themselves. They end up like you and Bev, not wanting to live apart and full of doubts that you can live together because you don't believe you can measure up to yourself or each other.'

'Then what's the answer? People don't change.'

'I used to think that. Now I'm not so sure. Perhaps what I've always called "compromise" is really change. Dr. Horney believes that we all have the capacity to keep reshaping and changing ourselves as long as we live. She calls it "the struggle for self-realization," meaning that everyone has a basic, continuous urge to develop his or her best inborn potentialities. We try to be what our culture expects of us, which can lead to a lot of neurotic, unhappy behavior. But if we could get past the stereotypes, some of us might do a lot better.'

'You mean Bev and I are both trying to be what the world expects, and not doing a very good job of it?'

'In simplified terms, yes. Look, dear, I'm not trying to play doctor. That would be lunacy. I'd just like to see you and Bev try to understand yourselves as well as each other. She loves you, Ed. Do you love her?'

'More than anything in the world.'

'Then that's where the answer really begins, doesn't it?'

'I don't know. No matter how much I love her, I can't live with her tolerance, her resignation, maybe even her pity. I'm a man, not a puppet.'

'Give it time. That's what I asked Bev to do. Think hard. See what the new job will do. Maybe it will help you reshape your thinking about things just as it may change Bev's.'

He sighed. 'But that's surface stuff, Mother. Underneath we need more of a bond than that.'

'Undoubtedly. But if you had a broken leg, Eddie, first I'd have it set. Then I'd begin to think about therapy to strengthen it so you could walk . . . and finally run. Marriages can survive a lot of broken bones if they have the therapy of love.' She smiled. 'Cheer up, sweetheart. Everything's going to turn out okay. I'm sure of it.'

She was doing it again, the thing she had confessed to Bev. She was demanding nothing of her son. She was coddling, overprotecting, shielding him from reality. She wasn't sure that things were going to be all right. She wasn't sure at all.

12

When she and Sylvia checked into the Dorchester, there was a letter from Ed. Bev opened it almost reluctantly. The few notes she'd received from him on this trip had been short, warm expressions of his love, filled with brief accounts of his daily doings and interlaced with constant reiterations of how much he missed her and how eagerly he awaited her return. She was sure this would be more of the same. The only variation would be more details about the upcoming promotion.

She had written little to him, pleading that the frenzy of Paris left her no time to do more than scribble a note. He accepted this without question, but then most men would. It is one of the many differences between the sexes. Women in love can always find time to write or telephone, a kind of reassuring communication that does as much for the sender as for the receiver. Somehow most men do not feel this need to stay closely in touch. There is something built into the male ego that precludes the need to reach out constantly to the loved one or to be disturbed, as women are, when the chain of contact is weak and spotty.

Bev knew, to her shame, that if it had been Arthur at home she would have written to him every day, as Sylvia did to Herman. But it was less the lack of love than the presence of guilt that made her unable to write often and freely to her husband.

The remaining week in Paris had been as joyful as possible under the 'new rules.' As she knew she would, she'd missed Arthur terribly during the two days he'd been in Lyon. He'd called her every evening at the hotel, presumably to make sure that she was having dinner in bed, which indeed she was. It was the only good thing about his absence. She was in bed each night at eight, exhausted. After Arthur's call she'd turn out the lights and fall into a deep sleep for ten hours. Even Sylvia's return from her dinner engagements didn't disturb her rest. The only thing that did disturb it were dreams in which she and Ed and Arthur were constantly in confrontation. Sometimes she woke up crying, terrified by nightmares in which she'd seen murder, though with the disjointed haziness of dreams she did not know the victim or the killer. It was strange. The dreams were always full of violence, yet they centered around people who were— inadequate words—'highly civilized.' She remembered hearing that dreams were always opposite. But she also knew that they frequently represented subconscious wishes. She recoiled from the idea. God knows she did not want to see any of them dead. Not even herself. The only close contact she'd had with death had been Geoff's. Perhaps that was somehow mixed up in these weird sleeping visions, even though she could not remember seeing him in any of them.

When he returned to Paris, Arthur had been true to his word. He did not again suggest that they become lovers in the literal sense of the word, but his actions were as loverlike as ever. She bargained for every day of happiness, every make-believe evening in which she pretended it was going to go on forever. When they left Paris it was like leaving another life, one that she knew she would never experience again in the same way. She might come back twice a year, but it would be different. No more the excitement of that first glimpse of the world's most beautiful city. No more romance, recklessness, joy. She made up her mind not to see Arthur in New York, even if he wanted her to. Next trip she would also stay away from him in Paris, difficult as that might be to manage.

Meanwhile she counted the days. Ten to go. Five in London and five more on the *Queen Elizabeth*. Then home to Ed, home to a different kind of adoration. Home, she told herself firmly and without pity, to duty.

She opened Ed's letter. It was an unusually sensitive one, written in the familiar, scrawling penmanship and dated the same day they'd talked on the phone.

Darling,

It is one o'clock in the morning, the end of a very eventful day that started with Joe Taylor's good news and ended with dinner with Mother! In between, of course, was the high point—hearing your voice. I could almost feel you here. I'm glad you're pleased about the upcoming promotion. I didn't expect it. But then I've never had your faith in me, one more evidence of what a stupid jerk I am.

Mother was happy about it too. Our evening was really good, Bev. I can't remember when we've talked like two adults. She told me that you'd been to see her last fall. I hope you don't mind that she told me, dearest. At first I was hurt that you had confided in her rather than in me, but I think I understand now why you couldn't. We got pretty philosophical about life. Too long to go into in a letter, but if she's right I guess there's a lot that you and I have never really understood about ourselves or each other. We have a lot to talk about when you get home. I hated the idea of your going away, but maybe it came just at the right time. I have a good feeling that things are going to be different.

The word about my new job probably will come through before you return. I'll have it stamped on a banner to wave at the pier! Meantime, I hope Paris was successful and that London will be less work and more fun for you. Go watch the changing of the guard for me. And be sure to see the crown jewels in the Tower. But remember that not one of them is as beautiful or precious as you.

All my love,
Ed

It was a letter that said very little and a great deal. Bev wondered what Ed and Jane had talked about that had impressed him so deeply. She was sure that her mother-in-law had not told him anything of the confessions Bev had made about the men in her life before Ed. Jane Richmond was not the kind of woman who betrayed confidences, even to her own son. Whatever it was, though, it seemed to have put Eddie on a straighter, more thoughtful course. But Jane had tried to do that for Bev too in that conversation some months ago. The trouble was that the inspiration hadn't had any permanent effect. Perhaps her own flesh and blood got more from Jane than she had.

There were two other letters from home waiting for her. One was Angela Thyson's, a boring recital of how cold New York was and how the weather made her rheumatism act up. Bev read it quickly and turned to the other envelope, addressed in a neat, feminine hand. It was from Ruth Eliason, and it enclosed a picture of Ed and Philip taken at the airport. It was an affectionate and grateful letter which said, in part, 'I can never thank you and Ed enough for all that Ed has done for Philip. He's gotten my poor, frightened little son to the point of going out to look at airplanes now, and I think before long he'll even manage to get him into one! Phil is a changed boy. Ed has a wonderful way with kids, Bev dear. But then he's an exceptional person—as who knows better than you!' The rest of the letter was full of small talk, quiet reassurances that she was picking up the pieces of her life, hopes that Bev had enjoyed the trip and that the voyage on the midwinter Atlantic wouldn't be rough. 'I miss you,' she said in closing. 'We've seen too little of each other in recent years. Let's make a pact to remedy that when you return. You've always been very special to me. You see, dear friend, I know the *real* Beverly. And I love her very much.'

Bev looked at the snapshot of her husband and the handsome child. They both looked so happy. The picture had a deep effect on her. Just let this new job of Ed's be good, she thought, and I *will* change. I'll give him the babies he wants and the wife he deserves. I've proved enough about my ability to make it in business. I can walk away from that now. No regrets.

At that moment she believed even the last part of her resolution. She wanted to believe it. She did not allow herself to face the real reason: She never wanted to come back to Paris, where the forbidden image of Arthur Powers floated in every glass of champagne.

After the second day, Bev had to face the fact that London was a disappointment. In years to come she would learn to love the dignified old city, but on this first trip the weather was raw and foggy. Her skin felt dry and her hands seemed always numb. Even Arthur noticed it when they were having lunch the third day.

'Something wrong, Bev? Besides this foul weather?'

'Just cold, I guess.' Aware that might seem an invitation that she knew she did not want to extend, she moved slightly away from him on the banquette.

'What you need is a little time off. Or are you booked for the afternoon?'

'Not really. Sylvia is checking sources for tweeds, but they all seem too heavy to me for American women . . . and American central heating.' She shrugged. 'I was going to the Tower of London to see the crown jewels, but wouldn't you know it . . . they're closed.'

'There are other ways of seeing English history, a lot more accessible and a lot more fun. Why don't you play hookey with me?'

He had paid the check, and without waiting for her answer he led her out of the restaurant. By now Bev would not have been surprised at anything he might have planned: tea with a duchess, a ride through the bleak countryside, or even a personal inspection of the Guards. Instead he directed her toward Old Bond Street, where shop after shop displayed in bow-fronted windows the finest of antique English furniture.

'These are still the best bargains in London,' he remarked as he held open the door for her at one establishment. Inside, everything was quiet. No one seemed in attendance, and they wandered for several minutes through the ground floor of the shop, Bev finding herself fascinated as Arthur discussed the different periods of what was on display. Her eye had been trained for fashion and color; this was something new. Certainly none of the homes she had been in had such beautiful things.

'Like my version of history?' Arthur was studying her, a faint smile on his face.

'I'm not positive about the history part of it.' Bev moved away from a mahogany secretaire reluctantly. The wood had felt good to her touch.

'But these aren't just antiques, Bev, or curiosities. These were all new once, made for people who were living and breathing as we are. With the same hopes and ambitions . . . and—well, yes, desires.' He regarded the long room thoughtfully. 'It fascinates me, wondering what their lives were like. Happy? Sad? Perhaps some of the emotions they felt still cling to these pieces.'

She had never seen him quite so reflective; this was not the romantic lover of Paris. London was affecting even him, she thought.

A man in a cutaway and striped trousers came slowly forward from the rear of the shop. He recognized Arthur, who was obviously a good customer, and as they started to talk Bev allowed herself to move away from them, looking at the various objects so carefully placed throughout the room. She wasn't sure she liked the idea Arthur had suggested, that inanimate pieces so beautiful to look at might still contain some of the emotions that had occurred in the rooms where they had stood over the centuries. She thought of the small apartment she shared with Ed. What memories would be there . . . and where? The bed they had shared, happily and then less so? But Arthur was speaking. . . .

'I said, which piece do you like the best?' He stood with the owner of the shop, both of them waiting for her reply. She glanced around, somewhat confused.

'Mr. Marbly is used to my game, Bev. I always tell myself I'm like a child in a place like this. I'm allowed to pick out one toy and one toy only.' He smiled at the man beside him. 'Except usually your prices are too high for me to afford it, aren't they, Marbly?'

While the owner made polite protests, Bev looked around again, with a much keener eye. It was just a game, of course. She knew from quick glances at the little tags she could afford nothing in this shop. But her own instincts for design had already selected several favorites. She moved farther away from the two men, walking toward the far wall.

'That,' she said, pointing up at the large gold-filigreed framed mirror hanging on the wall.

'Oh, an excellent choice, madam,' said the owner. 'Eighteenth-century Chippendale. Authenticated, of course.'

They spent a few more moments with the owner, discussing other objects, then Bev checked her watch. She'd promised Sylvia to go with her on a quick tour through the top department stores before evening, just to see whether there were any ideas that they might use at Welby's, and the afternoon was slipping away. Making her excuses to Arthur

156

and the owner, she went out of the shop, leaving the two men deep in a discussion of a sixteenth-century oak table. She was not even sure Arthur had registered that she was leaving. A curious man, she thought, not for the first time. Still, they would meet for dinner.

The next day had been a busy one. Dinner with Arthur had ended early. He had seemed preoccupied, and when she tried to get him to talk about what was on his mind, he deliberately stepped away from any discussion. Now, back in her room (Sylvia and she having decided to split their shopping excursions for greater efficiency), she was grateful to stretch out on her bed in the hotel room, happy to have a few minutes to herself.

There was a tap on the door. Sylvia must have forgotten her key again, she thought, as she got up to open it. But it was Arthur standing in the hall outside.

'Bev, could I talk to you for a moment?' His face seemed grim. Silently she stepped aside, letting him follow her into the room. She had no worry that something might happen between them. The look on his face had told her that whatever was on his mind, it was not desire. Besides, Sylvia would be back any moment.

'What is it, Arthur?'

'I . ... I can't make dinner tonight. In fact, I've just canceled my ticket to sail back. I'm flying to New York this evening.'

She knew she had not kept the disappointment she felt from showing on her face. 'Arthur, you look so worried. Is something wrong?'

'Marilyn. There was a letter yesterday, and I found a cable just now in my box downstairs. She's been in a bad car accident. She . . . she seems to be desperate to see me.'

Marilyn, the wife he had been so determined to get out of his system. Bev had formed a picture of her during their conversations: hard, cold, brittle, and selfish. But beautiful. For all of Arthur's protestations, the candle-lit dinners, the vases of mimosa, all Marilyn had to do was cable and back he ran to her.

'I'm sorry. For both of you.'

'I thought I was free of her, Bev. It isn't love or desire that's making me go back, she's found that with somebody new. Or so I thought. Only—well, now she needs me.' He

157

sighed heavily. 'I don't understand what I'm feeling. I don't understand why I didn't crumple the cable up as soon as I read it, go on with our plans just as before. Only I can't, somehow.'

'I understand, Arthur.' She touched his clenched hands gently. 'Perhaps it's for the best. We both knew we wouldn't be able to see each other in New York, that we each had our own lives and our own . . . obligations. Maybe it's better that we end it here, with nothing but good memories.'

'Don't say that, Bev. You know it isn't ended between us. I don't know what the future is, but it can't be over between us. Not now, not like this.' He reached for her, but she forced herself to pull back.

'I've never thought we've had a future, Arthur. I've never let myself think that. I have a husband who needs me. I can't let myself go back on my promises.'

'God, the terrible tyranny of the weak!' The bitterness in his voice startled her. 'I probably would have seen Marilyn anyway . . . just one more time. Just to be sure she was out of my system forever. But not like this. She was so proud of the way she looked.'

'Maybe . . . maybe she isn't injured that badly.'

He made no answer. At the door he hesitated. 'We do have a future, Bev. Somehow. Somewhere. I won't give that up.' He closed the door quietly behind him.

The trip back to New York was the opposite of the voyage to Europe in every way. On the way over she and Sylvia had felt buoyant and free like two schoolgirls on the first day of vacation, schoolgirls who were free to flirt and drink champagne and dance until after midnight. Now Sylvia spent most of the day in their stateroom, going over the designs they had selected, checking and rechecking the prices, convincing herself that they had chosen well. This was a task she preferred to do herself, shooing Bev away almost as a distraction. And Bev was wise enough to know that, if mistakes had been made, Welby's would blame the older woman and not her.

So Bev spent most of the days aboard the ship walking the endless circle of the deck. The weather was cold and raw, so most of the time she had the deck to herself, as she wanted. There was a lot to think about, more than she felt she could resolve in the five days she had before she returned to New York and her life with Ed. Sometimes in the late afternoon when she realized another day had gone by, she almost wished there were some way she could stop the huge boat and let it anchor peacefully in the middle of the cold gray ocean, until she could sort out her feelings, her emotions, and, more important, her obligations.

Ed. That was the center of it. She knew deep in the core of her being she loved him, loved him for the kindness, the patience, the endless devotion he had brought into her life, laying all of it at her feet like a gift that he would never take back. *But was she in love with him?* She was old enough now to know that was the only question that had to be answered. She had been once, she was sure. It had never been the quicksilver excitement she felt with Arthur, but that she already knew could be only a temporary thing. Perhaps what she felt had never been as strong and as deep, as trusting as what she had felt for Frank. First love, she thought, plunging her hands deeper into her pockets. Nothing is ever like that again.

Ed was different from Frank. He was a decent, honorable man who would never desert her, never take away his love. *But a puppy can give you that.* Instantly she shoved the unwanted thought out of her mind. Was what Sylvia had said true, that she wanted Ed to have money and prestige and, yes, power, as a frame for the kind of life she felt she wanted? She went over and over it again in her mind. Money she already knew she could earn. Prestige? What exactly did that mean? She had once dated a man who was determined to have his face on the cover of *Time* and *Newsweek* on the same week; that had been his definition of success. Only the following week somebody else's face would be there, she had thought at the time, dismissing him as a fool.

No, it wasn't reflected glory she needed from Ed. It was something deeper, something stronger, something of a permanence she could fasten her life to. If only he cared, really cared about anything, deeply enough to fight and sacrifice and struggle for it. It didn't really matter what: spending years building one perfect piece of furniture such as the ones Arthur had shown her, doing the quiet social work that filled Sylvia's husband's life, or even raising prize goldfish! Then she could respect her husband, love him, be in love with him. Only first he had to care about something!

But even as she let herself explore the thought, she knew he did care about something: her. Only it isn't enough, Ed, she said to herself. I can't live your life for you, I can't *be* your life. No one can be the sole reason for someone else's existence.

But as she started down from the rain-swept deck the last afternoon, she found herself softening the edges of her argument as she had so often before. Maybe this time it'll be all right. The promotion—maybe that's all he needs. . . .

Ed was at the dock to meet them. There was no banner in his hand, but Bev hadn't really expected it. His smile was as warm and reassuring as always, and with his help she and Sylvia were through customs and in a taxi in less than an hour.

'Listen, you two,' said Sylvia as they left the pier. 'I'm exhausted, and I have a feeling you both have a lot to get caught up on. And Welby's won't close if we take the afternoon off. So why don't you drop me and my luggage, and I'll see you in the office in the morning, Bev. Okay with you, Ed? Want to spend what's left of the day with your wife?'

'A great idea, Sylvia. I know now why you're such a success: an uncanny instinct for people.'

'That, and feet that can trudge through fifteen showrooms in one afternoon.'

Beverly had taken no part in this exchange; instead, she tried to catch the expression on Ed's face. There was something out of place about his manner, something she couldn't quite put her finger on. His greeting could not have been warmer or more loving, and yet every time she had tried to ask him about his promotion or his job, the conversation seemed to have shifted and she and Sylvia were telling stories of their time in London and Paris. Careful stories on Sylvia's part, Bev had noticed, with no mention of Arthur Powers. Perhaps this was the way she kept her own brief indiscretions from Herman.

After they had dropped Sylvia off and the taxi was starting uptown toward their apartment, Bev reached out for Ed's hand. 'Ed? Is something wrong? You've kept us chattering all this time and haven't said a word.'

He gave her gloved hand a squeeze. 'Tell you when we get home.'

He hadn't needed to say any more. Something had gone wrong with the promotion; she knew it without having to ask. Please, let it just be delayed, that's all. Just a delay.

Once inside their living room, he folded her in his arms and kissed her long and fervently. She tried to respond, but that was impossible with the questions forming in her mind.

'Ed? You said we'd talk about it when we got home.'

'Can't it wait for just a little bit? I haven't seen you for over a month.' He kissed her again, pulling her close. 'Your husband missed you. A lot.'

She allowed herself to submit to his kiss, but there was no warmth in her body and she knew he sensed it. Reluctantly he let her go at last and, dropping his coat on the sofa, pulled her down beside him. There was no desire in him now, no passion. He looked at her for a long moment, then down at his clenched hands as if he did not want to see the expression on her face.

'It's about that promotion I was so excited about.'

'Any . . . problems?'

'It didn't come through.'

Even though she had expected what he said, she was determined not to show her unhappiness. 'You mean, not yet? It probably will in time.'

'Not ever. Taylor . . . well, Taylor's not quite the big shot he thinks he is. In fact, he's not a very big man at all. He'd said something about one of the vice-presidents' having a nephew he was pushing for the job: young kid, one of those twenty-year-old know-it-alls. Well, Taylor's recommendation didn't work. The kid got the position.'

'Ed, I'm sorry.' She wanted to reach out to him, to comfort him if she could, but he just sat there staring at his hands, complete and separate from her. She tried to think of something to say that would help, something reassuring, only the words she chose seemed flat. 'There'll be other positions. Other promotions.'

'Not with that company.' He glanced at her, his eyes cold. 'You don't think after that kind of a double-cross I'd keep on working for them, do you?'

'Ed! You quit?'

'Of course!'

She thought of the long, numbing days he had spent before finding this position with the insurance company, the hopes he'd had in the beginning (as he had with all his previous jobs—how many had there been since their marriage?), then the dragging sameness of their lives as the work grew boring, the emptiness of their lovemaking at night. Now it would start all over again.

Something of what she felt must have shown, for his face flushed with anger. 'Bev, I couldn't have kept on working with them. Not after this! They as much as locked the door in front of me. "Tough luck, Mac, but you're not the type who gets promotions," ' he mimicked scornfully. ' "We need guys with connections." '

'It doesn't have to mean that, Ed. Everybody helps their relatives; it happens in every field. But to quit—'

'It isn't just relatives, Bev. Sonny-Boy apparently went to school with the sons of some very important people. And they might, just might, give our firm some of their insurance accounts. Taylor as much as told me that if I had the same kind of big accounts I could have had the promotion.'

Arthur, Bev thought. Arthur might know somebody who needed that kind of large-scale insurance. 'Could you get your job back? If you brought in some large accounts?' she said cautiously.

'Beverly!' It was rare that he called her by her full name, even rarer that he let her see his anger. 'I'm not riding on somebody's coattails!'

No, she thought. But you let me pay for this apartment. And the food on our table and the clothes you wear.

He flushed almost as if he heard what she was thinking. 'Do you know what Taylor had the gall to suggest? That you, being such a big buyer at Welby's, might be able to get us some of their insurance work.'

She sat back, a little stunned. Of course. Why hadn't she thought of that before? She would talk to Sylvia tomorrow, find out who was in charge in that area. . . .

'My God, Bev!' His eyes were studying her carefully, shocked by what he was seeing. 'You don't think I would consider that?'

162

'Why not? If it's connections, if that's what it takes, then let's use them!'

He stood and looked at her. The room was growing dark in the winter afternoon, but she could still see his face. This was how he would look as an old man. Tired, worn, already a little stooped. Only we're not old, she thought. We're young, we've got our whole lives ahead of us.

'Would *you* have done it, Bev? Taken a promotion at Welby's . . . if I had had the power to make it happen through *my* business? Would you have even taken a job there, if I had been the one who got it for you?'

Something inside her screamed out in silent pride, But I'm good at my job, I love it, I wouldn't have needed you! She forced it back, holding her lips tightly together.

'No, you wouldn't,' he went on. 'But then you've never needed help, not like that.' He picked up his coat. 'It'll be all right. I'll find something else. It's not as if I ever exactly had a calling to sell insurance.'

He stopped at the door, the coat still in his hand. 'I'd . . . I'd hoped you'd be on my side, Bev.'

Say something, she thought. Anything! He's hurt and unhappy and he needs a wife at this moment. That's what you promised to be. Only she could not force herself to say anything.

'Well . . . welcome home anyway,' he said, and when she turned to look at him he had already gone.

13

He did not come back that afternoon. Bev kept herself busy unpacking, arranging the gifts she had bought for friends and family, and dutifully called Angela to tell her she was safely home. Her mother as always was full of questions, but Bev found it almost impossible to make the full description of the trip Angela so clearly wanted to hear. When she finally put down the phone, she was tempted to call Jane, wondering if Ed had gone to his mother's for the sympathy and strength she'd not been able to give. But she couldn't make herself dial Jane's number. If Ed were there, it would be too difficult to talk. And if he weren't—well, she didn't want anyone knowing how worried she was becoming.

She tried to make the evening seem like any other. After a solitary supper she took a long hot bath, during which she firmly kept her mind on what she would have to do the next day at the store. Even later when she was in bed, trying to sleep, trying not to listen for Ed's key in the front door, she refused to let herself think about him. Or Arthur. Perhaps Arthur was the hardest problem of all.

When she woke up in the morning after another night of restless, threatening dreams, she found a blanket neatly folded on the living-room couch and a note from Ed. 'Came in too late to disturb you. Out on the job hunt. I'll be back tonight.'

So nothing had really changed. Wherever he'd been (and Bev couldn't see him in a bar or the apartment of some easy girl), he was still alive, still part of her life. Part of her problems.

Sylvia was in her small office at the store when Bev arrived. 'Anything wrong?' she asked after a quick look at

Bev's face. Bev shook her head. Sylvia knew enough not to ask any further questions. She pushed a small, beautifully wrapped package across her desk to Bev. 'This was here waiting for you,' she said.

Happy to have a distraction, Bev unwrapped the package carefully. One look at the bottle inside and she knew who had sent the present and why there was no card. She stood there, thinking of Arthur and Paris, the bottle unopened in her hands. She didn't need to smell the fragrance. She knew what it would be: mimosa.

The next days were full and busy. Bev plunged into her work. As always, it was easier when she did not have time to think. Ed had been at home that first evening, dinner prepared, making cheerful conversation that she tried to match. There were too many important things left undecided between them for either of them to want a serious conversation. Once they started, Bev realized, they might each say things that could never be taken back, that would split their marriage forever. And Bev knew neither she nor Ed was ready to take that chance.

Instead, Ed talked glowingly of the interviews he had lined up and, when it came time for bed, merely said he wanted to work a little longer on his job résumé and would probably 'sack out,' as he put it, in the living room so as not to disturb her. Bev nodded and went into the bedroom. She touched his shoulder gently as she passed him, hoping by the gesture he would understand that there was no anger between them.

The following afternoon he called and suggested they meet at Jane's. Bev agreed, wanting to spend the time after the store closed distributing the gifts she had brought back. She made her visit to her parents as quick as she could, her father as always understanding about the shortness of time, her mother protesting, her eyes full of questions even as she opened the box that held the scarf Bev had purchased in Paris.

The next stop was harder, for Ruth wanted to know all about her trip and was full of praise for the kindness Ed had shown little Philip. The boy seemed disappointed that Ed had not come with her, and after he left the room Ruth asked Bev pointedly about him.

'He's out of work. Again.'

'Bev, I'm so sorry. For both of you.'

'It's probably just as well. He never was terribly enthusiastic about selling insurance anyway. And he didn't exactly lose the job. He quit.'

'He didn't get the promotion?'

'You knew about that?' Ruth nodded. 'No. Somebody with better connections got it. Ed felt he couldn't continue with that kind of setup.'

'He has his pride, Bev,' said Ruth quietly.

'He also has a wife. And dreams of a family.' Bev could see Ruth was shocked by the crispness of her voice. 'Ruth, I'm not angry at him . . . exactly. Perhaps I think it should have been a decision for both of us to make, but maybe I'm wrong.'

'He'll find something else.'

'I suppose so.' She thought of the bleak past years, the fresh beginnings and the inevitable end to each of them. 'Only how much longer do we go on starting over? Finding "something else"? Ed's over thirty, Ruth. Most men his age are settled, have found a career, are moving ahead, making a life for themselves.'

'Perhaps . . .' Ruth hesitated.

'Go on.'

'He loves children so much, Bev. He's been wonderful with Philip, you know that. But all kids seem to like him. Maybe if he had a family of his own . . .'

'Ruth, he can't even support me. How is he going to support a family? God knows I'm not money-hungry, but we're still living in the same apartment I moved into when I left home. Can you see that tiny place with a crib? And me out of a job? Rent has to be paid, food has to be bought, and you can't do that if the breadwinner of the family is going to keep on looking for "something else."'

'Bev, you sound so—'

'Hard? Unforgiving? I don't want to be, Ruth. I love Ed, or at least I think I do. I want our marriage to work, but I can't do it all by myself.'

'You're not thinking about divorce?'

'I'm trying not to. I'm trying to find some way out of this tangle, and I just can't. Especially when I see there are . . . other ways of living.'

Ruth had known Bev too long not to catch what her friend was saying. 'You mean, another man?'

'No. Not really. At least, not yet.' Bev glanced at her watch. She still had half an hour before she was to meet Ed. It would be comfortable to settle back, finish the tea Ruth had brought her, and tell her about Arthur. Only what was there to tell? An attractive, powerful man, a series of romantic dinners, a bottle of perfume. She wondered, smiling to herself, how Ruth would react if she told her about the night in Paris and the bizarre and ultimately funny exhibition they had watched together. Probably Ruth would be shocked. Bev couldn't imagine Geoff having taken his wife to such a place, not if their marriage had lasted a hundred years. The differences between us, Bev thought, and resolutely got to her feet to go. She couldn't even allow herself the easy comfort of shared confidences with Ruth.

'Must you leave?' Ruth clearly wanted to share in Bev's life and help if she could. She'd missed having someone adult to talk to in the weeks since Geoff's death. Only Ed at dinner that one evening. She had her family, of course, and the boys, but she cared for Bev and hated to think there were areas in her life she was not going to be permitted to enter.

'Sorry, Ruth. I'll make up for it. But I'm meeting Ed at his mother's, and it's clear across town. It's not a meeting I'm looking forward to. I suspect Ed hasn't told his mother yet about quitting, which is probably why he wants me there, as a buffer.'

But to Bev's surprise the meeting she had been dreading turned out to be the easiest she had had since her return. Jane and Ed were both smiling, although Bev noticed a careful look in her mother-in-law's eyes.

'I've got a job, Bev!' said Ed exultantly after the greetings had been exchanged.

'Now, Ed, don't throw it at Beverly just like that. Besides, it isn't certain yet, is it?' cautioned Jane.

'More than anything I've had before,' said Ed. Quickly he told Bev his news. He'd contacted an old friend from his Air Force days, now living near St. Louis. The man had a growing air-freight business and was delighted to hear from Ed. His firm was expanding so rapidly he needed someone to open a New York office, and with a typical out-of-towner's distrust of New Yorkers had delayed in choosing the right person. Ed he knew and could trust, and as proof that the job was an actuality he was flying Ed to St. Louis the next morning for a conference.

'And you'll like this, Bev,' concluded Ed. 'It's for more money than I would have got even with the promotion at the insurance company.'

'Stop that, Ed. You're making Beverly sound greedy.' Jane at least had seen the stunned look on Bev's face while Ed was telling his news. She's not ready for this, she thought. Poor girl. She's not ready to let Ed suddenly be making the decisions. Her heart went out to her daughter-in-law, knowing the questions that must be going through Bev's mind.

For the next half hour the three of them went over the news. Bev, however, found it hard to join in the others' enthusiasm. As Jane had guessed, she was trying to sort out this new situation in her mind while still trying to be happy and encouraging. It sounded as if it were everything Ed had wanted. In all the years of their marriage she'd never seen him this alive and excited about the prospect of a new job, of starting over once again. She tried to remember if Ed had even mentioned the name of this man who was quite literally his lifesaver, and as the conversation went on, she realized he hadn't, although Jane seemed to know of him. How many other things had Ed kept from her during their marriage? she wondered.

When they finally left, Ed was in too good a mood to go quietly home. Instead he suggested an Italian restaurant they had often gone to in the days when he had been courting her. Bev determined to match him in his cheerfulness, and together they finished the bottle of wine Ed had insisted would accompany the meal.

Back in the apartment there was no question of Ed's sleeping on the sofa. Together they packed a suitcase for his trip to St. Louis in the morning, and when they were finished and he suggested a nightcap, she agreed quickly, hoping the alcohol would stop the questions in her mind and warm her body to his embraces. For the first time in months their lovemaking was not perfunctory. Ed was alive and passionate and patiently brought her to the point where at last she could forget their problems and join him as eagerly and openly as she had during the first year of their life together. Later, holding Ed in her arms as he slept peacefully, she refused to allow herself to worry about the future. They would work it out somehow.

The next day at the store she told Sylvia the news. One look at Bev's face and the older woman mentally crossed her fingers. If this was what Bev wanted, fine, only Sylvia wondered how many more emotional roller-coaster rides the younger woman could take in this marriage. As Bev was explaining that Ed would be away for two, possibly three days, the phone on Sylvia's desk rang.

'Mrs. Schlesinger,' said Sylvia. After listening for a moment, she handed the phone to Bev. 'It's for you.' Bev stared at her. She had long ago made it clear to her friends and family that neither she nor Welby's appreciated personal phone calls during business hours. As she took the phone, Sylvia whispered, 'Arthur Powers.'

Arthur! He was the last person Bev had expected to call today and frankly, in the mood she was feeling of being a dutiful wife, the last person she wanted to talk to. Aware that Sylvia was watching her and would be hearing every word, she greeted him politely.

'Arthur, how very nice to hear from you. I was just going to write you a note thanking you for the beautiful bottle of perfume.'

'Why not save yourself the effort and meet me for lunch instead? One o'clock, is that convenient?' He mentioned the name of one of the most expensive French restaurants in the city, a place where everyone in the fashion world made a point of being seen as often as possible. Beverly had never been there; that had been one of the many things she had planned to do in the future, but she had not expected to make her initial appearance there with a man as well known and important as Arthur.

'I . . . I really shouldn't, Arthur. We've a lot of work to do here at the store, having been away so long. I was planning on eating in.'

Sylvia silently mouthed the word 'Where?' Bev whispered back the famous name, and Sylvia instantly said, 'Go.'

'Well, perhaps I could get away.'

'Good,' said Arthur. 'I've a lot to talk to you about, a lot to tell you. And a small surprise as well, just to give you something to puzzle about through the morning.' He sounded cheerful and happy, confident and pleased with himself, the way he had been in Paris—not the haunted, unhappy man of their last meeting in London. 'I'll expect you to be wearing the perfume,' he added, hanging up before she could answer.

'So Arthur calls the morning Ed leaves town,' said Sylvia as Bev hung up. 'He must have spies at all the airports.'

'It's just a luncheon, Sylvia. He'll probably want to tell me about Marilyn.'

'He didn't sound to me like a man who wanted to wander down Memory Lane,' said Sylvia with some amusement. 'Anyway, enjoy yourself. I can cover for you if you need extra time.'

'Sylvia, you're impossible.' But there was a smile on Bev's face as she said it, a smile the older woman hadn't seen since Paris.

At one o'clock the affluent and the ambitious of New York's fashion world stopped whatever they were doing to gather at the restaurant Arthur had chosen. The cozy pink velvet banquettes were crowded with carefully tailored men and immaculately turned-out women. The air was heavy with the scent of fresh flowers, imported cigarettes, and expensive perfumes and noisy with the sound of fifty different conversations, all concerned with what was fashionable or what was about to become so. The highest names in the industry were dropped casually, whether the speaker personally knew them or not. The captain showed Bev through the tightly packed tables to the corner booth where Arthur was sitting. It was a sign of his power and prestige that he had this corner booth; it was one of the few places in the room where two people could have a conversation without being overheard (and, what was worse, finding the next day a report of their conversation in the gossip columns).

Arthur stood as she approached, offering her his hand. He was well aware that most of the people in the room knew him, knew of his romantic reputation, and would be curious about this young woman who was not instantly recognizable. He did not bend forward to kiss her on the cheek the way he might have with nearly any other woman in the room. After they were seated and had ordered, he knew the attention of

171

the people around them would be refocused on the next arrival. He could wait till then to allow himself to show the warmth he felt on seeing Bev again. She's not exactly beautiful, he had thought again as he watched her make her way through the restaurant to his table. But she had something that had nothing to do with looks or youth. There was about her a sense of dignity and determination, of clear, clean lines in the way she dressed and moved and thought. If he had ever thought that what had happened between them in Paris was just a little flirtation, easy to forget once he was back in New York, that thought disappeared in the few moments it took for her to reach him. I want her, he found himself thinking. And I'm going to have her.

The first few minutes of the lunch were spent in ordering, in light conversation, impersonal remarks. But after the captain had gone, Arthur put his hand out and covered Beverly's.

'I've missed you, Bev.'

She could feel her skin tingling at his touch, her body betraying her in a hundred intimate ways. She tried so hard to think of the lovemaking she had shared and enjoyed with Ed the night before, but, as always when she was with Arthur, it was hard to see Ed clearly.

'I've missed you too, Arthur.' She forced herself to remove her hand from his. 'So many times I've wondered what was happening. How you were. How . . . Marilyn is.'

'She's going to recover. Completely. According to her psychiatrist—the man she loves, or so she says—it was just a moment of complete panic. The fear that she would be scarred forever, that he couldn't possibly love her any more, that she would be out in the world with no alimony, nothing to rely on, her looks gone—well, I guess I became some sort of father figure to her.' He smiled a little cynically. 'She was even contemplating stopping our divorce.'

'But not now?'

'No. The good doctor got her the best plastic surgeon in America. She'll look the way she always has, maybe even a little better. Which means she doesn't need me.'

'So the flight back was for nothing?'

'I wouldn't say that, Bev. I told you in London I probably would have had to see her again, just once more, to be sure I was over her. Coming back early at least did that for me.' He smiled at her, looking directly into her eyes. 'So, little one, I'm a free man. Or will be as soon as the last legal papers are signed. Free in every possible way. Marilyn's just somebody who occupied my life for a couple of years and now has moved out. Permanently. With no bad feelings on either side.'

'I'm glad. For both of you.'

'It was so strange, seeing her in the hospital. I realized I had never once in all the time we were married been as close to her as I was with you when we were in Paris. Even though you and I, as they say, "behaved ourselves." With some reluctance, I might add, on my part.'

'And mine.' Before he could take advantage of her confession, she told him bluntly all that had happened between her and Ed.

'That leaves you . . . where? I mean, now?'

'I don't know, Arthur. If Ed gets this job, I can't very well walk out on him.' She had not told Arthur of the night before, when for the first time in months she and Ed had made love. Everything else she could tell Arthur as a friend, as a confidant, but this was something personal, something she could only share with her husband. To do otherwise would have been a betrayal she could not make.

'Why not leave him? If he gets this job, he'll be busy making a new life. He won't need you to lean on any more.' She started to protest, but he silenced her. 'Isn't that what he's done these past years? Isn't that what he's always done? First with his mother, then with you?'

She found herself flushing, aware how close he was to the truth but unwilling to admit it, even now.

'Look, Bev, I'm not trying to pry or to arrange your life. But I knew in Paris you weren't happy. And I don't think a new job for your husband is going to change that. You see, one of the things I've learned in life is that when something is finished, it's best to make a clean break. I think now is the time for you to do that with Ed.'

She was saved from having to answer by the waiters starting to serve their meal. She was not sure just what she could have answered. A clean break. It sounded so easy the way Arthur said it. Only could she ever do that with someone who had been so much a part of her life as Ed had been? Did she even want to break away? To what? She knew instinc-

173

tively that Arthur was not suggesting himself as an alternative. Three marriages had burned him too much to even consider such a thing again. And even if he did, sometime perhaps in the future, would she want him as a husband? It would mean, she knew, an end to any personal ambitions she herself had. He would never permit a wife to have a career, she was certain of that. It would be too much of a reflection on his status and his manhood. He was not like Sylvia's husband or, she had to admit to herself, like Ed, who could honestly rejoice in her achievements and successes.

'You're looking very thoughtful,' he said finally.

'There's been a lot to think about lately. I guess I'm in the position of the little girl in the poem who wants to be inside the house and outside at the same time.'

'You mean, you can't have everything? Don't you believe it, Bev. People can get everything they want, if they want it hard enough. Now, let's attend to this excellent luncheon, because I've got a little surprise for you before you go back to the store.'

Bev was curious about what he meant, as she knew Arthur wanted her to be, but wisely she decided to let him enjoy his mystery until he was ready to reveal it. The meal was excellent, but she would never remember what Arthur had ordered for her, so conscious was she of his sitting next to her, of the energy that radiated from his body across the distance that separated them, the magnetism, and, yes, she had to admit it, his sexual appeal. When at last they had finished, he signed the check quickly and led her out of the restaurant, barely nodding at the men and women who tried to catch his attention.

Outside was a limousine, the chauffeur jumping out as soon as he saw them to hold open the door to the back seat. As they got in Arthur said, 'You'll have to give him your address, I don't know it.'

'My address?'

He smiled again. 'Nothing improper, I assure you, Bev. Only my surprise is a little difficult to transport. I don't think you'd want to try and take it home on the bus from the store.'

More puzzled than ever, Bev told the driver and leaned back against the cushions of the car. There was no sign of any package in the limousine, and she was frankly confused by

Arthur's attitude. He was treating her a little the way her father used to do on her birthdays when she was a child, ordering her mother cheerfully to have Bev dressed in her best and then, without warning, taking her for a 'surprise.' Once it had been the circus; another time a matinee; once even a long excursion to the Bronx Zoo. Only, she reminded herself during the ride uptown, Arthur was not her father, and his surprises were likely to be a good deal less innocent.

When they arrived, Arthur insisted Bev go up first after having been told the number of her apartment. She looked around the small living room as she waited for him to follow her up. Had it always been this dark, or was it just the winter afternoon? She was suddenly seeing the place as Arthur would see it: small, impersonal even after all these years, neat enough but lacking in grace and charm—all the things he so obviously admired. She was almost tempted to close the door behind her and meet him at the elevator when she heard him tap on the door.

Outside in the hall the chauffeur stood behind Arthur, holding a large flat package in his gloved hands. He brought the wrapped package into the room, nodded at Arthur, and went out again without a word, closing the door behind him.

'Arthur, what is all this?'

'A surprise. Don't you like them?' He was working on the twine that held the wrappings together. In one sweep he ripped off the paper coverings. Bev could see what he meant now: the beautiful Chippendale mirror she had admired in London. She could hear herself gasp slightly as she knelt on the carpet to look at it.

'Arthur, is this for me?' She touched the delicate filigree of the frame. 'It's even more beautiful than I remembered it.' She stood up again. 'But of course, I can't take it.'

'You have to. It's very bad luck to give back a present. Especially a mirror.'

'You made that up!'

'Possibly. But that doesn't mean it isn't still true.' Something in his words surprised her. He was looking around the room as she had done minutes before, and she knew he was seeing it as she had. With almost an angry pride, she said defensively, 'I'm sorry, Arthur. It was very kind of you, but as you can see, it doesn't really belong here.'

'It belongs where you are. Maybe it's you who doesn't

belong here.' He made no move to step closer, but his words, the tone of his voice, were as intimate as if he were lying in bed next to her.

'I am here because this is where I can afford to live,' she said stiffly. 'Where my husband and I can afford to live. Now I think you'd better take that beautiful mirror and put it on a wall that deserves it. And I have to be getting back to the store.'

Afterward, she was to wonder what might have happened if he had done any of the dozen things she might have expected him to do: argue or attempt to hold her or joke at her pride. Any of them would have pointed out how clearly apart they were in their own levels of this city and in their professions. Instead, he picked up the mirror as lightly and casually as if it were an inexpensive lampshade and followed her down to the car. But once on their way back to Welby's, the mirror carefully packed away in the trunk of the limousine, Arthur began to ask her some questions: personal questions, but the way he phrased them was like a lawyer's —Did she like the building she was in? How long had she been there? How much could she afford to pay?—and they both knew he was referring to her paying for an apartment without Ed's help. Only Ed would be able to help, she kept reminding herself during the trip.

After they reached the store, he stood for a moment with her on the sidewalk. 'Bev, I'm not trying to rearrange your life . . .' He broke off with a small laugh. 'Well, maybe I am, but I don't want to be caught at it. I think I might know of a better apartment, well within your price range. One that the mirror would look well in,' he added.

'And what does a young woman have to do to get such an apartment?'

'No strings, Bev. I mean that. I'd like to give you a lot of beautiful things, you know that. But I also know you wouldn't accept them, not if there are . . . conditions attached. But I don't see any reason why as friends we can't help each other.'

'I can't help you.' She said it flatly.

'You have already. You got Marilyn out of my system. I don't think that would have ever happened if I hadn't met you. I owe you something for that, and for a lot of other things as well. And I like to pay my bills promptly.'

176

She took a deep breath. 'Arthur, you're a very exciting man. You've been wonderful to me, and very kind. But I think we'd better not see each other again.'

'I'd accept that, Bev, if I thought you meant it. But don't worry. What I want from you I'll never try tricks to get. I'll have it openly and honestly, and because you want to give it.'

She left him after that, not trusting herself to say anything more. She had tried to end it, tried as hard as she could, but she knew he was right. Whatever there was between them had not been finished by her behaving according to the rules by which she had been raised.

It was late the next afternoon when the phone call came. A polite female voice asked for Mrs. Richmond. Fortunately Bev was alone in Sylvia's office at the time.

'I understand you're looking for a new apartment, Mrs. Richmond. It so happens that one is coming on the market in one of the buildings our firm manages. Since you've been very highly recommended, I'd be happy to show it to you this afternoon if you could arrange to be free.'

Arthur hasn't wasted any time, Bev thought. But she found herself asking questions about the apartment, and when she heard the rent was only slightly more than what she had been paying and the location was at the end of 57th Street overlooking the East River, she could not resist arranging an appointment.

The apartment was everything anyone could want: a large living room with a fireplace (and a suitable space above it for the Chippendale mirror, Bev noted wryly), a comfortable bedroom, a kitchen larger than Bev's office, and a small second bedroom and bath. 'For a maid's room,' said Miss Lockley, who had been showing her the apartment. She glanced at Bev and corrected herself, as if realizing for the first time Bev's age. 'Or suitable for a nursery as well.'

Bev loved the place on sight. Although it was empty, the previous tenant had left behind thick wall-to-wall carpets, and the walls seemed as fresh as if they had been painted only weeks before. Carefully she asked about the owner of the building and was relieved when Miss Lockley mentioned a name she had never heard before. It would have been impossible if Arthur had been the owner, and instantly she knew he'd been prepared for that.

177

No strings. . . .

She knew Miss Lockley was surprised that she didn't make an instant decision—apartments like this were rare bargains, to be snatched at eagerly—but she promised to give her answer within twenty-four hours and hurried back to the store. Starting to dial Arthur's business number, not even aware that she was breaking the promise she had made less than a day ago, she noticed a message Midge had scrawled for her lying on the desk:

Bev, your husband called. He'll be home tonight, and he says he's got wonderful news.

Bev put down the receiver without completing the call.

14

That same afternoon Sylvia Schlesinger was experiencing something fairly rare for her: a feeling of guilt. She looked again at the afternoon paper on her desk. She'd finished her usual business lunch, with a manufacturer arranging for the models she and Bev had bought to be reproduced, and as always after a long and demanding business session she had allowed herself the small treat of glancing at the gossip columns before returning to the rest of the afternoon's work.

The item jumped out of Kilgallen's column. As Sylvia read it, she felt her cheeks flushing. This was no hot flash resulting from her age, she knew, but absolute and unmistakable embarrassment. Oh, God, she thought, what have I done? I practically threw that girl into his arms, and now look!

She read the few sentences again.

Arthur Powers, millionaire Lothario of the textile business and currently between wives, was seen having lunch with a new face yesterday. Insiders in the rag trade claim not to know his pretty companion, but a little bird whispered to me that Welby's must be giving one of its junior buyers longer lunch hours. Picking up something retail, Arthur? Or is it a new Mrs. P.?

Sylvia groaned out loud. That witch, she thought. Kilgallen did everything but spell out Bev's name. A fling in Paris, well and good, that hurt nobody, although only Sylvia knew that the meetings between Bev and Arthur were as innocent as the young woman proclaimed. But this . . . an item in the most widely read gossip column in America! Everybody who knew Bev would begin guessing. She wondered if Bev had

179

seen the column and suspected she hadn't. Twisting a fresh cigarette into her gold holder, she reached for her phone. After all, she had practically forced Bev into the lunch; she'd better be the one to break the news to her that most of their world of fashion was already speculating about exactly who Arthur Powers had with him . . . and what he got in return.

'Sylvia, don't be so upset.'

Bev looked at her boss, the newspaper still in her lap. She hadn't expected to be summoned to Sylvia's office this afternoon. They were both too busy preparing the French imports for production for a friendly chat, and Bev was more concerned when she got the call that she had made some error in the days since their return from Europe. She had gone over her business activities hastily as she rode up to the executive floor, and she was fairly sure she had handled all the jobs assigned to her as the older woman would have wanted. It was almost a relief to discover that the reason for the abrupt conference was only a blind item in a newspaper.

'Bev, I was an idiot. I should have known you couldn't be seen in that place with Arthur Powers without word getting out.'

'They don't mention my name, Sylvia. There are—what —twenty junior buyers here at Welby's?'

'None of them is Arthur Powers's type.'

'And neither am I.' Bev found herself smiling. Sylvia's concern was genuine, but it seemed slightly absurd to Bev. She had too many other things of importance to worry about today. 'Sylvia, listen. Even if they had printed my name, so what? We weren't necking between courses. It was a perfectly proper luncheon.'

'And later? You didn't get back until almost three.'

Bev found herself blushing. She had been glad the past days at the store had been so busy for the two of them that she had not had to discuss what had happened later: the unexpected and expensive gift she had had to refuse, his questions, and the offer of the new apartment.

'All right, Sylvia, I might as well tell you everything.' She told the other woman as quickly and concisely as she could of what Arthur had done and said. Sylvia listened impassively, making no interruption until Bev was through.

'God!' she said finally, in what sounded suspiciously like a moan. 'I didn't know I had gotten you in that deep.'

'Sylvia, you haven't gotten me into anything. The apartment is terrific. I can afford it—well, Eddie and I can afford it,' she added defensively. 'Arthur doesn't own the building, he's not involved. I don't even have to see him again if I don't want to.'

'And do you? Want to see him again?'

'I don't know.'

Bev got up restlessly and moved to the window of Sylvia's office. Although Welby's wasn't a skyscraper, the view from the top floor was impressive. The city lay before her, busy, energetic, full of people finishing the last hour of their workday. Soon the lights would go on in the fashionable apartment buildings all along the East Side, signaling a new night of parties, theater-going, elegant restaurants. Arthur's world, Bev thought. Not mine. Mine is to be home waiting for Eddie, hearing about the new job, pretending once more to be full of hope and excitement that this time things will really work out between us.

'I don't know, Sylvia,' she said again. 'I'm attracted to Arthur, I couldn't lie to you about that even if I wanted to. He's strong and exciting and—all right, a little glamorous. I like being with him. He seems to like being with me. How long that could last without our becoming lovers, I don't know. I don't fool myself that it's some great romance. I was just around when he was recovering from Marilyn. His ego was hurt; she didn't want him, she didn't even like being with him. But she's like some gloriously beautiful swan. And what am I? A sparrow, I guess.'

'A sparrow that keeps saying no,' remarked Sylvia dryly.

'For the moment, believe it or not, that's all I have been saying. How much longer I can hold out if we went on seeing each other, I'm not sure.'

'And then? Bev, you don't have any idea that if you divorce Ed, Arthur Powers is going to marry you?'

'Of course not, Sylvia.' Bev knew she sounded almost impatient. 'Marriage has never been discussed. He doesn't want it and neither do I.'

'Then what is it, Bev? Look, I'm not trying to pry. We talked about having a fling . . . it can liven up a marriage. But I meant something discreet, something out-of-town,

181

where nobody can get hurt and you can return to home base afterward with nothing changed. If you and Arthur start being seen around New York together, how much longer can it stay discreet? Even if the sparrow continues to say no?'

'Sylvia, I know all that! I've told Arthur we don't belong in each other's lives. I'm a married woman. I take that seriously.' Bev sighed. 'I guess I'm just saying if I weren't married, if I were free, I'd be wondering what to wear tonight and where we'd go for dinner and being more than a little excited about what would happen afterward.'

'And after the "afterward"? Listen to me, Bev. I've been around that track. The big dazzling love affair, no ties, everybody's free to be anything they want, go where they want. Only sooner or later you have to go back to your own home, and I think you'll find if there's no Ed there it can get damned lonely.'

'I know, Sylvia. Only sometimes you can be more alone even if somebody is there.'

'You mean if they're not the right somebody? Well, I can't argue with that. It took two husbands and a lot of other men before I found my Herman.'

Bev smiled. She could see the older woman was genuinely concerned. It gave her a good feeling to know she had one friend she could count on, no matter what the future held. 'Sylvia, stop worrying. By tomorrow there'll be a whole new column of gossip and all this will be forgotten. Ed will be back, the new job will be glorious, he'll love the new apartment, and Mr. Arthur Powers will be seen with some new face, undoubtedly more attractive than mine.'

'You really believe that? Or is it what you want to believe? Listen, Bev, you may be very smart about what the young women of America are going to want to wear—and you are. That's why I've been pushing for you to get ahead; you have a real feel for your work. But about men, I don't think you know as much as the dumbest college freshman.'

'I'm not totally without experience.' Unwillingly, Bev saw the faces of Frank and Neil. And then Ed, kind, patient Ed. . . .

There was something almost sad in her voice which Sylvia picked up instantly. 'I'm not saying that you haven't had your share of romantic problems. I'm just saying I don't think you know very much about the male psychology.' Sylvia lit another cigarette. 'Look, Bev, if you had gone to bed with Arthur in Paris . . . okay, I'd say no harm done and he probably would go on to somebody else. But you said no —and I believe you,' she added hastily. 'But that makes you something he hasn't owned yet, hasn't enjoyed. And if he's trying to get Marilyn out of his mind, "no" is about the most inflammatory word you can say to Arthur Powers. He's going to keep after you until he gets you, if it takes perfume, mirrors, apartments. . . .' Sylvia found herself unexpectedly laughing. Bev stared at her, puzzled for a moment, but as the older woman's laugh continued, she found herself joining in. 'My God, Bev, what do you think he's going to come up with next? I mean, what's left? Your own department store?'

'Sylvia!' By now she was laughing as hard as her boss. 'He's not going to come up with anything. I mean it. He's respected the limits I've placed so far. And that's as far as it's going to go.'

'Don't be so sure,' said Sylvia, suddenly serious again. 'I know a lot more about men like Arthur Powers than you do. If you think he's going to respect your marriage or Ed or what gossip can do to your reputation, you'd better do a little more thinking. You are his target at the moment, and no other woman is going to catch his eye until he adds your pretty little scalp to his belt.'

'My God, Sylvia, are you saying if I want to keep my marriage I should have gone to bed with Arthur, just to get him off my track?'

'I know it sounds crazy, but—'

'Crazy . . . and maybe a little negative?' For the first time since she had come into the office, Bev felt in charge of the situation. 'Did it ever occur to you that I might be good in bed? And that he might want more of the same?'

Sylvia gave her a wry smile. 'No matter what I suggest, I seem to get into worse trouble, don't I?' She took the newspaper from Beverly and deliberately dropped it into her wastebasket. 'Okay, Mrs. Richmond. I'll stop playing Mother Hen. You're a grown woman, and I guess you know how to handle your life better than I do. I just wish Kilgallen hadn't zeroed in on you so publicly.'

'You're making too much of it, Sylvia. There isn't a person

in New York who'll think anything of it. Or even remember it by the time they put the paper down.'

Only Bev was wrong. In different parts of New York several people she knew had read the column and not only guessed her identity but had come to their own conclusions about what was happening. In her smart dress shop, Marion read the column over and over again and found to her surprise that she grew angrier with each reading. She knew of Arthur Powers and his reputation, she and José had even seen him several times with his various ladies, and there was never any doubt in their minds what their relationship was. How could Bev had fallen for such an obvious wolf? She was wise enough to realize she wasn't just angry at her sister-in-law but at herself, for the way she had led her own life, the example she may have set Bev of the joy of freedom. And to her surprise she was also deeply, bitterly angry at Ed, knowing, without the details, that what she had predicted had happened, that he was the cause of the failure of his marriage.

Angela Thyson also read the column. There was no question in her mind that the girl mentioned was Beverly, although she hadn't the faintest idea who this Arthur Powers was. If he was in textiles it was probably a harmless business luncheon. Bev would never deceive a nice boy like Ed. She corrected herself silently. A nice *man* like Ed. Still, there was no point in alarming Beverly's father. She cut the whole page from the paper and, folding it into a neat little square, placed it at the bottom of the garbage can.

Jane Richmond read the column on the bus on her way home from work. She seldom bothered with the afternoon papers, but the woman sitting next to her had left the paper behind and as she still had fifteen blocks to travel she had picked it up. Like her daughter, Jane knew instantly that the girl referred to must be Beverly, and her heart sank. Don't let anything serious have happened, she prayed silently to herself as the bus continued uptown. Don't let it be important. Don't let it be anything more than idle gossip. And please, God, don't let Ed find out, he'd be so hurt.

Across town, on the East Side, two other people reacted in totally different ways. Ruth Eliason heard about the column at lunch. Two of the girls she and Beverly had gone to school with asked her out at the last minute, and it was only as the lunch progressed that she realized they had read the column and were anxious to pump her for every bit of information she might have about the rumor. Ruth sat through the meal stunned and a little sickened, trying unsuccessfully to change the subject each time it was brought up, stressing how little she knew about Bev's job at Welby's and whether it entitled meals with important millionaires. She also added, whenever she could, how attractive Ed was and how happy Beverly was in her marriage. But when the lunch was over she left by herself as quickly as possible, refusing a ride, determined to walk home alone. Only when she was safely out of sight of the other women's prying eyes did she find her own were suddenly full of tears.

Arthur Powers read the column while he was being given his weekly trim by his barber. The item was no surprise. The columnist, always thorough, had called him personally the night before to check on the identity of his luncheon companion. Without exactly revealing Beverly's name, he had revealed enough to arouse Kilgallen's curiosity. He'd counted on that. The next move would be Bev's, he thought. He found himself smiling.

Bev had not been home more than five minutes when the phone calls started, first from Ruth and then from her mother. Suddenly she was forced to realize that Sylvia had not been overreacting after all. Keeping her voice calm, she reassured her mother and then Ruth that while she was indeed the woman referred to, nothing but business had been discussed and she couldn't imagine how anyone could have misinterpreted it so crudely. Only when Jane called did she allow her defenses to slip slightly.

'He's just a casual friend, Jane,' she said on the phone. She glanced at the clock. It was well after seven by now, and the message she had received earlier from Midge had not said when Eddie was due back. The one thing she didn't want was for him to come in when she was explaining the column to his mother. That damn luncheon, she thought. What a fool I was! Everyone must have seen what I was feeling on my face.

'I met him with Sylvia in Europe. He's a very important manufacturer.' She decided suddenly to turn the incident to her advantage. 'Actually, Jane, he has friends in the real estate business. He had some suggestions for a new apartment for Ed and me, well within our budget, especially if Eddie has this new job. And we have been a little cramped here.'

'Of course,' said Jane, trying to let herself be convinced. 'It's a cute apartment for a single girl, but you and Ed really need something larger.' She hesitated a moment. 'When is Eddie due back?'

'Tonight, I don't know exactly what time. And I haven't done a thing yet about dinner.'

'I'll let you go then. And Bev,' she added, 'I'll be hoping the news is good.'

'Thanks, Jane. I'm sure it will be.'

Eddie Richmond had never felt happier in his life. As he rode up the elevator to the apartment, he knew he must be grinning with pleasure. So much had happened in just a couple of days. He had seen a whole new life, one he knew Bev and he could build a future in. George and his wife, Mary Jo, had been warm and hospitable, but more than that . . . It's this damn city, he thought as he struggled for his keys, holding his suitcase and the roses he had bought for Bev in one hand. That's always been the problem.

Bev greeted him warmly as he came in, pleased at the roses in his hand, and as she moved about, arranging them, he looked at her lovingly. She's thinner, he thought, and her eyes looked a little tired. He found himself remembering the soft-cheeked, bright-eyed girl of the day of their marriage. Part of the change was his fault, he knew. But he brushed that thought aside. Everything was going to be better now.

'Tell me about it,' she said, curling up on the sofa beside him. 'Or are you hungry? I haven't had much chance to do anything about dinner.'

'It's all right. They fed us on the plane.'

'And the job? Did you get it?'

'I've got it.' He accepted her quick embrace with pleasure, and any further discussion might have been delayed if she had not pulled back deliberately.

'Come on! Tell me everything. When do you start? What, actually, will you be doing? Are you going to have to set up a whole new office, or does this friend of yours have something here already?'

186

'Hey! Hold on!' For a moment, he was silent. So much had happened since he had left her, he realized she was totally ignorant of his new plans. 'Bev, the job we thought he wanted me to do—you know, a New York office for his air-cargo route? Well, we talked it over. I went over his figures with him, and while he wants to expand, it's more feasible at the moment to keep it strictly a Midwest operation.'

Her eyes were suddenly very serious. 'But . . . the job. You said you had it.'

'I have. Something better. George showed me all over his operation. He's got a fleet of seven planes, two more on order. Access to nearly fifteen small cities that aren't on any major trade routes, plus two planes for intercity passenger travel. It's a growing operation, and it's going to get bigger.'

'But what will you be doing?'

'That's the good part. I explained to him I don't have any money to invest, so I couldn't very well ask to become his partner or anything as grand as that. Not yet, at least. But he needs somebody to be in charge of the operation—the day-to-day work with the planes and the pilots—while he's out hustling new customers. Bev, it's perfect for me. For once I can really use what I've learned, the things I know and care about. And the salary's good. Not,' he added hastily, 'what we thought, by New York standards. But, Bev, you don't need that kind of money out there.'

'Out there?' she repeated. Suddenly she felt as if she had swallowed a cold stone. 'What are you talking about?'

'The new job. Bev, you're going to love it. They live in a section called Chestnut Hills. It's about thirty-five miles south of St. Louis, so you have all the advantages of a big city when and if you want them, plus the feeling of a small town.' He smiled a little. 'Although I don't think it's going to be a small town forever. George is predicting in ten years it'll probably be a suburb of the city. He's already got plans for real-estate developing. Land is still dirt cheap. I can get in on that too.'

He hugged her enthusiastically.

'Oh, Bev, it's a whole different way of living out there. I never realized it before. Hell, I've always lived in New York except for my days as a flyboy. Like everybody else here, I thought this city was the be-all and end-all of everything.

187

Well, it isn't! If you could see how George and his wife, Mary Jo, live! They've got this big old Victorian house that they're fixing up.' He grinned again, not noticing the look on Bev's face. 'Mary Jo says they do over another room with each year of profits. You'll love her, Bev. Even with their two kids she keeps up with the fashions, reads all the magazines. She showed me a couple of houses in the neighborhood that we could get cheap. . . . Bev.' His face grew serious. 'Bev, it was like I had suddenly come home. After all these years of wandering, I'd suddenly found the place where I belonged —where we both belong,' he added hastily.

'Ed, wait a minute. Are you saying you want us to move to someplace outside of St. Louis . . . just like that?' She snapped her fingers. He looked at her, puzzled. 'Ed, can you really be serious?'

'Of course I am. Bev, look, a lot of the things that have been wrong with our marriage have been my fault. I'd say ninety-five percent, maybe more. You married a man who was supposed to be your husband. Who was supposed to support you, take care of you, love you, and build a family with you. I haven't done that. You've said sometimes, when you couldn't keep it in any longer, that it was a lack of ambition. And I guess you were right. Only I realized flying in tonight it became more than that. It wasn't that I wasn't ambitious. I wasn't even functioning. Not as the breadwinner of the family.' He paused and looked at her before saying the one thing neither one of them had discussed in the past couple of years. 'Nor was I functioning very much as a man. It was beautiful the way we used to make love. Lately—well, isn't it time we faced it? I haven't been very good at that either.'

'And moving to St. Louis is going to change that?' she asked flatly.

'It can. Bev, it's a whole new beginning. I felt like a human being out there, I felt alive in a way I haven't felt in years. It's a job I know I can do. George is as confident as I am. There are good schools, plenty of room between the houses. Bev, it's starting to be spring out there already; there's green on the trees. We could start a garden, have our own vegetables and flowers by summer. It's . . . it's . . .' He stopped, trying to find the right words.

'It's Australia again,' Bev answered coldly. She moved

away from him. For one intense moment she honestly thought she would reach out and claw his face if he said another word.

'What?'

'You know what I mean. Another wild idea.'

'Bev, no! We'd be in our own country, with our own people. Our kids will be going to American schools.'

'Do you have a contract with George?'

He looked at her, his eyes hurt, as if she had slapped him. 'No, of course not.'

'So if it doesn't work out, he could fire you at any time, right?'

'Bev, he's a friend of mine.'

'Eddie! What kind of a friend is it that you haven't seen in over five years? I don't remember our sending Christmas cards to him. He wasn't invited to our wedding.'

He shifted uneasily. 'Bev, guys don't always keep up with each other the way women do. But he's a good buddy. He wouldn't go back on his word. And,' he added defensively, 'he won't have to. I can do this job, I know I can. It's not like being stuck in some office all day long, trying to be nice to people I can't stand, shuffling a pile of papers, not knowing what they are or caring, just knowing some more hours of my life have gone by that I hated to live through.'

'There's routine with every job, Ed. You think I don't know that?'

'Yeah, but it doesn't bother you. Bev, I can't stand it. I never could. I tried, because it seemed important to you. I wanted you to be happy. But I wasn't making you happy, was I? Let's be honest about that. I wasn't, was I?'

Silently, she shook her head.

'Now I have a chance. Bev, all the things we've talked about, dreamed about—we can have them now. A home, a future . . . and a family.' He planted his feet squarely as he faced her. 'I want that, Bev. I don't want to go through life just being Uncle Eddie to Ruth's kids or somebody else's. I want my own. And I want them with you.'

'That's going to be a little difficult, isn't it, if you're in St. Louis and I'm here in New York?'

For a moment they stared at each other in silence, both of them a little shaken by the coldness in her voice.

'Bev, I want you with me.' Eddie's voice was quiet, calm.

But there was no element of pleading in his words. Perhaps, Bev would think later, that was the thing that finally snapped her anger into the fury she never would have believed possible she held. He wasn't asking her, he was *telling* her.

'You want me with you,' she began. 'You want me to come with you to a strange city, to quit my job, to rely on you to support not only the two of us but a family, just because you want to get back to playing with airplanes again? You can make a decision like that by yourself, after four years of marriage, just as if I were some piece of furniture or a slave you can drag around anyplace you want to go? There aren't telephone lines between St. Louis and New York? You couldn't even call me?'

By now she could feel her body quivering with rage. She barely heard him interrupt.

'Bev, this wasn't something I could tell you on the phone.'

'No. But it was something you could decide by yourself. When am I expected to go?' she added bitterly. 'Tomorrow? The end of the week? Just walk out of Welby's, the position I've made for myself—the position, I might add, that has supported you in some comfort the last five years?'

'Bev, there are other jobs.' He could feel his anger rising to match hers. 'There's a department store in the town. Mary Jo was sure with your experience you could get a job there if you wanted to, after the kids were in school.'

'Mary Jo! My God, I never thought I could hate somebody I've never met. Mary Jo, with her garden and her magazines that keep her up to date and her prospect of getting me a job . . . doing what? Behind a counter selling stockings?' She raised her chin defiantly. 'Ed, I'm worth more than that. I'm better than that!'

'Bev, I'm taking this job.' The anger had disappeared from him. He was simply stating facts in a way Bev had never seen him do. 'I want you to come with me. I want you to be my wife. I can't imagine ever loving any other woman but you. But I am taking this job.'

'With or without me?'

'I have to, Bev. I have a funny feeling this is my last chance to have any kind of life that I can consider worth living.'

This was an Ed she had never seen before, not in the days of their courting, not in all the ups and downs of their married life. It was the man she had prayed he would

190

become, and now that it had finally happened she found she couldn't even bear to be in the same room with him. It was the hardest moment she had ever lived through, the hardest truth she had ever learned about herself, but with the courage that had never failed her, she faced it squarely.

'Ed, I'm not going to St. Louis with you,' she said quietly. 'I know it's what you want, I can see it in your face. I even think it's possible you may be right, that it is the right place for you, that the job will be all you want it to be.'

'What does that mean? I don't have a wife unless I stay here?'

'No. That would be threatening you. And I don't think either one of us would want that. I only know I've worked hard to get where I am, and I'm only on the first step of the ladder. I want to go further. I want . . . I guess, *more*.'

'You couldn't find a job in St. Louis? It's only thirty-five miles.'

They were talking like two strangers, she thought, planning a trip. 'I suppose I could. Maybe, with luck, in the same field. Only supposing this didn't work out, and the next old friend you contacted was from Seattle. Do I move there and start all over again a third time?' Her mouth tightened. 'Ed, I don't intend to be a salesgirl at forty.'

There was no look of a little boy in his face now. His eyes were steady and calm, as if they were looking into her heart and mind for the first time. 'Do you intend to be a mother by then? Or did you ever intend to quit your job long enough to have a family?'

Stung, she lashed back. 'Ed, that's not fair! Only today I looked at a new apartment, one we could afford, larger. It even has a room for a nursery. With a terrific view of the East River.'

'Damn it, I don't want a view of the East River! I want a wife! Now, do I have one or don't I?'

She could make no answer. Ed realized there really wasn't any need to. Her silence was enough. He picked up his suitcase and his coat. 'A good thing I didn't unpack,' he said, almost to himself. 'I'll be at my mother's until the end of the week if you want to think it over. Or talk to me. Only we don't seem to have anything left to say, do we? Maybe we never did.'

He hesitated, as if for one moment he wanted to come

near her, to reach out and hold her, but he stopped himself. She was to remember that moment for a long time, long after the door closed behind him and she heard the elevator going down. She was to remember it for years.

15

When she thought about it afterward, Bev was always a little surprised at how soundly and well she slept that night. According to all the movies and love stories she had been exposed to, she should have been pacing back and forth for hours, struggling with tears. It was only a long time later, when analysis had become so popular with New Yorkers that everything was discussed by everyone openly at every dinner party, that she realized what had happened to her that night. She had made up her mind. And as with any decision she made in her life, whether right or wrong, the making of it left her free and relaxed, rather as if she had cut through a tangle of ropes that had trapped her and were pulling her down.

Quite calmly, she called Miss Lockley as soon as she reached the store the next morning and told her she would take the apartment on the river. It would be a stretch, carrying the rent all by herself, but not that much of one. Arthur had probably counted on that. She asked the real estate woman to make out the lease and told her she would stop by her office at lunch to sign it. Almost as an afterthought, she added, 'Oh, and Miss Lockley, will you make the lease out in my name, Beverly Richmond? Not Mr. and Mrs. Edward Richmond.'

'Of course, Mrs. Richmond, but—'

'My husband may be traveling for a while, and I think, until our plans are settled, the lease had better be in my name.'

'I understand.' Miss Lockley put down the phone. Another marriage breaking up, she thought. What is the matter with young girls today? Without ever having met or seen the absent Mr. Richmond, she sided with him. At thirty-seven, she had learned that any husband was not easy to find. Her good years had been wasted in the Depression, when no man she cared about could afford to marry her, and then by the war, when they had all gone away. Well, she'd made a decent life for herself with her own agency, and there were worse evenings than dinner with girl friends. She started typing up the lease and within five minutes had forgotten Beverly. Except she had seemed such a nice young thing. . . .

The rest of the day Bev was too busy to have time to think of anything but the store. The first proofs of the fashion magazines had arrived, and she and Sylvia had a glorious hour of triumph when they realized that all the most expensive models they had chosen were going to be featured in the next issue. Full pages, most of them in color. It was clearly a big success for them; and Sylvia, for once not even thinking about Bev or her own private life, hurried the proofs up to the president of Welby's.

'Bev, this is going to mean a raise for both of us,' she said as she went out the door, her eyes gleaming. 'Or else!'

That would solve one problem, Bev thought, as she picked up her purse and started for the real estate office. She knew that only when she finally signed the new lease would she feel secure. When she came back, after having grabbed a quick sandwich, with the crisp paper in her purse next to the new keys, she found several messages from Jane. She took a deep breath before calling Jane at her store. It had to be done and she knew it, and as always with the things she disliked doing, she forced herself to face them directly, without delay.

'Jane? Sorry to call you at work, but I got your messages.'

'I should have waited until tonight, I suppose. When you were home.' The older woman's voice sounded diffident. Not sad or angry, but rather as if she were resigned to the situation, had perhaps already faced the pain involved a long time before. 'Ed told me what happened.'

'Jane, I'm sorry. I really don't think it's anything we can talk about on the phone. These are working hours, and anyone might come in at any time. And I'm not too eager to announce this right now.'

'Then you're not planning anything . . . immediate?'

For a moment Bev stared at the phone puzzled, not sure

what her mother-in-law meant. 'You mean, like a divorce?' she asked at last.

'I guess that's what I meant.' Jane sounded a little tentative now. 'Ed seems quite determined to go back to St. Louis for this new job. And I think I know how you feel.'

'Jane, I signed a lease for a new apartment at lunchtime. It's bigger than what we have now, but I don't think even if Ed changed his mind it would be big enough for the two of us.'

'Your marriage is really over?'

'I hate to say it, but I'm afraid so. But I'm not planning on doing anything about it. Not now. I think that would be rather foolish on both our parts.'

'There isn't anyone else, is there?'

Bev found herself smiling a little cynically. Sylvia had been right. News did get around. 'You mean like a "millionaire textile Lothario"? No, Jane. There isn't anybody else. That isn't really what this is about, and I think we both know that. I hope Ed does too,' she added.

'He only knows that he was extremely foolish to make this decision without you. That hurts him. He really is sorry, Bev. We talked about it a long time last night. But I'm honestly convinced he feels he has to do this.'

'I know he is, Jane. And I don't want to stand in his way.'

'Only you won't let him stand in yours either, is that right?'

'Jane, I really can't talk any longer. Tell Ed I wish him luck. I have no intention of doing anything . . . legal.' For a moment she saw her parents' faces, the look of sadness that would appear in her father's eyes, the horrified exclamations from Angela at the word 'divorce.' 'Maybe in six months or so, Ed and I will know a little bit more about how we both feel. If anything should be decided, we can talk about it then.'

'I'll tell him that, Bev,' said Jane softly. 'I think it'll make him feel better. Give him a little . . . hope as he starts this new job.'

For the first time since Ed had left the previous night, Bev felt tears forming in her eyes. She loved Jane; she'd been kind and wise and understanding far more than her own mother had ever been. 'Jane? I hope this doesn't mean I won't see you. I'd miss having you as a mother-in-law . . . and as a friend.'

'Don't worry, Bev. I'll be here whenever you need me.'
With that, she put down the phone. Luckily, she had a long
afternoon ahead of her. That would give her time to think of
the right words to tell her son, to offer him hope for a future
that might just possibly contain both this new position and
the wife he loved. She'd find the right words. She'd always
found them before.

Bev did not go back to her own apartment when she left
the store that night. Determinedly, she turned east and
started along 57th Street toward the new apartment. If she
had been a more reflective person she might have considered
each step as one toward her future, each one taking her from
the world and the security of the rules that had fought so
hard to form her. Instead, her mind was full of practical
considerations: how much was in her slim savings account,
how much of a raise might come through with the success of
the buying trip, which of the few pieces of furniture she had
picked with such loving care years before for her first
apartment she would want to bring with her now. Not very
much, she thought. What had Arthur said in London about
emotions clinging to furniture long after the people who had
lived with it had died? She hadn't much liked that thought at
the time, and she didn't like it any better now. A new life,
that was what she wanted, with new surroundings.

As always, her sharp eye for color and design was drawn to
the shop windows along the wide street. Antique furniture,
gleaming with years of polish, swaths of brightly colored
brocades for walls and drapes, thick carpets. These, she
thought. These are what I want to have, how I want to make
my world. She smiled a little at the thought, knowing her
meager budget probably wouldn't buy an ashtray in one of
these stores. But I'll have them, she thought. Someday.
Someday soon. The thought came into her mind swiftly that
without Ed to support she could put quite a bit away in the
next six months. In the meantime, she would make do.
Maybe one of the decorators at the store could help. Some of
the boys who worked on the display windows were ambitious, she knew. They all got along with her easily, maybe
because she looked young and vulnerable, although common
sense and the gossip she couldn't help hearing told her that
probably none of them was interested in her as a woman. Not

that it mattered to her. The last thing in the world she wanted at the moment was to get involved in the whole business of dating again.

Which brought her to Arthur. She stopped, waiting for the lights to change so she could cross First Avenue. For once, she had to admit, her courage had failed her. She should have called him right away, she knew that: yesterday after seeing the apartment, this afternoon when she had signed the lease. Only she hadn't. Anything she said he was bound to take as some kind of an invitation, and she wasn't ready to handle that yet. Probably he already knew. Miss Lockley must have told the owner of the building that she had taken the apartment, and he, being a friend of Arthur's, presumably would have called him. She'd telephone him at the office tomorrow, she thought, as she walked toward the end of the street, pleading that she hadn't wanted to say anything until she actually had the keys to the apartment in her hand. During business hours there wouldn't be much chance for him to ask about Ed, so she could keep the conversation light and impersonal. One thing she had already determined: This new apartment was not going to be some kind of a second home for Arthur, even if he wanted it to be. She'd had that before with Frank and all these years with Ed. This was going to be *her* home, no one else's, and if other people were there it would be because she had specifically invited them, not because they felt they had any proprietary right to be there.

She turned into the entrance of the building. A white-haired man wearing a doorman's uniform smiled and opened the door for her. She smiled back and introduced herself as the new tenant. His smile grew broader, and he accompanied her to the elevator full of suggestions of things she should know about the building and offering to be of help anytime she needed it. A good beginning, she thought as she rode up, and wondered if she had enough in her purse to tip him when she came down. She didn't want to start off on the wrong foot.

The apartment was even more attractive than she had remembered it. She walked slowly through the rooms, already furnishing them in her imagination. How wonderful to have space for things, she thought, surveying the deep closets with pleasure. To be able to buy a long sofa and not have to worry if there would be room to fit it in, to have her

197

clothes for the different seasons put neatly away and still have room for all the rest of her belongings. Things I don't even own yet, she thought wryly, and realized how much her life had been fashioned by the small space she had lived in these past years.

The wall-to-wall carpet in the living room was almost new, she realized when she finally settled in the living room on the step leading up to the bay window that looked out onto the river. She should have felt lonely or frightened at this step she had taken, but as on the previous day when she had first seen the place, she felt relaxed and completely at home.

When the doorbell rang she was not even surprised. Probably the man from downstairs with more advice, or maybe Miss Lockley, or even a first visit from neighbors. . . .

But when she opened the door she saw Arthur Powers.

'May I come in?'

'Arthur! What on earth . . . yes, of course, if you want to.' She stepped aside, letting him pass her. For a moment she felt a dart of anger that he had dared to presume, dared to arrive so blatantly in what she already considered to be her home. But there was no point in offending him. He'd been a good friend and, in his own way, had behaved honorably in all their meetings. And she could hardly continue to keep him at arm's length. Only that's where you're going to stay, she thought as she closed the door behind him. I don't come with this apartment, if that's what you have in mind.

Almost as if he could read her thoughts, he smiled somewhat shyly. 'I pass this apartment on my way home. I saw the lights on and wondered who had taken the place. I hoped it was you.'

'On your way home?' She raised a skeptical eyebrow. 'Do you have a houseboat on the East River? That's the only thing farther down the street.'

He laughed. 'All right. I'm lying. I knew you'd signed the lease. And I had a feeling you were avoiding telling me. So I decided it was time for the mountain to come to Mahomet.'

Now it was her turn to be embarrassed. He had, as he so often did, seen through her silence and the reasons for it. 'Come and take a look at the place. It's magnificent. Or it will be in time,' she added.

'Has your husband seen it yet?' he asked cautiously as he

put down his hat and the package he had been carrying on the bare window seat.

'No. Come take a look. There's a bedroom and heaps of closets. A real kitchen. Maid's room, bath . . .'

'I know the apartment,' Arthur said. He hadn't moved or taken his eyes off her since he had put down his things. 'I used to know the woman who lived here.'

So that was it. She wondered briefly who the woman had been—some girl friend or mistress, perhaps. It was time to disillusion him about the future status of the place and its tenant.

'She was my cousin.' He stepped closer, smiling a little at the confusion he saw in her eyes. 'No, Bev, this place doesn't have any romantic memories for me, if that's what you're thinking.'

'It crossed my mind. I'm afraid I haven't anything to offer you—'

'I have.' He unwrapped the package he had brought, bringing out a frosty bottle of champagne and two carefully wrapped glasses. The glasses, she noticed, were wrapped in the distinctive packaging of Tiffany's. Right down the street, she thought with some amusement. My neighborhood store.

'I thought . . . a small housewarming present.' Without waiting for her permission, he uncorked the bottle and poured it into the two long-stemmed glasses. 'The first of many presents, if you'll let me.'

'Arthur, I think we'd better get something straight right now.'

'Not just yet. First we toast the apartment.' Almost solemnly he handed her a glass and raised his own. 'To your new life, Bev. To your new home. And to your happiness.' He touched their glasses and took a deep swallow. In silence Bev did the same. She had had no champagne since the last time they had been together at lunch, and before that, Paris. A swarm of memories floated in her mind, and as she sipped from her glass she found herself looking at Arthur directly, seeing him as he really was. Not the powerful millionaire whose very presence brought her mixed feelings of desire and guilt, but simply an attractive man who cared for her, who had her interests at heart, who respected her and desired her and yet had never gone beyond the boundaries she herself had set. This was no greedy boy demanding a kiss

199

and as much else as he could get in return for buying her dinner. This was not even a man like Ed who could worship her but in the end would only make the decisions that gave him happiness. Never before had she met anyone like Arthur, and she was wise enough, standing there that late afternoon, to know she was not likely to meet anyone like him again. Ruthless? Of course. Determined to get his own way? She had never doubted that. But she realized they were a great deal alike, both of them single-minded, both of them trying to be fair and considerate of anyone they dealt with, but both determined to have exactly what they wanted, when they wanted it, fair or not.

It had to be faced at last. She knew it. She walked over to the mantelpiece where she had placed her purse. 'You only brought two glasses,' she said, breaking the silence between them. 'Wouldn't it have looked a little odd if Ed had been here with me?'

'No. I would have made the present to the two of you. And walked right back out the door.'

'For good?'

'No. Only until you were free. You are free now, aren't you?'

She kept her back to him. He had named the feeling she had had all day, using the one word she had not quite let herself even think. 'Yes,' she said. 'I'm free. Ed's going to St. Louis, the job's going to be there.'

'And you'll stay here.' It was a statement, not a question.

'Yes. It's not a divorce or anything. At least not yet. We don't know what our plans are going to be. It just seems better to wait for a while until we know if this job is going to be permanent.' Silly to put it like that, she thought. He must know I've signed the lease for three years.

'Only where does that leave you?' he asked quietly. 'On a very long string? Or really free?'

She looked at the gold ring on her finger, the ring Ed had put there four years before. Still with her back to him, she took the ring off her finger and slipped it into her purse. If she was going to start fresh, it wasn't just furniture she would need to leave behind.

'I think the string is cut, Arthur. For good.' She faced him now, holding out her glass. 'Could I have some more of that lovely champagne?'

He poured it for her. Then, setting down the bottle and his own glass deliberately, he put his arms around her. 'Don't be afraid, Bev,' he said softly. 'This doesn't change things. Not unless you want them changed.'

'But I do.' She could look up into his eyes. They were darker than she had ever seen them before, and his body, pressed tight against hers, was strong and alive with desire.

'I want you,' he said, barely whispering. 'I want you now.' He pressed his mouth against hers almost fiercely, his hands moving down her body, touching her intimately, holding her, moving with skillful authority over every part of her, still with his lips pressed against hers, open enough to let the tip of his tongue touch hers, sensing her initial shock, then sliding between her lips, warm and moist and tender.

She had known it was going to happen, had known it perhaps since the moment she had decided to take the apartment, but never had she allowed herself to imagine it happening like this: his hands loosening her clothes, his fingers moving past the nylon of her underwear until he could feel the secret place that gave the lie to any denial that she wanted him as much as he wanted her.

He stopped then, moving away from her calmly to turn out the one bare light in the empty room. She had removed her blouse and skirt by the time he had returned through the shadows, and had stretched their coats out on the thick carpet in front of the empty fireplace. He undressed swiftly in the darkness and lay down naked beside her. Even in the half-light she could see he was ready for her.

'Now, Beverly,' he whispered, his lips gentle and light as they moved across her face, down to her breasts. 'Now. . . .'

She could no more have refused him than she could have stopped breathing. Nor did she want to.

A mile north, Ruth let herself into her apartment. She'd had a restless day, working halfheartedly at her volunteer duties in the nearby hospital, taking a book cart around to the rooms of the patients, but her mind had not been on her activities. She'd been thinking about Bev, wondering about her future, knowing even from their brief telephone conversation the day before that something was seriously wrong. She debated calling her, but by now Ed would be back from his trip and they would want to be alone. She remembered sadly how it had been with Geoffrey. Good father as he had been, after his trips he needed time alone with her, time that they had both needed, that had added to the warmth and strength of their marriage. Now there would never be that time again for the two of them.

Instead of the silence she expected in the apartment, she heard squeals of laughter coming from the living room. Almost like the old days, she thought, startled for a moment. Almost like when Geoffrey was alive. She hurried down the hall to the living room. Rolling about on the floor were her three sons, engaged in some kind of wrestling match with Ed, all four of them pink in the face and laughing. It had been so long since she had heard them laugh like that. She was almost afraid to enter, knowing if she did the moment would be broken. Philip looked up and saw her hesitating in the doorway.

'Hey, Mom, look! Uncle Ed's here!' he shouted. He pulled himself free and ran to hug her. 'And he's got a great new job. He's going to be working with airplanes out in St. Louis someplace!'

In the babble of voices that followed, Ruth looked at Ed gratefully. The kindness he had shown her sons, all of them, but especially Philip! She would never forget that. There wasn't even any way to thank him. He had turned a frightened little boy, haunted by the death of his father, terrified of planes, into someone who could talk and laugh about them easily, almost as if he envied Ed the new job. But the job was supposed to be in New York, wasn't it?

Something in her face sobered Ed, and he stood, reluctantly freeing himself from her sons. 'Gang, I think it's time for your supper,' he announced. The boys protested, but he turned them over to Alma, the maid, who stood waiting at the doorway. 'Come on, you can't keep a pretty girl like Alma waiting.' Alma blushed as she always did when Ed was there. She was a shy girl, born in Yorkville and a present from Ruth's parents after Geoffrey died. 'To take over some of the work,' they had said, as if Ruth wouldn't have enjoyed having had even more to do to fill the empty hours.

'I'll come in and see you before I leave,' Ed promised as the boys were led away protesting.

'Ed? You said . . . a job in St. Louis?'

He nodded. 'Plans have been changed, Ruth. There's nothing much I could do for the firm here. And a lot I can do out there.'

'How does Bev feel about it?'

He hesitated. 'Ruth, I'm afraid it's all over between us.'

'Oh, no.' She said it so softly he didn't seem to hear her.

'Maybe not permanently. At least that's what I'm hoping. A very thin hope, I must say. But I need something to make me really try to get this job running smoothly. Maybe in six months I can get her to at least go out there, take a look at the place, see what our life could be like.' He signed heavily.

'She refused to go with you?'

'Yeah. I handled it with all my well-known grace and charm. Didn't even warn her, didn't ask her, didn't prepare her. Just sort of made it an ultimatum. And, Ruth, Beverly is not a girl you just tell things to.'

Oh, but she is, thought Ruth. She's wanted you to become strong, to make decisions. That's what she's wanted, needed from the very beginning! 'When do you have to go? Perhaps if you give her a little time—'

He cut her off abruptly. 'I'm going tonight. I'd told her the end of the week, but Ruth, I'm going to level with you. I'm afraid if I wait that long, if I think about it, if I start listening to people—you and my mother and, yes, maybe even Bev, if I could get her to talk to me—I might just cave in again. Do what's easy. Stay here. Try to find something else. Because I do love her. Inside me, I always will.' He sat down on the couch beside her. 'Only I can't let that happen, Ruth. I know what it would do to me. I've seen it happening these last couple of years, and it scares me.'

'You, Ed? Scared?'

'Sure, I know. Happy-go-lucky Ed. Only nobody's like that all the time, Ruth. I don't have to tell you what it's like to be unhappy. You've had more than your share. Well, I'm going through some of that too, and if I stay here I'm afraid it'll just get worse.'

He stood up, pacing the room restlessly.

'I don't belong in this city. I know it. I don't count the same things important that other people do. I don't want to live like them or talk like them or be like them. I want a simpler kind of life, with time for myself, for a family. I don't think a penthouse in the sky or the title of president of a corporation or having every headwaiter in town show me their best table means a hoot in hell.'

'Geoffrey felt like that too.'

'But he worked hard for it.'

'For the boys. For me. He wanted to make us happy. Secure.'

'Maybe if I'd had his family I'd feel that way too.' He stopped, his mouth tightening into a grim line. 'No. That's self-pitying and whining. I'm not going to use that as an excuse any more. That's one of the reasons why I have to go tonight. Ruth, I'm scared maybe I'm going to be trapped here. Maybe I know myself too well. Sometimes I feel like I can't breathe. Maybe because everybody's been too protective, too kind; it's like being smothered in cotton wool.'

'Ed, I can't believe it's over. I know how Bev feels about you. More important, I know that she needs you, more than she knows herself. You're decent and honest and good.' She thought for a second of the item she had read in the gossip column and wondered if Ed had seen it too. 'She won't find many men like that in New York.'

'Thanks, Ruth. But I don't deserve the kind words.' He stopped her with a gesture before she could interrupt. 'No, listen. Did you know I lied to Bev from the very beginning? I claimed I was doing some kind of executive work with an airline. I wasn't. I was a steward. And you know something, Ruth? I was happy being a steward. Only Bev would never have fallen in love with a guy like that, and I knew it. So I lied. From the very first date.'

How much that confession must have cost him, Ruth thought. 'It wouldn't have mattered to Bev.' But even as she said it, she knew she was lying and that Ed knew it, too.

'Maybe not for a guy she was dating. Maybe even a little love affair. But marriage? Never. Bev belongs in a different world, Ruth. She belongs with this city, maybe even this particular time of the century. I don't. And what makes it impossible between us is I don't even want to belong. So . . . I'm clearing out. I packed my bags this afternoon, left them at the terminal, and came here to say goodbye. I couldn't go without that.'

'Bev doesn't know?'

'I left a note.' He stepped closer, his eyes searching hers. 'Ruth? Will you keep an eye on her for me, please? You're her oldest and best friend. She'll listen to you. She may kick and struggle a little, but she'll listen.' His eyes were sad now. 'I don't want her to end up some hard-boiled career woman with a part-time man like my sister, Marion. I don't think anybody is meant to live like that. Bev's not used to stubbing her toes. And she will sooner or later, if there isn't something more than just her work and getting ahead to live for.'

Ruth tried to smile, but she knew he could see the effort it cost her. 'Ed, aren't you being a little . . . premature? If you both love each other, and this new job works out, in six months things could change. She might feel different about the store then, about New York. She wants a family, I know she does. Every woman does.'

'Not necessarily, Ruth. Not every woman is like you.' He was standing close to her, close enough for her to reach out and hold him, comfort him as she had so often done with Geoffrey when the outside world had disappointed him, when the goals he had set for himself had seemed impossible to reach. Only of course she couldn't touch him, not ever, even in the kindest of ways. He belonged to Bev.

'The boys will miss you, Ed. Especially Philip. And . . . so will I.' That was as close as she dared come to saying what she felt. Only she felt nothing, she told herself sternly, except that he was unhappy and upset, and she'd learned through the years that men take that much worse than women.

'I'll miss you too, Ruth. Geoff was my best friend. In a funny kind of way I feel like I'm deserting both you and Bev.'

'We both want you to be happy, Ed,' she said carefully. 'That I do know. And if this is what it takes, then I think both of us want it for you.'

'Thanks, Ruth.' He leaned forward and kissed her gently on the cheek. 'Take care of yourself. Now, I think I'd better say goodbye to the boys. My plane leaves at seven-thirty.'

He walked swiftly out of the room. Ruth made no move to follow him. You won't be back, she thought. It's all come apart and there's nothing I can do. She stood there without moving. After several minutes, though she did not hear the door close, she knew he had left the apartment.

It was nearly seven by the time Bev reached her apartment. Arthur had dropped her off in his limousine. They had both made the ride in silence, not wanting to talk in the presence of the chauffeur in the front seat, even with the glass partition closed behind him. Arthur's hand had reached out for hers during the ride, but after a few blocks she removed it gently on the pretext of looking for her keys in her purse. He made no further attempt, although he studied her face curiously for a moment. When they reached her building, he didn't get out, letting the chauffeur open the door for her.

'Dinner tonight?'

'Thank you. I'd like that.'

'Shall I pick you up?'

'Better not.'

'The Stork Club, then? Eight o'clock?'

'Wonderful.' She reached forward and took his hand impulsively. It felt warm and strong as it had all through their lovemaking. Only now he seemed distant, a stranger she had met at some party who had been kind enough to see her home. Afraid what she was thinking might show on her face, she got out quickly and hurried into the building.

On the way upstairs she allowed herself to think back to their lovemaking. He had been everything she had desired, everything she had never quite allowed herself to dream about: strong and ardent and patient. It was only afterward that they had seemed separate, in a way that had never happened when she and Ed had made love in the good years. Or even the way she had felt with Frank. But she hadn't known Frank. Maybe she had not even known Ed. She let herself into the apartment, surprised for a moment to find it dark and empty. Even before she saw the note on the table she knew from the empty closets that Ed had gone, collecting his things sometime that afternoon, leaving nothing behind, not even a half-finished tube of shaving cream. She picked up the envelope and opened it.

Dear Bev,

I know I said I'd stay until the end of the week, but put it down to one more case of my being unreliable. Mother has the address of where I'll be working if you need to reach me. I hate leaving like this, but I don't know that there's anything more we have to say to each other. At least, not at this time. If there is, I'm taking the seven-thirty American flight to St. Louis, and you can page me at the airport. Only I don't think you will. Maybe I don't even think you should. Perhaps, in time, when I have proved I can stand on my own two feet, you'll let me run back to you and hold you and carry you off into a life we can both share. Until then, all my love, my beautiful princess.

Forever,
Ed

Automatically, she glanced at the clock. He would have expected her home earlier, after the store closed. She would have been if she hadn't gone to the new apartment. There was still time to try and reach him. Only he was right, she wouldn't do it.

She read the note a second time. There should be tears in my eyes, she thought. Tears for all that had been between them, the life they had started so bravely, so happily, which had dwindled down through the years to the single piece of paper in her hands. But she felt no tears. It was just a letter she was holding, one that someday she would make herself throw away. Only not quite yet. Not tonight. She put it carefully in the bureau drawer under her handkerchiefs.

She forced herself to take a deep breath and looked at the clock again. His plane would have left by now. And she'd have to hurry if she was going to be on time for Arthur.

16

It was eight months before Bev heard from Ed again, not six, and then only indirectly, through his mother. Jane called one Saturday morning in December and asked if she could see her, and Beverly agreed. They hadn't talked in the months that had passed, and Bev sensed a slight uneasiness in herself after she hung up the phone. She had meant to stay in touch with Jane, but perhaps they had both known there was nothing either of them could say at this time that would have been any help. From Ed, there had been no word at all.

Bev moved quickly around the apartment that day, getting it in order, filling the glass bowls with flowers, expensive in December but necessary to present the place as she wanted her mother-in-law to see it. Gerry Lawson, one of the window dressers at Welby's, had helped her decorate, steering her away from the inexpensive reproductions just beginning to appeal to the American public.

'Stay with good things,' Gerry had said. 'And if you can't afford them just yet, wait. It'll be cheaper in the long run.'

Arthur had offered his help and, more than that, money, but she had been firm in refusing him, accepting only as a housewarming present the beautiful mirror he had bought for her in London. It was unquestionably the finest piece in the apartment, settled securely in place over the mantelpiece as if it had been designed for it. With bright colors and full drapes at the windows, the apartment looked serene and almost elegant. The vacant spots, waiting for furniture she could not yet afford, Gerry had filled with pots of plants and leaves. 'The place is big enough so you won't look like you're living in a jungle, and we can get rid of them without pain when you buy what you really want.' The only big new purchase had been a bed, wide and comfortable, that she could sleep in with no memories.

As she waited for Jane it seemed to Beverly this was the first time in months that she'd had time to think of what her life had become. She looked at herself critically in the mirror over the fireplace. Was she different? Nobody had commented on it particularly, certainly not the people she saw frequently: Ruth, her parents, Sylvia and her other friends. Arthur always told her she was lovely. Naturally thin, she had lost a few pounds; perhaps that's why her face seemed more distinct, more clearly defined. Or perhaps it was because the face she saw was no longer that of a young girl but of a grown woman.

It had been an exciting year, she thought, moving restlessly around the apartment. The results of her first trip to Paris had been enormously successful, and she and Sylvia were both honest enough to know a large part of it had been due to Beverly. Before the trip, Welby's had a reputation of being a very elegant store for women of a certain age and a very definite amount of money. But with Beverly and the arrival of the decade of the fifties, a new market had opened up: A young market, interested in style and color and change, a market Beverly understood very well. Many women who came into Welby's now were her age. They didn't just want the 'good black dress' that their mothers bought religiously every year. They wanted clothes that moved and flowed, that showed their naturally lithe bodies to the best effect, that had been designed to reveal firm young skin and not just to cover the parts of a woman's body that gave in first to time. They were the girls who worked, not to fill time before a suburban marriage but because they had brains and energy and talent. It was the beginning of the time of the youth culture in America, and subconsciously Beverly understood it perhaps better than anybody else in the fashion field.

She had made a second trip with Sylvia in the summer and had been gratified to see the dresses and suits she had picked were being copied all over the country, to the outraged howls of the manufacturers who had bought the original designs and claimed with absolutely no truth at all that they were being 'ruined.' Full skirts were still popular, making manufacturers of textiles and designs like Arthur even richer than before.

Arthur. Bev wondered how much of the change she saw in the mirror was due to him. The last eight months had been the most exhilarating, most vibrant, and, if she were to be honest, the most educational of her life. He was knowledgeable about everything from wine to lovemaking. Their relationship was not a courtship, if it had ever been that. Nor was it an affair such as Ed's sister had with José. There was no permanence in their commitment to each other, no steady days that were set aside exclusively for them to be with each other. A week might go by without a phone call, and then he would see her four nights in a row. They went to the theater, to the best restaurants, to the opera. The columnists had long ago given up reporting their appearances; they were old news by now. Beverly suspected that on the nights he did not see her he saw other women but to her surprise she found she did not mind. And perhaps the fact of her not minding was what kept him coming back after their few quarrels. For there were quarrels, and they were always the same.

'Everybody's entitled to a vacation! Of course you can take a week off and come with me to Bermuda!' Or San Francisco or that interesting little inn on the Cape.

When she refused, using the store as an excuse or saying that her parents would be hurt or even that technically she was still married, he would storm out of the apartment, slamming the door behind him. His quick temper was something she had suspected even when she first met him —that and his impatience—but now they had become part of her life, to be handled coolly and calmly, knowing as she did it was a guaranteed way to infuriate him even more. I must enjoy it, she would mutter to herself after one of his exits, finding herself smiling. It was not that she was not attracted to him, not that she didn't desire him and enjoy as much as he did the long sensuous evenings they spent together, but somehow with Ed's departure she had found herself growing some sort of emotional shell. No man would ever hurt her again, she told herself. No man would ever be that close or that important. Instead, the love she might have lavished on a husband and children went into the store, and each day she found it more exciting. She was shrewd enough to know her work was a bond that was stronger than desire between her and Arthur. For once there was a woman in his life to whom he could talk about his business, who understood it, who was as excited by it as he, who knew the questions to ask and had answers to questions he had not yet considered. The other women he knew were concerned with their figures, their faces, whom they saw, and what their friends did. With Bev there were none of the supposedly clever sayings of children to be repeated endlessly over dinner tables while the other guests waited impatiently to report what their children had said. Dinner with Bev was exciting and dazzling and occasionally infuriating. And so he kept coming back.

Only now it was Jane who was coming. With word, she said, from Ed.

'How lovely you look!'

'Thank you, Jane.' She took the older woman's coat, giving her a moment to collect herself. Jane seemed older than she had remembered her; there were tired lines on her face that Beverly had not remembered seeing before.

'And the apartment . . . with that magnificent view!' Jane moved to the window seat, as guests always seemed to do when first arriving. 'It's certainly lovelier than what you had.'

'Yes. It's nice to come home to.' Bev busied herself with the tea things, keeping her face away from her mother-in-law. Jane watched her carefully. She hoped there might be a hint of loneliness in her voice, but she was far from sure. She knew from Marion that Bev was often in the company of Arthur Powers these days, and she had made it her business to find out, as discreetly as possible, a little more about the man. No marriage would ever come of it, she felt, and wondered if Bev knew that as well.

'I've . . . had a letter from Ed,' she began carefully once they were seated. 'After I read it, I called him. He wanted me to talk to you.'

'How is he?'

'All right. I think. He's not in St. Louis anymore. He's in San Diego.'

Bev looked at her. 'Didn't the job work out?'

'Fine, apparently. But, Bev, you knew he was in the reserves. With this Korean business he's been called back in.'

'He's back in the service?'

Jane nodded. There was a sick feeling in her stomach again, the same feeling she had had when he told her. It was too much to have to worry about your son going off to war twice in one lifetime, she thought.

'But . . . will he be sent overseas?' The Korean police action that had begun that summer had seemed millions of miles away to Bev; she had never thought of it in terms of Ed. No one in her life had been affected by it.

She was, she realized that December afternoon for the first time, too old to know any of the college-age boys who were being drafted. And the other men in her life, Arthur and Ruth's friends, were either married or exempt from being called back again.

'He doesn't know where they're going to send him. At the moment they're short of navigators, so he's teaching at this base on the West Coast. But he said everything is bound to be pretty uncertain for the next couple of months. That's why he wanted me to see you.' She took a deep breath. 'Beverly, he feels it would be a good idea if you two were officially divorced.'

She had expected it from the moment Jane had called, but all through the hours of waiting she had pushed the thought to the far corner of her mind, not willing to examine it or unleash whatever emotions she might feel about so final a break.

'Is there . . . another woman?'

Jane smiled. 'Oddly, it's me. He wants to make me the beneficiary of his insurance. Apparently there's some kind of red tape that if he's still married it automatically goes to you. He said he thought you could probably take care of yourself, and he was worried about my future.' She smiled slightly. 'It suddenly seems to have occurred to him that I'm not getting any younger.' She reached for her purse. 'He . . . he sent the papers. He said all you have to do is sign them and he'll file for the divorce in California.'

Bev held the crisp legal papers for a long moment. 'I suppose I should have expected this,' she said at last.

'Beverly? I think if you don't want the divorce, Ed wouldn't push for it. Not even for the insurance. It's just if he goes overseas and anything should happen—I mean, it's not like he feels any different about you. He doesn't. I could tell that on the phone.'

'No. It's the . . . sensible thing to do.' She reached for a pen and without looking wrote her name on the pages. The spaces had been carefully marked with a penciled X. 'How . . . how has he been? Did he tell you?'

'I think very happy, Beverly. He liked the work, he seems to have made a lot of friends there. He plans to go back once he's out of uniform again. Of course, whether there'll be a job for him then or not, I don't know.' Suddenly her composure deserted her. Bev looked up to see the tears rolling down Jane's cheeks; Jane, who never cried. 'Oh, Bev, it's not what I wanted, not what I wanted at all! I wanted the two of you to be happy, to be together, to have a family. There won't ever be one now. I'll probably never see grandchildren.'

Bev reached out to hold the older woman, noticing for the first time how thin Jane's shoulders were. She is older, she thought. Ed's right to worry about her. Gradually Jane stopped her tears, but she made no move to break away from Beverly's embrace. 'I'm sorry,' she said at last. 'I didn't mean to let go like that. Only there's something about a divorce that seems so final. I haven't done very well as a mother, have I? Ed in his thirties, divorced, going off to war again with nothing to come back to. Marion divorced, as well as involved with that awful man. . . .'

This was the first time Bev realized that Jane had known about her daughter's long affair with José. It had been the one thing never discussed between them.

'He won't marry her, you know. Even if he were free. And she's wasting these years when she should be making a life for herself, planning a future.'

'She seems happy. She has her own business, she's making her own way.' Bev's answers seemed hollow even as she made them.

'That's fine for now. I've never tried to make judgments. But what happens five years from now? Or ten? José won't be there. If he can't be faithful to his wife, I doubt if he'll be faithful to Marion. There'll be somebody younger. And the good years will be gone for Marion and she won't be able to get them back.'

'Jane, I know you're worried. And I'm shocked about the news of Ed. I . . . I wish there were something I could say to change it.'

'Bev, is it over with you two? Completely? Do you feel it in your heart? Because if you're not sure, I have a feeling it would mean everything in the world to Ed if you flew out to see him.'

'I can't, Jane.' She thought of Arthur. He was due to arrive in an hour to take her to Ruth's cocktail party, the first party she had given since Geoff had died. But it wasn't Arthur or that she couldn't arrange time to get away that made her say no. 'Things are just beginning to heal, Jane. At least for me. I think they must be for Ed, too. I'll always love him, I guess. In some kind of way. But I can't go back to what we were. And I don't think it's fair for him, with whatever may happen in the future, to have a wife to worry about.'

'You're right, I suppose.' Jane stood, putting the papers back in her purse. 'I knew it even before I came here. I guess I just couldn't resist trying one more time. Shall I send any message to Ed for you?'

'Tell him I wish him all the best. That I'm sure he'll be all right. This police action can't last forever. Maybe they won't even send him overseas, but if they do, tell him I'll be praying he'll come back well and safe.'

'I'll tell him that. And please, Bev, let's stay in touch.'

An hour later Beverly and Arthur were in the middle of the worst quarrel they had ever had. Between them on the floor lay a long box, crisp tissue paper spilling out the sides and in the middle a full dark-mink coat, thick and sensual, an 'early Christmas present,' as Arthur had announced when he handed her the box.

'For God's sake, Beverly, don't be an idiot! You're not a child. You know I can afford it. Why on earth shouldn't I give you a mink coat if I feel like it?'

For once Bev's calm control deserted her. Perhaps it was the conversation with Jane, perhaps she had a sudden cold feeling that her life might easily go as Marion's had, but all her tact and cleverness deserted her. Arthur was staring at her as if he had never seen her before, and she realized she must look like some sort of wild woman, all because she was refusing a coat worth thousands of dollars. She struggled for control but knew she wasn't succeeding.

'Arthur, I can't take a gift like that! We're friends . . . all right, we're lovers. Or at least part of the time.'

'What does that mean?' His face was cold.

'You know perfectly well. We're not married, we're not likely to be married—'

'Is that what you want? A proposal, the day you sign your divorce papers?'

Bev had told him of Jane's visit when he arrived. He had taken the news with a grunt, and she began to realize in some sort of way this might have seemed as if she were trying to maneuver him into a different position in their relationship. After that he had offered the coat almost casually, and the tension each was feeling had flashed like lightning striking dry wood.

'No! I don't want a proposal from you, Arthur! I've never wanted it or expected it. I've never wanted anything more from you than the times we've spent together. *When* it was convenient for both of us, when we wanted each other, when we wanted to be with each other. That is all I have ever wanted. So if you think I'm trying to become the fourth Mrs. Arthur Powers, forget it completely and totally and forever!'

He switched his tactics instantly, lowering his voice and leaning forward, eyes warm and sincere. 'Then why act like this? Why not let me give you the presents I want to give you?'

The anger left her as suddenly as it had come. 'That's the whole problem, Arthur. They're what *you* want, not what I want. This coat isn't because you want to keep me warm for the winter. And it isn't to get me into bed.' She noticed him sitting back at this, almost, she thought with some amusement, as if she had shocked him. 'I love going to bed with you, and you know it. I hope it will go on happening for a long time, as long as we both want it.

'But this coat is something different. The caveman going out and dragging back the pelt to his lair to show he owns the lady. No, don't interrupt. You want me to wear this coat because you like to be seen with rich, well-dressed people. Every woman you know, I suspect, has a mink coat. And you want one for me so I don't disgrace your reputation.'

'Bev, that's nonsense. My God, all this fuss over a Christmas present!'

'And what am I supposed to give you in return? A chance to show off your latest acquisition? Well, I'm nobody's acquisition, Arthur.' She thought of the times she had seen

Marion with José, the diamonds he had given her glittering at her ears and clipped to her dress. But never one for her finger, she thought, remembering what Jane had said. And there never would be. Whatever happened in life, nobody was going to force her into that role.

'I'm not something to be possessed, Arthur. I thought we both understood that, right from the beginning. I'm not going to be one of that army of East Side ladies whose possessions come from some gentleman finding them attractive for a season or two. If I want a mink coat, I'll work hard for it and I'll get it . . . and it will be mine.'

Reluctantly, he found himself almost amused at her independence. 'As a sign that the cavewoman can go out and skin a pelt just as easily as a man?'

She laughed. It was going to be all right between them after all. 'Something like that, dear Arthur.'

'I'm going to look an awful fool taking it back,' he grumbled.

'Tell the saleswoman I'm holding out for sable. That ought to impress both of you. Now, if you don't mind getting my winter coat, we're late for Ruth's party.'

Ruth had been uneasy all day. It had been nearly a year since Geoff's death, and she knew she had to come out of the grayness she had felt all these months or Christmas would be forever spoiled for the boys. A holiday open house—it had seemed so simple when her mother had first suggested it, to put up a tree and get her sons excited about the prospect of presents, the way they always had been before when Geoff was alive. Even Amory Phelps had agreed to it, strong, solemn Amory, one of Geoff's law partners. She wondered, as she smoothed her hair in front of her bedroom mirror, how she would have got through this past year without him. He was a more serious man than she was used to. There was none of the energy that so characterized her late husband, none of the warm simple naturalness of Ed that had helped her son Philip so much. She missed Ed more than she should. This whole past year might have been easier if she could have seen more of him—and, of course, Beverly.

But she had learned by late spring that even the closest friends eventually pull away from someone else's grief. It was as if death, especially a death by accident, were some sort of contagion, something people did not want to be around for too long in case it spread, reminding them that they, too, would someday not be alive and vital and here.

She had taken up volunteer work then, not out of any enthusiasm. She was as guilty as the others, she realized, in that hospitals were a constant reminder to her of the impermanence and unhappiness of life. But she had to do something to fill the days with the boys in school and preschool, and lunching out and shopping were not enough. Any small idea that she might train for a job or a career had been firmly squashed by her parents and Geoff's. He would not have wanted her to work, all of them said. It would seem like a reflection that he had not left her well off, and that of course was not true.

If Ruth had had some special talent, even a desire to move into the working world, the unhappiness of this year of mourning would have stopped her from taking even the smallest of first steps. And now when the grief had settled down into a kind of numbness that she realized was going to be part of her life for a long, long time to come, she was too shy to consider how to move out into the world again. She'd loved her home when Geoff was in it, loved her young sons, had never desired even for a moment the kind of life that Beverly found so exciting and necessary. All her life decisions had been made for her, and because they had been made with care and love, she had accepted them gratefully, not realizing that in the process she was becoming nearly as helpless as a baby.

And now, if she wanted, she could be safe again forever —if she still believed in such a word as 'forever.' Amory had been kind at first. There had been dozens of business details to handle regarding Geoff's estate, papers to sign, meetings to be held. But during the summer Ruth realized his feelings for her were changing. He began to ask her out for dinner, and, grateful for adult companionship, she had accepted. Privately she had to admit to herself that some of the evenings seemed very long. Amory had no particular gift for conversation, and his interests were almost rigidly narrow. Theaters and concerts seemed a waste of time to him, although as a member of a wealthy family he felt it his duty to support the Philharmonic and the opera with yearly subscriptions and to attend, rather as if it were a duty, like church, something he was expected to do but not to enjoy. His reading was almost completely limited to the field of law. Still, he was moderately good-looking, a man of strong character, and quite obviously attracted to her. Even her parents had noticed it and as tactfully as possible suggested he might be an interest worth encouraging.

Only one thing seriously troubled Ruth about him. He was not comfortable with her sons, and the boys, normally so cheerful and energetic, became subdued and silent when he came to the apartment. Ruth thought of how happily they had greeted Ed, the joy they had found in roughhousing with him and the affection he had so clearly given back. But perhaps, as Amory said, the boys were running a little wild. She sighed and started for the living room when she heard the first doorbell ring. She didn't have to think about making a decision about Amory yet. At least, not tonight.

By seven the apartment was full, the boys wide-eyed with delight as the guests continued to arrive, most of them bearing packages to be placed under the tree, carefully marked with each of their names. Amory had muttered, 'They'll be spoiled silly before the holidays are over,' but for once Ruth refused to let his disapproval matter. She was pleased to be surrounded by friends again; after this long, empty year it was good to have cheerful voices in these rooms, have decisions to make concerning feeding and entertaining them. Alma, flushed with the unexpected excitement, hurried among the guests carrying canapés, and the bartender in the dining room hadn't had a moment for a cigarette since the first half hour.

Ruth was particularly pleased to see that Bev had arrived with Arthur. There had been one uneasy dinner with the four of them that fall, when it was clear that Amory did not approve of Arthur, and the other man found him a stuffed shirt. However, they were all making polite conversation together beside the glittering tree, and Ruth allowed herself a moment of hope that all of them could become, in time, friends. She herself was none too sure about Arthur. She had heard all the usual gossip about him, and a past that included three ex-wives was not very encouraging for Beverly, but when she had mentioned that, somewhat hesitantly to Bev over lunch one day, Bev had merely laughed.

'Ruth, I've no intention of marrying Arthur. Or anybody else for that matter,' she had said and changed the subject.

But Ruth hadn't believed her. As Bev approached her thirties, she would want children and a solid family life. Every woman did. If she waited too long . . . still, there was always the chance Ed would come back.

'Ruth, it's a lovely party,' Bev said as she came up, and then, pulling her to one side, 'Can we have a minute together? I've had some news about Ed.'

Ruth nodded, and together the two women disappeared through the crowd into her bedroom. They did not notice that as soon as they left, by unspoken but clearly mutual consent, Arthur and Amory each headed for opposite sides of the room. Vulgar, thought Amory as he moved to the side of a girl he had been escorting casually since her debutante days. Goddamn prig, thought Arthur, attracted to a buxom blonde in a low-cut dress.

'What's the news? Is Ed well? Is he still in St. Louis?'

'Ruth, I'm sorry. I probably should have waited. It's not exactly party news. But I know how you and the boys feel about him. It seems he's been called back into service, this Korean mess. I thought you'd want to know.'

'But he'd been doing so well with his new business!'

Now it was Beverly's turn to be surprised. 'You've heard from him?'

'Not often. And not me, exactly. But he'd send postcards to the boys. He's always been a big hero to them, especially Phil. Pictures of the house he had rented, the airfield where he was working. He really seemed to be making a success of it.' She hesitated. It was hard sometimes to talk to Bev about anything really close to her. 'I'd sort of hoped that . . . well, this being the holiday season, maybe he might even come to New York, talk to you about the future.'

'We don't have one, Ruth. Jane came by this afternoon. Ed wants a divorce. He feels we should both be free in case he gets sent overseas again. And there's the matter of his insurance. Naturally I want Jane to have it if anything . . . should happen.'

'Bev, I'm so sorry. I guess I'm a romantic. I'd always rather hoped—' Before she could continue, the phone on her bedside table rang. She excused herself to answer it and almost at once looked back at Bev, her face pale, her mouth opened in shock. 'Bev, it's for you. It's your mother.'

'It's all right, Ruth. I told her I'd be here tonight.' But the look on Ruth's face frightened her. 'What is it? What does she want?' Without waiting for an answer, she took the phone from Ruth. 'Mother? What is it?'

Angela's voice sounded very far away. 'I'm at the hospital. Your father didn't feel so good about an hour ago. I called the doctor and they got an ambulance. The doctor thinks he's had a heart attack. Oh, Bev, can you come, please? Can you come right away?'

Frightened as she was, she got the instructions from her mother as quickly as possible, grabbing up her coat as she did. 'It's all right. I'll be right there.' She put down the phone. 'Look, Ruth, I have to go. It may not be serious, but I can't take any chances. Arthur's got the car outside. Don't tell anybody else. I don't want to ruin your party.'

She hurried out of the room. For a long time Ruth couldn't move. It was all so similar to last year. The phone call saying that Geoff had crashed. Damn Christmas, she thought with sudden vehemence. Damn all holidays when you're supposed to feel happy and secure and loved. She wondered bleakly what this last year would have been like if she hadn't had her parents, hadn't had anyone to lean on. And yet they were no younger than Bev's parents, they wouldn't be around to help her forever. Carefully she smoothed back her hair. She would leave all that to Amory. If he stayed on after the others had left the party and proposed to her again, this time she would say yes.

17

When they reached the hospital, Bev, who had been silent throughout the ride, told Arthur abruptly she didn't want him to come up. She would call him. Without waiting for his reply, she jumped out of the car and ran into the hospital. Arthur leaned back in his limousine, watching the doors swing shut behind her. It was starting to snow, and even inside the car he could feel the cold December wind.

'Where to, sir?'

'I don't know, Leonard,' he said to the chauffeur. 'Give me a minute.' He'd planned on dinner with Bev this Saturday night. There were reservations at 21; she'd be happy wearing the new mink coat, having shown it off first at the party; it had had all the makings of one of their best evenings. Now everything was changed. He had to admit she was more than a little right about the coat. He did like to see his women chic and well dressed. He realized she was probably the only woman who had seen through the gift to his own selfishness.

He was grateful to Bev that she hadn't asked him to come up with her to the hospital room. He hated illness, his own or anybody else's. Sickness had always seemed to him some kind of flaw and he preferred it kept out of his sight, like dirty dishes or a piece of broken furniture. Still, all this didn't solve what he was going to do with his evening. He was aware that Leonard was watching him in the mirror over the dashboard. He could return to the party, but he already had the phone number of the blonde he had been talking to when Bev reappeared and he couldn't very well go back and claim her, at a party given by Bev's best friend. He could imagine what that snob Phelps would say about that. Of course there were plenty of other girls he could call for dinner, even this late, ranging from elegant divorcees to younger, more compliant models. But somehow it all seemed a little too much effort.

'Just take me home, Leonard,' he said finally. 'You can have the rest of the night off. I'll turn in early.'

As the car started through the park, Arthur wondered—if something did happen to Beverly's father—how it would affect their relationship. This whole fight over the mink coat might only have been because she was worried over what her father might think. Not that Arthur cared; he could probably buy and sell her father a hundred times over and never notice it. It was only later that night after he had turned off his bedside lamp and was preparing himself for sleep that Arthur had another thought. Was it possible Beverly hadn't wanted him to come up to the hospital room because she was ashamed of him? He dismissed the thought almost as soon as it occurred. Only for once he found it difficult to get to sleep.

'Dad? Can you hear me?'

He opened his eyes slowly. He seemed so frail in the sterile white bed. She found herself thinking of Jane that afternoon. It was almost too much for one day that two of the people she had depended upon, leaned on, were suddenly to appear old and helpless, needing *her* to lean on. I'm not ready for that, she thought, as she sat by her father's hospital bed, not knowing she was facing the same fear Ruth was facing, that happens to everyone whose parents live long enough. That moment when you realize, no matter how far apart you have grown, that they are not always going to be there to depend on, to give definition to your life. Harry and Angela's daughter. That's what she'd been. Ed's wife. From now on, she thought bleakly, she would just be Beverly Richmond.

The doctor had warned her it was serious, serious enough that he had kept the sobbing Angela out of the room, leading her to the solarium at the far end of the hall where Bev had found her, staring out at the falling snow, her eyes wet and red. But the doctor could see Bev was in control, and he allowed her to go into her father's room.

Harry Thyson lay quietly in the bed, not moving, mysterious tubes in his thin arms, a hospital gown over his body.

When his eyelids flickered for a second, she had leaned forward, taking his hand.

'It's Bev, Dad. Are you in pain?'

He tried to smile, but it took too much effort. 'Don't worry, Bev. I'll be all right.'

He tried to swallow, but his mouth was too dry. She reached for the glass on the table and, holding up his head, put the straw in his mouth. The water seemed to refresh him.

'I'm sorry I'm being such a . . . problem.' He let his head fall back against the pillows.

'That's okay, Dad. I'm right here.'

'It's my heart, isn't it? Old Dr. Webster warned me about that a long time ago, but I didn't think . . .' His voice grew stronger and his eyes focused on her face sharply, the way he had when she was a child and he suspected something had made her unhappy. 'Are you all right?'

'I'm fine.'

'Where's Ed?'

'Ed's . . . away, Dad. I told you. He's starting a new business.' She had told her parents that much and no more in the spring, and there had been something in her voice that had told them not to inquire further.

'He's a good boy, that Ed. Maybe not for you, but a good boy.'

She nodded, not trusting herself to speak.

'Only he hasn't made you happy, has he?'

This was the first time her father had ever spoken directly to Bev about her marriage, and here in this silent hospital room, perhaps the last room he would ever be in, his eyes staring into hers, Bev knew she couldn't lie any more.

'Not always, Dad. We seem to have different ideas of what's important in life.'

'I guessed that.' He let out a long breath, harsh, rasping. 'One of Nature's tricks, I suppose. You're attracted to what's your opposite, only sooner or later you discover you can't live with it.'

'It wasn't like that with you and Mom, was it?'

'No.' His voice was weaker now, and she had to lean forward to hear him. 'But there was another girl, a long time ago, before I got married. I loved her, Bev. I . . . I don't think it can hurt now to say I loved her more deeply than I've ever loved anyone except you. Only I knew it couldn't work. Not for a lifetime.'

Bev felt his grip tighten on her hand. This was something she'd never thought of, that there could have been other people in her parents' lives. They had always seemed so close, so much of a couple. How foolish she'd been, to take them for granted as if they had only been born to be her family, never to have seen them as a man and a woman with their own needs and wants and desires.

'Mother never knew about this girl?'

'No. She may have guessed. Everybody loved Rita. That was her name, Rita. She was bright and charming and wild. Only I knew it couldn't last. So I broke it off deliberately and married your mother. It was hard, but it was right.'

'And you think I should have broken it off with Ed before I married him?'

'Only you can answer that, Bev. And if it has to be broken, even now—well, there's still the future.'

Bev wondered suddenly if her father suspected the existence of Arthur in her life. Only she couldn't ask him, not tonight, maybe never.

'Bev?' His grip on her hand was weaker now, and she could see the effort it cost him to speak.

'Please, Dad, try to rest. . . .'

'No! Let me speak. I want you to have a great life. I want you to fly as high and as far as you can. If it can't be with Ed, then face it. You are your own person. And if you have to stand alone, I know you'll find the courage to do it.'

'Nothing's been decided, Dad,' Bev lied, hoping her face was as reassuring as her words. 'Now, you shouldn't talk any more, the doctor won't like it.'

'I just want you to know I never regretted leaving Rita.' His eyes closed wearily for a moment, and when he spoke again his voice was as soft as a sigh. 'If I'd married her, I wouldn't have had you. You gave the heart to my life, Bev.' He tried to smile. 'Stronger than what they put in bodies, I guess.'

'Daddy, I love you—'

'And I love you. But sooner or later you'll find the only thing you have to hold on to is your own self, your own courage. It's the only thing that won't fail you. Remember that.'

'I promise, Dad.'

Harry died that night, slipping first into a coma, his hand still in Bev's and then an hour later she knew it was all over. Through the weeks that were to follow she was grateful to him for his last gift, the strength to face the finality of her divorce and the knowledge that that part of her life was finished as completely as the years she had spent as his daughter.

She tried to spend as much time as she could with her mother, but as the days passed she realized how little they had in common. Always it had been her father she had turned to, who had encouraged her right from the beginning, who had made her independent and strong, able to face the world. Her mother had been the cautious one, the one who worried and anticipated the worst of accidents, and though Beverly knew her mother wanted nothing more than to move in with her, she could not offer the invitation. So she kept delaying any decision, until finally, after the long wet spring, Angela made her own choice.

'Cousin Marjorie is alone too, you know,' she remarked one night after a dinner that had seemed endless to Bev. 'Out in Tucson. Since Aunt Margaret went into the nursing home. She's written to ask if I'd like to come for a while. It would be just a visit, of course. At least at first. Till we see how we get on. But I think it might be good for my rheumatism. And Marjorie and I always did get on well.' She looked at Beverly, hoping her daughter would say something. 'It's not as if there were anything to keep me here.'

'I think it might be a very good idea, Mother. To try, at least. You know what my life is like at the store. Sylvia says I'm due for another promotion . . . I'll be a full buyer. That means I'll have even less time than I do now.'

'I know. Your father was very proud of your success, Bev. I just hope it's enough to make you happy.'

It was May by the time her mother finally left and Bev had the time to pick up the pieces of her own life. Arthur had called during the weeks since the funeral, but she sensed it was more out of duty than desire. They had dinner a few times and sometimes, but not always, had ended the evening making love in his apartment. She sensed she was more restrained with him than she had been before, less pliant, less giving since her father's death, almost as if she felt more guilt being with Arthur now than she had during the months when, legally, at least, she had been Ed's wife. Somehow in that long winter, Arthur's lovemaking had become almost a duty to be endured. She tried as skillfully as she could to hide that feeling from him, but it was a definite relief the night he told her he would be making a month-long tour of factories in the South.

At any other time her feelings might have puzzled or even worried her, but the longed-for promotion to full buyer had finally happened that same spring, moving her from the small office she had shared with two other junior buyers up to the executive floor, with an inside office next to Sylvia's. Gerry decorated it in bright colors so that you hardly noticed the cubicle had no window of its own.

'Well, kid, you finally made it,' said Sylvia. She put down the plant she had brought as a present on the clean-lined modern desk. 'The youngest full buyer Welby's ever had. How's it feel?'

'Just great, Sylvia,' said Bev simply. 'This whole winter's been like a long tunnel I'd never get out of. I'm finally beginning to feel like it's spring in the city.'

'Well, if you want to be sure about it, feel free to come into my office and look out a window. And I've got our tickets for the summer showings. You'll be pleased to know that Welby's thinks highly enough of us that this time they're flying us over and letting us have separate rooms at the Ritz.'

'The Ritz?'

'Yes indeedy. Right across the street from Mademoiselle Chanel. You can draw what conclusions you want from that.'

'But . . . the Ritz. Sylvia, they never let the expense account go that far!'

'I know. And guess what? You'll be right close to your old buddy. I hear Arthur Powers is going to be in Paris at the same time. And isn't he always at the Ritz?' With a wave of her hand, Sylvia disappeared back to her own office.

In the weeks left before they went, Bev debated whether to call Arthur. She wasn't exactly sure where their relationship stood, or even if it could still be called that. She knew he had been seen with other women. Once in a while his name would make the columns, and some 'good friend' in the store would manage to leave a copy of the paper, the item clearly marked, on her desk. Bev suspected Karen Landers, one of the girls she had started with who had never concealed her envy of Bev's rapid rise. Midge had finally left the store after the first year when her pregnancy had become obvious. She was the only one of the girls Bev had been close to, and yet, because seeing Midge always reminded her of the crazy nights of her affair with Neil, she had never really felt comfortable with her. Maybe she had never really felt all that comfortable with any of the other people at the store except Sylvia.

But as the days drew closer to the date of her flight to Paris, Beverly knew she would have to make some gesture at least of friendship toward Arthur. If those frozen weeks after her father's death had hurt or offended him, she owed it to him to try and explain. The few times she had tried to phone him, he had not been in and she had left no message. Finally she decided the simplest, most tactful way was to send him a note telling him of her coming trip and where and when she would be in Paris. To do any more would seem to be pursuing him, and that could only drive them farther apart. Now if he wanted to see her, it would be up to him. Although, as spring flowered in the city around her, she was beginning to come back to life again, and she was too honest not to admit to herself that a very important part of her life was her relationship with Arthur. If it still existed. . . .

The flight over was smooth, and the rooms she and Sylvia had at the Ritz were comfortably large. The expense account wasn't enough to place them on the Place Vendôme side. Instead, they stared down at the narrow street that held Chanel's shop. Sylvia had filled her in on the many stories of that exceptional woman's life, and now that she was again reclaiming her position as the leader of French fashion, Bev was eager to meet her. But the showing of her line was packed with hundreds of women squeezed onto little chairs, the air was heavy with the smoke of French cigarettes, and if the tiny lady who had created her own fashion empire met new people, they were far more important than a young buyer from Welby's. Clutching her pad with the figures of the styles she had admired, Bev let herself be shoved out onto the street after the showing.

Standing on the curb opposite was Arthur.

'You look exhausted,' he said, without a greeting. 'How about a drink? Or is it too early?'

She agreed to a drink, and with authority he moved them through the crowd and into the Ritz, settling in a corner booth that had clearly been reserved for him. George the bartender had already started mixing their drinks when he saw them enter, and Bev barely had a minute to study Arthur before they were left to themselves. He looked as he had the first time they had met in Paris, and she felt again the excitement, the sudden unexpected rush of desire she had known in those precious days. We should always meet in Paris, she thought, and smiled a little to herself.

'That's more like it,' he commented. 'You looked absolutely grim outside there.'

'It was quite a showing. And it's been quite a winter.'

'I know. I've missed you, Bev.'

'I've missed you too, Arthur.'

He reached out for her hand on the table. Again she could feel the electricity in his fingers, in his whole body. There'd been no other man in the months since they had been together. She hadn't wanted it, had not even missed it. The store and trying to handle Angela's dependency had taken all her time and energy these past months. Now once more Arthur was back in her life, alive, sensual, disturbing. Only this time she was not the self-contained, rule-bound young woman she had been on that first trip to Paris. There was no reason to hold him off, no husband to demand her first loyalty, no family to be shocked by anything she did. For a swift moment she felt almost frightened—she, who had faced all the challenges of her life head on. But the old rules by which she had been raised, rules of conformity and fidelity that had been like bars of a cage for so much of her life, bars that had held her in and bound her actions with their hundreds of 'Thou shalt not's,' had also, she realized, offered her a safety that these new days would never provide and never could again. For a girl who had been positive at eighteen that she was an adult, she now felt, nearly ten years later, as if she were more of a child than she had ever been before.

'Bev? You're very far away.'

'Not really.' She squeezed his hand gently and then removed it to reach for her glass.

'I'm going to be here for the next couple of weeks. Can we see each other?'

'Of course.'

'Dinner tonight? I've a reservation at Tour d'Argent at nine.'

'That would be perfect.' She had heard of the fabulous restaurant with its glorious view of Paris and the Seine, and the superbly served ducks, each bearing a special number dating all the way back to the beginning of the restaurant's career. It had been on her list of places to see, though she knew if she went there with Sylvia that two women alone, if they were admitted at all, would be placed at the worst table in the most crowded part of the establishment. It would be different going with Arthur. Captains would smile, waiters would bow, the service would be impeccable. All because she had a man, a powerful, wealthy man, to handle all the arrangements. She could understand Ruth's desire to marry somebody like Amory. It could be so simple to settle back and let life be directed for you.

Across the bar she saw a familiar face, and she touched Arthur's arm to get his attention. 'Arthur, look over there. Isn't that José?' She hadn't seen much of her former sister-in-law or her Spanish friend this past winter, but she was positive she recognized him. He had half risen to greet a tall, very thin redhead, a girl she was sure she had seen less than an hour before modeling the beautifully cut clothes at Chanel's showing. Their backs were to her and Arthur, but there was no mistaking the proprietary air with which José had touched the girl's shoulder as he had seated her.

'That's José,' said Arthur briskly as he reached for the check and signed it.

'That's not his wife?' said Beverly, already knowing the answer.

'No. And it's not Marion either. But you didn't really think he was totally faithful to anybody, did you?'

'That would be naive, wouldn't it?' She thought of what Jane had worried about that afternoon at her apartment. A wise woman, Jane. She wondered bleakly if that was what lay ahead for her with Arthur. Would she, too, allow herself to get so used to him, so used to the comforts he could arrange for her life, that in time she would be as helpless without him as she knew Marion would be without José? She was determined not to let that happen. For a moment she was tempted to cancel her date with Arthur for dinner, but before she could speak he leaned forward and whispered in her ear.

'How about coming up to my suite? It's still early. We'll have time for some champagne before we have to dress for dinner.'

She knew if she refused him it would be the end of their affair. He would smile understandingly, probably still take her out to dinner that night, but whatever there was between them would end, and forever, right there at the table in the bar. She didn't want to refuse him, she knew that. Every part of her body was ready for him, eager for his touch, his skillful lovemaking. She had missed his companionship as well, the challenge of his ego against hers, the strength of his stubbornness, the excitement of his constant desire for all that was new and exciting in life.

And yet she dared not let herself become a Marion or a Ruth. As she had learned only too well, she had only herself to depend upon: her own mind, her own choices, her own freedom. It would be difficult to achieve all that, to take as well as give, and not be turned into a caricature of the hardened, tough businesswoman or the opposite, a compliant vine needing someone to wrap around for support and comfort and a reason for living. And yet men stood alone, were expected to do it every day, and as Bev sat there at the bar in the Ritz she knew somehow she and a whole generation of women her age were going to have to learn the secret as well. Oddly, she felt exhilarated. This she knew she could handle. It was as if a door had opened suddenly in a solid wall and she saw for one brief moment the world outside as it really was—saw it and knew it was hers for the taking, if she had enough courage.

'I think some champagne would be wonderful, Arthur.' He took her arm and led her to the door. As they passed José, he did not look up.

This time their affair was different, and it was a long time before Arthur could date the change back to that afternoon in Paris. Beverly was as he had remembered her, ardent and alive and full of curiosity and as sexually arousing as any woman he'd ever known. But something had gone or changed, and while at first he did not notice it, gradually he found himself in a relationship that bore no resemblance to anything he had experienced before. They were lovers, of course, but it was not an involvement that could be taken for granted. With Bev there were none of the teasing turndowns he had experienced with his wives and other women. No headaches or pleas that their hair had just been done, the feminine wiles he had grown used to that could only be placated with an expensive gift or the promise of a fashionable outing. When Bev did not feel like going to bed with him, she said so, clearly and directly, but with enough charm that he could not argue with her. If she, as she often did during their time in Paris, had to refuse an invitation to dinner or the chance to take off for an afternoon to drive through the countryside, it was because she meant what she said: She was here for business, and that came first.

He knew she enjoyed his company, he knew he amused and interested her, and he knew, in a way that was extremely flattering after the years with the icy Marilyn, that she found him in every way a perfect partner in bed. But there remained something of her he could not reach, could not dominate, and it was only on their last Sunday in Paris together, while they were walking aimlessly through the quiet streets of the Left Bank, gazing at the antiques in the closed shops, that he finally understood what had happened. With no lessening of the sexual desire that still flamed as brightly as it had at the beginning, they had, somehow, also become friends. It was a curious feeling for Arthur. He had never known a woman as a friend. Businesswomen like Sylvia, of course, and warm fresh bodies to go to bed with, yes. Hostesses at his dinner parties, objects to display or ignore as his wives had been at various times, but never had he found simple companionship with a woman before, and in a curious way he was finding that it strengthened the bond between them. I should have married someone like Bev, he thought to his surprise, instead of the three very different women who had shared his name. He was not wise enough to realize that women like Bev had not existed when he had been a young man. But he was clear-eyed enough to know that if he should in some wild romantic mood propose to the

233

woman at his side, there was every possibility she might say no.

It was a staggering thought to a man as self-centered as Arthur, and he was hard put to make conversation as they continued their walk while he considered it: a woman who didn't need him, who wasn't trying to trap him or exploit him, a woman who was with him simply because she enjoyed his company in bed and out.

If Arthur had been older, less spoiled and indulged, more aware of the changes going on in the world of men and women around him, he would have accepted what he realized that Sunday as the finest compliment Bev could have paid him. He did appreciate it, but at a time when in any other love affair he would be growing weary or bored, he found instead that the woman at his side had become a challenge, one he was determined to win.

18

It was several years before Beverly got her first mink coat. Her salary had grown as rapidly as her responsibilities and she could have afforded it sooner, but consciously she had put it far down on her list of desires. The money she made went into her apartment. Each trip to Europe for Welby's she found time to search out the antique stores she had grown to love, and with careful advice from Arthur and from Gerry, who had left the store to start his own decorating firm, she managed to find bargains that would be impossible ten years later. The plants in her apartment, except for a few favorite ones, disappeared, and the vacant spaces were filled with the gleaming furniture she had once so eagerly admired and reluctantly known she could not afford.

She had found other interests as well. Through Arthur she had met Lazlo Vladchek and his round little wife, Hansi. Lazlo ran an extremely successful art gallery on Madison Avenue, started when he had arrived in New York penniless after the war. An elegant man of fifty, with a head of silver curls and a clever European face, he had taken to Beverly from the first moment Arthur had brought her into his gallery. His was such an open, honest, direct appreciation of her that she had found herself laughing with pleasure even as he called his wife over.

'Hansi, look! Isn't she lovely? Dressed like a European and yet with that marvelous skin and legs only Americans have with their vitamins and orange juice. Hansi, I am definitely going to make a pass at this girl. You must understand and forgive me. In advance.'

'Lazlo, Mrs. Richmond happens to be with me.' Even Arthur was amused by this open approach.

'Don't think that protects her,' remarked Hansi, looking Beverly up and down carefully. 'My dear, I warn you right now, what Lazlo wants, he goes after. However, I should tell you, if by any chance you should weaken in some careless moment, I have not the slightest intention of giving him a divorce. Nor will he ask for it. I've been very careful to keep the lease to the gallery in my name, as well as the most important paintings. And if you only decide on a fling and find that this aging Hungarian has stolen and broken your heart, I shall offer you no more comfort than to say "I told you so." '

Lazlo made a sour face like a thwarted child. 'You see, Mrs. Richmond? The practiced charm of generations of my family, wasted on this plump little shrew. Does she allow me a moment of glamour? Of mystery? A chance to gaze into your eyes and charm you with a suggestion of an assignation? No.' He sighed theatrically. 'She treats me like a slightly backward little boy who should not be allowed to cross streets alone.'

'When I do,' Hansi replied equitably, 'you invariably go off the wrong way.' She smiled at Beverly. 'The man has absolutely no sense of direction.'

'Except in the tango,' interrupted Lazlo. 'I do a superb tango.' Right in front of his wife and Arthur, he seized Beverly and moved her through a complicated dance step. 'You see? Hansi, we must see more of this creature, she moves beautifully.' He released her as abruptly as he had grabbed her. 'And now I suppose to throw Arthur off the scent of this unbelievable new passion of mine we shall have to show him the new Picasso lithographs, although he clearly does not understand Picasso or appreciate him.'

'I like Picasso,' Arthur said with a smile. 'But if you're painting a lady with two eyes I think it helps to put a nose between them.'

'Infidel! However, you have excellent taste in women, so I shall have to forgive you.'

That was the beginning of the friendship that built between the Vladcheks and Bev, a friendship that was to ripen as time went on to include dinners in which they roared with laughter over Hansi's succulent chicken in paprika, cutthroat games of cards, excursions to odd lofts around town to examine and (very rarely) buy the work of new artists. It was a world Bev had known had existed in New York but that neither Arthur, the store, nor her own friends had ever shown her. She found she fitted into it as easily as a dress made especially for her. Oddly, it was a world in which Arthur was never completely comfortable. It was a world of artists who had little respect for people who had only money. People like Arthur were valuable, of course, to finance a concert or set up a fund for the education of a promising new singer or dancer, but they were not to be taken as people of importance. It was a world that realized a limousine was certainly more comfortable than a subway, but if the subway was faster and took you where you wanted to go, what did it matter?

Her friendship with Lazlo and Hansi didn't happen all at once. But over the months she began to realize that while they liked Arthur well enough, it was she who had become their friend, laughing off Lazlo's romantic advances, always announced at full voice and in the presence of his wife, and it was she who would stay behind to help Hansi clear up the dishes when the rest of the party had gone off to a political fund-raising or a demonstration of a new way of silk-screening posters. Often Bev would catch Hansi looking at her when Arthur was present, her dark eyes shrewd, her tiny mouth slightly pursed as if there were things she would have liked to tell her but decided with European prudence to keep to herself.

Bev suspected she knew what was in both of the Vladcheks' minds: that Arthur was not the right man for her. He would not have been comfortable at the impromptu picnic in Central Park they gave to celebrate the first real day of spring the following year—not unless there had been a servant to put out chairs, the wine was poured into Baccarat crystal, and the picnic basket catered by one of his favorite restaurants.

But Bev was happy with the Vladcheks—more than happy. They brought a color and gaiety to her life that in all the early years of working at the store and worrying about her marriage and her career she had never quite allowed. In the proper world of Ruth and Amory and their friends, she knew that to be a career woman no matter how successful, with a broken marriage behind her and no immediately eligible man in her life, was to be a failure. To Hansi and Lazlo she was more like a younger sister that they would not have changed or improved in any way. So through them, she entered a world of art and artists, learning to appreciate the drive of young talents, the discipline and dedication they gave to their lives, even as she did to her own work. Through her new friends she learned not only to collect and judge art but to keep a fresh eye for fashion, to see the excitement of clothes that were not rigid or coordinated but chosen for casual living. As one Madonna-faced harpist proclaimed one evening, 'Why should a table wear a lace cloth and not me? Besides, it doesn't wrinkle if someone suddenly decides to make love without warning.' The others had laughed and Lazlo had rolled his eyes in a perfect imitation of suppressed passion, but Beverly had caught the sounds of a new, freer world, and she would remember it as she selected designs in the future.

Not that she completely separated herself from Arthur and his world. She knew she enjoyed that world and always would. She relished the comforts of his way of life, but she never allowed herself to make them necessary for her own happiness. And one of her greatest satisfactions at the parties they attended was that she was no longer being looked at as 'Arthur's girl' or 'friend' or whatever was the current word for that season. She was beginning to be known not just in the world of fashion but as one of a new wave of women who were making their own name and place in the world of business. Men who might simply have eyed her appreciatively at cocktail parties in the past once they found out her position at Welby's began to talk to her of business, of financing and the economic future of the whole intertwined world that produced the clothes, cosmetics, and perfumes that American women wanted and, wanting, bought. There was change in the air, a shift of power. Styles still originated in France, but other countries were beginning to enter the market: Italy with its fluid silks and supple leathers, Britain with the first stirrings of its mod designs, German craftsmanship. And moving quickly and firmly ahead of them into the lead, America. The old days when what one wore or put on one's face or used as a perfume was decreed only by a tiny cluster of European arbiters was ending. Women from all over the globe were snatching up the better-made American creams and lotions, the simpler clothes in newer man-made fabrics, the opulent furs that only American designers seemed to know how to handle.

Welby's had its own fur department by now, and deliberately Bev had refrained from examining it, though she knew every other department of the store thoroughly. Perhaps she sensed what she saw there would be a temptation she was not quite willing to accept. Fur coats for women like Bev were what their mothers bought, especially the more expensive furs. The era of 'fun furs' (a phrase Beverly was to grow to hate) had not yet begun. To her, a fur coat was dark and heavy and solidly constructed, the clear and definite sign of an affluent husband and one's own middle age. But when Sylvia, now promoted to be the only woman among Welby's few vice-presidents, arrived lavishly draped in mink, Bev could not stop a gasp of appreciation.

'I know, I know. I swore I'd never get one,' said Sylvia as she held the coat out wide, parading back and forth across her office. 'But they're predicting a cold winter, and what the hell, a vice-president ought to have something besides an attaché case to show she's arrived.'

'What do you think Herman will say?' asked Bev with a small smile, knowing not a penny of what he earned had been spent on the purchase.

'Not a darn word. Especially since I'm having a zip-out liner in beaver made for his new raincoat. I think the damn thing is going to cost more than this. That's what we get for not having a men's department.'

This had long been one of Sylvia's complaints against the store, and Bev was reasonably sure that her recent promotion to vice-president was a sign from the entrenched and conservative management of Welby's that they were about to change their mind.

'Incidentally,' Sylvia went on, 'it's time you got yourself down to the third floor and saw what's going on in the fur department.'

'I know,' said Bev. 'Pastel mink stoles and Persian lamb blazers. No thanks.'

'They're doing a lot more than that. And maybe it's time you stopped looking like Little Miss Ingenue around here. I happen to know there are big plans in the making, *money* plans. And any woman who wants the next rung up had better start looking successful. Luckily, you're a small size so it won't take as much fur to cover you as it does me.'

Bev was far more interested in the rumors Sylvia was hinting at, but she knew this afternoon at least her chances of finding anything out other than about the growing fur salon were minimal. 'All right, Sylvia. I'll take a look. But I hate spending that kind of money on a status symbol.'

'Listen, don't knock status symbols. That's the only respectable way women can impress some people, people we may need to impress in the near future. And I do mean "we." '

This intrigued Bev even more, and that afternoon when she had finished approving the ads for the Sunday *Times* she took the elevator down to the third floor. Forty minutes later, thanks to her store discount and the fact that they had a model in her size, she had taken one more step into looking like what she called privately 'the world of Arthur's women.' She deliberately arranged for the coat to be ready on a day when he planned to take her to dinner, calling him to say she would meet him at the restaurant. Whatever his reaction to her independence would be, she could handle it better in a public place.

They were to have dinner that night at the currently most successful restaurant in New York, decorated with huge and mythical portraits of the Roman Caesars. As she came through the doors she saw Arthur standing at the bar. She hesitated for a moment, waiting for him to look up first, wondering what his reaction would be. He stared at her and then slowly started to smile.

'Well! Either I have been supplanted by a wealthy and more persuasive man or our Beverly has joined the ranks of the Philistines.'

'Don't be so sure. When I take the coat off, I might be wearing a hand-woven blouse from the Village. Just to keep everything in proportion.'

'You look wonderful.' He leaned forward to kiss her on the cheek. This was rare for him. His kisses were private, passionately on the mouth and the brisk prelude to lovemaking. Almost never did he kiss her in public, even the social kissing on the cheek becoming the fashion even among enemies. He stepped back and looked at her appraisingly. 'Who finally persuaded you to take the big leap?'

'Arthur, stop it. You're talking as if I'd been going around looking like a drudge.'

'You've been going around, as you call it, looking like a very attractive young woman who works for a living. Now you look like somebody who hires and fires people. Something tells me the store must be involved in this. Shall we discuss it at our table?'

As they started toward the maitre d', they became aware that this rather aloof personage was in the middle of a scene with a highly indignant couple. Bev had, over the years, seen such arguments often in the restaurants Arthur had taken her to, couples who had made reservations, usually weeks in advance from out-of-town, and on the evening they had arranged were being turned away as the captains and managers of the chic restaurants gave their tables to more frequent and favored customers. It always made her slightly embarrassed as she passed these frustrated diners, knowing that often Arthur had not even bothered with a reservation but had merely arrived, confident that the best table would instantly be made available for them.

Tonight, however, the argument was more heated than usual, blocking their entrance into the main room of the restaurant. The manager, in the black and white of his profession, with a nose as proudly Roman as any of the portraits on the wall, was trying to calm an extremely indignant woman as her silent husband stood back. It was the woman's outraged voice as well as her Southern accent that caught Bev's attention.

'Ah think this is an absolute outrage! That reservation was made by our hotel the day we arrived. Ah've never heard of anybody being treated like that! Why back home—' Frustrated, she turned to her husband. 'Frank! Don't you just stand there! Say something to this man!'

Maybe it was the name, although later that night Bev realized she must have heard that name hundreds of times in the years that had passed, but she looked at the couple more closely, touching Arthur's arm to make him stop.

The man ahead of them looked uncomfortable. His hair was thinning, and his dark suit had obviously been purchased at a time when his figure had been leaner, with no incipient flesh to strain the button at the waistline of his coat. Clearly he was between two antagonists, neither of whom he felt prepared to handle. 'Sally,' he said hesitantly, 'let's not make a fuss about it. We'll find another restaurant.'

'I don't want another restaurant! I told all the girls back home we were going to eat here and I'm not going back to say some snooty Eye-talian tried to keep us out!'

Bev knew him then, knew him instantly, seeing through the marks that more than fifteen years had left on his face. Impulsively, she stepped forward. 'Frank? Frank Burroughs?'

He looked at her, almost frightened, as if he could not take being attacked from one more side. His wife stopped in mid-sentence, her eyes narrowing as she studied Bev carefully. Bev did not even notice Arthur or the captain watching her as she stepped forward.

'It is Frank, isn't it? Frank Burroughs? I'm Beverly. Beverly Richmond—well'—she smiled at Frank's wife— 'Frank would have known me as Beverly Thyson.'

'My God . . . Beverly!' He shifted uneasily, obviously not sure whether he should shake her hand or kiss her and, unable to make a decision, simply bowed slightly. 'You look wonderful!'

She reached out and took his hand in hers, knowing his wife was standing there seething with speculation over who she was. Obviously he had never told her about them. The clear envy in his wife's eyes was better than a mirror. Thank you, Sylvia, Bev thought gratefully. Thank you, fur department at Welby's and Arthur, for being better looking than Frank and having a reserved table, and thank you, Jean-Pierre, for having done my hair for tonight.

'Arthur?'

She looked at him with a sweet smile on her face. She knew he knew her well enough to realize there was more to this casual reunion than she was letting on, and she also knew he would be full of questions later. But she didn't care. For the next couple of hours she intended to taste what she expected to be the sweetest dish in the world: revenge.

'Don't you think that nice captain could find a table for all of us? I haven't seen Frank in years. And I've never met his wife.'

She must have loved him once, Arthur thought as he made

the arrangements. Loved him probably more than she'll ever love me. There was a glitter in her eyes and an air of modest triumph about her as she took her place beside the frumpy woman this guy had married. It should be an interesting evening, Arthur thought, as he ordered the special champagne he knew Bev loved. Although what she could have seen in this poor wimp he couldn't possibly guess.

'Two children now. A girl and a boy.'

'Let's see, they'd be how old?'

'Thirteen and twelve,' Sally interjected. She didn't know what Frank's relationship with this cool, poised woman next to her was, but she intended to find out, if not during this dinner then definitely later. She tried to smooth out the skirt of her dress, but she knew it was too tight, as was her girdle under it. Pink had always been her good color, but she realized Beverly and most of the other women in the room were in simple black. New York women! Well, at least her garnets were good. They'd been her grandmother's and everybody could tell what they were, which is more than could be said for the strings of pearls that every other woman in the room seemed to be wearing. You can buy pearls in a five-and-dime, she thought as she tried to maneuver the large menu around so she could keep an eye on her husband and Beverly. Garnets are something you only get from family.

'Oh? You've been married that long, Sally?'

'Longer. We didn't have any children for the first couple of years.'

Bev forced herself to smile. 'How wise,' she muttered. So Frank had been trapped by a lie! All these years she'd wondered about that, and she could see by the look on his face that it was still a live and aching wound inside him. Ah, Frank, she thought. You fool! With all your talk of honor. You were tricked by the oldest female ruse in the world. Or were you? Was the lie from you . . . and not from her?

'What field are you in, Frank?' Arthur decided that if Bev wanted answers, somebody outside whatever the two of them shared was going to have to ask the questions.

'Frank works for Daddy,' Sally said, not giving her husband a chance to speak. 'He started out to be a lawyer, even had all kinds of wild ideas about our moving up here, but

243

Daddy and I soon put a stop to that. I mean, Daddy has this big furniture business. It's been in our family for simply years. And he knew somebody was going to have to take over someday, what with him and Mama not having any sons. So I persuaded Frank to come into the business.'

I'll just bet you did, thought Beverly. So much for Frank's dreams of the quiet, dignified practice of law.

'Not that Sally's father really needs any help, even today,' remarked Frank. 'He's a very healthy man. He'll be around forever.' It was obvious to everyone at the table but Sally that he did not regard the fact with total joy.

'I certainly hope so! Lands, a business like Daddy's needs somebody who can really take charge.' That ought to stop them, thought Sally. Let them know that they weren't just anybody, that the Crawfords counted for something down home. 'And it's so comfortable in Virginia. I mean, everybody knows who really matters. Not like up here. New Yorkers are so pushy sometimes. They just think they about own the earth.'

'A lot of them do,' remarked Arthur dryly. 'Or at least the more valuable parts of it. Frank, I think you're ready for another drink.'

Arthur was tactful enough not to come up to her apartment after they had dropped the Burroughses back at their hotel. Whatever she intended to tell him about Frank could wait for the future. The triumph she had expected throughout the evening obviously had not happened. Sally had never stopped talking, interrupting with complaints about the food, the service, New York, and New Yorkers in general with pointed questions.

'You said "Mrs. Richmond"? Where would Mr. Richmond be?'

'We're divorced. He was called back into the service, but he's back now, out in the Midwest.' She thought of the joy in Jane's voice when she had called with the news. No matter how many years passed, Ed was still Jane's little boy, and Bev knew the relief she felt in having him safe again. The divorce decree had finally come through and rested securely in Beverly's safety deposit box, and, with the exception of her monthly calls to Jane, she had almost succeeded in blocking out the years of her marriage. And now this loud,

244

vulgar woman was pulling at the scars again, scars she had thought had long since disappeared.

'Why, that's a shame, honey!' Sally said with obvious false sympathy. ''Course, down home we still think divorce's just about the worst thing that can happen to a woman. But I guess we're old-fashioned. And I know it's not easy for a woman when she gets to a certain age to find herself another man.'

'Oh, she's found one,' Arthur interjected smoothly. 'I keep proposing and proposing, and she keeps turning me down.' All right, Bev, he thought, you owe me one for that.

'Is that so?' Sally was momentarily deflated. 'I just don't know what gets into these modern career women these days.' She glanced at her husband, who was holding up a slightly unsteady finger to beckon the waiter. 'Frank, you're not going to have a fourth martini, are you?'

Bev closed the door behind her, letting her new coat drop on the couch. The draperies were not closed, and there was enough light from the street below to show the contours of the room. What an awful evening! She remembered a saying she had read or heard once: 'Revenge is a dish best tasted cold.' They were wrong, whoever had thought that. Revenge should be taken when you're first hurt and angry, when quite literally you feel yourself capable of murder. Not like this, so many years later. If she could have wished for one thing at that moment, it would have been that she had never seen Frank again. Before, at least, there had been memories, bad ones at times, but gentle ones, too, full of all the hopes and dreams she had once had, of a home and a husband and children.

Strange. She hadn't really thought about Frank for a long time. Perhaps during the early years with Ed she had compared the marriage she had to the one she had been cheated out of, comparing it always, she had to admit, to Ed's disadvantage. And perhaps, with Ed gone, there had still remained some sort of goal that one day she would set out to achieve, once she had established herself and her career. She had never fooled herself that a marriage to Arthur would fulfill that dream. She knew him too well for that, although she could have hugged him for the graceful lie he had told at dinner tonight. But like many women of her age, the old hopes could still come back and haunt her on the sleepless nights that everyone has, the nights when you toss in your bed, wondering where your life is going, whether you have made the right choices, wondering even if there are any choices left to make.

Beverly realized that night as she sat in her dark apartment that she was no longer the same woman she had been even that afternoon. Some small part of herself had died this evening. Without sentiment, she faced it. She was never going to have her own family. There would never be the perfect white house, the handsome, sensible adult husband, the years of watching her own children grow. Whatever happened to her, and she was young enough to know that many possibilities still remained, that kind of marriage, of complete and total linkage with the past, with her parents and grandparents and their grandparents before them onto a future of the following generations, that was over forever. It was not just her age or that she had seen so clearly the disaster of Frank's marriage. She had been forced to look deep into herself and realize it would never have happened to her even if Frank had been loyal or Ed the man she had hoped he would become. She knew now Frank had been some impossible dream, and perhaps he too had known it, so that it didn't really matter whether the lie that had hurt her so cruelly had been his or Sally's.

She was too much of a realist, she knew, as she sat there in the dark, to think she would have made Frank any happier than Sally. There had always been a weakness in him, as there had been in Ed, only both times she had been too much in love to see it. The energy that surged through her would probably have turned Frank into what she had seen tonight, a frightened, bitter drunk. She had no illusions now that she could have shared a life with him peacefully, protecting him from the buffets of the world that he had not the strength to face. She had failed to do that with Ed, and Ed at least had loved her, at least had been willing to try.

She looked at her life as it stretched behind her. She had been so young, so ignorant when she had argued with Ruth that a woman could have everything in life, a career and a marriage, both of them working together like the wheels meshing in a watch. Ruth had known better, although her choices had not made her happy, what with the death of

246

Geoff and now this oddly cold marriage she seemed to be having with Amory.

Bev allowed herself that evening the self-indulgence of memory. The end of the war and Frank slim and young and passionate, the terrible destructive guilt she had felt after she had given herself to him and he had left her. That had taken her to Neil for punishment. She wondered what had happened to the musician. She suspected with the wildness of his life he was already dead. It didn't really matter. But because of Neil she had married Ed, warming herself with his decency and love until once more the reality of life made her face the fact that she could not match her life with his. And now there was Arthur, sensual, selfish, often arrogant, generous with his time and his money when he felt like it, but cold and locked in his heart. Where are the men, she wanted to shout that night? The men that had been promised to the women of her age by their mothers and the movies and the novels they had read? Strong, kind, decent men, ready to move into adulthood, eager to become husbands and fathers? Only she knew that night they didn't exist, any more than the girls who had been promised to them existed: sweet and simple and demure with passions that only would be turned on, like a light switch, once some man had said 'I do' in front of a congregation.

It's been a lie, she thought. There was no cynicism in her, and no desire for tears. I suppose, in a way, I've even become part of it, selling clothes and cosmetics and illusions, dreams that an eyeshadow or a mink coat or a new way of wearing your hair will bring you total happiness and fulfillment. Well, let other people be fooled by the illusions; she had choked them in herself forever.

Time to go to bed, she thought as she hung up her new mink coat. Tomorrow she knew she would get a phone call from Frank at the office, a phone call made not from his hotel room but from a public booth, trying to arrange a secret meeting. His leg had pressed against hers more than once during the dinner, and it had not been by accident. Well, she would have the receptionist put him off, even after the inevitable flowers arrived. She knew quite clearly what he would want: a short, brief sexual encounter, to be followed possibly by hurried, future visits up from Virginia on 'company business,' as he would explain to an increasingly suspicious Sally. Bev suspected it had happened already with other women. Well, she would not be one of them. Sally was welcome to him. What interested her far more was what Sylvia had hinted about the future of the store.

19

The store was to be sold. Sylvia had been hearing rumors for some time and with a mixture of discreet questions and private snooping had discovered most of the details of the operation long before they were announced. There was considerable outcry about the sale; shocked elderly customers who had been outfitted there from birth to old age wrote protesting letters to the *New York Times*, and there was even talk by some of the younger employees of picketing on the sidewalk, something so totally alien to Welby's respectable tradition that the idea was dropped almost at once.

The new owners, a Midwestern conglomerate named Rales Incorporated, hurried into public print with announcements that they had no intention of changing any of the quality and service that had made Welby's an important name in American fashion, but Sylvia—and Beverly, when she heard the news—was too sensible to be fooled by such obvious public relations.

'The changes will be small at first, I suspect,' said Sylvia, one afternoon after the news had been announced. 'After all, what they're buying is the name, the tradition of quality. They're not going to turn us into a cut-rate department store.'

'What about the building itself?' asked Bev. Each day it seemed a new skyscraper was being constructed around them, and she was well aware that the dignified old store was sitting on a piece of real estate that could only increase in value.

'They're keeping it. I don't mean to say twenty years from now we'll still be here, but at the moment we're going to be the flagship of their attempt to control the quality fashion market. They're already negotiating with a couple of textile houses . . . I wouldn't be surprised if Arthur's is one of them. And they've got feelers out to some of the fashion magazines that haven't been doing too well. There's even talk of putting out their own line of cosmetics. Big bucks, Bev.'

'And us? Where do we fit in?'

'That's what's going to be interesting to find out,' said Sylvia, fixing another cigarette in her holder. 'They're going to need us,' she added grimly. 'If they think a regiment of accountants in three-piece suits are going to be able to pick what the American woman wants to wear a year from now, they're in for a big surprise!'

The next few months were the most nerve-racking Bev had spent with the store since she had started there as a salesgirl. New executives came and, almost as quickly, went. It was clear that the last descendants of the original founders of the store were becoming little more than figureheads, shuffling meaningless papers in their offices and waiting for phone calls from the center of the organization in Chicago. Whoever was the actual power that controlled the giant organization, if indeed there was one, neither Bev nor Sylvia could find out. They pored over Rales reports, trying to tie the various names listed with the changes that were occurring in the store itself. That there was some kind of power struggle going on they were both aware, but for the first months they felt they and the store they worked for were like some giant indigestible meal a dragon had swallowed and could neither digest nor spit out.

It was the beginning of an age of commercial acquisitions. Old family firms that had contentedly been doing business in some cases for over a century were suddenly and bewilderedly reporting to Texas bank presidents. Oil money, rich and apparently endless, was gurgling into nearly every vein of American business, consolidating, enlarging, opening shopping malls and branches of quality stores in areas that only a short time before had been the barren acres surrounding big cities.

Bev and Sylvia and a few other executives at their level were able to ride out the changes. After a few disastrous independent decisions ('Made by a computer, I'll bet,' Sylvia had said of one with disgust), fashion was once more placed in the hands of the people trained to shape it. By the end of the first year, Sylvia was made executive vice-president of the store itself, a title that obscured the fact only to outsiders that she was in all but name president of the store.

'Of course they won't give me the title,' she grumbled. 'Some man will have that. But I think they've learned from their damn sack dresses and Nehru jackets to keep their nose out of what they don't know.' She was referring to two of the biggest failures the industry had known, failures that had been minimized for Welby's and the Rales conglomerate by Beverly's having had the sense to buy extra material in Europe, enough to market the loose, unpopular female fashions by adding hastily constructed self-belts to define the slender waists American women refused to conceal. Still, Bev was shrewd enough to realize that loose, comfortable fashions could be attractive on a woman with a figure problem, and years later when caftans were first making a tentative appearance on the fashion market she supported them vigorously, ordering them in beautiful colors and flowing, soft materials that instantly became popular.

But after the first year she found she was still in the same position she had been before. The corporation had raised her salary at Sylvia's insistence, and she had Sylvia's old office now and her own secretary. But like many executives at her level whose companies had been absorbed, she was facing the fact that at barely forty she was apparently at a dead end.

'What is it, Sylvia?' she complained one afternoon in the early 1960s when the two women were alone in Sylvia's office. They had kicked off their shoes and were relaxing over a cup of tea. Most of the afternoon had been dissipated by a company luncheon they had been forced to attend, honoring the promotion of a junior vice-president to the much higher position of Rales district manager, in charge of all the many enterprises involved on the entire East Coast. 'Am I using the wrong toothpaste? Is it "something my best friends won't tell me"?' she said, quoting the popular ad. 'Why should that know-nothing Andy Treblett get that promotion? If they gave him a company watch I'll bet he wouldn't know enough to wind it!'

'He's a man,' answered Sylvia. 'Listen, Bev, let's not kid ourselves. American businesses don't like women. Not in top jobs. The guys get scared. Oh, they claim they have a lot of other reasons. That we're unreliable, that five days every month we're going to poop out on them, that we'll get married or pregnant or burst into tears. But the real reason out there is they're frightened. They've been running the world for centuries, and they and we both know what a mess they've made of it. So they're hanging on to their turf with all the strength in their greedy little fingers.'

'It's got to be more than that, Sylvia,' Bev persisted. 'I'm free, I'm able to travel, I know every aspect of the fashion world, and as far as I know I haven't stepped on any precious male egos. I should have had that job. I'm trained for it, I can handle it, and I don't mind saying I'm damn mad I didn't get it.'

'Well, just say it to me, honey. Don't say it outside there. If it's any consolation, I agree with you. It should have been your promotion. Hell, it doesn't matter to me. I've got what I want. It would be nice to have the title of president, but I can live without it. I don't want to go any further, and Herman doesn't want it either. He hasn't been as well as he should be, and I can see a time ahead of us, and not too long from now, when it's going to be a nice little apartment in Florida and goodbye nine-to-five forever.'

'Could you take that?' Bev looked at her with honest amazement. She was so used to Sylvia she never thought of her in terms of time or age, but she realized that Sylvia would have to be fairly close to retirement age. After all, last June she herself had turned forty, something she had thought would be a terrifying milestone but which had turned out glorious. Arthur had unexpectedly joined her two days before in Mexico City, and together they had driven to the topsy-turvy village of Taxco, where she had made a successful deal to buy silver jewelry for the store. They had had dinner in the patio of a little inn, and that night, after warching the moon rise over the old cathedral, had made love with a joy and enthusiasm that neither had experienced in a long time. 'Could you really bear to stop working?' she asked more pointedly.

Sylvia sighed. 'I don't think I'm cut out for retirement, exactly. But I owe Herman something. I don't know how many more years he'll have—how many more any of us have, for that matter. He never complains, but I know he hates the winters up here. He gets this bad cough starting the first of

November and it doesn't seem to leave until May.' Her face was serious. 'I need him in my life, Bev. I want him well and happy. And if it means giving up the rag trade, maybe that's a decision I'm going to have to make.' She smiled at the worried look on Bev's face. 'Hey, don't frown. It causes wrinkles. Let's get back to you. If I did retire, I would have said last week you would automatically take my place. Now, after Treblett's getting this promotion, I'm not so sure. There might be something more than just a little antifeminism going on here. I think I'd better snoop around and find out what's happening. Meanwhile, if I were you, I'd put out a few feelers on my own with other companies. Just in case.'

Bev knew exactly what she meant. She had seen it happen before, bright executives inexplicably dead-ended in their careers. If they submitted, the next step was generally to fire them. It's all wrong, she thought as she went back to her office. I've worked harder than anyone else in this organization, I've given more of my time and my energy. I know more about what will sell and what won't . . . I even know why. Well, Welby's isn't the world, and if I can't rise here, maybe it's time I found a place where I can. Never for a second did she doubt that she could find another job if she had to. Rather, it seemed like a new, challenging game to be mastered. Over the years she had met many important people in all the different aspects of the fashion world: cosmetics, advertising, magazine reporting, textile design.

That brought her thoughts to Arthur. Over the past couple of years they hadn't seen much of each other. There had been no clear break, just that they had both been busy and somehow their worlds had become more separate. With the exception of the time in Mexico, their business trips had not coincided, and while they still met for dinner at least once a month, more and more often it was only for dinner. Whatever happened at Welby's, she was determined not to tell Arthur. The last thing she wanted was to have him feel he could use his influence on her career or her life.

That afternoon she made a careful list of the fields where she might find the kind of position that she would enjoy, and that would pay her the comfortable salary she was receiving from the department store. For all her knowledge and contacts, she was surprised to find how short the list actually was. She had no hesitancy about her abilities to handle a wide variety of jobs. She had long since grown into more areas of responsibility in the store than just choosing the designs for the following season. But at this period in the sixties she was finding, as many capable women were, that the salaries they could receive were in no way comparable to what a man would get in a similar position. In fact, it was almost a classic joke at one of the glossiest of fashion magazines that attracted young, eager women with each June graduation that there was no way they could afford to work there without a generous allowance from their families.

It was a week before Sylvia called her into her office for another private conference. She told Beverly to close the door, and when she was sure they would not be overheard or interrupted she plunged right into the problem.

'You're not going to like what I've got to say,' she began. 'And I could be wrong, but I don't think so. What I'm hearing comes from a couple of different sources. All very subtle because they know we're friends, but I'm getting a picture and I don't much like it.'

'I never expected to get this far without making enemies, Sylvia. What are they saying? That I'm watering the perfume? Or taking kickbacks from the designers? Because I can stand up to any business charge they want to make.'

'They know that. No, it's a little nastier than that. You remember Karen Landers?' Bev thought back to the girls she had started with at the store. Karen had been the only one who had continued on at Welby's, rising slowly to a position of some responsibility but never making a total success of her career or her life. Twice married and divorced, both times she had left Welby's, tried other jobs, and come back to the store again. Slightly older than Bev, she had never gone higher than being an assistant buyer and probably never would. Shielded in her private office, Bev had not been aware of the world of gossip that went around concerning the executives, but if any rumors were being started about her life she was not surprised to find Karen behind them.

'What's she up to now?'

'A nice messy little affair with that guy from the Rales home office. You know, Charlie What's-his-name, who comes to town once a month. Married, wears those awful silk suits, about twenty pounds overweight.'

'I know who you mean. What's that got to do with me?'

'She's handing him an earful. Apparently, in between the nightclubs and bed they talk. Or rather, she talks and he listens. And what he hears he takes right back to the big boys in Chicago.'

'Stop beating around the bush, Sylvia. What's she telling him?'

Sylvia hesitated. She knew what she was going to say would hurt Beverly, probably more than anything that had ever passed between them over the years. And it was so damn unfair! The typical rumor that envious little men and women attached to anybody successful, to make their own failures in life more acceptable to themselves and the people around them.

'Did you know Rales has been trying to buy Arthur Powers's firm? And that he's turned them down?'

Bev stared at her, puzzled. 'What's that got to do with me?'

'Did you also know that Arthur owns a good chunk of Welby's stock? So that when the store was absorbed by Rales he made a very good profit?'

'No, of course I didn't!' She thought back over her conversations with Arthur. With his advice she had invested in several stocks and watched them grow successfully, but he had never once mentioned that he had any financial interests in her store.

'The rumor is that Arthur turned down Rales's offer because an insider tipped him off that they would up the ante if he did.'

'And . . . I'm the "insider"?' Bev felt a little sick.

'Not just that. Apparently the big boys in Chicago have it in their pointed heads that your rise at Welby's has been because of Arthur's influence. That the two of you are not just "great and good friends," as the magazines put it, but that without his push over the years you'd just be another salesgirl.'

Bev took a deep breath and forced her voice to remain steady. 'That sounds like our little Karen's version of the news.'

'Anyway, Rales is a very conservative group, expense-account lunches or no. And they've got it in their corporate heads that you're some kind of fluffball who couldn't be

255

trusted to find her way to the ladies' room without somebody guiding you.'

'Sylvia, of all the rotten—!'

'Wait a minute, Bev. It gets worse. Apparently somebody at Rales even talked to Arthur about this, and while I'm not absolutely positive, the implication was that he didn't exactly deny it.'

'I don't believe it! Arthur would never do a thing like that! He—' She stopped abruptly. Arthur would indeed have done a thing like that, just a little lesson to keep her in her place. She thought of all the nights she'd had to refuse his invitations because of work, the trips she'd turned down, the phone calls she had sometimes forgotten to return under the pressures of business. She had never had any illusions that he was an easy man or a forgiving one or that his pride and ego were not enormous and quickly injured. But this! This was the act of an enemy! He'd never loved her enough to hate her that much, had he?

'You going to be sick, Bev?'

'No. I'm just . . . stunned, I guess.' She looked at Sylvia. 'How do I fight this, Sylvia? Show them the profit sheets? The decisions I've made? Force Arthur to tell them the truth?'

'Hold on, Bev. We don't know that Arthur had anything specific to do with this. He's not my favorite person in the world, but I'd never accuse him of deliberately lying about you. It's just that when gossip starts, there doesn't seem to be any end to it.'

'Oh, there's an end to it, Sylvia.' Bev's voice was cold and controlled. 'Right or wrong, I've made a big mistake in letting myself be linked with Arthur all these years. I made up my mind to that years ago in Paris, but I guess I've been careless. You know I've never asked a single favor from him. I never let him turn me into one of his possessions.'

'You even bought your own mink coat,' remarked Sylvia dryly. She was glad to see the way Beverly was taking it. She should have expected that. She knew the younger woman was strong, but anybody could be expected to cave in at least momentarily when confronted with such a pack of lies. And while Bev might not think Arthur capable of spreading rumors, Sylvia wasn't so sure. Arthur was getting older too, and power was important to him—power over his company, over people. Bev was the one person he had never been able to control.

Bev stood up, her face set. 'All right. No more Arthur. Any suggestions on what I should do next, Sylvia? Because I'm going to fight this, and hard.'

'I think maybe it's time you had a little more of what the press calls "visibility." Let's see if I can arrange a couple of articles in the fashion magazines about your rise to success. Pictures of you, your office, your life-style, the apartment.'

'Not until I have redecorated, I think, Sylvia.' Bev was surprised to hear the edge of bitterness in her voice. 'I'm getting a little tired of wall-to-wall carpeting anyway.' She had changed the carpeting, of course, since that first afternoon so many years ago, but with a combination of practicality and perhaps a little sentiment, she had kept the style. Now was the time to be done with it.

Later that evening, when Sylvia had finished dinner with Herman, she told him what had happened. He listened to her patiently and with interest, as he always did whenever she brought the problems of the store home.

'It's just so damn unfair,' she said, summing it up.

'She's a strong woman, Sylvia. She'll survive it.'

'Surviving isn't living. And what else has she got in her life?' That was what really hurt. Bev had made her own choices, and tonight she must be realizing, perhaps for the first time, that with all she had accomplished, she still only had half an existence.

But Bev was not spending the evening with regrets. She left the office promptly at five, early for her, and went straight back to her apartment. Ruth had called her earlier, saying she wanted to discuss something, and Bev wanted to be sure the place was in order before she arrived, as well as give herself time to arrange her own thoughts. Breaking with Arthur would be no problem emotionally. She had a strong instinct that the wild story Sylvia had told her was perfectly true. In a curious way she could even understand his thinking and why he might have allowed the rumors to spread, if not actually starting them. She had found him enjoyable over the years as a friend and exciting at times as a lover, but she never doubted that at this critical stage of her life and her career she could break away from him forever without regrets.

The question was how to make the break public, sufficiently so that the whole of their small fashion world would know she was her own woman and, she hoped, realize that she always had been. Coldly, practically, as she waited for Ruth, she considered her alternatives. There weren't many. She could hardly take an ad in *Women's Wear Daily* proclaiming that she no longer knew Arthur, and any attempt to fight rumor with rumor would only succeed in making her look defensive. No, there was only one clear option. Arthur would have to be supplanted in her life by another man. Ed, you would have come in handy here, she thought wryly. Even an unsuccessful husband as a constant and public escort, host to future parties (Sylvia's advice about publicity was excellent), would establish her own independence. But it had been a long time since she had spoken to either Jane or Marion, almost by an unspecified mutual consent between the three of them. Not that she had any illusions that Ed would come running after all this time. Or that she would want him even if he did.

No, she would need an affair with someone here in New York. Deliberately, she opened her address book to look for a possible candidate. There had been brief episodes with other men in the past years, never lasting more than three or four meetings, nothing that had affected her heart or her plans. The first had been a young composer that Lazlo and Hansi had introduced her to, about to have his first major concert in New York and literally terrified at the prospect. She had comforted him one evening and on impulse had invited him off to the country for the weekend before the concert. He had been grateful and loving, his confidence in himself reassured. The concert had been an enormous success, and afterward he had been invited to conduct his own music with many major orchestras around the world. She didn't even know where he was at the moment. She seemed to remember the Vladcheks saying something about Italy.

There had been other men, not many, but a few. One or two were married but not working at it seriously, and after a busy night at a trade showing she had sometimes allowed herself to sleep with them, knowing it was not important to either of them. One of what Sylvia had called 'little flings.'

Obviously, trying to renew a relationship with any of them, even if they both wanted it, would leave her no better off in terms of rumors than the one concerning Arthur.

She hesitated when she came to Ralph's name. Ralph Pearce had come into her life the year before, when her building had gone co-op. He had been the man she dealt with at her bank, arranging for the money to purchase not only her apartment but the studio next to it, so that she now had two full bedrooms, one of which she could and did use as an office, plus the maid's room and bath, as well as the large and elegant living room. She knew Ralph was interested in her and that much of his life outside the bank was quietly unhappy. She had heard him say enough to realize that his long and childless marriage was not a good one; his wife was in and out of various alcoholic sanitariums several times each year. She liked Ralph as a person, respected the way he never allowed himself to say a word against his wife or wallow in self-pity over his situation. He was a convenient man as an escort and certainly would be a guest at any party she gave, but his position ruled him out for her purposes. A successful banker was not what she needed to show the world she was making her life on her own. Perhaps Ruth would know of some single man that would be right.

The two women had not seen each other for several weeks, and at first Bev was shocked at Ruth's appearance. The soft, plump contours of her friend's face seemed to have disappeared; her eyes were restless, and there were dark circles under them.

'How's Amory?' Bev asked at last.

'He's . . . all right,' Ruth answered evasively. 'Actually it's rather difficult to explain, but in a way he's why I'm here. Ever since he decided we should move to the suburbs, there seem to have been a few more problems than usual.'

Bev had a fairly sharp idea of what the problems were. Amory had insisted on the move a year before, buying a large and, Bev thought privately, hideous mansion in Connecticut. The reason he had given was that Ruth's boys were growing up too unruly in the city, that they needed to be out in the country where life would be simpler, and presumably there would be enough room so that they would not get on his nerves. However, almost immediately after the move he had

259

enrolled the boys in boarding schools, leaving Ruth alone much of the time. She had never fought him on these decisions. Early in their marriage she had tried, unsuccessfully, to reason with him, but Amory was far different from her first husband. Whenever she had questioned his decisions or even some tiny detail he had proposed, he would grow icily cold and refuse to speak to her at all, sometimes for as long as a week. After the first two years of their marriage he had taken to sleeping in his own room, so that the silences between them had a way of growing into something almost menacing. Ruth had learned the only way to keep even the semblance of cordial relations alive between them was to instantly give him his own way. Like all bullies, he had grown more demanding as a result, and much as Ruth missed her sons, she could not honestly wish them to be in the same house with their stepfather for any length of time. She loved the boys deeply and knew without their speaking that they were as unhappy with Amory as he was with them. Still, she never seriously considered leaving her second husband. The boys were young and healthy, they would survive the harshness they had found, and at least Amory was providing them with excellent educations. As for herself, she could endure her life and knew, after the death of her parents, she basically had no other choice.

'It's Alma, actually,' said Ruth. Alma had first come into her household after Geoff's death, a bright-faced, cheerful young girl. She knew how much the girl had given her family over the years, and now, with Amory being so inflexible . . . 'Amory's never really gotten along with her. He seems to find something new to pick on every day. Either she didn't iron his shirts right or his egg was too hard. You know how fussy he can be.'

Bev knew exactly. Her private opinion of Amory had never been high, and through the years of his marriage with Ruth it had sunk with each meeting. He was a petty little tyrant who had probably always been jealous of his law partner Geoffrey and had thought by marrying Ruth and acquiring their sons as an instant family he would somehow become as loved and admired as Geoff. It hadn't happened, of course, because there was nothing in him to give, and the resentment he must have felt had turned him into a crabby, difficult, rigid autocrat. Poor Ruth, thought Bev, he must make her life hell.

'I'm surprised Alma hasn't quit.'

'She'd like to, but Bev, she's been with me and the boys since she was nineteen. I think she's scared of the outside world, afraid every man who's the head of the household is going to turn out—well, like Amory. And now he's talking about . . . well, he thinks we should have a couple working for us. Something a little more grand than Alma. So that he can entertain more.'

Bev could see him now, fussing over the decanting of the wine with a butler, playing lord of the manor. No, Alma would definitely not fit into that picture.

'How do you feel about all this?'

'I don't know, Bev.' She sighed a little. 'Maybe if we entertained more he'd be home more. He works awfully hard, you know,' she added hastily. 'And often it's too late to make the trip out to the country. Maybe if I could make life a little more comfortable for him he'd relax a little.'

'If you're worried about Alma, Ruth, I could think of a dozen households that would be happy to have her.'

'She doesn't want strangers, Bev. She'd like to work for you.' Ruth watched her friend carefully. This had been Alma's idea, the first nontearful sentence she had uttered after Ruth had tentatively spoken to her about another job. 'You know how she's always liked and admired you. Now that you're so successful, and with this big apartment . . . well, don't you really need somebody on a permanent basis?'

Of course, thought Bev. This would happen the day she found her career at Welby's was being deliberately stopped, when she would probably have to resign and spend months looking for a new position, when she had committed herself to redecorating the whole place. And now Alma, with a full-time salary!

But she didn't hesitate. If she could at least take that sad look out of Ruth's eyes for one moment, the struggle would be worth it. 'Of course I'll give Alma a job, Ruth. And be damn happy to have her, just as soon as she wants to come. Since I'm going to redecorate this place anyway, ask her what color she wants her room to be.'

20

After a talk with Ralph at the bank, Bev felt a little easier. He had watched her investments for her carefully, and while she was far from being a rich woman, she found she could easily manage Alma's salary and the redecoration of the apartment and still continue to contribute to her mother's support out in Arizona. As long as I keep my job at Welby's, at least, she thought. But even without that salary she could easily live for nearly two years in the same style without worrying about an income.

Alma quickly became invaluable. Quiet and subdued when she first arrived, in a few weeks she had taken charge of Beverly's apartment and many of the time-consuming private details of her life. Gerry had thrown the staff of his now-impressive decorating firm completely into the project of redesigning the apartment, and he and Alma cheerfully took over the details, leaving Bev free to concentrate on her work. Or, as she was beginning to find more and more, the lack of it. At the store, areas of responsibility were being removed from her control, gradually at first and then more abruptly. To whatever degree the gossip affected the Rales organization or whoever had started it, it was beginning to acquire a momentum that Bev found alarming. Decisions she had had approved weeks before were suddenly canceled, reports that should have reached her desk were being sent to other managers, and while Sylvia continued to back her completely, Bev found that her worst fears were becoming reality.

I won't quit, she reminded herself over and over again. They're going to have to come right out and fire me if they want me out. With a good healthy settlement. In the meantime she used all her skill to remain patient and tactful with the people at the store and the executives who came in from Chicago for the Rales organization. Abruptly scheduled meetings, sudden long-distance phone calls that forced her to stay late were accepted cheerfully and with a smile, although it meant canceling theater tickets, dinner parties, and quiet evenings by herself or with the Vladcheks. Only once did she fail to agree, and that was when a vice-president of the Rales Corporation wanted to meet her in her office late one evening. Not only did he have a bad reputation as a woman chaser—she had no intention of being alone in her office with him at that hour—but he had picked the day when she had finally arranged a meeting with Marion.

As she walked up Madison Avenue toward Marion's shop, Bev tried to remember just how long it had been since she had seen her former sister-in-law. There had been no open break, even when the divorce became final. They had simply moved into different worlds the way friends can in a city as crowded as New York. With Arthur no longer the glamorous, ardent suitor he had been, Bev seldom went to the places where she might have seen Marion and, if the affair was continuing, José. The expensive restaurants were now, in Bev's case, for business lunches. The quiet brunches she had shared with Marion in the early years when José was with his wife had gradually ended. Marion always had a good excuse when Bev called. Bev, however, had decided that at this stage of her career it was time to renew their friendship if she could. She was honest enough to admit it was partly because Marion had always been a valuable source in the past of what was happening in the world of fashion: who was being fired, who needed an assistant, what firm was succeeding and which was not.

Marion's voice had sounded the same on the phone when Bev had called to set up a meeting, suggesting that Bev come by the store after work. She probably knows what's happened to me already, Bev thought. That would make it easier.

But when she got to the store she was surprised to find large signs in the nearly bare windows: SALE. GOING OUT OF BUSINESS. She tried the handle of the door and then tapped on the glass. Marion appeared from the back of the store and opened the door for her. For a moment the two women merely looked at each other in silence. She's changed, thought Bev, and she instantly wondered, as anyone would, if she herself had changed as radically. Marion's first words relieved her of that worry.

'Bev, you look beautiful! Come in.' She led her into the store, turning on a few lights as she did. 'Sorry everything's such a mess, but this closing business seems to be taking forever. Come into my office where we can talk.'

Following Marion, Bev tried to pinpoint the differences in the woman in front of her. She was older, of course; they all were, although that was not what she had first noticed. Always Marion had been vibrant—stunningly dressed, hair curled, makeup perfect. Today she seemed almost austere. If she was wearing makeup, it was too subtle for Beverly to discern, and her suit was dark and plainly tailored. Even her hair was different, pulled back severely and the first traces of gray allowed to show. She looks like Jane did when I first met her, Bev thought with surprise.

'Marion, you're going to have to fill me in. I had no idea you were selling the business.'

'It's been a rather sudden decision.' She smiled, and for the first time Bev saw a trace of the old Marion. 'And from what I hear, things have been too hectic at Welby's for you to have heard any outside news. Congratulations on your promotion, by the way.'

'Oh, that.' The newness had long since rubbed off her title. But Marion's commenting on it probably meant she had not heard the more recent gossip. 'Why are you closing? You've always done so well!'

'I'm getting married.' Marion said it flatly.

'Congratulations!' Bev was honestly pleased, but the look on Marion's face puzzled her. There was no gleam of happiness in her eyes or sound of it in her voice. 'To . . . José?'

'No, Bev. José's been out of the picture for some time.'

'I . . . I didn't know.'

'Neither did I for a while. I suppose I should have known it couldn't last, but you tend to fool yourself.'

'He went back to his wife?'

'He never really left her. No, he's found himself a very pretty blond starlet. Swedish, I believe. Twenty-two.'

Bev found herself remembering the Chanel model in Paris and the conversation she had had so long ago with Jane in which the older woman had predicted just this ending. She wanted to ask about Jane, but she knew this was not the moment. 'Are you very unhappy about it?'

'I was. Funny, I always thought I was so independent, that I didn't want to be tied down, that I wanted to make my own life, my own way. I didn't take into consideration, I guess, that years pass, and if a man like José wanted to go out with a middle-aged woman he'd take his wife, not me.'

'But . . . you're getting married?'

'Yes.' She mentioned the name of a well-known movie designer. Bev tried to hide her reaction. The man was extremely successful but notorious in the industry for his sexual preference for other men. 'Since Claude is working almost completely on the West Coast, it seems simpler to close the store and move out there with him.'

'But Marion, I . . .' Bev didn't know how to continue. Surely Marion had heard the same gossip she had, must have known the man's past. And yet if she didn't, was it for Bev to mention it?

'You're thinking about his reputation, aren't you?' Marion's voice was cool. 'I know about it. We've discussed it frankly. A lot of it is highly exaggerated, but he admits the tendency is there. Probably always will be.'

'And that doesn't bother you?'

'A little, perhaps. But not as much as you might think, Beverly. I've had quite a lot of lovemaking in my life, and very seldom was it all the songwriters make it out to be. If I spend the rest of my life living without it, I'm not so sure it'll be that much of a loss. You look surprised. Why? I've had a couple of decades of being Marion the Free Woman. I think it's going to be a comfortable change just being settled for the rest of my life.'

'Do you . . . love him?'

'In a way. I have enormous respect for him. He's a very talented, tasteful man. He's extremely wealthy; don't think I'm ignoring that either. He likes me, he has a beautiful home. He enjoys entertaining. I'll be very good at that.' For a second she allowed her voice to have a faint edge of bitterness in it. 'And I'll never have to worry about him leaving me for a younger girl. If he's in another bed, at least it won't be with anyone he can marry.'

'Marion, you're a very attractive woman. You could have
—'

'I could have *what*, Bev? I'm over fifty. I'm still reasonably
good-looking. I go to a lot of parties. What sort of man is
around to share my life? The three-martini-lunch boys who
want a free trip to bed? The seventy-year-old widowers
who'll expect me to be their live-in nurse when they have
their next heart attack? Or the men like Claude? And there
are a lot of them around.

'At least Claude's honest about what he is and what he
likes. On a purely practical basis, it would stop a lot of gossip
if he had a wife. Not to mention that I know the fashion
business thoroughly. I'll be able to help him. He wants to
expand, to start his own California design house. We'll make
a very good partnership.'

'I . . . I wish you all the luck in the world.'

'Thanks. But I don't think I'm going to need it now.
Marrying Claude will solve a lot of problems.' She rubbed
her forehead wearily. 'I want to get out of this city, Bev. New
York does something to people. I don't know, maybe it's all
right for men. But it chews up women sooner or later. And I
don't just mean me.' She raised her head and looked at Bev
shrewdly. 'It's already starting on you, if what I hear is
correct.'

So Marion did know! 'Things have been a little . . .
strange since Rales took over Welby's. I can't deny that.'

'From what I've heard, someone's out with a hatchet to get
you.'

'I've heard that too. That's why I'm doing a little looking
around. Nothing specific. But if something else did turn up,
I wouldn't necessarily say no.'

'So that's how it ends. You gave a lot to that store. To your
career.'

'I'm not exactly out in the street, Marion.'

'No. But you're not exactly happy either.' She looked
directly at Bev. 'Do you ever think about Ed?'

'Sometimes.' This was uneasy territory for Bev, talking to
his sister. 'First of all, tell me how Jane is.'

'Getting older. Like all of us. I've tried to persuade her to
stop working, but I think she's afraid of having to sit home
alone all by herself. She's awfully thin and tired, it seems to
me. Don't ever tell anyone, but she's one of the reasons I'm

marrying Claude. I think maybe I can get her to move out to California, get her to take a good rest. Maybe see a doctor. She hates anybody fussing over her, but I'll make it seem like I need her to run the house. And there'll be enough money.'

'I'll miss her,' admitted Beverly. 'We haven't seen each other much the last couple of years, but it was always good to know she was just a phone call away.'

'And Ed? Aren't you going to ask about him?'

'Of course. How is he? Jane told me he'd come back from Korea all right. Did he go back to St. Louis?'

'Yes. It seems home to him now. Although the company he was working for got absorbed into a larger firm while he was away. Still, he seems to be doing fairly well in real estate, and I gather from his last letter that something else may be in his future. In the same place.' She smiled knowledgeably at Bev. 'I think his wandering days are over.'

'I'm glad he's all right.'

'A little more than that. He writes that he's thinking of getting married again. To the younger sister of George's wife . . . you know, the man he went out there to work for.'

Mary Jo. How many years had it been since she had stormed at Ed that night about George's wife, and she still remembered her name. And then she thought of Ed, the way he had been when he first married her, warm and loving, the times they had spent together, the line in his last letter that he would love her always. She'd never told anybody, but she had kept that letter, even after the divorce. It was sealed in a plain envelope in her safety deposit box, marked *To be destroyed unopened on my death*. Tomorrow she would make a trip to the bank and destroy it herself, not opening it. Not that she needed to. She had never forgotten what he had written about coming back for her. Her eyes were suddenly stinging, but she raised her chin defiantly. The sensible part of her knew there was nothing to cry over. All that had been finished a long, long time ago.

'Bev? I think he'd forget about her if you went back to him. Even now.'

'Marion, don't be absurd. It's been—how many years? He wouldn't even remember what I looked like.'

'Don't fool yourself. I've never had a letter or a phone call from him, and neither has Jane, that he hasn't asked about you. Bev, be honest with yourself. He's never gotten you out

268

of his system, and I don't think he ever will. Sure, he's lonely now, he's feeling time passing, too. But in all these years he never married again even though I know, and so do you, how much he wanted a family. I think he feels this is kind of his last chance for that. Why not go out and see him? See if there's anything left between the two of you. It sure as hell would beat fighting the politics at Welby's.'

Go back to him. She could do it, Bev knew. She could have him back; he might never even find out that she would be going to him out of fear, fear of all the things Marion talked about: of age and loneliness and, yes, if she were honest, the fact that the career she had found so exciting when she was young was no longer hers to control. Only she couldn't do it. Call it pride, call it determination, she would never go begging to anyone, even if she were the only one to know she was begging.

'Marion, you've been seeing too many bad movies.' She deliberately kept her voice light and cheerful. 'People don't get together again after all these years. Besides, contrary to all the talk, I'm still a vice-president of a very important store. And that store is still here in New York. So . . . nothing has changed in our lives. I'm very glad Ed's found somebody. Send him my best wishes. I hope he'll be very happy, I've always hoped that. And I wish the same for you. Is there any chance I could give you and Claude a party before you head west? They'll be finished redecorating my apartment in a week or two, and I'm wild to show it off.'

They talked a little longer, and Beverly felt she had concealed from Marion the thoughts that had gone through her mind all during their conversation. She shouldn't have been surprised at the news about Ed, she told herself as she walked home. It was bound to happen sooner or later. The fact Marion had hinted that he might still be in love with her was . . . interesting, that was all. She wasn't going to run to him, like a little girl who had fallen down and scraped her knee. She had never done that, and she wasn't going to start now. Only she couldn't stop herself from thinking as she walked of what life would be like if she were with Ed. Not now, of course, but if she had gone when he had wanted her. Probably there would have been children. Her energies would have been used in keeping a home together; she had no illusions, looking back, that the major part of that job would not have fallen on her shoulders. She would have managed, she had no doubts about that, but what would have been the price? Years of bottled-up anger, making herself believe in Ed's dreams? Or would she have somehow had the courage, as his mother and sister did, to let him be the man he was, decent and kind and good, happy without ambition? That much courage she knew she could never have had. Good luck to you, dear Ed, she thought, as the doorman touched his cap when she entered her building. May your life be happy.

Sylvia kept her promise. With a tactful word here and a subtle hint there, she pulled all the many strings at her command to turn Bev into a personality in her own right in the fashion business. The party for Marion and Claude was reported in all the gossip columns, the apartment made the cover of the most expensive design magazine in America, and in a listing of the most important women in America, done yearly by one of the news magazines, Sylvia with persuasion and some very delicate threats made sure that Beverly was listed instead of herself. But her greatest coup was to have Beverly nominated for the annual Fashion Leader of the Year award. Sylvia had won the honor herself twice, and she was determined to get it this year for her protégée. This, she found, was an easier task than she had expected. A lot of people had known and worked with Bev over the years, and she had built up a considerable number of friends and allies, more than she realized. Many of them were aware of the rumors that were circulating and knew how false they were. And seeing that a person of Bev's standing in the business could be destroyed by vicious gossip was a cold reminder that the same thing could happen to them as well. So the fashion ranks closed around her, protecting their own.

A week before the banquet, Arthur called. Clearly he expected to be Bev's escort to the party. She had hoped that she might be able to slide out of their relationship without a serious break between them, but with his phone call she realized that was impossible. To arrive with him that night would merely confirm the rumors and destroy all the careful planning she and Sylvia had done. When she tried to hedge on the invitation he became almost angry, and she knew she would have to meet him. She refused his invitation to dinner. There would be no more public appearances of the two of them together. Instead, she invited him for a drink at her newly decorated apartment. Thank heaven, she thought, and not for the first time, for the presence of Alma. He would have to behave himself if there were another person there.

'Very attractive.' He looked around at the Regency striped walls, the gleaming silver, and smiled slightly. 'I'll miss the wall-to-wall carpeting, though.'

'Not fashionable any more, Arthur.' She handed him his glass. Alma had appeared and taken his coat, and if he was surprised to see a maid Arthur had made no comment.

'I saw the pictures, of course. When you gave the party for Marion and Claude. As a matter of fact, I was a little surprised I wasn't invited.'

Bev had planned several approaches to this meeting, planned them and, exasperated, discarded them, hoping finally as she dressed that evening that, whatever had to be said, she would think of the right words when the time came. Now he had given her the opening she needed.

'I couldn't invite you, Arthur. And I rather suspect you know why.' He raised his eyebrows but made no answer. 'Apparently there's been a lot of gossip about us—'

'That's hardly new, is it?' he interrupted.

'The *kind* of gossip is a little different. That my career has been solely based on your help, that without you I'd be some sort of salesgirl. Not very flattering, but then gossip never is.'

'You'll rise above it.'

'I intend to. Unfortunately, it means I can't see you any more. At least not for a very long time. You know the upheaval we're going through at the store. I don't want any more wild rumors going back to the head office of the Rales organization.'

'That bunch of little pipsqueaks,' he grumbled.

'Not so little that they didn't make you an offer for your firm. Which you turned down—the rumor being that I had told you they would offer you more.'

'They have. And they'll go still higher, mainly because I don't intend to sell.'

'I think you're making a wise decision. You're a little young to retire.' Actually, that wasn't quite true, she realized.

271

Arthur would have to be in his late fifties, although he certainly didn't look it. All his life he had taken care of his appearance, and the man that faced her that evening seemed in the prime of middle age. 'But you can see continuing my relationship with you would put me in an impossible position with the Rales people.'

'And you'd sacrifice our relationship . . . for them?'

She kept her voice calm. 'Arthur, we've been friends. We've been lovers. I've enjoyed all of it. But there comes a time when I have to face reality. I've worked hard for what success I've made. I don't intend to let it be laughed at or sniggered about as some boardroom joke. You know—although one of the rumors is that you haven't said so—that I've never taken anything from you, not money or mink coats or even your influence. But I intend for the world to know that as well. And if to do that it means we say goodbye here and now, yes, I'm prepared to do that.'

'God! I never realized what a cold, tough bitch you could be.'

'I'm being sensible, Arthur. You know it as well as I do.'

He looked at her for a long moment, his eyes hard. 'There are other places to work besides Welby's, and other conglomerates besides Rales. You want a career? Come and work for me. Tomorrow. I'll start you as a vice-president. I thought for a while my sons might come into the business, but they're too busy spending the dividends on the stock they got from their mother. I think you'd work out fine.'

'Arthur! You haven't heard one word I've said! It may be very generous of you to make this offer. Maybe that's the way it seems to you. And perhaps I should be very grateful. Only I'm not! I'm not going to be flaunted as your mistress or concubine or possession or whatever you think you can make of me. I've made my own life and my own decisions, and I intend to keep on doing it.'

'Your way! Always the way you want things to be!'

'I have not been ungenerous to you, Arthur. Nor have I ever wanted to be. But you must see my side of it.' She could feel her jaw tightening. 'You would if I were a man.'

'This wouldn't have come up if you had been a man.' It was a small attempt at humor, but neither of them could smile at it.

'All right.' He stood and looked down at her. His face was

carefully controlled, but she knew him well enough to realize he was furious. For a second she allowed herself to wonder if perhaps he really had been behind all this. 'I hope you'll never be sorry about this decision.'

'Arthur, please! Don't let's part enemies.'

'Some things, Bev, even you can't control.'

21

Ilyena, Baroness Von Falkenberg, was looking at her fingers. She had spread her short stubby hands out on the top of her antique desk after her personal manicurist had left, and with occasional glances at the small gold clock at her side she was timing how long it would take for her nails to dry. Each nail was in a different color, or rather a different shade of the same sort of dusty rose that she and the other cosmetics manufacturers had, without conscious agreement (beyond the rumors they all had from their spies in the competing companies), chosen to be this spring's new color. The nails on Ilyena's left hand were from her firm, differing only slightly in color. One of them would be her choice for a major promotion by the end of the afternoon. Or, as the manicurist reported wearily, perhaps not. The Baroness was perfectly capable of scrapping months of work and sending a stiff note to the experts in her laboratories to try again.

The fingernails on her right hand were each painted with the product of a different competitor. There was the shade the Maxon brothers had chosen, a rather pallid pink, the color of a Jordan almond at Easter. It *was* drying faster than the others, just as her secret reports had told her. It was cheaper, too, as were all the brothers' products. Cheap didn't bother the Baroness; she had long known that women were not impressed by bargains when it came to beauty products. What they got inexpensively they tended to consider trash. Still, the 'degenerates,' as she always referred to the Maxon brothers, were professional about their products. Nobody was quite sure why Ilyena had chosen that name for them, as both gentlemen lived with perfect rectitude with their wives and families in the suburbs, but the label had spread through the industry anyway. Two other fingers were by new firms. The Baroness knew to the penny how much each had allowed for an advertising budget for this new shade. They would be no match for the amount she was prepared to spend. Still, there was a gloss to one of them that would bear looking into. She would have to find out what they had added that gave it that particular luster.

The longest finger of her right hand she had reserved for the shade produced by her arch-rival, a lady whose appearance of an overbred duchess concealed a brain as shrewd as Ilyena's own. This woman was spoken of only as the 'housemaid,' having democratically revealed in an interview years before during World War II that because of the servant shortage she often washed her own dishes. Ilyena had seized on that item with glee, and no matter how many honors the lady won, how many of her horses successfully captured the Kentucky Derby and how many charts of her pedigree were embossed on the boxes of her products, the 'housemaid' was what she remained to the Falkenberg staff. Ilyena noted with deep pleasure that the housemaid's polish was the last to dry. As for that new Paris-based company, it was of so little importance she had relegated their shade to her thumb. Trivial, underpublicized, it would take at least a generation before the firm could make any serious inroads in her market. And by then she would probably not be here to see it.

Superstitiously she raised her hand and crossed herself in the traditional Greek-Orthodox way. She was not afraid of death, she told herself, she had seen too much in her long life to be afraid of anything ever again, but there was no point in bringing the subject up, even to herself. Throughout the decades of her successful career, she was aware there had been constant guesses about her age, a subject she dismissed as unimportant. No one could possibly know, since she herself did not know. Having fled a Greek uprising in the arms of her mother, who died before she herself had learned to talk, there was no possible way she could be sure of anything about her birth, neither when it took place nor where or even who her family was. In the top right-hand drawer of her desk there was a pile of passports, each from a different country and each with a contradictory birth date stamped inside, the only tangible results of five marriages and a variety of new beginnings. She kept them, not because she lacked faith in the stability of America, which had not only taken her in and made her a citizen but had also blessed her with a fortune so large even she did not know exactly how much she was worth. Still, it never hurt to have a few escape hatches, just in case. She had seen too many seemingly imperishable nations crumble into revolution in her lifetime, destroying the fortunes of those foolish enough to consider anything permanent, to let herself ever be placed in that position.

Her left hand was now dry enough for her to move the appointment book on her desk closer. She had few vanities left in life and even fewer illusions about her own appearance, but she resisted the wearing of glasses almost as fiercely as she would have gone into combat with a rival firm. Glasses reminded her of age, and she was in the business of fighting that off, not only for herself but for millions of women across the world. Martin, her male secretary, aware of her weakness, always filled in her appointments with bold-print letters in a thick-pointed pen. Beverly Richmond was her next appointment.

The Baroness glanced at the clock again and allowed herself to lean back in her thronelike chair. Mrs. Richmond would already be outside, but it never hurt to let people wait before an interview, and during it Ilyena knew she would make herself sit up straight, helped by her formidable corsets, keeping herself six inches from the back of the chair as nobility had long been taught to sit. The fact that her 'nobility' came from a marriage long past and not from birth made no difference whatsoever.

She reviewed in her mind the information she had on the woman she was about to meet. She knew, of course, her position as a vice-president of Welby's. It was a store that over the years had resisted all her attempts to dominate their cosmetic section, giving equal space to her and her rivals. There are battles and battles, and Ilyena was clever enough to know this was one she was not likely to win. It did not, however, stop her from continuing to try.

While she had known Beverly casually through the years and had read of her being given the Fashion Leader of the Year award a few weeks before, it was not until Lazlo Vladchek mentioned her that she began a serious study of the woman. Years ago she and Lazlo had had a brief affair in Paris—or perhaps not, she couldn't quite remember—but he had remained a fringe part of her world, advising her on her extensive collection of art from time to time and discreetly passing along information as to what other collectors were buying. It was at his suggestion that she was seeing Beverly, and in the week between making the appointment and today she had managed to uncover a great deal of information about the woman.

'It's a pleasure to see you again, Baroness.'

Beverly had also prepared herself for this meeting, gathering every scrap of material she could from Lazlo and Hansi, even spending an entire afternoon at the public library, collecting all the facts she could find. She knew exactly why the Baroness had kept her waiting for a quarter of an hour. Lazlo had warned her of this, and she could tell in one glance what the empress of the cosmetic industry had been doing to fill the time. Thanks to Lazlo, she even knew that the left hand was painted with Falkenberg products and the right with those of rivals.

Ilyena had not taken her eyes off Beverly since she had been shown into her office. So this was the woman Arthur Powers had not been able to control to his own satisfaction! Her careful investigation had shown her just how groundless the gossip was. With or without glasses, she could read sales figures faster than any accountant in her employ, and she knew the choices and decisions that Beverly alone had made while working for Welby's. As for gossip, it had never bothered her in her life; all it had ever meant was inexpensive publicity from small-minded people. The question was, how could she use this attractive woman who sat with such composure in front of her, enduring her careful, silent scrutiny with a poise that the Baroness respected. This Mrs. Richmond was not too tall, which was always good for a lady executive. Ilyena had absolutely no illusions about men, especially men in the business world. She always needed women who could stand up to them in carrying out her orders, but it was better that they not be physically intimidating as well. It was much easier, if you had to make a man do something he did not want to do, for the woman giving the order to look up at him while doing so. It at least gave him some lingering feeling that he was still in charge. Ilyena knew the rumor was that she only chose women executives who were shorter than herself because it made her feel powerful. It had given her one of her few rare moments of laughter. How idiotic most people were!

'I understand you're looking for a job,' said the Baroness finally.

'Yes.' Bev had known this would be the Baroness's first question and had decided any kind of evasive answer would be both timewasting and irritating to the other woman.

'You're a vice-president at Welby's.' The old woman's eyes narrowed. 'There's no position I could offer you that would pay anywhere near that kind of money.'

'It's also highly unlikely that any group of Midwestern businessmen would ever be able to overrule you.'

Ilyena chuckled. 'Good! That puts our cards right on the table.' She spread her hands out before her. 'Speaking of that, which shade do you like?'

'I'd better like the ones on your left hand, hadn't I? Those are the Von Falkenberg products, I believe.'

'Outspoken, aren't you? Lazlo must have told you. Only why did you tell me? I might have been impressed by your taste if you hadn't.'

'Because I expect you would know that Lazlo had instructed me. And I don't think you're a woman who could be deceived or would very much appreciate it if it happened.' Beverly leaned forward and scrutinized the hands before her. 'The middle finger is the clearest rose. But I like the luster on the little finger of your other hand.'

'So do I.' The Baroness abruptly closed her hands. This Richmond woman was intelligent; there would be no need to play any more games with her. 'I may delay putting out my new shade until I can find out just what gives it this shine.'

'I wouldn't, Baroness. Rose is going to be the shade for this spring, but I suspect it won't last beyond the autumn. As for glossy finishes, we've been experimenting with them slightly at the store and they haven't caught on yet. I'd say it would be at least another year. That would give you time to incorporate them into your next shades.'

'Thank you.' Those two words were seldom uttered by the Baroness in any language, and she found herself almost amazed they had come to her lips. 'Now, for you. What exactly is your situation at Welby's? You have a contract?'

'No. It's never been a store policy. And with the Rales organization taking over, I doubt if it's likely to be.'

'That's probably wise. There are many stupid people in the world; why tie yourself down to them? You will find, if we get to know each other, that I am impatient with dumb, boring, unrealistic people. A sinner can repent, but stupid is forever.'

'I'm not stupid,' said Beverly calmly.

'That I understand. Although it was probably not the height of wisdom to become mixed up with Arthur Powers. He can be a very difficult man, I hear.'

'So do I. However, I am not, as you say, "mixed up" with him. And, contrary to the rumors, I haven't been for a very long time.'

'Rumors! Foolish people who gossip when they have nothing intelligent to say. I ignore them.' She tapped her fingers restlessly. The housemaid's polish, she noticed, was still not quite dry. 'Still, Mrs. Richmond, I'm wondering what help I can be to you?'

'Yours is a major company, madame, involved in many fields. I'm experienced in all aspects of fashion, from the right photographers through advertising layouts to packaging, promotion, and shipping. I've been handling a lot of that for Welby's for years.'

'The Rales people made a mistake. You, they should have put under contract. Are you free to travel? I have displays in over a thousand stores in America alone. They need constant supervision. Sometimes my products are not placed where the customers can see them.'

'Not at Welby's, Baroness. I think you'll find your percentage of sales there has been up this last year—since the display was moved to the center aisle.'

'Your decision, Mrs. Richmond?'

'People like your products. It was simply basic common sense.' Bev had a good idea that the old lady watching her knew to the penny how much she had made in sales at Welby's, not just in the last year but the years before. 'As far as being free to travel, yes, I can go anywhere at any time.'

'There is no Mr. Richmond?'

'I'm sure Lazlo told you that I am divorced.'

'And no other man in your life?'

'No, madame.'

'Very unwise of you. With this gossip going around, you should be seen with someone new. Someone younger than you, I think. Handsome. That will make the vindictive Mr. Powers even more furious. More important, anything further that is said will merely make him seem old and foolish. That will stop the rumors. Be sure the new man is somebody very unimportant. Talented but not yet a success. That will make it seem as if you are helping him. When people gossip about that, you will seem very powerful.'

'Very good advice, madame.' Bev did not mention that she had considered the same solution. She had long ago learned that everybody loves to feel they have offered an original suggestion.

'Men are a nuisance, of course. Still, there are times when they can be useful. Come and see me again next week for lunch here at my office. In fact, I think we'd better make a habit of having lunch at least once a week. Naturally the rumors will start that we are nothing but lesbians. Still, it will not be accepted. I've paid too much in settlements to too many former husbands for that particular slander to work.' She opened a drawer in her desk and rummaged around in it, finally pulling out a piece of rather dingy embroidery. 'Here. I want you to have this tea cloth.' Bev would have protested, but the Baroness paid no attention. 'A gift makes one a friend,' she continued. 'One of my former in-laws embroidered it. She hopes to become my favorite with such gifts. Stupid, of course, but then she was always a stupid woman. It's even badly done.'

For the first time in the interview Beverly was at a loss as to what to say. The gift was a gesture, but then to describe it so rudely made taking it almost an insult. However, to refuse it would be even worse.

'Thank you, Baroness. My housekeeper is always complaining my linens are too plain. She will see that this is treated with care.'

'Very tactfully put. Now, if you could possibly arrange for slightly more display space at Welby's . . . for my new rose shades?'

Beverly knew that to commit herself would put her forever in the power of this woman. But to turn her down flatly would make an unnecessary enemy, and the most important lesson Bev had learned was not to make an enemy if you could avoid it. With a smile she said, 'Nothing is impossible, madame. Shall we wait and see how your spring line goes?'

The older woman sighed. 'Ah, well, I didn't really expect to bribe you with a tea cloth. Shall we say lunch here next Wednesday?' As Bev nodded and started for the door, the Baroness called after her. 'And get yourself a handsome young man! Considering the trouble they cause, you might as well have someone good to look at.'

After Bev had smiled and left, the Baroness allowed herself to lean back in her thronelike chair again. Mentally she ran through the list of managers in her corporate staff all over the country. There was no one she needed to replace at the moment, but this young Richmond woman was worth cultivating. She wondered idly if Beverly knew the Rales organization was also after her empire. She would have to ask her that at their next meeting.

For the next few months Beverly saw the Baroness often, usually at business lunches; occasionally she was invited to the gigantic apartment on Park Avenue. The meals were served on the finest of damask linens and gold plate, but the food was so sparse and badly prepared she found it sensible to have Alma prepare her a snack before attending. She had not known that Rales was after Von Falkenberg Cosmetics at that first meeting, but she was not surprised when the Baroness told her. As word of their friendship spread, she found herself in an interesting position. Obviously the Rales organization learned of it almost at once. How, Bev was not quite sure, but she suspected Sylvia had carefully dropped the news to Karen. Gradually, the attitude the conglomerate had shown her in the recent past began to thaw. Clearly her friendship with the Baroness made her seem an important lever in their plans for a takeover of the old lady's company, and while the subject was never discussed between the two women, the headquarters of the organization in Chicago could not know that. And always, after every meeting, the Baroness would press a gift on her, as if it were some ritual the meaning of which she had long since forgotten but which she retained out of habit, rather than friendship. Sometimes it would be expensive, a Georgian silver inkstand; sometimes nothing more than a piece of crumpled lace, obviously the worse for years of wear. Unable to match such generosity, Beverly made it a habit to learn the Baroness's favorite flowers and after each meeting sent her the best selection she could find.

'A gift makes one a friend,' she was to remember.

The other advice the Baroness had given her and which she had already decided was necessary happened almost by accident. Ben Ellis entered her life that spring, arriving at her office with two purposes: to get Welby's to advertise in his fast-growing bi-weekly newspaper of the fashion world and to interview her for their next edition. He did not get the advertising until two months later, but the interview was so probing and pleasant that it stretched beyond store hours into a dinner at a restaurant that Bev suspected he could not quite afford and then, surprisingly for her, into an invitation to see his apartment and, after a brandy, his bed.

She did not fall in love with Ben, although if she had been his age, ten years younger, she might have. His lovemaking was brisk and efficient, but it was almost as if it were something he felt they both needed to do before they could get back to what was really important, talking endlessly about the world of fashion that bounded both of their lives. He was handsome enough to make a room full of women all turn and stare when he entered, and he had cheerfulness and energy about him that did not make other men jealous. Clearly he was a young man headed for success, and if Bev ever allowed herself to think that he might possibly be using her and her position to achieve that goal, she did not let it interfere with her pleasure in being with him. After all, in her own way she was using him. Her life had always been so carefully organized, she realized, both in the years with Arthur and in the business world, she had forgotten, except for the happy evenings with the Vladcheks, what fun there was to be found in the sort of spontaneous excursions Ben planned. He had one of the first lofts in Soho, the section below Greenwich Village, giving him lots of space and light. Beverly began to find herself in the position Arthur had been with her when they had first met. She enjoyed giving him gifts: a dozen good shirts that he reveled in, a flowering plant the size of a small tree, a pot of caviar and a bottle of champagne they could share in bed.

He was a new breed to her, a type of man that could only have evolved out of the sixties and seventies, cheerful, lighthearted, and deadly serious only about his work. With him Bev could leave off her designer clothes and wear jeans and a sweater. Always slender, she knew she could still get away with such outfits where many women her age could not. Together, she and Ben explored the city, eating hot dogs on the street (his favorite food, for all the famous restaurants they went to), attending dance concerts given in barely converted basements, behaving, she realized privately, as if she were twenty again. But she did not make the mistake of many women who become involved with younger men of trying to be his age. She knew part of her attraction for him was that she was not like the college graduates he knew. She was an adult woman in her forties, a success, knowledgeable and not without power. Perhaps her power was the most potent of her charms. Using the Baroness's advice deliberately, she cultivated that hold on Ben. He became her escort at all the best parties, she was never beyond subtly helping the success of his growing newspaper by recommending it to important firms to use for advertising, and she made sure that the photographers at the events they attended always pictured them together and, more important, got his name correctly. Through all of this Ben accepted what she did happily, never asking anything for himself, confident that what she was doing was something he undoubtedly deserved. Their affair would have begun and, at least for a short while, continued without her efforts, without the gifts she so enjoyed giving, but she knew her attentions to his well-being and his career were what kept them together after the first few months. Oh, Arthur, she thought one night as she was dressing to go home, Ben naked and asleep on his wide platform bed behind her, I understand you better now! It's fun to show the world to the young and eager, fun to help them toward their goals.

The stories of her and Arthur had almost completely disappeared, she knew, helped by the fact that most of that spring and summer Arthur was in Europe. In honesty, she did not miss him. With her work, the weekly meetings with the Baroness, and long summer weekends with Ben her life was fuller than she had ever known it to be. And while she was careful to keep her emotions completely under control, she had to admit that Ben was becoming the best and most satisfactory part of her life. Alma had taken to him at once, insisting that like all young men he needed to be fed, and often when Bev came home from the store she would find the two of them cosily chatting together over freshly made strudel in the kitchen. Tactfully and then more openly with the security of her new position, Alma suggested the young man should be Beverly's husband. Bev only laughed at that, but with the growing permissiveness of the times, she would occasionally allow Ben to stay the night in her apartment. Alma's only comment was to wink happily when she brought in two trays in the morning.

Bev had known it could only be an affair, brief, romantic, and due to end in time, but she had not expected how the end would come. She had spent a leisurely lunch with the Baroness, consulting with her about the latest of the Rales organization's moves. She had been summoned to a management meeting in Chicago the following week, along with Sylvia. They each had made previous trips to the center of the conglomerate during the period of time Rales had taken over the store, but this was on a higher level and Sylvia was positive it meant they were at last going to be taken into the inner councils, the first women, at least from the New York branch of the organization, to be so included. The Baroness thought so too.

'They have made me a very interesting offer, my dear Beverly. One that in conscience I may not be able to refuse. I would still run my company, still choose my own people, and they would back all of my ventures, laboratories, experiments, losses . . . for a fair share of the profits. Most interesting.'

'That happened at Welby's too, Baroness,' cautioned Beverly. 'And the original family found themselves completely out of power within a year.'

'Because they were foolish enough to give them control. I shall retain seventy percent of the stock. A very good offer. I am tempted.' She looked at Beverly carefully. 'Naturally, I will have approval of whoever they choose as liaison with their organization. I think they might consider it a good idea to name you, my dear.'

This had been in Beverly's mind for a long time, but she knew that to suggest it to the old lady would be a serious error. Much better for it to have come, at last, from her.

'It would mean leaving the store,' she answered thoughtfully.

'It would make you a very important executive as well. A large salary; hold out for that. Stock options. Control not just of my world, but invaluable to them through their entire network of companies. You will not ask for the position, of course.' She allowed herself the smallest of smiles. 'As you have not allowed yourself to ask for it of me. Here, I have a present for you.' The Baroness removed a large twin topaz ring from the little finger of her left hand. The ring was a special design, almost a trademark of the Baroness's. She had had the same design duplicated in emeralds, sapphires, and rubies as well as in a series of less expensive stones, one for every color outfit she chose to wear. She maneuvered it off her heavily knuckled hand and, with the metal of the band still warm from her skin, handed it to Beverly.

'Your highness, I couldn't possibly . . . this is worth a fortune!'

'Nonsense. I was very careful to wear one of my less expensive ones today. Besides, it will be a sign, the way the popes used to send their ring with one of their emissaries. You will wear it to the meeting. You will continue to wear it. And the message will be very clear to the men at Rales that you are my choice. Besides, it is August, much too hot for a mink coat. And these are the sort of men who only recognize the obvious symbols of success.'

Bev smiled, thinking back to when Sylvia had said much the same thing to her when Welby's had first been purchased by the conglomerate.

'I thank you, Baroness. You have been a very good friend to me.'

'And you will be to me,' Ilyena answered calmly. 'I shall want twice what they intend to offer me for my stock, so start preparing them.'

When Bev reached the street, even the heat of the August day seemed lighter, easier to bear. It was a Saturday afternoon, and practically all the people she knew had left town. Ordinarily, she and Ben would have spent the weekend at the house she had rented in the Hamptons for the summer, but because both of them knew a luncheon invitation from Ilyena was nothing less than a command, Ben had agreed they would stay in town. He was to pick her up later for dinner in someplace strongly air-conditioned, but, elated with her gift and the prospect of her new position, Bev decided not to wait to tell him her news. The gift of the Baroness's ring would certainly make an interesting item for one of his gossip columns; if he agreed, they could revise his own personal column in time for it to make the next edition, which she knew would be read from cover to cover by the men she was to meet the following week. That wouldn't hurt, just in case madame's signature ring was not as well known as she thought.

On impulse she hailed a cab and directed the driver downtown. Almost like an omen, there was a hot dog wagon at the corner of Prince Street where Ben lived, and she stopped to pick up two of the fragrant rolls, not worrying if the onions and mustard dripped on her summer suit. She let herself into Ben's building and started up the dirty stairs. One thing about a younger lover, she thought as she climbed, was that they seldom had the money to live in elevator buildings and their endless stairs kept you in good condition. She knew he would be as excited about her news as she was, and as she paused on the landing outside his door to catch her breath she knew what his reaction would be. It was always the same whenever he was in a buoyant mood. He would take her to bed and then, happily satisfied, propose marriage. Neither of them took it seriously; it was as much a 'thank you' as anything else, but this time she might surprise him. It wouldn't last, of course. Not longer than two or three years at most, for underneath the cheekiness and ambition she knew Ben was a deeply conventional man, one who would only really marry for home and family no matter how much he might stray from the domestic life afterward. Still, at forty-five a second marriage, even a brief one, could do her no harm, and he *was* fun. It would bear thinking about.

She opened the door to his loft with the key he had given her. It was a cavernous space, divided into parts by movable partitions. Draperies had been pulled across the windows, closing out the hot afternoon sun, and she took a moment to adjust her eyesight to the gloom. It was then she heard the voices.

She knew very well the area they came from, the large bed at the back of the loft. Ben's voice was instantly recognizable, but it took a moment for her to identify the girl with him. Vanessa, of course. His tall, personable assistant. But her usual drawling, elegant, Radcliffe-trained voice was different this afternoon. She was moaning, moaning with pleasure, and the words Ben was saying to her were the same that he had used with Beverly only two nights before.

She stood there very quietly, without moving. Then she stooped down and placed the two hot dogs neatly, side by side, on the bare wood floor. Closing the outside door behind her, she started very carefully down the staircase, her fingers trailing along the wall as if to guide her. She would go to the Vladcheks' tonight. They would be pleased with her news. And if Ben was not clever enough to understand what she had left on his doorstep, Alma could tell him she had gone out of town.

It was only when she had safely reached the street that she thought to put on her sunglasses. A woman her age did not cry in public.

22

The meeting in Chicago went exactly as the Baroness predicted. Beverly and Sylvia were put up in a lavish suite in the newest hotel. 'It looks like a cross between Versailles and San Simeon,' quipped Sylvia. They each had their own room, and there were lavish gifts of flowers and fruit and liquor from both the Rales organization and the hotel. 'Something tells me the boys are in trouble,' said Sylvia, and as usual her predictions were correct.

At the corporate meeting the next day, and then later with the board of directors, the two women realized why they were being treated as honored guests. Studying the conglomerate's annual report, they had been astute enough to realize that only the fashion side of Rales was showing a profit. In the three days of consultations and bargaining that followed, the two women emerged with what they wanted. Sylvia was to have the title of president of Welby's. Beverly was advanced to the position of a full Rales vice-president, in charge of all the various fashion companies and operations Rales owned. The newest and most important of these acquisitions would be Von Falkenberg Cosmetics. As further proof of her importance, the organization offered her a contract. As she and Sylvia flew back to New York after the last meeting, the contract rested unsigned in her purse. She had been polite, charming and tactful, but had made it very clear to the board that her lawyer would have to examine the document. Her lawyer and, she thought to herself privately, Ralph as her banker and the Baroness as her friend. It was a generous offer and she knew all her advisers would consider it such, but it was time the men of the board were made a little uneasy for a while. They had done their share of that to her in the past years.

'So we all have what we want,' said Sylvia as they sipped their martinis in the first-class section of the plane. 'I finally get the title, and you—did you realize that when you sign that contract you're going to be the first and probably for years the only woman member of their precious board of directors?'

'*If* I sign,' said Beverly absently.

Sylvia looked at her. Bev had been quiet this trip. Sylvia had put it down to the pressures of the conferences, but now she was beginning to wonder. 'Something wrong with it? It'll make you rich. It also makes you one of the top women executives in the country. Isn't that what you wanted?'

'Yes.' But the one word sounded more like a sigh to Sylvia.

'Not still thinking about young Mr. Ellis, are you?' Beverly had told Sylvia what had happened. In the days between that Saturday afternoon and their trip to Chicago he had called several times, and while Bev had been polite, she had refused to see him.

'No.' It was true, she thought. After the initial pain, she had found she hardly thought of him. Maybe when she had time she would regret what had happened, but she knew whatever scars he had inflicted on her were more to her pride than to her heart.

'Good. I always thought he was too much of a hustler for you. You sure don't have much luck with men. That shark Arthur Powers. Frank What's-his-name. Ed—'

'Did I tell you Ruth heard from Ed? He's married again. They're expecting a child.'

'Does that bother you?'

'No, not really.' Bev looked out at the thick white clouds that surrounded the plane. 'It's just that sometimes I wonder. . . .'

'Don't look back, kid, something may be gaining on you. Isn't that what the old baseball player said? Anyway, it's good advice for all of us.'

It was advice that Bev took. The next years were the busiest of her life. The contract that she finally signed gave her many benefits, but the Rales conglomerate was not doing it out of kindness. They expected to use her and her ability to the fullest, and Bev was willing to give them all her skill, her knowledge, and, with the emptiness of her personal life, as much of her time as they wanted. At least once a month she traveled outside the country: Europe for fashion showings, Hong Kong for silks and skilled workmanship, South America to open new markets and explore investment possibilities. If the Baroness had thought Beverly would be devoting the majority of her time to Von Falkenberg Cosmetics, she was to be disappointed. The cosmetic firm was only a small part of Bev's responsibilities. Every other week when she was in the country she had to attend a directors meeting in Chicago. She was proud that under her control the returns on the fashion side of the organization continued to grow steadily, through fads and slumps, good years and bad.

Gradually the men who controlled the board began to treat her with the respect they would have shown for any equally successful male. At first there had been a sense of uneasiness among them—chairs held, doors opened for her, dinner checks paid by other members of the board. One or two of them, after coffee, would hint at something more sexual, but Bev, not even slightly tempted, turned down all offers diplomatically but definitely. On her own she made it her business to meet the wives of the members of the board and tactfully ask their opinions of various Von Falkenberg and Rales products. While making friends, she learned a great deal. What an untapped supply of energy! she thought, driving back from a luncheon with some of the wives in the suburbs of Chicago. The women she had been with were all highly intelligent (quite a few more so than their husbands), alive, vital, full of talent and ideas. Most of them were her age, which meant their children were out of the house. But because of their husbands' prominence and position, they could not consider taking jobs. A few of them had gone back to college for courses in subjects they were interested in, subjects they had put aside in the years when they were raising families. But whatever they learned could only be used as a 'hobby.' All of them were involved in various charitable works, and more than a few devoted long hours to voluntary political work. But none of them were paid, none of them even expected that. They had been chosen young by their husbands, and now that their duties as mothers were over they were filled with restlessness, a desire to be considered as professionally competent as the men they had married. Bev knew that many of them envied her, and she redoubled her efforts to make them friends.

As one of them had said to her while they sipped wine before the luncheon, 'How lucky you are, Bev! To be considered a real person, not just some kind of an append-age: "Charlie's wife," "Carol's mother," "B. J.'s daughter"! Sometimes I have the feeling I'm just a shadow, that I don't exist if somebody isn't standing out there in the sunlight, making the shadow.' Bev remembered how she had felt at her father's deathbed. Hard as life had been at times, at least she had escaped that fate.

It was a feeling Ruth Phelps knew very well. For a long time she had known her marriage to Amory was a mistake. There was nothing tragic about it, she told herself often. He didn't drink to excess or hit her, and as the boys grew to young manhood he began to treat them with the same polite respect he showed the junior members of his firm. All three boys had done well in school; Philip especially had pleased her with his decision to become a doctor, specializing in children's diseases. How much of that, she wondered, came from those terrible days when he had lost his father? It was almost as if some secret determination had been planted in him then, with the help of Ed Richmond, to give aid and care to other children someday. But the year she turned fifty-three, Ruth found the security she had known most of her life was as much of an illusion as the movies she and Bev had argued over years before when they were teenagers.

Amory wanted a divorce.

Ruth knew she should have been prepared for it, should have suspected it might happen, and braced herself for the destruction it would mean to her life. They had not been involved sexually for a long time, and yet she knew those drives were strong and important to him. But it had been easier not to confront him with what she suspected: that he was going to other women. Instead, she had made herself as much of a partner in their marriage as he would allow her to be, exercising to maintain her figure, making sure their home ran smoothly, entertaining his clients and business contacts carefully and with strict attention to every detail. He always treated her with perfect politeness, thanking her for each successful dinner, never forgetting their anniversary or her birthday, each year with a more expensive gift. But each year she knew they had grown further apart. He spent most of the week in the city now, in an apartment he had chosen for himself, not even suggesting she help decorate it. Vacations together, even if either had wanted them, were a thing of the past. He would state that he couldn't get away from his prosperous law firm and suggest she travel by herself. Several times she had accompanied Bev on one of her business trips. It meant being alone in the daytime in strange cities, but she had forced herself to see whatever famous sites were available and would listen to Bev's details of her day each evening with as much interest as she could manage. Someday she knew Amory would have to retire, and they would be more in each other's company than either of them wanted or was prepared to handle. But she had put off that thought as she had put off so many others in the past which she knew she could not solve.

Only now it was not to be. He stood before her in the long living room of their suburban house, a yellow legal pad in his hands. All through dinner he had been silent, even more than usual, and when it was finally over, instead of retreating into his den he had asked her to join him in the living room.

'Ruth, I don't know of any tactful way to say this. Perhaps the best way is just to get it out in the open. I want a divorce.'

She stared at him as if she were seeing him for the first time. His hair was graying, his waistline was thicker, the glasses he wore had to be changed each year for a stronger prescription. He handed her a glass of brandy and sat down on the couch opposite her. Obviously the pad contained his list of how to divide their possessions. He was that determined.

'Have I done something . . . wrong?' she said finally, more to break the silence between them than for any other reason.

'No. Of course not. This isn't anybody's fault. Well, mine, I suppose, in a way. We probably never should have married.'

'You said you loved me,' she said dully.

'I did. In one way I still do. But maybe I just didn't know what real love was then.'

'And now you do?'

'I think so. My lawyer—I'll be using Sanderson at the

office, by the way—advised me against telling you this. But I don't want to start out on a new life with lies or trickery.'

'Do I know her?'

'I don't think so. Her name's Leslie Hunt. She's a banker.' He mentioned the name of one of the most powerful banks in the country. 'We met last year while working on old Mrs. Tremont's estate. We've been seeing each other somewhat steadily since then.'

'A businesswoman. Somehow I never thought of you being involved with someone like that, a woman with a career.'

'Neither did I. But she's bright and charming—'

'I'm sure she is,' Ruth cut in. 'How old?'

'Thirty-one.' He hesitated. 'I know what you must be thinking—'

'I doubt it.' Ruth almost smiled. In over twenty years of their marriage she wondered if she had ever before interrupted Amory twice in one conversation.

'It's fairly obvious, I expect. The middle-aged man trying to recapture his youth with a younger woman. The oldest cliché in the world. Only it isn't like that with us, Ruth. We share so many of the same things, the same goals, the same interests. The same things make us laugh.'

'You don't have to go on about it, Amory. I remember very clearly all the signs of being in love.' It was strange to think of Amory laughing with anyone. 'Didn't we have interests in common?'

'Ruth, you were here with the house. What was I supposed to talk about when I came home at night, crabgrass and the ladies' sewing circle?'

'It was *you* who wanted the house!'

'I know. Now I want something else. Please understand. I think Leslie and I can have a real marriage. I'm not sure we've ever had one all these years. . . . I think maybe Geoffrey stood between us.'

Stung, she lashed back at him. 'That's not true! All these years I've been a good wife to you, and you know it!'

'Ruth, I don't want to argue about this.' He took a deep swallow of his brandy. 'One thing is right about the old clichés. When you reach the middle fifties, you suddenly become terribly aware of time, how quickly it's going by. I don't know how much more of life I'm going to have, Ruth. I want to share it with Leslie. And to my enormous surprise, she wants to share it with me.'

'I wouldn't put yourself down, Amory,' she answered coolly. 'You're a very wealthy man, from an excellent family. Even a bright, clever career girl of thirty-one will start thinking of settling down. You see, Nature has a funny way of evening things out. Pretty girls—and I think you'll agree I was pretty, Amory—we had it all our own way until about . . . what, thirty-five? The flowers, the phone calls, the "I can't live without you" speeches as men reach for your body. But after thirty-five, you boys come into your own, don't you? It doesn't matter if you're balding or fat or have high blood pressure. Some woman will always want you. You don't even have to be particularly wealthy, it's just that by that time women start realizing the merry-go-round has slowed down. It may be our last chance when we get into our thirties to get the brass ring.'

'Leslie isn't like that, Ruth. I think she'd be content if we went on just as we have been.'

'Don't fool yourself, Amory. It's bad enough that you've fooled me.'

Amory left that night, with one suitcase, after instructing the houseman as to the careful packing of the rest of his clothing. He was, for him, surprisingly generous when they finally settled down to the business discussion of the ending of their marriage. Ruth was already comfortably well off with what her family had left her, and the terms that Amory was prepared to offer made her an extremely well-to-do woman. That should have provided the security she had always needed, but as she sat in Beverly's apartment the following afternoon she was more depressed than she had been since the tragic death of her first husband.

'What do I do now, Bev? I feel so . . . strange. So lost.'

'You never really loved him that much, did you?'

'Bev, it doesn't have anything to do with love! I made my life around him, the way I did with Geoff, the way I did with my parents when I was a schoolgirl. I probably became dull. Only I thought that was what he wanted. It was what I was supposed to do, wasn't it? To be a good little girl, do the right thing, marry a man and share his life?'

'Ruth, I know you don't want to hear it, but Amory's no loss, believe me.'

'No, I don't want to hear it! I feel somehow I've been cheated. Oh, not by Amory. I should have guessed this was going to happen sometime. I feel cheated by life. I followed all the rules, and what did it get me? I'm fifty-three. My boys are grown, with their own lives. I wouldn't marry again even if somebody asked me—and after two decades of trying to even up men and women at dinner parties, I assure you, nobody's going to ask me. I'm healthy. I'll probably live another twenty-five years at least. So what am I to do with a third of my life? I've no skills for a job, even if I could get one at my age. The only thing I know how to do is run a house.' She laughed. It wasn't a pleasant laugh. ' "Housewife." That's what you put down when you fill out a form. And suddenly you discover it's true. The man walks out and what are you married to? The house.'

'You could buy an apartment in this building.' Bev tried to sound cheerful. 'I'll share Alma with you.'

'No, thanks. No, I've got to start over, and I don't want any reminders of the past. Not even Alma. Bev, it's like having been an invalid. I'm going to have to learn how to walk all over again. And without leaning on anybody.' She looked at her oldest friend. 'The way you learned to walk by yourself, Bev, a long time ago.'

'A career doesn't always make you happy, Ruth.'

'Does anything? *Can* anything?' She stood. 'Well, I'd better try to find out. I'm storing the furniture, putting the house on the market. I never liked it anyway. And then I'm going to take a trip. A long trip. The lawyers can handle all the details without me.'

'I'll be going to Hong Kong next month. If you want to, come with me.'

'No, Bev. I've got to be alone. All by myself. Think things out without anybody to lean on for company. Or strength. I've never really done it, you know. Go off by myself. Find out if there really is a Ruth Phelps. A Ruth Wells Eliason Phelps. And find out what she does with the rest of her life.'

Ruth left the next week, not seeing Bev again before she left. She was flying to San Francisco, she wrote, to join a cruise ship. She would be gone for several months, and she asked Bev not to worry about her.

When she returned it was late spring, and Bev was delighted to find her friend had a new serenity about her. Ruth took an apartment near Béverly, but not so near that there was any hint of her leaning on Bev for companionship, and refused Alma's reluctant offer to return to working for her. As the months went by, Bev found that somehow, from inside herself, Ruth had found the resources necessary to weather this storm in her life. Charity work that she had done so reluctantly after Geoff's death years before she now seemed to find fulfilling. She contributed heavily, both in time and money, to artistic and political causes, but instead of its seeming, as Bev had feared, merely a frantic attempt to occupy her time, Ruth genuinely enjoyed what she was doing. Once when Bev was storming over a member of the Rales board who took over an idea she herself had proposed, Ruth looked at her with a wise smile.

'Someday, Bev, you may find that a lot of good can be done in this world if you don't care who gets the credit.'

But Bev did care about the credit. It was she, not Ruth, who felt unfulfilled the next two years. The Baroness died, and the Rales organization took over the cosmetic firm completely, absorbing it into the conglomerate, shifting Bev more and more into executive decisions. Her life was busy and exciting, or so it must have seemed from the many articles written about her during this time: in the *Wall Street Journal*, the fashion magazines, the gossip columns. If she found no one man to replace Ben and Arthur, there were still eligible males eager to please her. The experience with Ben had warned her that a great deal of the attention had to do with her position, and while she allowed herself to enjoy the company of the men she met, increasingly she would end the evening with a firm handshake after dinner and take her own taxi home. Never promiscuous, she found that to make love with a stranger, whether a suave Italian or a more direct American, was more often than not an experience that left her lonely and unsatisfied. It was not that a period of her life was ending; it was merely that the sexual act seemed to have lost meaning if she herself had no genuine feelings for the man involved. And that seemed impossible now.

As she had so many times in the past, it was Sylvia who rescued her. She arranged a meeting with Bev in her office the following autumn and, when the younger woman arrived, greeted her as always with warmth. Bev had been in and out of Welby's often in the past years since her promotion to the Rales board, but her visits had been on business. Riding up in the elevator, she remembered the first days she had come to work at the store and the feeling she got from the executive floor. Now the whole store seemed warm and familiar to her. Perhaps too familiar. Nothing seemed to have changed since her departure. And change was vital in luring customers into an establishment that had to be ahead of every fashion trend.

'Sylvia, you look great! And the store seems busy.'

'Busy, yes. Prosperous? I'm not so sure. The quality trade is off, and the recent slump has been hurting us. Plus all those damn cut-rate places that feed off the mistakes we made, the suits we ordered by the hundreds instead of the dozens, the dresses that won't sell in the large or small sizes. We have to dump them to make the books balance, and the young crowd is snatching them up—even if they have to go all the way out to the suburbs to buy them.'

'Welby's has weathered that before. It will again.'

'Maybe. And what about you? Do you mind hearing an old friend say you look a little tired?'

'Six weeks in Hong Kong and the Red-Eye Special from Los Angeles this morning. You know I can't sleep on planes, and there wasn't time for a nap before the office. End of the week I'm off to Rome again. Emilio is a month behind on his shipments: labor trouble. The Chicago boys are expecting me to solve it.'

'Sounds glamorous. Still get excited by traveling?'

'Not at fifty-five.' Sylvia was one of the few people Bev allowed herself to admit her real age to. Not out of vanity, merely that she knew in the business world there were too many young contenders for her position. None of them were beyond using their youth as a selling point for their ability to cope with problems. 'I tell you, Sylvia, before I go to bed at night I have to put a piece of hotel stationery by the alarm, just so when I wake up I'll remember what city I'm in.'

'And California? No chance for a rest?'

'I had an evening with Marion and Claude. And Jane.' It had not been an easy meeting. Marion was gracious and Claude, as always, polite and charming. But Jane was clearly not well, and when Bev had talked to Marion privately later, her former sister-in-law had to admit that the move to California had not achieved the desired results for her mother. 'Jane's awfully thin, it worries me.'

'How's the marriage working? If you can call it that.' Sylvia had long known of Claude's sexual preferences and firmly believed that Marion had made a mistake in marrying him.

'All right. At least on the surface. That's all I saw.'

'No over-friendly houseboy or male secretary in swim trunks?'

'Claude's too much of a gentleman to do that, Sylvia. No, in a strange way I think they're happy. I think he's discovered he needs her. And that's something Marion hasn't had in a long time.'

'That's how they get us, the old "I need you" routine. And we swallow it every time.' Sylvia lit another cigarette. 'Any . . . new word on Ed?'

'Yes, Sylvia. Apparently he's with some kind of factory in that suburb of St. Louis. The manager of it, no less.'

'Wasn't he supposed to be getting married again?'

'Yes. They had a daughter.' Odd how saying that word hurt. 'How's Herman?'

Sylvia took another puff on her fresh cigarette and then squashed it out deliberately. 'Not good. November's always the start of his bronchitis. Actually, that's why I wanted to talk to you. While you were out there in Hong Kong a couple of things came up, and I wanted to get to you before the Rales boys did. First of all, did you know the store's going to be closed?'

'For good? I knew there were rumors, but—'

'I figured you'd probably heard some of them. No, it won't be permanent. At least that's the plan at the moment. But it turns out this prime piece of real estate is just too juicy for a six-story building. The boys have decided to tear it down, put up a thirty-story skyscraper, and incorporate the store into it. But only if they think they can make more money that way than by renting it out floor by floor. That's why this next year's going to be important before they close us down.'

She leaned back in her chair. Bev had never seen Sylvia so

quiet, almost contemplative. 'Bev, I love this store. Crazy, isn't it? Six floors on a noisy street in Manhattan. But I've given a good chunk of my life to it. I'd hate to think of its being wiped out by a bunch of wreckers, just one more reminder of how this city destroys anything of value. So I've had to come to a decision, and that's where I need your help.' She leaned forward. 'Bev, I want you to take over Welby's as president for this next year. If anybody can make it show a profit, it's you.'

'Sylvia! You mean . . . you'd quit?'

'It's time, Bev. Maybe it's even past time. Herman's over seventy. To be perfectly frank, I'm not much behind him. The place needs somebody alive and energetic. I don't think I can do it any more.'

Beverly was stunned. All these years Sylvia had been a symbol of strength to her, a symbol, she realized, of the store as well.

'Bev, look, I haven't said anything to anybody about this. Just Herman. That guy is so decent. He's been wanting me to quit for years now, but he would never say it, knowing what it meant to me. Anyway, the boys at Rales don't know, at least not yet. I know it's kind of a step down for you to go from being a full vice-president of the whole organization to come back just to run the store. It's also really putting your neck on the line. If you don't turn a profit before the store closes, that's not going to look too hot on your record.'

'I don't care about that, Sylvia! As a matter of fact, I'd sort of welcome the challenge. Not to mention being able to sleep in my own bed every night. If I never see another suitcase, it'll be too soon.'

'Then you agree? I know if we both ask for it, the board of directors can't very well say no.'

'When would you want me to take over?'

'As soon as possible. I want to get Herman down to Florida before the first of December. And it's not as if I had to break you in or anything. Hell, you know this store as well as I do. Maybe better.'

'Sylvia, will you answer something honestly? I know you're worried about Herman. And none of us are getting younger. But do you really think you can turn off your career like this? Stop working forever?'

'Bev, I honestly don't know.' Sylvia got up and went to the

window looking out over the wide avenue below. 'Sure, I guess it's been a career. Not like inventing penicillin or painting the *Mona Lisa*, but effective. Only maybe you reach a point where you just don't care any more whether next year's pleats go right or left or even sideways.'

'Somehow, I can't quite believe that.'

Sylvia smiled. 'You always could see right through me, couldn't you? Maybe why I've never quit all these years is that I'm a little scared. Not of being with Herman all the time. He'd love me if I'd sat on my behind from the age of twenty. I think. But I just don't know about me. Maybe I don't really know if there's a "me" there, if it's not connected with the store or work. Now is a good time to bow out gracefully and find out.'

The words were familiar. Bev could hear Ruth's voice saying almost the same thing. She, at least, had come through. Although it was warm in the office, she found herself suddenly shuddering.

'Something wrong, Bev?'

'I guess I was just wondering what I'll do when I have to face that decision myself.'

'You'll find an answer, kid. It may not be the one you want, but I've got a feeling you'll survive.'

23

Beverly became full president of Welby's three weeks later. It was too late to do anything about the Christmas displays. They were, as usual with the store, dignified and old-fashioned. But she immediately began making plans for after the first of the year. It was not that anything was wrong with the way Sylvia had run Welby's. It was just no longer news. Sylvia had been accurate in her judgment: The entire store needed to be shaken up and pointed in a fresh direction. Bev spent many hours in planning.

Her first step was to get publicity. With the help of Lazlo and Hansi, she planned a benefit for young musicians, for the first time using the store itself for the event—a banquet, followed by a short concert and dancing. For this she arranged to strip most of the next-to-the-top floor. Using Gerry and his interior design staff, she had it draped in bright cloth from the store's fabric department. With an almost fierce determination she spent December combing through her address books for anyone in New York or outside who could be of help to her. She had long before made a social peace with Ben Ellis, attending his wedding to an adoring ex-debutante two years before. Bev privately suspected the girl was more in love than Ben, and the fact that the bride's father had a publishing empire hadn't lessened the girl's charms in Ben's eyes. Certainly his paper had grown in power and influence, and she did not hesitate to call him for publicity for the benefit she was planning. Almost grateful at being able to do something for her, Ben plugged the occasion in almost every edition of his paper. It became the fashion event of January, and the expensive tables were almost completely sold by Christmas.

Meanwhile she persuaded all her friends among the wives of the officers of the Rales conglomerate to fly in for the evening. From her contacts at Von Falkenberg Cosmetics she arranged for donations of cosmetics as party favors for the women and the introduction of their new aftershave lotion for men, with small bottles for each male guest.

Only one person was she reluctant to contact: Arthur Powers. Lazlo and Hansi brought it up more than once, but she had made some excuse each time without definitely making up her mind. It had been too long since they had seen each other for any of the gossip to be revived, but she had not forgotten the anger he had shown when she refused his offer to work for him. Finally, Hansi took matters into her own hands and announced that Arthur would be a guest at the table she and her husband had taken. In a way, Bev was relieved. Not to have asked him would have been even more obvious than to have called him for a favor. It would make it seem as if she still felt some antagonism toward him, and as she dressed the night of the benefit she realized in a strange way that it was gone. She had missed seeing him over the years. Perhaps for that reason she took extra care with her appearance; even Alma noticed it as she fastened her evening gown.

'You look very beautiful, ma'am,' she had said. Alma loved gala evenings like this. The last few years since young Mr. Ben there had been too few of them.

'Thank you, Alma.' The door chime sounded and she answered it herself. Ralph was her escort for the evening, his wife once more hospitalized after having been allowed home for the holidays. The banker had not revealed any of the details, but Bev suspected the reprieve from the sanitarium had been a disaster. As always he looked handsome in his tuxedo, his eyes bright with pleasure at seeing her. Attractive as he was, Bev still found it difficult when they had not seen each other for some time to remember what he looked like. I guess that's the ultimate test of whether you are attracted to a man or not, she thought, as he helped her on with her fur cape. She determined to make an extra effort to be charming to him that night.

The benefit was an enormous success. Photographers from all the papers stood outside the store entrance, brilliantly spotlit for the evening, waiting to take pictures of the celebrities as they arrived in their limousines. Bev's work had paid off. There were two extremely popular movie stars in attendance, making their first public appearance together after months of a much-gossiped-about romance. An exotically elegant duchess had flown over from France, paying her own way for a change, determined not to miss the event, and the highest-paid people in the fashion industry had all turned out, as much to be seen as to check on how the competition looked. The concert and the dinner had gone well, and at midnight Bev for the first time in the evening was allowing herself to relax when Arthur came over to her table.

'May I have this dance?'

She smiled, made her excuses to Ralph, who for all his attractions as a steady escort was not a very good dancer, and joined Arthur. She had seen him earlier at the Vladcheks' table, but in the crush of trying to keep the party moving she had not had a chance to speak to him. He looked much older than the last time they had met—thinner, his face heavily lined. He must be almost Sylvia's age, she thought, as he led her onto the crowded dance floor. And for the first time in her memory, she had to admit he looked it.

'It's a very successful party, Beverly.'

'Thank you. It was good of you to come.'

'I've missed seeing you these last few years. I don't have to ask how you've been; you look great. And you've done very well with your career.' He added, without bitterness, 'Without me.'

'I never wanted it to be like that, Arthur. But you know the position I was in.'

'You thought I was responsible for the rumors, didn't you?' She could make no honest answer that wouldn't lead to another argument, so she said nothing. 'Well, maybe it's time to admit that I was. At least, I did nothing to stop them.'

'I know, Arthur. Anyway, that's ancient history now. How have you been? You're looking very . . . trim.'

'I'm turning into a scrawny old man, and I don't like it one damn bit. I guess you must have heard. Your wonderful Rales Corporation is trying to pull a stock raid on my company.'

'I didn't know, Arthur. I've been totally involved with Welby's for the last three months.'

'They think they can get me this time.' His face was grim. 'All because I gave my ex-wives shares in the company. And they're all determined to sell out, my sons included. The lazy parasites!'

'Is it a bad offer?'

'Hell, no! They're too smart for that. It's six dollars a share over the market price.'

'Then maybe—'

'Take it? And do what with the rest of my life? Bev, they're trying to force me out of my own company. And I'm not taking that. I'm not so old I can't fight back. And I will.' He stopped dancing and looked down at her. Nothing had changed, she thought. The anger and ego and pride that had dominated him all his life were still there. 'So tell that to your bosses back at Rales.'

With that he left her, marching through the crowd on the floor for the exit, not even going back to make his farewells to Lazlo and Hansi. She watched him go and wondered if she would ever see him again. So much had passed between them, and now once more he was a stranger.

The party achieved everything Bev had hoped. The papers and fashion magazines covered it extensively, and from then on Bev pushed her campaign to revive the store with undiminished zeal. Hardly a week went by without Welby's hosting some event that made the papers: fashion shows, jewelry collections, even contests among the city's art schools for the best window displays. Welby's once more became *the* store for high fashion, but Bev was careful not to exclude the young woman's market, and business grew rapidly. By the following August, when her mother came to town for one of her rare visits, Bev had put the store firmly in the black, and the official word from Rales was that Welby's would be rebuilt in the new building when it was constructed and that they were prepared to give her a contract as its president for as long as she wanted.

'It's a real triumph, Mother,' she said to Angela, as they sat together in her office on the top floor of the building. Angela had spent most of lunch talking about Arizona and relatives that her daughter had almost completely forgotten. Bev had to admit the move had been good for her mother. She was tan and thinner than she had been before, and while she still had minor complaints about her rheumatism, the change in climate had obviously been the best thing that could have happened to her. In her late seventies, she looked ten years younger.

'I can see that, Beverly. Your father would have been so proud of you.'

'And you? Aren't you proud?'

'Bev, what can I say? I know it's probably narrow-minded of me—old-fashioned, I guess—but this was never the life I wanted for you. Now, don't make a face. It's a wonderful career. Did you know your cousin Marjorie and I have a subscription to *Women's Wear Daily*? All the way out there in Arizona. Every time your name is printed, Marge shows it to the girls at the bridge club. We're both very proud of you.'

'Only? I have a feeling there's an "only" coming up.'

'Bev, I know sometimes I've made you impatient, talking about your personal life. Your father was always the one who understood your ambitions. But I guess I wanted more for you.' Before Bev could interrupt, Angela went on quickly. 'Oh, not more than this. It's exciting and wonderful, I know. You've used your talent and your ambition, and you've used them well. I've kept up with the magazine articles about women and careers, and I realize now there was a lot that was bad about the old way of looking at what a woman should do with her life.

'Bev, I was wrong to try and persuade you otherwise. Only . . . I can't help worrying about your future. I can't exactly say I approve of divorce, but I know you had your reasons. And I'd hoped all these years, maybe I've even prayed about it a little too, that you would marry again. Life isn't much fun if you don't have someone to share it with.'

'You stayed married to Dad, Mother. And you end up just as much alone as I am.'

'Yes. But I think your father's death came from putting too much of himself into his work. Those Depression years—you were just a child—they took an awful toll. I should have made him retire. I think I could have if I'd spoken out about it. Been firm. Shown him a little more fun in life. There was a girl once, before he married me. Rita. I've forgotten what her last name was. She could have done that.'

Bev thought of the story her father had told her the night he died. So all these years, her mother had known!

'Only I guess I didn't know how,' her mother went on. 'I just wasn't like that. I was always so afraid of things, afraid to argue, sure the worst was going to happen. And then it did: He died. And I found I had to pick up the pieces and go on alone. Thank God for Marjorie. We get along well together. We've both been able to make another life. But that isn't what I want for you, Bev, just a pasted-together kind of existence. I want you to be as successful as a woman as you are as an executive.'

'I have plenty of friends,' Bev said defensively. What was it about her mother that always turned her back into a rebellious teenager? And yet she knew her mother was talking calmly, sensibly, about the very things she and Ruth and Sylvia and, yes, even Marion had all had to face.

'Yes, I'm sure you have friends, dear. And beaux. I see all those nice-looking men with you in the fashion photographs. I suppose you've even had affairs, too.' She stopped and smiled, a little shyly. 'Good heavens, I think I'm blushing! Don't worry, I don't intend to ask you about them. In my day you didn't even imply you did things like that with your husband. Only now—oh, dear, I don't know how to say this —but I so wish you had someone in your life who loved you and cared for you.'

'I've heard from Jane,' said Angela somewhat tentatively as Bev sat there in silence.

'Is she any better? I saw her last year and I was worried.'

'No, I don't think she is. She said something about having an operation, but I don't think it was successful. I think it's cancer, and I'm afraid she feels there's nothing she can do about it.'

'Mother! How awful! I was very close to Jane. I thought she hadn't been well for a long time, but you know how private a person she is. I couldn't ask questions.' Bev was wondering as she said this if there was any way she could arrange time to fly out to see her former mother-in-law.

As if she had guessed her thoughts, Angela said, 'I don't think she wants anybody to know. Marion must, of course. But I don't think she wants sympathy or visits or anything like that. The reason she called me was to say that Ed's wife had died.'

'Ed's wife?'

'A car accident. Just before Christmas. I have a feeling

Jane told me because she knew I would tell you. I think she wants you to know.'

'Mother, Ed and I have been divorced for years. He married again, has a daughter, has apparently found the life he likes—why on earth would he want to see me? Of course I'm sorry about his wife's death, but that doesn't change anything between us.'

'Are you so positive, Bev? I don't think he ever got you out of his system. I don't think he could have. I never saw a man so much in love. And as for you—well, you never married again. And you must have had chances.'

For a moment Bev sat there in silence. Had there been chances she could have taken? Arthur had been the closest to her in all those years, but he had never proposed, and she suspected even if she had wanted it he still would not have asked her. Her other beaux, they had all talked of love, but had any of them really wanted to make a commitment? Of course, she had never encouraged it, never wanted it, but would any of them have asked her to be his wife?

'Bev? Have I said something wrong?'

'No, of course not, Mother. I was just thinking. Maybe Ed did have something to do with my not getting married again. Only not perhaps the way you think. Maybe I was afraid whoever I chose I'd try to shape him into the kind of man, the kind of life I wanted. The way I did with Ed. Maybe learning that it didn't work stopped me in some way.'

'You're both in your fifties now, Bev. Maybe it's time to stop changing people and just accept them the way they are. Ed was a very decent man. He must be awfully lonely now.'

'So I should go out there and thrill him with my New York glamour? Oh, Mother, what good would that do?'

'I suppose you're right. I'm just being sentimental. Still, Beverly, a career can't fill every moment of your life, can it? You're at the top of your profession. But you must know that ten, fifteen years from now somebody else will be sitting in your place, making the same decisions, doing your job as well, or maybe even better. Even your friend Sylvia had to retire eventually. Only she had a husband. What will you have?'

Beverly changed the subject after that, and for the rest of Angela's time in New York she was careful to keep their conversations on general topics. But what her mother had said made a deeper impression on her than she liked to admit. For the first time in years she started to have nightmares again. She would wake up in the darkness, her skin damp, trying to remember what it was that had frightened her. It was like the dreams she had had so long ago, before she had left Ed—or, rather, let him leave her. Dreams of fog and people fighting, dreams of death and murder; only she was never able to remember who was being threatened, who was being killed in the fog. She would lie there in her bed, angrily blaming her mother for bringing up the past, but she knew it was not all Angela's fault. She had read enough to know that conflict in dreams usually reflects some sort of conflict in your conscious life that you are unwilling to face.

It was Lazlo who brought her the news. He appeared in her office late one afternoon that September, walking in unannounced, his face grave.

'Lazlo, what on earth . . . ?'

'Sorry. I didn't even give your secretary a chance to announce me. Very attractive, too. I should have been more polite.' There was a buzz on the desk intercom. 'That's probably her wondering if I'm some kind of madman. Only I had to see you.'

'Sit down.' Bev reassured her secretary over the phone that her visitor was welcome and asked that she not be disturbed. In all the years she had known the art dealer, he had never come in like this, and she knew it must be important for him to do it now. 'Is something wrong? Hansi?'

'No, no, she's fine. It's Arthur Powers. Or have you heard?'

'I've been reading about the stock fight he's been going through. Apparently the Rales offer was more than the majority of his stockholders could refuse.'

'Ach! Those sons of his! Spoiled rotten. Thanks to the settlement he made on them and their mother—plus his other wives—they outvoted him. It's no longer his company now.'

'He must be taking it hard.' Beverly remembered the anger in his face when they had parted the night of the benefit. The idea that anyone could have control over his life must be the worst punishment Arthur would ever have to endure.

'Beverly, he's had a heart attack.' Lazlo leaned back in his chair, almost as if this statement had exhausted him. He was older than Arthur, and this reminder of the illnesses and weaknesses of age frightened him.

'Lazlo! Is it serious?'

'Pretty bad. I might never have known except we have the same doctor. He called me. Arthur's practically alone in that big apartment. He won't go to a hospital. He's afraid if word gets out, all the people still on his side will be convinced he is too old and sick to run his business. He's like some kind of hurt animal, lashing out at anyone who tries to help him.'

'When did it happen?'

'Night before last. He'd been trying to line up stock votes, even though everybody told him he had already lost. He was in a wild temper; you know the way he can get. He left his boardroom, and then down on the street he saw the headlines that his company was being sold. He barely made it to his limousine. The chauffeur had the sense to take him straight to the doctor, but he insisted on going home afterward. He's there now. The doctor gave him some sedatives, but he's still furious. We're all afraid—Hansi and the doctor and I—if he keeps on like this he'll have another attack, and that would be fatal.' Lazlo leaned forward. 'Beverly, would you go and see him? You're the only person strong enough to talk sense to him. You two go back a long way. I think perhaps maybe you were the only woman that was ever important to him. He'll listen to you.'

Bev stood. 'Lazlo, of course I'll go. But I don't think it will do any good. He probably won't even let me in. We didn't part on very good terms in January, and we hadn't seen each other for a long time before that.'

'There's no one else, Bev. His children hate him. He was never very good with friends. He told the doorman not to let Hansi and me up. There isn't anyone else who can reach him.'

'I'll try, Lazlo. I don't know if I have anything to say to him that he'll want to hear. Still, I owe it to him to try.'

Lazlo dropped her off in front of Arthur's building, one of the largest and most impressive on Fifth Avenue. It had been a long time since Bev had been there. Images of a dozen parties in the past flashed through her mind as she crossed the sidewalk to the entrance: of parties, of nights spent together, of the fire and passion he had brought into her life, and the pride and need to dominate that had separated them. She gave her name to the doorman, who looked doubtful but called the apartment anyway. After several minutes he came back, a surprised look on his face.

'Mr. Powers will see you, ma'am. It's the penthouse, the elevator on the left.'

'It's all right. I know the way.'

The houseman showed her into Arthur's den. He was seated at his desk, a pile of papers in front of him. He did not rise or even look up when she came in.

'Come to look at the corpse?' he said. The afternoon light was dim, but Bev could see he was very thin. His hair was now completely white, and his skin sallow.

'No,' she said, taking a seat near him. 'I've come to see an old friend.'

' "Old" is certainly the right word for me. I don't know why I let you up here. Or have you come to gloat like everyone else?'

'Arthur, you have a lot of friends. Nobody's gloating. We're all concerned about you. Lazlo, Hansi—' She broke off, not able to think of anyone else.

'And that's all, isn't it? Except for the doctors and lawyers and bankers? Nobody else gives a good goddamn whether I live or die!'

'Arthur, don't get excited! I'm sorry about what happened to the company. I know how much it meant to you. But it doesn't have to be the end of the world for you. The sale has made you an even richer man. You can do anything you want, go anywhere—'

'Bev, stop talking like a fool! Whatever else you were, you were never that. Where am I supposed to go . . . that I haven't already been? What am I supposed to do . . . if I don't have a company of my own? Play checkers in the park? Hell, if I follow the doctor's advice I won't be able to eat what I like, drink what I like. I'd be afraid to go to bed with a pretty girl, presuming I could get one. Even with money.'

'Aren't there other things in life you want?'

'Not after seventy years of "eat, drink, and be merry,"' he grumbled. 'I can't exactly see me on my knees, praying in a monastery, can you?'

She laughed, hoping this sour remark meant at least a small respite from the deep rage he had been feeling. 'No, I can't see a monastery. But I could see a lot of other things you could do. Your collection of antiques: Any museum in the world would come crawling to get them. You'd be on their board of directors, probably chairman by the end of the first year if I know you. You've always been interested in art; I could see you backing Lazlo in a new gallery, discovering new artists.'

'Retirement activities. That's what you're talking about, isn't it? Well, I don't want to retire, Bev! I want life to go on as it has. Just the same as it has. No changes. And for that I want my company back. I built it into what it is. No one has the right to take it from me.'

'You mean you want "everything," Arthur? You told me once—remember?—that one could have it if one tried. Only we didn't realize that "everything" isn't forever, did we?' She tried to make her voice as soothing as possible. 'Nobody can go back, Arthur. We both know that. Maybe the secret of a happy life is to not even want to go back.'

'Hogwash! That's only if you haven't enjoyed your life! And I have.'

'Then enjoy the rest of it! Arthur, you're sick and hurt and angry at the moment. I understand that. But there can be a lot ahead of you. You were never a narrow-minded man in your interests. If it's work you want, you have more than enough money to start a new business—'

'And have them take it away from me, the way they did this one?'

She smiled. 'Don't give any stock to ex-wives in the next venture. That way you'll be protected.'

He smiled back at her at last, but the smile faded quickly. 'Who am I kidding, Bev? I'm too old for a new business. And too young to sit around eating custard and waiting for my hair to fall out.'

'You'll find something when you feel better.'

'Bull! You don't believe it any more than I do.' Bev could sense his anger returning. 'And you needn't feel so superior. You'll end up the same way. Fighting to hang on to what you've achieved. Stubborn. Proud. And they'll knock you out too.'

It was a harsher version of what Angela had told her, but Beverly knew it meant the same thing. 'It's already happening. They're going to start tearing down the Welby building next month. The store is supposed to reopen in the new building, but who knows? I hope I'll have the courage to face it if it doesn't. And to let go gracefully.'

'Don't kid yourself. You'll fight it just as hard as I have.' He stood and walked over to her. 'You know I was a damn fool, Bev. I should have married you.'

'Maybe I wouldn't have had you.'

'Oh, I had my charms in those days. I think I could have persuaded you. Together we could have owned the world. Instead, I picked three clinkers. And let you get away.'

'I'm still here, Arthur. And I'll be here when you want me.'

'You know, Bev, the last couple of months, during all this fighting, I've been thinking about you. About the two of us. We've had a lot. Love and friendship and anger. You've been good in my life. But maybe for the first time I wondered if I've been good for *you*.'

'I wouldn't have missed the times we've had together.'

'I wonder. If I hadn't met you in Paris all those years ago, you might still be married. Did you ever think of that?'

'I think you're giving yourself too much credit, Arthur. Ed and I probably would have been divorced sooner or later. Maybe this way was better.'

'But if you hadn't met me? I pulled a lot of strings to get that apartment for you. That was what did it, wasn't it?'

'And I've always been grateful. But you didn't pull any strings to get me, Arthur. I wanted you.'

'Your decision? Not mine?'

She smiled again. 'A little of both, perhaps.'

'Tell me something, Bev. Did you ever really love me? I've never known.'

'How many years have you been my lover, my friend, my good companion?'

'That's no answer.' He shifted a little so he could see her face clearly. 'Were you ever *in* love with me?' Then he snorted, as if he realized the sentimentality of his question.

314

'God, I sound like some kid wanting to be thanked for the gardenia he brought on prom night!'

'It's not a question to be ashamed of, Arthur.' She hesitated for a moment, thinking. 'I've admired you. I've desired you. You've made me happy and furious, excited, puzzled, thrilled. You've been ruthless enough sometimes to make me hate you. And thoughtful enough sometimes to make me forget everything else.' She smiled, a little ruefully. 'And you've made me laugh. Maybe that's the best gift.'

'And cry?'

'Oh, I suspect there were a few tears over the years. Does that satisfy you?'

There was a look of tolerant amusement on her face; in the past it had often irritated him but now, for some reason, it pleased him. Old friends, that's what they'd become. Then he remembered.

'You still haven't answered my question. You were never really in love with me, were you?'

'Arthur, you're impossible! After so many years? "Love" or "in love" . . . is there a difference? Was there something you wanted me to give you that I didn't?'

'Yourself.' His words were quiet, so low she could hardly hear them. For a second she found herself thinking back across the years to the night she had sat beside her father in that hospital room. But Arthur wasn't dying; his spirit, under the pain and anger, was still alive—she could hear it in his voice as he went on speaking. 'I mean that. Totally and completely. I never had that, did I? First I thought it was your husband that stood in the way. Then your career.'

He moved away, turning his back on her to look out at the park below, already beginning to grow dark with the long shadows of the trees at twilight. 'I wonder now, Beverly. Did I miss the most important part of life with you? Maybe with everybody?'

She walked over and stood beside him. 'How can I speak for everybody? I don't even know if there was more of *me*. Oh, Arthur.' She took his arms and turned him so he faced her. 'After all these years . . . you're still the unhappy little boy, aren't you, who wants to know if there's more? More surprises . . . more birthday presents? Dear Arthur, I gave you the best of myself, and I don't regret it. But I think only now do I understand that all these years I've had to give

315

myself to you carefully, or you'd break my gifts. And me. Let's be honest, Arthur. I don't think you or any man wants somebody totally.'

She stepped back from him and he could see that, for a moment at least, she wasn't thinking of him but of the other people in her life.

'I suppose saints give themselves totally to God. And artists to their work. For the rest of us it's too heavy a burden. All of another person, all of the time.' She smiled at him lightly, back with him again. 'I think I learned that years ago with Ed.'

'And I got what was left over?'

'No, Arthur. If it hadn't been for Ed, I see now I couldn't have loved you. And having loved you, perhaps now I can look at Ed in a different way too.'

'You're not thinking of seeing that guy again, are you?'

'I have no plans of any kind now, Arthur. Except to see you well and happy. And I promise to do anything I can to help.'

'Nice speech, Bev.' She could tell from his voice that the bitterness had come back. 'It almost sounds as if you finally feel yourself free of me.'

'We're both free now, Arthur! Maybe more than at any time in our lives. Free to give exactly what we want. And to take what we want. And not have to worry any more: is it enough? We've gone past all the guilts and the regrets. You'll see. It's one of the good things about getting older.'

She touched his arm gently and helped him back to his chair.

'Now why don't you try and get some rest? We'll have dinner together as soon as you feel up to it and discuss the future. It's going to be a lot happier than you think.'

That night was the first time in weeks that Bev slept without nightmares. In the morning she wondered why, until Alma brought in the breakfast tray with the morning paper on it. She suspected when she read the news story on the front page that she would never have those nightmares again—and perhaps none of her happiest dreams, either.

Arthur Powers had died during the night of a second heart attack.

24

Welby's officially closed the following week. Except for the brief memorial service for Arthur, Bev seemed to have spent every waking moment at the store attending to the thousands of details involved in closing the huge organization. There would be time in the future to grieve for Arthur, and she knew she would. Time to face what each of them had done for—and to—each other, to measure the man who had shaped so much of her life and to accept that she would never see him again.

She found herself almost glad that her hours were filled, arranging for the storing of unsold goods and the redistribution to other Rales stores all over the country of what could still be marketed. There was an employees' party. All this took hours of time, leaving Bev no moment to think of Arthur, so that when she was ready to leave the last day it was almost more with a feeling of relief than of regret. For the next months—or, as she privately expected, next years —until the new building on the location was finished and the store ready to open again, she would once more be part of the Rales board of directors, not with a specific assignment but in charge of their wide-flung fashion empire. For the first weeks she would not even have an office of her own but would be working out of her apartment.

It was after seven when she left the office for the last time, an overstuffed attaché case under one arm. The secretaries had long gone, and the store had been officially closed to the public since noon. Each floor had a night watchman; the man on the executive floor had already stopped in twice to check if she had left. At last she was ready. There was no sentimental rush of memories as she walked the thick carpets toward the elevators this last time. She tried to bring some to mind as she waited. It's over, she thought. Nearly all her working life had been spent in this building, starting as a teenage salesgirl and leaving as president of the company. She realized how empty that title was. A president should be of something important, something permanent. Only now the building was coming down, at the desires of men in a boardroom a thousand miles away, and who knew when it would reopen again? Or even if? Would the Rales people still want her? She was realistic enough to know their contract could be broken if they suddenly decided she was no longer of value to them. It had happened to other women, and it could happen to her. It was as if Arthur had tried to warn her of that, as had her mother. But it had never been the future that frightened her, only the rules and patterns and mistakes of the past. Unlike Arthur, she didn't want more of the same. She was ready for the new, for what lay ahead for her in life. What had Ruth said, 'a third of my life still to live'? Perhaps not that much, but more than enough. She was already making plans when the elevator doors opened.

Once on the main floor, she stopped to look around. She had done it for years, ever since she had risen to the level of an executive office, almost like a housekeeper checking to see everything was in order before she went to bed. The movers would not come until the following Monday, so the store looked much as it always had. She walked along the deserted aisles, touching a dress on a rack, straightening a bottle carelessly replaced in a display case. So many things to buy. So many beautiful things that had surrounded and shaped her life, and now, perhaps for the last time, she was seeing them in what was *her* store.

How many jokes had been made over the years, she thought, about women shoppers? The jokes must go back for centuries, only they seemed to have reached their peak in describing the American woman, a cliché known worldwide, the voracious, never-pleased shopper. But it wasn't caprice that made women into this tired butt for every comedian's humor. She realized it standing there, perhaps for the first time. Beverly had never been philosophical about her work. But this store, and all the stores all over the world, had perhaps been the only place millions of women had ever been able to exert one of the most basic of human needs, a

318

need men exercised every day of their life as a natural right. The need for some kind of power. Perhaps power was the wrong word. *Choice*. That was closer, she thought. Men for centuries had been allowed to make decisions that affected millions of lives, the fortunes of whole countries. Only in a place like Welby's could a woman satisfy that need. It would have seemed trivial to any man, Bev knew. Any of them would laugh if she ever tried to put it into words. But just the right to be able to say, 'No, I don't like it in blue, I'd like it in brown,' or, 'Do you have a size smaller?,' knowing you could walk out if you were not pleased, was all that generations of women had ever been allowed.

We should have stayed pioneers, Bev thought. Then we were needed, not put on pedestals that we never wanted, to be treated as dolls, without a chance to contribute to life. She had been lucky. She, at least, had chosen her own road, walked it to success, and been fulfilled. But perhaps any road you choose yourself is the one that's right for you in the end. As she walked down the long, deserted aisles, she thought of the women she had known, each of whom had fought her way through to a personal life, some of it to friendship as her mother had done, some in sacrifice as Jane and Marion had chosen, some in simply surviving to find their own lives independently, no matter how difficult, like Ruth. And now it was her turn. Her mother had been right. In fifteen years, probably less, somebody else would have her job, would care about it as she had and perhaps be even better at it than she had been. Time to move on, she thought, twisting the double topaz ring on her finger that the Baroness had given her so many years ago. She had once said, 'We are the sum total of all we have experienced in life . . . minus the vanity.' A wise woman.

'Mrs. Richmond?'

Bud, the nightwatchman, came up to her, his guard dog under firm control at his side. 'I might have figured you'd be the last person to leave the place. Going to seem kind of funny not having you and Welby's around.'

'Let's hope it's only for a while, Bud. Still, you never can tell.'

'You've been here a lot of years. Bet you have a lot of stories to tell.'

'Just about people, Bud. And people don't change that

much.' She smiled a little. He reminded her of that nice young book editor she had sat next to at a dinner party the week before. He'd said the same thing, practically challenging her to write a novel, even sending her sample books from his publishing house to pique her curiosity. It was something she had never thought about, but now perhaps there would be time. Certainly the novels she had read had never been about the women she had known.

'You going to take a vacation? Now that the store is finally closed?'

'I might, Bud. But I still work for Rales, and I suspect they'll soon have me on the road again.'

'I guess that's exciting. They got places all over the world, haven't they?'

'Oh, I don't think I'd go that far, Bud. Maybe just to St. Louis. I've been hearing it's very pretty out there.'

'Saw it once. Didn't care for it much. Still, I suppose if you've got friends there—'

'I used to have. Anyway, who knows? We never expected the store to close, so who knows what the future will bring?'

'That's right. You take care of yourself now, Mrs. Richmond.' He unlocked the revolving door to let her go through one last time.

'I will, Bud. You do the same.'

As she had for so many nights of her life, she turned right and headed east toward the river. Even though it was only September, there was a hint of the coming fall in the air, and she found herself smiling, her steps growing brisk and energetic as she walked toward the future. She had a feeling it was going to be a lovely autumn.

THE END